MW00763573

THE LEGACY

THE LEGACY

BOOK ONE OF
THE CUSTODES NOCTIS

MUFFY MORRIGAN

three ravens

THE LEGACY. Copyright © 2008 by Muffy Morrigan.
All rights reserved. Printed in the United States of America.
No part of this book may be used or reproduced in any manner
whatsoever without written permission except in the case of brief
quotations embodied in critical articles and reviews.

Second edition, 2011

three
ravens

The Three Ravens Books logo is a registered trademark
of Three Ravens Books

www.threeravensbooks.com

Cover design by Georgina Gibson

Library of Congress Cataloging-In-Publication Data
is available upon request.

Chapter One

Galen Emrys had been eighteen when he learned the truth. He'd been told the truth before, but he'd been eighteen when it was brought home in all its bloody glory. He'd been eighteen when it all began. He'd been eighteen when it ended. He'd been eighteen when he denied all he was meant to be.

He'd been eighteen when he died.

The alarm blipped and the rich sounds of a Boccherini quintet filled the room, echoing off the high ceilings. Galen groaned and lay listening to the music for a minute, the nightmare from the night before still playing behind his eyes. *Ten years and still that dream nearly every night.* The bitter thought formed as he rolled over and stared up at the light playing on the wall. *It has been ten years. Funny, sometimes it feels like just yesterday. I still expect to see...* He pushed himself up before the depression that thought always caused pulled him down.

The wood floor was cold as he wandered through the apartment to turn the coffee on before heading into the shower. The kitchen opened off the huge space of the living room, one of the advantages of living over a retail space was former warehouses make huge apartments, if you weren't too picky about bad flooring. He stopped to pull a splinter out of his bare foot. Turning on the coffeepot, he walked to the window looking out at the gray day. The Northwest in early winter was an unending stream of gray, rainy days. He sighed, the day was starting off on a bad note.

Walking back to the bathroom he stopped in front of the mirror, tugging on a strand of light brown hair. The length of his hair was a continual source of discussion. He liked it shorter, the guys in the band wanted it longer. He picked up the scissors, then set them down again. *Not today, in the mood I'm in I might do something I'll regret and have to let grow out later.* After his shower, he grabbed a cup of coffee and headed down the stairs to the herb shop below.

As he walked down, he looked out the back window, making sure no one had left anything—or anyone—outside his door. *Nothing... yet.* Galen put his coffee down on the counter, pausing as he always did to enjoy the quiet and the rich mixture of smells of his shop—dried herbs, incense, beeswax and coffee. He straightened the jars on the shelf behind him, putting the jar of vervain he'd left out the night before back in its place, then walked to the front door and unlocked it, turning on the open sign and pushing open the curtains.

The coffee had cooled by the time he got back to it. He considered heading out to the espresso stand across the street, a nice mocha mixed with the flirting of Becci was definitely a draw. At twenty-six, Becci had purchased the small stand across the street, after three unsuccessful months she hit on the idea of Hot Babes Coffee, dressed herself in lingerie, hired four other women and had nearly overnight success. Luckily, she made good coffee, too.

The lure of fresh coffee became too much and Galen wandered out of the shop and over to the stand. He turned back to look at the shop. He'd inherited it from his father, who had inherited it from his father, and so on, back to when the family had first arrived from Europe. His father left it to him, but Galen stepped into the role as proprietor a little uneasily. He couldn't refuse the shop any more than he could refuse the Gift.

"Morning Galen," Becci said, leaning over the sill, perky breasts held in check by a bright pink bustier.

"Hi, Becci, can I get a mocha?" he said.

"Sure, hon." She turned, started the coffee and leaned back out the window, smiling at him. "Your eyes are really green today. Like fir trees in the rain."

"Writing a song, Becci?" he said, smiling back at her.

"Could be. I could sell it to you and Flash," she giggled. "When's the band playing next?"

"Friday, I think, we got a gig down at Rat's Nest," he said, taking the coffee.

"Oooh. Can't wait." She waved the money in his hand away. "I still owe you for taking care of Sandi, keep your money to yourself."

"Thanks." Galen walked back across the street and into the store, the rich smells flowing around him as he walked in. He sighed. Somehow the shop always smelled like...home. He hadn't really stayed there until he was thirteen. The family followed the strict codes of fostering laid down in antiquity and he'd only visited from his adoptive family on weekends, but this place had always been home.

In keeping with the traditions, when he turned thirteen, he'd gone to live in the apartment over the shop, back in the care of his birth parents and his father's brother. His mother died when he was fifteen, leaving the large apartment to the three of them. *Except on weekends when...* He shoved the memory away, taking a moment to check the cash register.

A woman walked into the shop, wandering around the edges of the store picking up items and putting them back down. After a few minutes, Galen walked over to her. "Can I help you?"

She looked at him with a sad smile. "Are you Galen?"

"Yes."

"I, uh, I heard that you might know something about herbs and healing?" She quickly glanced out the window then looked back at him.

"Depends, I guess, on what you are looking for," he said carefully.

"It's my, uh. This is stupid," she said, turning back towards the door.

Galen put out a hand to stop her without coming into contact with her. "What is it?"

She looked at him again. "My daughter is sick and they don't know what to do. The doctors don't even know what's wrong with her. I ran into a nurse in the hospital cafeteria, and she said you might be able to help."

"Again, it depends," he said.

"Would you talk to her?" The woman looked at him with a combination of hope and suspicion.

"Of course, how old is she?" Galen said.

"Thirteen," she said. "She's in the car, can I bring her in?"

"Sure." He watched as she walked out of the store. The woman came back in, leading a thin girl with long blond hair. "Hi," Galen said with a smile.

"This is stupid, mom, no one can help," the girl said, her tone bleak.

"Kristy," the woman said, a warning tone in her voice.

"Kristy?" Galen said, smiling at her. She smiled back. It wasn't much of a smile, but she tried. "Can you tell me what's going on?"

"I don't feel good," she said with a shrug. "I keep getting worse."

"Worse how?" Galen said, putting a hand on her shoulder to steer her to the back of the shop. Pain lanced up the touch, the black spot hovering over her heart took his breath away. He dropped his hand, took a deep breath and looked at her. She looked back with a little nod. *She knows how bad it is, she understands she's dying. Only thirteen and that calm.*

"Can you help?" Kristy met his eyes.

"I'm not sure how much I can help. I will try, though," he said. "Can you come to the back? Your mom can have some tea, and I'll get some herbs for you."

He led them to the curtained room off the back of the shop and motioned Kristy's mom to sit at the table. He made some tea and went back into the shop to gather herbs. Galen put heart's ease, elder, hawthorn and motherwort into a bag. He looked at it for a moment, wondering what else to add. Those herbs felt right, he tended to go with his gut instinct when dealing with any facet of healing. He closed the bag and walked into the back. Kristy was sitting in the recliner with her eyes closed. Her mother had tears running down her face.

Galen walked over to Kristy, and with a look, asked permission. When she nodded, he put a gentle hand on her forehead. He relaxed and let the light flow. *It's your Gift.* He heard his father's voice. *"Like mine, like my father's. It's part of who we are, what we do."* The pain was building behind his eyes and in his chest when he finally pulled his hand away.

Kristy sighed under his hand. "Thank you," she whispered. She opened her eyes and smiled at him. "Thank you," she repeated, and stood up, swaying a little until her mother put a steadying hand on her elbow. "It's going to be okay, mom," she said calmly, still smiling. Galen saw the tears start. He knew she understood he couldn't heal her all the way, but he'd taken away most of the pain and given her a little more time. He walked out into the shop to give them a moment together.

The door banged open and he looked up. "Hey, Rhiannon," he said to the fortyish woman striding into the shop.

"Galen, we're having a party tonight, thought you might like to come along," she said with a feral smile.

"Party?" Galen said with an answering smile.

"Yeah, down at the park, something's been taking late-night visitors, and we thought we'd stop by and see what's going on," she said. "Do you mind?" She grabbed the tongs and dug a piece of candied ginger out of a jar.

Galen shook his head. He'd met Rhiannon Ross ten years before, and since then she'd appeared on a regular basis. She was a killer, pure and simple. She specialized in things that killed children. She'd lost her daughter and learned the truth. After that she'd become a killer, going after the lesser beings that took people away from the light into the recesses of the dark.

The truth did that to some people, the sudden flash of knowledge that there were things most people denied lurking in the dark corners of the world, hiding in the shadows of the night. There were too few people left to fight them, fewer still who faced the big things—those things that the creatures of the night fled from. *I'm supposed to be one of those people, one of those who fight the dark the night fears. Me and...* He stopped "Come by and get me when you're heading down there," he said with a smile.

"You okay?" Rhiannon looked him over with searching eyes.

"Why wouldn't I be?"

"Your birthday, of course," she said gently.

"We'll see when the day arrives, I guess." He turned as Kristy and her mother came out of the back.

"How much do I owe you?" Kristy's mother asked.

"Ten fifty for the herbs," Galen said with a smile at Kristy, the girl blushed. Rhiannon chortled.

"Is that all, but what about...?"

"No charge for that," he said, taking the money from her and dropping it into the cash register.

"Thank you again," Kristy said, giving him a hug and dashing out the door. Her mother followed her with a grateful smile at Galen.

"Another success?" Rhiannon said with a raise of the eyebrow.

"No, not really, I just made her more comfortable. I couldn't help her, not enough," Galen said sadly.

A gentle hand was laid against his arm. "It's okay. You can't save everyone."

"I can't even save most, Rhiannon, honestly."

"Saved a few of us, though." She laughed a little. "You're damn good at those tiny stitches, hardly leave a scar, better than I ever got at the ER."

"Don't tell Mike Silva that." He grinned back at her.

"I have, many times." She perched herself on the counter. "You planning anything special for the next few days?"

"I was thinking about starting with a large bottle of tequila and a few limes."

"Does it worry you?" She looked at him with her searching gaze.

"Does what worry me?"

"It's been five years since Parry and Bobby were killed and ten years since…"

"Don't, Rhiannon, please," he said, surprised at the desperate note in his voice. His heart was pounding as sudden memories flashed before his eyes. *The quirky smile of a thirteen-year-old slyly mentioning his birthday, the happy laughter in his voice when he'd opened the package Galen gave him. "This makes it official, doesn't it?" he'd said with a proud grin. Galen grinned back. "Yeah, Brat, it does."*

"Galen? Honey?" Rhiannon's hand was back on his arm, she gave it a little shake.

"Sorry." He blinked. "What're we after tonight?" She stared

at him for a long moment, he'd gotten used to the looks over the years and calmly started straightening the items in the display case.

"Not sure. Demon of some kind? Ghoul? Werewolf? Does it really matter? Whatever it is, it dies tonight."

"I just wondered what I should bring along."

"One of each?" she said, hopping off the counter. "I always do."

"Yeah, you do." He laughed. She gave his arm a little squeeze, and headed out of the shop.

As she left, a customer walked in and then another. The shop was surprisingly busy, a steady flow of customers. Most were looking for herbs or vitamins. Several came in for more unusual items. Galen catered to an interesting mix of people. One seventeen-year-old came in looking for a love spell for her boyfriend, and an older woman looking for a spell of protection for her house.

One of Galen's favorite customers, Mrs. Barkley, came by for rosemary, candied ginger, the healing Galen offered for her arthritis and five ounces of catnip for her cat. At ninety-seven Mattie Barkley was spry, funny and very active. Galen shook his head as he watched her get in her car and head home. He sighed as the 1939 Ford Coupe edged away from the curb. Galen had to admit to himself he coveted the car, still in near perfect condition.

"Excuse me?" A voice broke into Galen's musing.

"Yes?" He looked up at the medium-sized man standing in front of the counter.

"I heard..." He cleared his throat and ran a hand through his hair. "I heard about you the other day and I was wondering..."

Galen smiled encouragingly. "Yes?"

"I've tried other people, you know. No one can actually

help, they say they can , but they're just snake-oil salesmen, you know?"

"Yeah," Galen said, stopping a shrug.

"But then I heard about you, a friend said you might be able to help me." He glanced nervously around the shop.

"Maybe," Galen said, sliding his hand across the counter and letting his thumb brush the man's hand. Pain seeped through the contact, but it was something other than illness that Galen sensed. The pull of the moon, the hunger for flesh flowed into him from that touch. He met the man's eyes. "How long?"

The man chuckled, a bitter note in the laughter. "Just like that? No judgment, no 'kill the werewolf', just 'how long'?" He shook his head. "They said you were different. It's been years. I didn't even know at first that I'd been infected. I just thought it was a dog bite, then I thought nothing could be done." He frowned. "Can you cure me?"

"No," Galen said gently. "I can't cure it." The man turned to leave, Galen grabbed his arm. "I can help."

Hope flared in golden eyes. "You can?"

"Yes. I can give you a spell to help, and you need to come in on the days before the full moon. I think with the spell, and some healing, we can control it."

"It doesn't bother you? What I am?" the man said as Galen led him to the back of the shop.

"If we'd met under different circumstances, maybe. I'll be honest, I've killed your kind, but I'll help if you ask. I have more than a few non-human clients." Galen smiled and gestured to the chair. "Sit down and we'll get started."

The day had gone by quickly. At closing time, Galen locked the front door and put the till in the small safe in the back of the shop. After double-checking the door, he headed up to the apartment. The sun was down and the large room was dark when he opened the door. A noise from the kitchen made him stop. He stood still, listening. The heater gave its little knocking sound again. Galen relaxed and laughed at himself, wondering if he should go out at all, considering his heater had made him jump.

He threw some leftovers in the microwave and headed to the closet to pick out what he would take with him tonight, pausing by the small shelf on the living room wall. He looked at the picture of his father and uncle and then glanced up at the plaque on the wall, ancient, heraldic, with the words *Custodes Noctis* on the coat of arms. At the end of a long list of names were his father's and uncle's, Paracelsus and Robert Emrys.

"Going out tonight, Dad," he said to the photo, to the room at large, in case his father had decided to haunt the place after all. "Rhiannon came by. Asked me to go along. I think she's worried, considering what's coming up, you know. Gods, I miss you two." He smiled sadly at the picture. "I know, it's not enough, is it? But you agreed when it happened, Dad. You thought it was for the best, too."

He sighed, walked into his bedroom and opened the closet. It served as a weapons locker of sorts. Galen ran his eyes over his collection, wondering what to take with him. Swords, a bow, several guns and a large super soaker water gun were on shelves. *Oh, that'll look great, sword, gun and purple-and-blue water gun, still if it works.* He ran a hand over the two swords at the front of the closet, moving down the cool leather of the scabbards, lovingly repaired over many centuries. The gentle hum of the swords resonated against his palm. The lines of the ancient ritual played in his head. *Hand to hand...* He stopped himself, then with a sigh, he grabbed the falcata—his favorite sword—the 9mm and the water gun. He'd just closed the doors when he heard someone on the stairs, he froze for an instant, senses reaching outwards until he recognized the tread on the stairs. He walked back into the living room as Rhiannon opened the door.

"You about ready?" She smiled when she noticed the weapons in his hands. "Don't forget that all-purpose first aid kit of yours."

"Never," he said with a laugh, the exhilaration that always hit him before a "party" already brewing. Galen walked into the bedroom and grabbed the satchel with the first aid kit. Bandages, sutures, antibiotic creams, herbs and a few magical items to treat the kind of wounds the things they played with could inflict. He picked up the small knife from the bedside table. It had a small blade and a sterling silver hilt, more a ritual knife than practical in any way, but it had been a gift. And he always carried it as a token of the giver. He had received it the day it all began, nine days before it all ended. *Do you like it?" Questioning eyes met his, unsure. "I saved up for a long time to get it." Galen remembered smiling. "It's perfect." An exaggerated sigh met that statement. "Oh, good."*

"Galen? What are you doing in there?" Rhiannon's voice broke into the memory.

"Coming," he said, shoving the knife in his pocket. He threw the satchel over his shoulder and walked back into the living room. "Are you eating my dinner?"

"It was just getting cold in the microwave," she said, spooning another mouthful of chili out of the bowl.

"I did plan on eating that before we left."

"Oh, sure." She took one last spoonful and handed the bowl to Galen.

He looked down at it, then back at her. She was grinning. "Sometimes I swear, Rhiannon." He laughed, then with a shrug finished the chili. "Let's go."

* * * * *

The park was quiet, the trees casting odd shadows in the light from the streetlamps. A soft whisper of wind rustled the leaves on the bushes as Galen and Rhiannon walked silently along the trail. A dark shadow separated itself from a tree. Galen nodded at the large man who slipped quietly up beside them.

"Good to have you join us," Greg Alexander said solemnly, nodding at Galen. "It's always a pleasure when you come along to play."

"Thanks," Galen said by way of greeting. *Always he is so reverent, so aware of who I should be, not who I am.*

"I heard something down by the gardens," Greg said.

"Okay, how do we handle it?" Rhiannon said, settling down to business.

"There are four main paths," Galen said. "Two from up here, two from below. If one of us comes from below we might be able to cut off whatever it is." He looked through the shifting shadows towards the gardens, full of empty branches. "I'll head down there."

"Be careful," Rhiannon said.

"Always." Galen walked silently down the path, sticking to the shadows, instincts honed in his youth serving him well. His senses were alert to every sound, shift of light and scent. He paused for a moment, something had moved off the trail to his left. A fat raccoon crossed the path in front of him, stopping to look at him for a moment before moving on.

Galen reached the lower paths to the gardens, glancing up the hill, he saw Rhiannon moving, ghostlike, down the hill. He was getting ready to move when someone screamed. Galen ran towards the sound, towards the back of the gardens where the leafless bushes were thick, obscuring his view. It was there, whatever it was, dragging a woman through the rosebushes. A shrill whistle let him know Rhiannon was behind him and to his right, the barking cough was Greg up and to his left.

Not a werewolf. Galen slowed down, drawing the falcata. "Let her go," he said quietly. The thing turned black eyes in graying flesh towards him. It hissed at him. He smiled. "Okay, time to play, then," he said, excitement buzzing through his hand. He caught sight of Rhiannon out of the corner of his eye and nodded slightly as she moved up behind the thing. Galen took a step forward, swinging the blade in front of him.

It let go of the woman and stood, looking at Galen for a moment. It reached a bony hand towards him. "Keeper," it hissed.

"Not anymore," Galen said.

"Yes, you are Keeper. Always Keeper." It took a step towards him and paused. It sniffed the air, breath rasping into its lungs. Without warning it dove for him, knocking him off balance. Galen recovered, dancing away and brought the falcata up in an arcing swing. It launched itself at him again, one gray hand closing over Galen's wrist. It let out a harsh sigh. "You're *that* Keeper?" Galen ignored it and sliced down, cutting the arm off at its wrist, the hand still clinging to his arm. He shook it off with a grimace. It came for him again, diving, the one claw-shaped hand outstretched towards his throat. It laughed, the odd dead voice full of glee. "Good," it hissed. "*That* Keeper, here. The time is coming. The echoes build."

"No." Rage boiled out of Galen mixing with the exhilaration of the moment. He lashed out with the sword. The thing ducked, the blade swung through empty air. Galen shifted his balance, preparing for another swing. It came at him again, a knife in its remaining hand. He dodged the blade as it stabbed towards his abdomen. The movement unbalanced him enough for the body-blow of the thing to carry him down to the ground. "Shit!" he said, pushing himself out of the way as it brought its blade down towards his throat.

"Galen!" Rhiannon hit the thing, carrying it away from Galen. She didn't move out from under it fast enough, he saw the blade sink into her flesh. She cried out, shoving it off of her. Galen saw a crossbow bolt shoot out the back of the thing. It screamed and stood, clawing at its back. Out of the corner of his eye he saw Greg grappling with another one of the creatures. *Well, if you can call turning it into hash grappling.* Galen pushed up off the ground and launched at the creature in the same movement. He caught it that time, neatly severing the head from the neck. It dropped to the ground and after a huge convulsion lay still.

Galen ran to Rhiannon. She was trying to push herself up, one hand covering the bloody wound high on her shoulder. He pushed her hand away to get a better look at the wound. Black tendrils had already moved out from the wound. "Hold still," he told her firmly. She stopped moving and looked at him, a questioning look in her eyes.

"What?" she said.

"Just don't move until I tell you, okay?" He focused on the wound, "feeling" it carefully. Galen was still aware of the end of Greg's fight, still aware of the thing he had killed on the ground. He dug through his first aid satchel and pulled out bandages and an herbal cream. Galen smeared a liberal amount of the cream on the wound before pressing the bandages in place.

"What's that?" Rhiannon asked, her nose twitching as she caught a whiff of the cream.

"Clover, St. John's Wort, vervain, betony and dill. It should stop the spread of the poison until I can deal with it at home."

"Not here?"

"No," he said, looking at the wound again. "It might be a little rough, I need to know we're safe before I heal it."

She nodded, understanding. "How'd we do?"

"All finished," Greg said, coming up behind Galen. "Although the woman's dead. The one I killed grabbed her before she got away. Throat's ripped completely open." Galen glanced up at the other man, Greg had splatters of the thing's black blood on him.

"Damn," Galen sighed, then grinned at Greg. "Nice work finishing it."

"A little messy, I know. Not like you." Greg grinned back. "One swing. Nice, neat. Takes a bit of skill." He laughed and Galen laughed with him. He always felt a little drunk after a successful party. Regret flowed on the heels of the exhilaration so quickly he barely had time to catch his breath. He shoved the memories away.

"Give me a hand with Rhiannon," Galen said, pulling her to her feet. He and Greg half-carried her back to the parking lot and slid her into the passenger seat of her pickup. She mumbled a little as they buckled the belt around her.

"Will she be okay?"

"Yeah, I just need to get her home to finish treatment." Galen slapped the other man on the shoulder. "Thanks for inviting me."

"Any chance to party with a Keeper," Greg said.

"I'm not a Keeper," Galen snapped.

"Yes, you are, and it's an honor when you come out with us. A Keeper helping us?" the older man said kindly. "I know why you always say that, I understand. But it's really who you are."

"Who I was, Greg, not anymore." Galen smiled and walked around to get into the truck. "I'll give you a call and let you know how she is."

"Thanks, and I'll call you for play-time again really soon," Greg said, grinning.

"Sure." Galen turned the engine over and put the truck in gear. "How are you doing?" he asked Rhiannon, she smiled without opening her eyes. "Pain?" he said. She nodded. "We'll be home soon."

He pulled the truck out onto the dark road, the streetlights making glaring stripes on the hood of the pickup. *It's nearly midnight. It's nearly...five years since Dad and Uncle Bobby, ten since... I wonder if Rhiannon is right, that I should be worried. I have wondered about it. I thought I felt... and the scar has been acting up, twisting at night. Ten years, it might mean something, but what...?* He shook his head and glanced at Rhiannon. Her eyes were open, watching him. He smiled. "Almost home."

Chapter Two

Galen pulled the truck up behind his building, bringing it to a rattling stop. He grabbed his first aid kit and jumped out of the truck, walked around it and wrenched open the passenger door. "We're here, can you help?" he said to Rhiannon. She opened her eyes with a wan smile and nodded, swinging her legs out of the truck and putting an arm over Galen's shoulders. He helped her the rest of the way out and up the stairs to the apartment, dropping her gently on the couch before flipping on the lights.

"Time for the whammy?" she said, her eyes trying to focus on him.

Galen nodded, kneeling by the couch and rubbing his hands together before laying one on the wound on her shoulder and the other over her heart. He let the light flow, her eyes drifted close as he felt his hands heat up. Galen let his eyes close as he focused on the movement between his hands waiting until he felt the black poison from the blade recede. He pulled away and dropped back on his heels.

Rhiannon opened her eyes. "All fixed?"

"Mostly, the wound isn't knitted, but it might need to drain a bit."

"You know best, doc," she said, pushing herself into a sitting position.

"I'm not a doctor." Galen stood and wandered into the kitchen. The healing left him a little light-headed, as always. He pulled a sparkling water out of the fridge and took a long drink.

"That fancy piece of paper on the wall says doctor."

"It says Ph.D. not M.D.," he said with a laugh, grabbing another water and walking back to the couch.

"I remember when you got into grad school, Parry was bursting with pride."

"He was a little embarrassing about it sometimes," Galen laughed. "He and Bobby both. Even though...I still went and...I think they were a little sad, too," Galen said suddenly. "It was a little symbolic of the break, that I continued even after what happened."

"He was proud, he and Bobby both. They were planning such a party..." She stopped herself, looking at him. "Sorry."

"Five years ago, right? I know. Right before my birthday, right before It came for me again."

Rhiannon smiled gently. "It is today isn't it?"

"One in the morning," he said quietly. Memories were crowding in, pressing against him.

Rhiannon put a gentle hand on his shoulder. "Galen?"

He looked at her. "Yeah?"

"What happened to Parry and Bobby wasn't your fault."

"It was though, they were protecting me. Shit, the Emrys line of Keepers ended that night, five years ago."

"The line isn't ended, Galen."

"It is," he snapped out. "And Dad and Uncle Bobby died defending that end. Defending me. It came for *me,* Rhiannon. I...I couldn't even save them." Galen sighed and got up again. He walked to the cupboard, and dug out two shot glasses and a bottle of tequila. "Since it is today." He poured them both a shot and held one out to her.

"To Parry and Bobby," she said, clinking her glass against his.

"When will we get there, Galen?" The bright smile beamed from the passenger seat. Galen took a deep breath, a lump forming in his throat, the loss suddenly fresh. "To Rob."

"To Rob," Rhiannon acknowledged quietly. "Galen? In all

these years, I've never really asked, but do you want to tell me? How it began?"

"You were there."

"About halfway through the beginning."

"The beginning of the end?" He heard the bitter note in his voice. Galen poured them another shot. Suddenly the need to talk materialized as the old wound in his chest gave a hard twist.

"Galen?"

"It's okay…" He took another slow breath, the past crowding him. "You know that as *Custodes Noctis*—Keepers—we're raised by adoptive parents until we're thirteen?"

"Yeah, you told me. And always brothers."

"Brothers." He sighed. "Five years apart. Always the same birthday. Like Dad and Uncle Bobby. At thirteen, we come to live with the older Keepers, to learn about what we do, to train for our lives as *Custodes Noctis*."

"Protecting the world from the night?"

He nodded, they went over it every year, a familiar ritual, comforting. "*Custodes Noctis*, Keepers of the Night, the ancient line, keeping the world safe and protected from those things that the creatures of the night fear." The words flowed off his tongue almost as a chant, a lesson learned and repeated hundreds of times.

"And ten years ago you…"

"I went to pick up Rob from his adoptive parents. Down in California. It was supposed to be a three-day drive. We were taking it in easy stages. We had gotten to know each other over the years, he came here for weekends and part of the summer, but that was the big move and I went to get him, the way the older brother always has, since the *Custodes Noctis* began."

"A hero's journey," she said gently.

"I don't know about that," he said. He could hear the bitterness in his voice, the old emotions consuming him as the tequila loosened his tongue. "It was our second day on the road..."

PAST
TEN YEARS BEFORE
Day One

Afternoon was moving into early evening, the traffic thinned after they passed through the last town and the radio had given way to static. Galen was trying out various music choices, most met with disgusted grunts from the passenger seat. He finally gave up and slammed "Jupiter" into the tape player.

"When will we get there, Galen?" Rob asked after several minutes of Mozart. Galen looked over. His nearly thirteen-year-old brother smiled at him with a bright, carefree smile.

"When are we going to get where?"

"You know." His brother rolled his eyes.

"We'll be there tomorrow night," Galen said and Rob sighed. Galen waited for a minute or two, but couldn't stop himself from smiling at his brother's repeated dramatic sighs. "Don't worry Rob, we'll be there in time for our birthday." He knew Rob was asking about more than just their birthday.

"Promise, Galen?"

"Yeah, Rob. I promise, like I did yesterday and the day before..."

"And the day before," Rob finished for him. He grinned at Galen. "And it's a big day all around, isn't it?"

"Yeah, you start your training with me the next day." He grinned back at Rob.

"The formal training to make me *Custodes Noctis*, right?"

"No, the training to make you shut up sometimes," Galen said, giving his brother a little shove.

"Yeah, right." Rob shoved back. "At thirteen we leave our first family, begin our training with our brother and we learn how to use our Gift. We take the first steps into the night, the place others fear, but we walk. Right?" Rob had repeated most of it in a little sing-song. A lesson repeated many times over the years.

"Right. Our family has been Keepers since before Rome, since before the stone circles. We have protected people from the night and the things even the dark fears," Galen went on.

"Always brothers, always of the same family."

"Right."

"We get to get stay at a hotel again tonight, don't we?" Rob changed the subject with a sly grin. The trip was a huge adventure for him, and he was making the most of time with just the two of them. It had been sparing in the past, except for late nights talking in the privacy of one or the other's room. The time had been filled with lessons and the first of their training.

"Yeah, we'll get to stay in a hotel tonight, Rob. We'll pull off for dinner first, how's that sound?"

"Can I pick, Galen?"

"Sure, what do you want tonight?"

"Burgers? We had pizza last night and tacos the night before."

"Keeping track of everywhere we eat?"

"Yep, I don't want to repeat until after our birthday," he said, smiling at Galen. He took every chance to remind Galen their birthday was just around the corner.

"What happens if we repeat?"

Rob shrugged. "I don't know. Just seemed fun, you know." Rob's smile faded just a tiny bit. Sometimes leaving his adoptive family hit him, and a slight sadness crept into his voice.

"Sure, something different is always good." Galen smiled at

him. Rob's smile brightened again.

"Can I have dessert, too? A sundae?"

"Yeah, Rob, sure." Galen noticed exit signs coming up. "Want to stop here? Or later?"

"Now? I'm kind of hungry now, Galen, if it's okay?" His brother still sounded a little sad, Galen could sense the edge of Rob's uncertainty.

"Wouldn't have asked if it wasn't." He followed the exit down to a small town. "What do you think about Pat's Burgers?" Galen said, pulling into a diner alongside the road. "Hey," he said, putting a hand on Rob's arm before the other could get out.

"Yeah, Galen?"

"I know it's not quite our birthday, but I thought you might like this." Galen pulled a small package out of his pocket and handed it to Rob.

His brother took it with wide eyes. "Can I open it now?"

"That's why I gave it to you," Galen said, smiling.

Rob ripped the paper off and carefully opened the box. His eyes lit up as he reverently pulled the copper, silver and bronze bracelet out. He laughed happily, a joyous sound. "This makes it official, doesn't it?" he said with a proud grin.

Galen grinned back. "Yeah, Brat, it does." Galen slid the bracelet over his brother's left wrist. The design remained unchanged from the first ones made millennia before, the badge of the Keeper, *Custodes Noctis*. Each design was unique to a given family line. "There's more."

Rob pulled the cotton aside and gave a low whistle. He pulled the small knife out of the box and smiled as he slid the blade out of the scabbard.

"Brother to brother," Galen said with a gentle smile. "Happy birthday. What?" Rob was grinning at him. His brother handed him a small package, carefully wrapped in the Sunday comics.

26

"What's this?" Galen asked.

"I've been doing my homework," Rob said, a little shyly. "Brother to brother," he solemnly repeated the formal phrase.

Galen smiled a little quizzically. He opened the package, a small silver-hilted knife rested on the bright paper. A Celtic knot wound its way down the hilt and scabbard. It was almost identical to the one he'd given Rob. He was silent for a moment as he held the gift. "You have done your homework, the traditional gift for when we start training together."

"Do you like it?" Rob asked quietly. Galen looked up, questioning eyes met his, unsure. "I saved up for a long time to get it."

"It's perfect." He smiled at Rob.

"Oh, good," Rob said with an exaggerated sigh.

"We're a good team already, Rob."

"Really?" Rob beamed at him. "And I've been reading the sagas. I know the ones about the First Emrys and the Legacy by heart now, Galen."

"You do?"

"Sure I do! In modern English, Latin and Anglo-Saxon. I was planning to start on the Old Norse and Irish, but I didn't have time. I didn't know if I'd get quizzed by Dad and Uncle Bobby on that. The sagas pretty important to the family."

"More than just pretty important."

"Will they ask me about the Anglo-Saxon?" Rob said eagerly. "Will I get extra points?"

"I'm not sure. They never asked me."

"Ah, shit." Rob looked over at him with a quirked eyebrow.

Galen laughed at that. "Ready to eat, Brat? And you might want to watch your language around Dad." He tucked the two knives carefully into the glove box.

"Yeah, right. How's it look?" Rob held out his wrist, the cuff bracelet sparkled in the streetlight. He held it next to Galen's arm, looking from his bracelet to his brother's.

"Looks good."

"Yeah, it does." Rob pulled the sleeve of his sweatshirt back down. The day had cooled as the sun set.

They got out and went into the restaurant. It was bright and faux-fifties. Galen shook his head when Rob declared it "Kinda awesome." They were seated at a booth in the back; a pretty, young waitress came over to take their orders. "What do you want Rob?"

"Cheeseburger, and can I have a milkshake, Galen? It'd be a nice treat before my birthday," Rob said with an innocent smile.

Galen laughed. "Okay, I'll have a burger and coffee."

"Wow, it's going to be your birthday? We'll get you that milkshake for free," the waitress, her name tag said Ashley, said. "How old will you be?"

"Thirteen, day after tomorrow."

"Really? That's interesting. There's a full moon that night, too." The waitress smiled at Rob and Galen felt the hair on the back of his neck rise.

"Rob," Galen said with a frown.

"Yeah?" Rob pulled his eyes from the waitress, he had been staring at her. He caught Galen's look and just smiled at Ashley-the-waitress until she left.

"What is it?" Galen said softly. "What did you see?"

Rob frowned as he thought about it. Galen watched him. "She had black spots."

"What kind? Like illness? Like your grandmother?"

"No, not like that, like, I don't know. It felt wrong," Rob said, carefully choosing his words.

"You can tell me more, Rob," Galen chided gently.

"I'm not sure what it is. She looks wrong somehow."

"Okay. I trust you. We should eat up and go on to the next town tonight, Rob. We'll be that much closer to home, you know?" Galen saw the waitress head into the kitchen. She reappeared with the pot of coffee and Rob's milkshake a few minutes later.

All through their meal the sense of something wrong kept growing. Galen could feel his back muscles tensing in response. He watched Rob looking at the waitress, the frown of concentration on his face. Galen wished his brother could tell him more of what he saw, but Rob was still learning to use his Gift. The ability to "see" things as they were, evil, illness, good, health, was the younger brother's Gift. It was difficult to learn, to use and control, at least according to their uncle.

Galen watched Ashley go back and forth between the tables. Another waitress, older—maybe in her early thirties—had come on shift as well. She, too, was watching Ashley, and when Ashley was busy with three men sitting at a table at the far end of the restaurant, she headed over with a pot of coffee.

She bent over towards Galen as she filled his cup. "Get your brother and get out of here. He's in danger."

"What do you mean?" he said quietly.

"Kids his age disappear around here. Two months ago my... my..." She stopped and looked at him. He could see a tear run down her face. "My daughter—it was her thirteenth birthday and she disappeared. They found her, four days later."

"I'm sorry," Galen knew from the way she said it that her daughter was dead. "Do you know what happened?" he said as softly as possible, smiling at her like he was thanking her for the coffee.

"She was cut up, mutilated, there were marks drawn on her, symbols of some kind. The police..." She stopped when she saw Ashley heading back across the diner. "Just go."

"Thank you." He looked over at Rob. His brother heard what she said and stopped eating. "Did she have black spots?"

"No," his brother said quickly. "Galen?"

"Time to go." He stood up and casually tossed a twenty down on the table. They walked slowly out of the restaurant. The parking lot where he had left the car was dark. Galen had purposefully parked under one of the large lights. The jeep was new, a present from his father and uncle, and he had no intention of letting it get stolen on its first road trip.

"Rob?" he said, keeping his voice nearly soundless. His brother closed the gap between them. "When we get to the car, get in and lock your door. Okay? No matter what happens."

"What?" Rob sounded a little scared.

"Just do as I say, it will be okay, trust me."

"Of course I trust you, Galen. Duh."

Galen fished in his pocket and pulled out the keys. He used his body to hide the action as he handed the keys to Rob. "Start the car for me."

"Galen?" Rob said, fear beginning to color his voice.

"It's just a precaution, Rob. Be prepared, right? But you need to get into the car, make sure your door's locked and get it started, no matter what." He repeated it emphatically, hoping the training they had would be enough to help his brother through whatever was about to happen.

"Yeah, sure," Rob said, moving to Galen's side.

As they approached the car, the three guys Ashley-the-waitress had been serving stepped into their path, trying to block their way to the car. Galen shoved Rob behind him, towards the car. "Rob! You know what to do!"

One of them made a lunge for Rob and Galen dove towards him. He grabbed the guy, hit him hard and felt the guy's nose squish. "One down!" Galen said, letting Rob know he was okay.

He heard the car door slam closed, a second later the engine roared to life. The two remaining men were trying to get to the vehicle, to get to Rob, but Galen had no intention of letting that happen. Galen moved towards the door. One of the men blocked his way, a knife in his hand. The other came up on Galen's left side. Galen saw something flash and felt the blade plunge into his chest. He was slammed against the side of the car.

He heard a sound—the car window rolling down. "Galen, move!" He slid towards the back of the car to avoid a blow and the jeep's door exploded outwards, propelled by a thrust from his brother's legs. Galen dove into the driver's seat, threw the car into gear and floored it.

"Rob, sit down," he said to his brother who was leaning over the backseat. Rob slid back down into his seat with a towel in his hands. He folded it carefully and handed it to Galen. "Thanks," Galen said, pressing the towel to his side. He could feel the warm flow of blood across his stomach, already soaking the top of his jeans.

"Galen?" Rob was looking at him, his eyes wide, frightened.

"I'm okay, Rob. Good thinking with the door. You did good." He smiled over at Rob. "Real good."

"Thanks, Galen. Are you hurt bad?" He sounded panicked.

"I'm okay."

"It's a lot of blood, Galen. The towel's already soaked."

"It'll be okay, Rob. We just need to get out of here first." He tried to focus on driving. He was getting a little light-headed and starting to get cold, starting to go into shock. Rob must have realized something of the same thing. He reached over and turned on the car heater. Galen looked over at Rob. "You okay?"

"Yeah, I'm okay. Galen!" he yelled, looking out the window.

Galen turned and saw the truck blocking the road. Slamming on the brakes, he put the car in reverse and turned around.

Another truck, without lights, had come up behind them. Another car and another. They were trapped.

"Shit!" Galen looked over at his brother. "Rob, listen to me. As soon as you get a chance, you run. Find a phone and call Dad and Uncle Bobby. I need you to do as I say," he said as calmly as possible.

"Galen?" Rob was scared, Galen could hear it in his voice. "You're coming too, aren't you?"

"I am, but I need to know you're going to try and get away, too. We're a team, but I need you to try and run. I'll be right behind you, okay? But you keep running, no matter what."

"What do you mean?" Rob said, his eyes filling with tears.

"Just get yourself safe." Galen said, watching a group approach the car. He leaned over and grabbed his nine millimeter handgun out of the glove box. "Rob?" He looked over at his brother.

"Yeah, but Galen…"

"Rob, you heard the waitress. They're after someone your age. That's why you need to run."

"But…"

"Don't worry, just run, no matter what you hear, no matter what."

"Galen." The tears were running down his brother's face.

"Rob, gods damn it, just do what I say!" He saw hurt flare in his brother's eyes. "Sorry, Rob. I'm sorry." He gave his brother's arm a gentle squeeze. "Trust me?" Galen asked. Rob nodded. "Ready? Now, run!" Galen threw the door open and swung the gun up, firing off three rounds in rapid succession.

He sensed, rather than saw, his brother's flight. A dark shape moved to block Rob's dash, Galen turned. "Rob, down!" He knew Rob would react to that command without thinking, they had been working on that one since he was five. Galen fired at the dark shape. He saw one go down, then another, and then the hammer came down on an empty chamber. One of the men in front of Galen jumped towards him and drove a fist into his side, the pain exploded and dark spots danced before his eyes. Galen collapsed to his knees.

He heard Rob's terrified shout, "No! Galen!" and heard Rob screaming at the edge of his awareness. "No!" And his brother's voice was cut off.

Galen tried to struggle to his feet. Another punch to his side, he didn't even see it coming. It put him down. He thought he felt someone kicking him. His whole focus, what was left of it at least, was on his brother. Galen reached out with what was left of his strength, trying to reach Rob, but his sense of his brother was completely gone. He needed to know what was happening. His last vision before blacking out was Rob, limp, unconscious, tossed into the back of one of the waiting cars, then the darkness rose up and claimed him. "No, Rob, no."

* * * * *

"No, Rob, no." Galen heard his voice, heavy with grief, suddenly loud in the quiet room. He opened his eyes, Rhiannon was looking at him, tears on her cheeks.

"I'm sorry, Galen," she said softly, laying a hand over his.

"Usually I wait until you leave to work myself into this state," he said, the laugh still bitter. His head was resting on the back of the couch as he looked at her. "Sorry." He reached for the bottle again.

"I think you've had enough, honey," Rhiannon said, pushing herself up off the couch. "It's almost five and I have to work part of the day."

"Yeah." Galen tried standing up, only to drop back onto the couch again. Rhiannon laughed gently and pulled him up, letting him lean on her. He realized she had maneuvered him into the bedroom and pushed him onto the bed. As he dropped down onto the mattress, she pulled the blankets over him. He remembered mumbling something about putting a note in the door of the shop before he was asleep.

He was running. They were chasing him. Terror was pounding through his veins like blood in rhythm with his heartbeat. He had mistakenly run into a small alley, it cost him. As he came out from behind a large dumpster, they cut him off. Hands grabbed him and tried to pull him away, fists connecting with him, a voice calling out to leave him alive. Then, suddenly, sirens, feet running and someone asking if he was okay, he couldn't answer, pain and blood prevented the words from forming.

Galen shot upright in bed, his heart pounding from the nightmare. His hands were shaking with fear as the room came slowly into focus. "Oh, not good," he groaned. Galen grabbed his head and stumbled out of bed towards the bathroom. Once there, he rummaged through his medicine cabinet for the homeopathic remedy for a hangover, *Nux Vomica*. He pulled the small tube out and dumped several pellets under his tongue. After splashing cold water on his face, he walked back into the bedroom and shoved the curtains all the way closed. It was gray outside, the light still too bright. *How much did I drink? I don't even remember.* Galen sank back into the bed with a sigh. *That nightmare, it felt a little like…No.*

Pulling the pillow over his head, he went back to sleep.

Chapter Three

The phone was jangling from the living room. It stopped, but not before it had wormed its way through the pillow and straight into Galen's brain. He pushed the pillow aside and peered blearily at the clock, it was just before noon. He was sure he'd told Rhiannon he'd open the shop at noon. Groaning, he stumbled into the bathroom, dosed himself with the *Nux Vomica* again and climbed in the shower, letting the hot water ease his pounding headache. "Never again," he said to his reflection in the mirror, then laughed, knowing he said it every year. The water had started to cool when he finally got out.

The store was quiet as he walked through, he unlocked the door and headed straight for the espresso stand. "Hey, Becci," he said quietly.

"Galen!" She bounced over to the window, red bra and panties bright against her light skin. "You're late today!"

"Yeah, sorry, late night. Anyone been by the shop?"

"Someone came by about seven, looked in the windows and left. And Flash came by about half an hour ago, he read your sign, though, and said he'd be back," she said, handing him a coffee. "I put in an extra shot or two, you look like you could use it. Don't tell the boss," she said with a wink.

"Thanks," Galen said, sipping the coffee. "Not too hot."

"Figured you needed to drink it fast," she said, leaning over the sill.

"Good guess." He smiled at her and walked back to the shop. He turned the open sign on as he walked in and settled behind the counter, resting his head in one hand, holding the coffee in another. *I should just close the store on these days. I'm in no shape to work, really, and with the scar acting up like it is...I'll close early tonight.* He took another sip of the coffee. His head was still aching. Something in the pain made him stop for a minute. It felt familiar.

"You alive?" Flash said, walking into the store and carefully closing the door, keeping one hand over the bells so they were muted.

"Mostly." Galen smiled as his friend put another large coffee in front of him. "Thanks."

"Thought you might need it, all things considered." Flash dragged a stool over behind the counter, sat down and peered at him. "Man, you look like shit."

"Thanks for the coffee." Galen glanced at him with a grateful look. He'd met Alvin "Flash" Lynch auditioning for a band. Neither had liked that group and had decided to leave and form their own. With the addition of keyboards and a drummer, The Urban Werewolves had been born. Galen and Flash had formed a fast friendship over the last four years.

"I started a little earlier than usual last night," Galen said with a grimace.

"I figured as much when the store was locked up this morning."

"I meant to be down sooner." Galen shrugged. "Didn't make it."

"How are you holding up?" Flash looked at him closely. "I know the fifth anniversary of my mother's death hit me really hard for some reason."

"No worse than usual."

"You're lying to me, Galen."

"Probably. I'm not sure."

"You coming to practice later? We do have that gig at Rat's

on Friday. He said that we'd get half the take."

"If the money actually materializes it'll be some kind of epic miracle." Galen snorted. They had played Rat's Nest three times, always promised cash, but always something came up, the bar tab, breakage—something—and Rat never got around to paying. "His nickname's a little too appropriate."

"I don't know," Flash said, grinning. "Seems kind of mean to the rats out there."

Galen laughed with him. "Yeah. I'm not sure if I'm up to practice, Flash. I can't seem to shake this headache."

"You need more coffee." Flash got up off the stool.

"I haven't even finished my second."

"Uh…"

"Did Sara just get to work?" Galen said, grinning at the blush that suffused his friend's face.

"Maybe. I'll be right back." Flash was out the door before Galen could raise another protest.

As the door banged closed behind Flash, Galen closed his eyes, trying to focus a little healing inwards. His father had scolded him once or twice for using the Gift to cure hangovers, but this time it felt different. He took a deep breath, letting himself relax. *"It's harder to heal ourselves than others, Galen," his father had said to him. "Why?" Galen asked. "I'm not sure. The Gift is focused outwards most of the time. We can do it—it's just much harder, and the bigger the need, the harder it is."* The headache wasn't diminishing. Galen shifted his focus from healing to diagnosis, trying to figure out what was causing it. The realization it was coming from somewhere outside himself caused his heart to beat a little harder than usual. The scar gave a painful twist, hard enough to take his breath away.

"You okay?" Flash had a hand on his back.

"Can you go in the back and grab the dark red bottle? The

one with the poison sticker on it?"

"Sure." Flash was back a few seconds later with the bottle in hand. "One of your weird-ass concoctions? You know that whole fucking shelf, most of the bottles have poison stickers on them."

"Yeah, they do." Galen took a sip of the bitter liquid, pausing as it moved out through his body, stilling the twisting of the scar. "I thought people might be less likely to try them that way." The ache in his chest receded, but the headache didn't.

"Got you another coffee. Mocha or latte?" Flash held out two cups.

"Mocha, thanks," Galen said, taking the cup.

"Bunny?" Flash said, sitting back down beside him.

Galen grinned. Since forming the band, they had spent many happy hours looking for an imaginary lead singer whose name would go well with the band. Bunny and the Urban Werewolves was the last in a long, long list of possibilities. "Bunny works, but I was thinking the other day about Heather. Nice blond name. Cheerleader type."

"So's Bunny."

"True, I guess the search goes on." Galen sighed, taking a sip of the mocha.

"Hard losing your Dad and uncle the same day," Flash said suddenly, apropos of nothing.

"It was." *Especially considering they died for me. It came for me again, we thought It was gone after I…but It came again, five years after. Looking for me, looking for…Sometimes I think we didn't make the right decision, maybe we should have…Coulda, shoulda, woulda, doesn't get me anywhere now. I couldn't save them.* He sighed.

Flash had been watching him. "Come out with us tonight, man, even if you don't want to practice, let's go out somewhere away from here, that way you can't brood."

"I'm impressed you got all that out without taking a breath."

"If I stopped to breathe you would've interrupted me."

"Thanks. Let me think about it?" Galen sighed as Flash rolled his eyes. "If someone comes in and needs to be zapped I'll be in no state to go out, you know that." Zapped was Flash's word for the healing Galen did. Flash still didn't quite believe it, even after Galen had healed him after a serious accident on stage.

"I know, I just don't want you hanging around all by yourself doing that brooding thing you do," Flash said.

"I don't do any brooding thing. The last time you accused me of that, I was preparing for the defense of my dissertation."

"You were brooding about it and I fixed it."

"You took me to a strip club and got me drunk, the night before my defense."

"You felt better afterwards. And don't frown at me, *Doctor* Emrys, you got through just fine with your boring old musty degree."

"Yeah, yeah. Go away, Flash, I have customers coming in." Galen smiled at Flash as the other rose and headed towards the door.

"I'll be back tonight."

"Fine. We'll see you then." Galen turned to the man who came in the store. "Can I help you?"

"I'm looking for some frankincense," he said gruffly.

"Tears or powder?" Galen asked, shifting his shoulders a little. Something about the man set him on edge, he couldn't put his finger on it, but there was something. *Sometimes I wish I'd gotten the Sight, being able to "see" people would be very helpful.* The man followed Galen as he walked back behind the counter.

"I'd prefer tears," the man said.

Galen turned to get the jar from the shelf, the sudden sense of unease growing as he turned his back on the man. He pulled the jar down and put it on the counter, glancing at the man's hands. They were bruised, the skin broken on one knuckle. "How much?"

"Do you have half a pound?" the man asked with an odd grin.

"Of course." Galen began measuring out the resin on the scale. He often wondered why he carried frankincense at all. *I can still smell that stuff they were burning before the ritual... Frankincense was part of it.* "Here you go. That will be fifteen dollars," Galen said, dropping the sack on the counter.

"Right." The man dug a grubby twenty out of his pocket and handed it to Galen, letting his fingers come into contact with Galen's hand. A slight shock, cold, like the touch of death, ran up from the point of contact. Galen jerked his hand back and set the change on the counter. The man smiled at him, a mocking look in his eyes. "See ya soon." He turned and walked to the door. Pausing at the entrance, he laughed. "Very soon."

The door slammed closed behind the man. Galen realized his hands were shaking. Something had shivered up that touch, something that felt like the thing that had killed his father and uncle, that felt like the thing that had taken his brother. *Can It be back? A five-year cycle of some kind? In all my research, I still don't know all that much about It,* the thing had existed in various forms since forever. *In the first form those people worshipped It, after those first days...It was so much worse, what It became, what It did to all of us.*

He stopped, drawing a deep breath and focused, using just a tiny bit of the healing to drive the tension away. He laughed at himself, as the tension in his shoulders eased, even though the headache was still there.

Galen put the jar of frankincense back on the shelf. The bells chimed on the door again, he turned quickly, already preparing for the worst. "Hi, Lana," he said, mustering a smile.

"Hello, Galen. Do you carry chasteberry?"

"Yes." He walked over to the large shelf labeled "women's herbs" running his eyes over the various bottles on the shelf. "Do you want pills? Capsules or tablets?"

"Of course I want pills. Tablets, please, capsules make those awful-tasting burps," she said with a look on her face like she was smelling something very unpleasant. "Those sleeping pills you sold me were terrible."

"They worked, didn't they?" He was still smiling.

"Well, yes, they worked, but I didn't know how long I could stand it."

He pulled the bottle of pills off the shelf and walked back over to the counter, still with the fake smile pasted on his face. He rang her up, put the bottle in a little bag and handed it to her. She gave a little humph and left the store.

A delivery truck pulled up outside. Galen went out to meet the driver and direct him where to put the boxes in the back of the store. As the driver was leaving, another customer came in and then another. It was nearly an hour later before Galen got back to his boxes. He cut the tops open and started inventorying the shipment of herbs.

"New goodies?" Rhiannon asked. She'd come in moments before, bringing the smell of fast food tacos with her.

"Some herbs, a few magical items I've been waiting for, some other stuff."

"And the big, long box?" She handed him one of the bags she had in her hand.

"The box that looks almost like it might have something pointy in it?" Galen said with a laugh.

"That's the one." Rhiannon had picked the box in question up and brought it over to him. "Something sharp and pointy?"

"Very." Galen laughed at the look of pure glee in her eyes. "I meant to wrap it." He shrugged. "Open it if you want."

"What? For me?" she asked, meeting his eyes.

"Ten year anniversary, thought I should get you something." Galen handed her the box cutter. She eagerly opened the box, whistling as she pulled out a archer's falchion. Galen had chosen the short sword with her height in mind. She ran a loving hand over the scabbard before pulling the blade out and taking an experimental swing with it. "Do you think most women get that turned on by a sword, Rhiannon?"

"If they don't there's something wrong with them." She grinned. "You didn't have to, honey."

"Yes, I did, Rhiannon, I would've never made it through without you," he paused, looking at her.

"You would've done fine without me."

"No. You were so calm, so strong, even after everything that had happened."

PAST

TEN YEARS BEFORE

Day Two

He was cold, cold and wet. That was the first thing that crept into Galen's awareness. The ground was hard under him and he could hear sirens in the distance. He was still lying on the road, the cold seeping up from the pavement.

"Hold still. Help is on the way," a woman's voice said. Galen opened his eyes. Well, actually he opened his right eye, the left one didn't want to open. A woman with soft ginger hair was holding his hand, gently patting his wrist, and a man with white hair was kneeling beside her. "What's your name?" the man asked.

"Uh, Rob?" Galen said, confused.

"Your name is Rob?" the woman asked.

"No, Galen. My brother, Rob, is he here?" He felt panic twisting in his chest. He tried to sit up. Pain stabbed through him. He could feel his side burning.

"No, no, lie still," the man said, pushing him back down. "There was no one else here. I looked around. I called the police, they're on their way. An ambulance, too. What happened?"

"They took my brother. We were at the diner and then, they took him." Galen stopped, unable to go any further. "My Dad, I need to get a hold of my Dad." Galen could hear the sirens, they were quite close now. He tried to reach out for his brother, but couldn't stretch beyond his body. With a small groan, he tried to focus some of the healing to give himself a little more time—he knew he only had a minute or two left of consciousness. "Call him, his number is two zero..." He couldn't hold on anymore.

The next time awareness raised its head, Galen was in a hospital. He could tell by the smell. They'd given him something, he had an odd feeling of disconnect he suspected must be coming from painkillers. Galen looked around. His left eye still wouldn't open very far. He was alone in a room, the IV stand beside the bed had a bag of blood hanging from it. Something was wrong. He floated on the drugs for a minute, casting around, trying to figure out what it was. The answer slammed into his head with a near physical force. "Rob!" he heard his voice in the quiet room.

Galen took a deep breath. When he sensed a little of his strength had returned, he reached out for his brother. He slowly extended out beyond himself, letting the hospital room dim as he searched for Rob. After a minute, he thought he felt the tiniest hint of his brother—pain, a confused rumble of thoughts, fear. Over it all was fear. *"Rob?"* He'd never managed to communicate actual words to his brother, but he tried this time. *"Rob? Can you hear me?"* For just an instant he thought he felt a sliver of recognition, he wasn't sure. *"I'm okay, Rob. I'm coming."*

He tried to sit up, only to discover restraints on his wrists. He pulled against them. They wouldn't budge. He tried to stay calm. The need to find his brother and his own fear of being restrained were creating something very close to a panic attack. Galen ran through his training, trying to find a way out of the restraints. Finally, he relaxed, letting the muscles in his arm go limp and he started easing his hand out of the restraint. He'd nearly worked his left hand all the way free when the door opened.

"We're awake," a woman who looked to be in her forties said, smiling as she came into the room.

"Yeah, nice." Galen said, relaxing. "Can I get these things off?"

"I'm not sure, they said you might be violent," she said, hesitating.

"Who said? I'm not." He smiled at her. "I'll be good, I promise." He held his breath as she hesitated. The nurse reached to take his pulse, he let a little of the healing light flow out onto her hand. She suddenly smiled at him. "Please?" he said softly.

"Okay, if you promise to be good."

"Of course," he said, still smiling at her. She unbuckled the restraints on his wrists. He could feel the ankle ones, but now that his hands were free they didn't worry him. "Thanks." He rubbed his wrists. She peered at the monitors, took his blood pressure, checked his temperature and smiled sweetly before she left.

Galen waited for ten minutes. He watched them creep by on the clock. Satisfied that no one was going to come in for awhile, he sat up and undid the restraints on his legs. His father and uncle had told him many times that if you act like you are supposed to be somewhere, doing something, people just assume that's what's meant to happen. *I wonder if that works for escaping from hospitals?* He waited for a moment as a wave of dizziness washed over him, pulled the IV out of his hand and swung his legs out of bed. His clothes were in a bag on a chair by the door. As he changed, he focused a little healing into himself, trying to numb the aches enough to let him get out of the hospital unnoticed.

Galen opened the door and looked down the hospital corridor. Luckily, the room he was in was only one door down from the elevators. He heard it ding and walked casually there as the doors opened. As he stepped into the elevator, a couple, visitors judging by the teddy bear, stepped out. He smiled at them and they frowned.

"Are you okay?" the woman asked.

"Just got released," Galen said, still smiling, counting the seconds. The doors finally closed. He punched the button for the lobby and hoped he could get out before anyone checked his room.

His luck held. He managed to get out of the hospital before the alarm was raised. Galen stood at the entrance for a minute, wondering how he could get back to where he'd left the jeep. As he stood there a taxi pulled up and a man got out. Galen opened the door and got in the back of the cab.

"Where're you headed?" the driver said, looking at him with the same frown the couple in the elevator had given him. "Should you be leaving?"

"The doc said it was fine. I got drunk last night and left my car out on the road. About four miles out of town, heading west." He smiled at the driver.

"Get in a fight, too?" the driver said, pulling out. He just sounded curious, not like he was trying to get information.

Galen forced a laugh. "Yeah, there was this blond." He whistled. "But her boyfriend didn't approve."

"What a bitch," the driver said. Galen wasn't sure if he meant the blond or the situation.

"Yeah." He leaned back into the seat. He wasn't in very good shape. The knife wound was stitched, but still bleeding a little, he was pretty sure at least one rib was broken and he looked at his reflection in the cab window. His left eye was black and mostly closed, he had a large bruise over his right eye and the left side of his jaw and neck were purple. *Gods, my face is a mess. No wonder people are looking at me a little weird.* Galen focused the healing inwards, trying to shore up his defenses a little until he could get a hold of his father and uncle.

It took ten minutes to get back out where he and Rob had been trapped. "That your car?"

Galen sighed. The jeep was still parked beside the road. The cops had chalked a pick-up time on the back, but it was still there. "Yeah, thanks." Galen got out and paid him. He waited until the taxi was well down the road before getting in. *Just in case. I don't really know who are the bad guys right now.* Galen put his hands on the wheel and reached out for Rob. He could sense nothing of his brother.

Galen turned the car around and headed back towards town. There was a rest stop off to his left, nestled under several large trees, far enough from town to be surrounded by woods and fields. He pulled in and headed to the phone, unable to shake the increasing sense of panic. He needed to call his father and uncle and let them know what was happening. *Hopefully, I'll find Rob before they get here.* He looked at his watch. It was just past six, he knew his father and uncle were out getting things for Rob's arrival. On the off chance they were home early, he dialed the number. When his father's voice answered, Galen took a deep breath, then realized it was the answering machine. "There's a problem, Dad. I'll call back in two hours." He walked slowly back to the car. *That waitress, the one who warned us, I need to talk to her.*

He parked the car where he could see the backdoor of the diner he and Rob had eaten at the night before and sat watching the employees come and go. Finally the older waitress came out. He got out of the car. "Hey," he called softly.

She jumped and looked around, then spotted him. "Oh my god. What happened?"

"They got my brother." And he had to stop. Somehow saying it made it a reality.

"What?" She looked at him, then seemed to make a decision. She walked around the car and got in the passenger seat. "How can I help?"

"What?" Galen got in and looked over at her. "Are you sure?"

"My daughter's dead. I don't want that to happen to your brother." She put her hand lightly on his arm. Her despair and grief flowed out from her touch. Galen opened himself a little to get a sense of her sincerity. *She's telling the truth, she's not one of them, she only wants to help me find my brother. Rob said she didn't have spots like Ashley. Even though he isn't quite sure how to use the Sight, he could see that.*

Oh gods, Rob. Galen could feel tears in his eyes. *They killed her daughter. They killed her, she was Rob's age.* "Can you tell me anything? Anything at all." He smiled. "My name's Galen, by the way."

"Rhiannon," she said with a sad smile.

* * * * *

"You changed my life a bit too, Galen," she said, laying a gentle hand on his cheek. Galen snapped back to the present, the remembered pain suddenly fresh. "You know that." She sat down, the sword still clasped in her hand. "Doesn't feel like ten years, does it? Since Megan, since Rob…"

"No, it doesn't."

"How do you feel?"

"A little hungover. I have a headache I can't shake."

"There's more."

"Someone came in today. I thought I felt It." Galen put an emphasis on the word. He always did when talking about the thing that had killed his father and uncle.

"What?"

"I'm not sure, but this man came in looking for frankincense and when he handed me the money, I swear he meant to touch me and let me know what was there. Then when he was leaving, he said 'see you very soon' and every warning bell in my head went off all at once." He laughed. "Of course, I'm probably just being paranoid, a little hangover can do that. The scar's been acting up too."

"The scar's acting up? Bad?"

"A little more than usual," he said quietly, knowing she'd understand.

"Galen, maybe you should be worried," Rhiannon said anxiously.

"I'll be careful, how's that?" He sighed and then smiled at her as he picked up the garbage from their meal.

"Five years, Galen, it might mean something."

"It might, Rhiannon, I know, it's just I can't…" He stopped as a guitar riff started playing. Galen pulled his cell phone out of his pocket, glanced at the caller ID and flipped it open. "Hey, Mike. What's up?"

"Galen, hi. They brought someone in this morning, a John Doe, no ID, thought I should call you." Mike Silva was an Emergency Room physician Galen had known for years. He called occasionally when he had a difficult case, or when something out of the ordinary came into the ER.

"I thought you didn't like me playing in your sandbox," Galen said with a laugh.

"I don't, usually, but this guy has a bracelet like yours," Mike said.

"I'll be right down, meet you in ER?"

"Sure, see you in fifteen."

Galen flipped the phone closed. "That was Mike Silva. Sounds like a Keeper was brought into the ER this morning. Whoever he is, he has a bracelet."

"What's wrong?"

"I'm not sure I'm in the mood for the lecture. As soon as other Keepers find out who I am, I get the lecture," Galen said with a sigh. "I deserve it, just not sure I'm in the mood for it."

"Want a ride?" Rhiannon stood.

"I think I'll drive, that way I can hide out for a bit, Flash wants to take me out tonight."

"Strip club?" She shook her head. "The Flash panacea." She gave him a quick hug. "Call me if you need me."

"Thanks, I will." He locked the front door of the store after her and grabbed his keys. Heading out the back door, he thought he saw someone out of the corner of his eye, but when he looked over the shadow was gone. Galen paused by the jeep and looked over the parking lot one more time, unable to dispel the sense of unease building between his shoulder blades. With a shrug, he got into the car and turned the engine over, idly flipping through the radio stations while the car warmed up. Settling on the classical station, he pulled out and headed towards the hospital. He worried about the fact it was only one Keeper at the ER. They came in twos and if the other was dead, Galen knew this one wouldn't last long. The image of his father holding his uncle's body played in his head.

The lot was full when he got to the hospital. He pulled his car up to valet parking and hopped out, taking the token from the kid parking cars. He chuckled to himself, the attendant looked about twelve. Galen wandered through the hospital, winding his way through the maze-like hallways until he ended at the ER. He walked up to the harried-looking nurse sitting behind glass under the "triage" sign.

"Can I help you?" she said, looking up at him.

"Hi, I'm Galen Emrys, I'm here to see Mike Silva, he's expecting me." He smiled at her.

"Oh, yes, he told me you'd be here." She stood and came out the door. "Follow me," she said as she led the way back into the ER. "Wait here." She left him standing in a quiet corner of the hallway.

A scream came from the room next to him, someone a couple of rooms over was crying quietly, a nurse was laughing. Galen let it all flow around him, trying to ignore his increasing headache. Finally, he saw Mike come out of a room down the hall from him. Mike smiled as he saw Galen standing in the corner.

"Were you chewing gum in class?" Mike said with a laugh. "Got stuck in the corner?"

"Ha, ha, Mike. I was abandoned here by a nurse." He followed the doctor as he walked quickly through the ER.

"I get abandoned by nurses all the time," Mike said with a sly grin as they stopped at the elevators.

"I'm sure you do." Galen grinned back. They got into the elevators. "We're playing at Rat's on Friday."

"I'll bring Linda, she likes that sort of thing."

"Linda? And that sort of thing?"

"Yeah, I met her a couple of weeks ago, friendly." Mike wiggled his eyebrows. "She likes going to bars, hearing live music."

"Right." Galen laughed. "Want to tell me, Mike?" he asked, dropping the light, bantering tone.

"They brought him in early this morning. He's not in good shape. He got worked over, cops chased the attackers off. I took over right before they sent him upstairs, noticed the bracelet."

"No one's been in looking for him?"

"You mean like last time?"

"Yeah." Galen remembered the call from Mike eight months before. "How old is he?"

"Hard to tell, he's a mess, but early twenties would be my guess," Mike said. "Why?"

"It's hard when the healer of the pair is wounded, hard on the younger brother. We saved the last one, I hope we can again. We'll need to start looking for his brother. If the brother's dead..."

"What?" Mike cut him off.

"He's dead, too. We can save him now, maybe, but he won't last long. Is there anything else?" Galen could sense hesitation in the doctor.

"Well, for an instant I thought he looked a little like..." Mike shook his head. "Never mind." Mike smiled at the nurses sitting at their station. "Checking on my John Doe." He led Galen to the room in the corner of the ward. Pushing open the door, he gestured Galen in ahead of him.

Galen looked at the figure on the bed, bruised, unconscious, an IV snaking into his arm. Something in Galen suddenly shattered, the world coalesced for an instant and something snapped. He felt it as a physical sensation. "How bad?" he managed to whisper.

"What?"

"How bad, Mike?"

"Not good, I told you. They worked him over good," Mike said, looking over at him. "Galen?" Concern colored Mike's voice.

"Will he live?"

"Galen?" Mike grabbed his arm. "What is it?" When Galen remained silent, Mike shook him a little. Galen turned, meeting the concerned gaze of his friend. "Do you know him?"

"Yes and no," Galen said quietly.

"Yes and no? What the hell does that mean? Who is he?" Mike demanded.

"My brother, Mike. He's my brother."

Chapter Four

The room was silent except for the hiss of oxygen and the soft beeping of the heart monitor. Galen could hear his own breathing, it sounded harsh in the quiet room. He idly wondered if Mike could hear the pounding of his heart.

"What?" Mike asked.

"My brother, Mike. Robert Emrys. You can change the paperwork and bring in whatever I need to sign, okay?" He still hadn't moved, standing just inside the door, unsure, thinking if he moved the spell would be broken and it would be someone else on the bed. The truth was there, he knew it was Rob, he could feel his brother's pain radiating across the room to where he stood by the door. *Something happened. The block is gone.*

"Your brother? You have a brother?"

"Yeah." Galen tore his eyes away from the bed and looked at Mike, the doctor had a shocked expression on his face. "Kid brother, five years younger. Same birthday."

"Like your Dad and uncle?"

"Exactly like them," Galen said, forcing his feet to approach the bed. He looked down at the still form of his brother, bruises covering his head. "I guess that explains the headache I couldn't get rid of. How bad?" he asked, as he did he laid a hand his brother's arm "feeling" what was there. Pain shot up from the touch, exploding behind his eyes, stronger than any reaction he'd had in years.

"Galen!" Mike caught him as he started to fall.

"Sorry." Galen steadied himself and stood up straight. "I forgot." He smiled sadly. "You wouldn't think I would, would you?"

"What the hell are you talking about?" Mike said, looking into his eyes, one hand against Galen's wrist checking his pulse.

"Family, it hits you harder. And brothers, well, the Gift's designed for them more than anyone else." Galen sighed, aware of the throbbing pain in his head. *Rob? Is it really...* He stopped himself. *No, I can't deny it. It is you, isn't it?* The bond that had been broken, hidden away, was suddenly there again, pounding in his chest like a slowly healing wound.

"It'd be nice to know what you are talking about sometimes. You get that funny look in your eye and I lose you."

"Thanks, I think." Galen snorted. "And as bad as it normally is for brothers, it's worse for Rob and I. Something happened when we were younger, but even before that the bond was much stronger between us. We could...Usually it takes years for the bond to form, it was always stronger in us, I think even more than Dad and Uncle Bobby, even before...when we were kids and then after..." Galen swallowed. "After...Well, the bond was...We had to break it after..." He stopped, unsure how much more he should share with Mike.

"After whatever it was that happened that you never told me about, that your Dad was silent about, that left those scars on your body? The ones that look like symbols, the ones that look a little like you were..."

"Yeah."

"He has them, too. I noticed when I examined him. It's not something you all have?"

"No." Galen heard the bitter tone in his laugh. "No, we're special, Rob and me." He stopped himself. "Can I stay?" Galen ran his eyes over his brother. "Is this a mistake? Letting him know I'm here?" he said softly, more to himself. "No. Something tells me my death is over. I'm tired of being dead, I want life. I hope he can forgive me someday. I...It's too late anyway. He probably knows I'm here."

"What did you just say?" Mike asked.

"He probably knows I'm here already."

"No, before that."

"Did I say something?" Galen looked at the doctor.

"Are you okay, Galen?"

"I'm not really sure. Can I stay?" Galen repeated.

"So you can do whatever it is that brings people back from the dead?"

"I can't do that, damn it," Galen snapped, then laughed a little. "Yeah, so I can do that thing I do, but I want to be here when he wakes up, too."

"How long has it been, Galen?" Mike said, putting a hand on his shoulder and giving him a gentle squeeze.

"Ten years."

"I'll let the nurses know, so they don't try and chase you out later. I'll be around for a few more hours. I'll check on you before I leave."

"Thanks, Mike." His friend gave him a quick slap on the back and left the room. Galen turned back to the figure in the bed. His brother's hair was curly. Galen smiled, remembering long-winded complaints about the natural curls in the brown hair, half a shade darker than his own. *He's tall. I told him he'd be tall. He was always so worried that he wouldn't grow.*

His smile faded as he looked at his brother. Rob's face was bruised, there was a gash in his forehead. Galen could feel some of his brother's pain, radiating off Rob in a wave. *He looks terrible. I need to know how bad it is.* He laid a gentle hand on his brother's head, "feeling" a little more this time, bracing himself against the flash of pain long enough to get the impression of broken blood vessels, pressure and agonizing pain. Something else was simmering there too, an undercurrent that, even unconscious, flowed through Rob's body. "The nightmare this morning, I thought it felt like you for a moment. It must have been you after all," Galen said quietly.

What had remained of the bond between the two had let him know over the years when Rob had been seriously ill or injured. Knowing how serious it had to be to get through the break, it had been all Galen could do to keep his promise to stay away. Once, before his father died, Parry had gone to heal Rob. After his father was gone, it had been more difficult, knowing Rob was ill, and being unable to help.

"It was so hard to stay away, Rob," Galen said as he dragged the chair over to the bed. "Once I couldn't. It was after that car wreck three years ago..." He carefully lowered the rail on the bed. "I knew how bad it was, you were...I knew..." he sighed. "So I came, how could I not? I waited until everyone was gone from the ICU and slipped in. I've always wondered if you knew I was there."

He rubbed his hands together for a moment before taking a deep breath and putting one hand on Rob's forehead and one over his heart, pain ran up his arms. He kept his hands in place this time, letting the light flow, feeling the familiar resonance of his brother. Dropping into a deeper state he guided the healing light through Rob's body, then carefully layered in gentle sleep to finish the healing process. He pulled shaking hands away, leaning back in the chair, black spots dancing before his eyes. "I haven't done anything quite like this for awhile. I take more risks with you. I always have," he told his brother.

His headache was back full force, his hands were still shaking. He put a hand down on Rob's arm, letting his thumb run along the deep scar in his brother's forearm. Galen glanced down looking at the faint scars on his brother's arms, ones that mimicked the scars on his own. "Ah, Rob. Ten years, and still the scars are here. I hoped they'd fade, after what I did. I'm so sorry." He stopped. "That man today, my scar acting up more than usual and now you're here. Rob? What does it mean?" Galen paused, realizing he was instinctively reaching out to his brother, speaking to him as if he were awake and able to hear.

He closed his eyes. The healing had left him vulnerable, memories were crowding back against him, from the moment he'd met Rhiannon and seen the pictures of her daughter, the overwhelming fear for his brother as he'd looked over the pictures of the child suddenly blending with the undercurrent of emotion radiating from Rob. *Megan had been...* He drifted off to sleep.

PAST

TEN YEARS BEFORE
Day Two

It was quiet in the parking lot, customers coming and going without noticing the two people sitting in the car parked at the back of the diner.

"Rhiannon," she said with a smile. "I'm off shift, let's not stay out here."

"Good idea," Galen said as he pulled the car back onto the road. "Where was your daughter found?"

"About six miles from here." She looked at him. "Take the next left. You look pretty bad. Are you alright?"

"No. But I have to find my brother. Alright or not, no choice." He took the turn. It was a single lane road, winding through the trees. "You said when they found her..." He stopped.

"She was cut up, mutilated, and had symbols drawn on her, yes. They were drawn in blood and something that looked like black ink. I...This is going to sound really strange, but I have the crime scene pictures in my purse. I have a friend who works at the daily paper and he got them for me." She was looking out the window.

"Not strange, maybe a little weird, but if you're looking for answers, it makes sense."

"Here, pull over. I'll show you where her...her...where they found her."

Galen pulled over and turned the car off. "Would it be okay... Can I see the pictures?" He needed to get a good look at the symbols she was talking about. Maybe he could recognize them or be able to describe them to his father and uncle.

Rhiannon pulled an envelope out of her purse. "They aren't pretty. I only looked once. I was going to take them to the university and see if anyone in the anthropology department could recognize the symbols."

"You seem to be handling it okay."

"Not really," she said, looking at him. "I take a tiny bit of solace from the fact they said she hadn't been sexually mistreated in any way. None of them had been, you know."

"What do you mean?"

"None of the poor things were hurt that way. You know."

"What?" Galen said, looking at her, she opened her mouth to say it all again and cut her off. "No, that actually had never occurred to me. What I meant was you said *them*. More than just your daughter?"

"Five others. My daughter made six."

"And nothing's been done?"

"We were all strangers, passing through town. I stayed after it happened because I had to know. I just needed to know—to find closure. That's what everyone said, 'find closure, it will heal you.' But that's not true and everything's pretty much gone now, the grief, the tears. All that's left is rage. White-hot rage. It will consume me, I'm sure, but for now I can keep it in check, most of the time."

Galen nodded understanding and pulled the pictures out of the envelope. When he looked down at the first one his hands started shaking. "Oh, gods," he whispered. He tried to get a good look at the symbols, he couldn't see well so he flipped over the next picture, and the next. He didn't realize he was crying until a tear dropped on the photo he was holding. He brushed the tears away and looked again. He concentrated, trying to memorize the symbols. He turned over the next photo. "Oh, no, I'm so sorry." He was pretty sure his heart stopped. It wasn't just symbols. He looked at the photo again, at the small arm devoid of skin. He cleared his throat and handed the pictures back to Rhiannon.

"Let's go," Galen said, getting out of the car. He was unsteady on his feet and leaned against the car.

"Can I give you a hand?" she said, standing beside him. "You look terrible. It's quite a hike from here."

"I'm okay, at least for now." He pushed himself off the car and followed her down a path. He had to grit his teeth to keep going. The sun was starting to set, bathing the forest in an eerie red glow. *That might be symbolic, and that doesn't make me feel better.* She'd stopped in a ring of trees.

"They found her here. I don't think this is where she was killed. The police didn't say anything, but I have this feeling, you know?"

"Yeah, I understand," he said as he started scouting around the small clearing. There was nothing there, nothing looked disturbed or had any evidence of a ritual being performed. Galen closed his eyes and focused on the resonance of the forest. "You're right, it wasn't here, something dumped your daughter here." He was just about to turn and leave when something stopped him dead in his tracks.

A scream carried across the forest. "No! Galen!" His brother's voice was terrified, anguished.

"Rob!" Galen shouted. He turned to run in the direction of the shout. Trying to reach out and get a feeling for where Rob was, panic flowed back from his brother, panic that was quickly becoming terror. Rhiannon grabbed his arm, he turned on her in his desperation, reflected fear from Rob coloring his reactions. "Let me go!" he growled dangerously.

"It echoes here, you can't know where that came from."

"Please, let me go, please." He ran out of the clearing in what he thought was the right direction. The forest was getting dark, and the path he was on ended abruptly. He turned back and tripped, going down hard. Galen just lay there, unable to get up, pretty sure he'd done some new injury to himself. A hand touched his back. "Rob sounded so scared. I have to find him," Galen said, hearing the desperation in his voice.

"Galen?" Rhiannon said gently. "Come on. We need to get you out of here."

"That was my brother, he must be here, somewhere."

"Sound carries out here. It echoes. I'm so sorry." She helped him to his feet and held his arm until he stopped swaying. "I know this won't make you feel better, but they said my daughter…the timeline, she'd been killed on the full moon. That's tomorrow."

"I don't know…" His watch beeped. *I can't leave. I can't. He's here somewhere. No, I have to talk to Dad and Uncle Bobby. I need them here. I need their help. And the full moon's tomorrow. Maybe, just maybe, he has a little time.* "I need to get back to the rest stop." He turned and followed the path back to the car. *"Rob?"* He reached out for his brother. *"Hang on, I'm looking for you."*

* * * * *

A groan from the bed woke him. Galen blinked the familiar nightmare away. Nearly every time he slept for the past ten years he relived those days. The room came into focus. It was late, the hospital had the hushed quality of night. He could hear the nurses talking quietly at their station, and somewhere a TV was on, the harsh canned laughter carrying down the hallway. He laid a hand on Rob's forehead and guided him back into healing sleep.

"How's he doing?" Mike asked from the door.

"You tell me." Galen stood and stretched, leaning on the bed rail as the room spun. "Aren't you off already?"

"Things got exciting downstairs. We had a shooting and then someone found a kid all cut up." Mike scrubbed a hand across his face. "Poor thing looked like someone tried to bleed her dry. Someone heard her crying, they found her buried in a pit south of town."

"Really?" Galen said absently. "People are sick." He was watching as Mike examined his brother. "Well?"

"He's good, I think the bruises are even starting to fade."

Galen closed his eyes as relief washed over him. "Thank every god in the pantheon."

"Covering all the bases as always?" Mike said with a little laugh.

"Always." Galen smiled. "Thanks, Mike. I'll walk down with you. I need something to eat." He put a hand down on his brother's arm. "I'll be right back."

"He can't hear you," Mike said as they walked out of the room.

"Yes he can, trust me in this, you can hear a lot."

"Sounds like you're speaking from personal experience."

"Yeah, I am." He let the subject drop as the elevator opened in front of them. "What?" Galen said, Mike was shaking his head.

"Sometimes I'm a little in awe of you. I wouldn't have given the guy a snowball's chance in hell. He hadn't stirred since he was brought in. I was sure I'd lose him."

"Rob?" Galen said, frowning. The sudden anger surprised him, but he clamped it down, knowing the source. *They thought they were doing the best.*

"Yeah, sorry, I should have told you, I didn't know what to say."

"It's okay, Mike."

"But he's going to be alright, I'm not just saying that, hell, he'll be able to go home tomorrow."

"Tomorrow? Good. Want to join me? My treat?" Galen said. He enjoyed Mike's company, and when they weren't talking "shop" they usually had a good time. Sometimes shoptalk got a little heated.

"Sure." Mike wandered through the cafeteria and ordered for both of them. Galen waited by the cash register and paid the ticket. "You need to eat meat," Mike said, shoving the tray towards him.

"Sorry, can't."

"You always say that."

"Well, I can't." Galen shrugged. "I told you."

"I don't know why," Mike said with a shrug. "I've smelled burns."

"Burns, after the fact, Mike, not while they were burning. And this one was different," Galen paused. "It's not just that. The smell of blood bothers me, too."

"You'll have to tell me the whole story sometime, Galen," Mike said, frowning at him with concern.

"Someday, but for now accept I don't eat meat."

"Your loss, my gain," Mike said, biting into his burger. Galen laughed and they settled into a discussion about various bands playing in the area. Mike was a long-time supporter of The Urban Werewolves and Galen was grateful for his support. The doctor, for all that he was only twelve years older, had kind of adopted Galen, offering support, encouragement and the occasional smack on the head.

Mike was laughing at an off-color joke a new intern had told him, Galen laughed along, his mind elsewhere. Something was bothering him. *What?* A flicker of something awakened in his brain. He sipped his coffee trying to figure out what it was. *Something, but what?*

"I need to hit the sack," Mike said, yawning. Galen focused back on his friend. "I have a lunch date tomorrow with Brandy."

"Brandy?" Galen laughed at the doctor. "You're a bit of a slut, Mike."

"I resent that," Mike said, punching him lightly on the arm. "I'm more than a bit of a slut."

"Right." Galen walked out of the cafeteria, to the elevators with Mike. The doctor got off in the lobby and Galen went up to the third floor.

"Someone stopped by looking for you," the nurse said, coming out of Rob's room. "He said he was your uncle and wanted to know if your brother was okay. I didn't say anything, patient confidentiality. I didn't even say if he was on this floor."

"Thank you," Galen said, the alarm bells ringing in his head. "I'm back, Rob. You know, I wonder if that's what I felt earlier. I think It's back and looking for me again, looking for you to finish what It started ten years ago."

He dragged the chair around the bed to the side by the window. It was away from the equipment the nurses needed to check on a regular basis. Galen lowered the railing, settled in the chair, laid his hand on his brother's arm and carefully put his feet on the bed. Despite the coffee he had consumed, he was asleep within several minutes.

His feet hit the floor when he rolled over, pulling him out of a deep sleep, filled equally with nightmares and comforting dreams of home. Galen opened his eyes, gingerly moving his neck, stiff from sleeping in the chair. Light was filtering in from behind the curtains. He stood up, stretching and rolling his shoulders. Walking over to the windows, he looked out at the parking lot behind the hospital. He idly watched people as they arrived, most seemed to be staff, getting out of their cars and striding purposefully across the lot.

"Hello?" a light baritone voice said, sounding confused.

Galen's heart started pounding. He swallowed and, taking a deep breath, turned around. "Rob," he said, walking over to the bed.

Rob looked at him, the color suddenly draining out of his face. He frowned, tears at the edges of his slate-blue eyes. "Galen?" he whispered.

Galen sat on the edge of the bed. "Hey, Brat."

"Galen?" The tears escaped Rob's eyes and were trickling over the bruises on his face. He held his hand out towards Galen.

The gesture was reminiscent of Rob's thirteen-year-old self. It was too much for Galen. He reached out and pulled his brother up and into his arms in a fierce hug. Rob let out a soft sob, Galen felt his brother's arms go around him. He felt the tears start as the ache in his chest, an ache that had been there for ten years, was suddenly easing. "It's okay, Rob" he said softly. *It's okay. Staying here, letting him know, it is okay. I think we were wrong.*

His brother pulled away, looking at Galen, the tears still on his face. "You're dead."

"I was," Galen said, swallowing the lump in his throat. "I'm better now."

"Galen," Rob said, his voice hoarse with emotion. "Are you sure you're alive?"

"Yeah." Galen laid a gentle hand on his brother's leg, opening himself to Rob, letting the bond slowly repair itself. "I'm pretty sure I'm alive."

Rob swallowed again, a frown on his face, the tears still trickling out of his eyes. He looked around the room. "Hospital?"

"You were brought in yesterday morning," Galen said, allowing the change of subject. He scrubbed the tears off his face.

"Yesterday?" Rob blinked, looking at him. "What happened?"

"You were attacked, the police brought you in."

"I don't remember." He frowned. "Can we go?"

"We need to get you checked out by the doc first, then we can go."

"I don't like hospitals, Galen," he said, swallowing. "You know why."

"I know. I'll go see if I can find someone, then we can go home."

"Home?" There was a note of longing in his brother's voice.

"Yeah, Rob. Home."

Chapter Five

The hospital corridor was busy as Galen rolled Rob down towards the entrance. His brother had been quiet since he'd come back with the doctor. Galen sighed, watching people walk towards them. A nurse turned the corner and headed their way. Rob sat upright in the chair.

"Galen," Rob said softly, his voice barely more than a whisper.

"What?" Galen said, dropping a hand down on his brother's shoulder. A shiver of anticipation ran up the contact. Rob's heart was beating fast.

"That nurse, coming this way." Rob glanced back casually. "She…"

"Okay." Galen maneuvered the wheelchair into a group of people. As they passed the nurse, she looked over and met Galen's eyes. What he saw there caused his heart to speed up as well. He thought he could see the reflection of It on her face, lurking behind the sparkling green of her eyes. Galen pushed the chair quickly to the entrance and handed the token to the valet. Rob stood up, still a little shaky, and waited beside Galen while the valet fetched the car. "We'll be home soon," Galen said.

"Home," Rob nodded, he smiled as the valet pulled Galen's jeep up. "You still have it?"

"It's only ten years old. It was new for my eighteenth birthday, you know." Galen walked around to the driver's side of the jeep. He slid behind the wheel and smiled over at his brother, the bright carefree smile he remembered was on Rob's face. "Low miles, I've taken good care of it. They wanted to get me something else, something new, when I turned twenty-one, but I couldn't give this up. It was the car…"

"Yeah, I know," Rob said. He was playing with the tuning on the radio, flipping through the stations, stopping briefly on the classical station. "Mozart at Eight" was on, the DJ chattering about J.C. Bach.

"It was Mozart." Rob's voice was soft.

"What?"

"That day, Mozart, 'Jupiter.' I remember. You put it in right before we pulled off. Right before you gave me my bracelet." Rob looked over at him, his eyes searching Galen's face.

"It was. And I haven't been able to listen to it since. I took a date to an evening of Mozart, she was mad when I left during the encore." Galen chuckled. "Rob…" He stopped himself, not ready yet. "Did you drive?"

"Yeah, I left my car…" Rob frowned, Galen saw the confused look on his brother's face out of the corner of his eye. "I think I stopped for coffee? That might be it."

"Okay, well, what kind of car is it?"

Rob looked over, his face turning red. "It's, uh, a lot like this one."

Galen smiled, ignoring the little twist in his stomach. "We'll get someone looking for it. I have a few friends who can find anything, anywhere." He laughed. "Anything, anywhere. I mean that."

"Anything, anywhere?" Rob asked with raised eyebrows.

"Yeah," Galen smiled. "I have some, hmm, interesting contacts here and there."

"Like Dad's and Uncle Bobby's? Not all human, not all living?"

"Something like that. Although I think we'll start with the humans. They can find it, I'm sure, without bothering anyone else."

"Good, I'd hate to lose it."

Galen pulled up behind his building and hopped out of the car. Rob stepped out slowly, looking up at the building, an expression of disbelief on his face. He glanced over at Galen and then walked to the door. Galen unlocked it and they went upstairs. He opened the door to the apartment and Rob walked in, still with the look of disbelief.

"It's still awhile before the shop opens. Why don't you grab a shower? I'll find something for you to wear. You're close to my size, I think I can find you something."

"Sure." Rob walked towards the bathroom. Galen watched him go. He went into his bedroom and dug through the dresser, pulling out a change of clothes. Walking to the bathroom, he heard the shower running. He knocked before opening the door, then dropped the clothes on the closed toilet lid and quietly closed the door.

Galen stood outside for a moment before turning and walking back to the bedroom. He got himself a change of clothes and then sank down onto the bed, his head in his hands. The emotion that was setting in surprised him a little. He could feel the tears in his eyes, an ache in his chest and a lump in his throat. "I think It's back, that nurse, the man in the shop yesterday," Galen sighed. "Dad? Uncle Bobby? Rob's here, but you both know that, don't you? He's actually here," he said to the quiet room. His father suddenly felt close. "He's really here. Does it mean something? If it does, what? I think It's back, I need you two. We...Rob and I, need you two." He heard the catch in his voice as he said it. Weight settled on the bed beside him and a warm arm was placed over his shoulders.

"Galen?"

He looked up at his brother. Rob's eyes were a little red around the edges. "Yeah?"

"I…"

"It's a lot to take in, isn't it?" Galen said softly.

"A little." Rob smiled. "I left you some hot water."

"How are you feeling?" Galen ran his eyes over the bruises still coloring his brother's face.

"Sore, but mostly okay. Of course, you know that," Rob added with a laugh.

"Yeah." Galen sat quietly for a moment longer, aware of the warmth resting on his shoulders. With a sigh he stood up. "I'll be right out."

Rob was waiting for him when he finished, standing in front of the pictures of their father and uncle. His brother smiled at him and they headed down to the shop. Galen stopped to look out the back door. "Always have to check, people leave things out there sometimes."

"Things?" Rob asked as they walked through the shop.

Galen shrugged. "Yeah, things."

"Like?"

"Oh, you know, people, animals…" Galen smiled. "My shop functions as a clinic, sort of…I can stitch a wound and things like that, people come here sometimes."

"Or drop the victim off outside?"

"Yeah, that too," Galen said, opening the front door. "I need coffee, you?"

Rob laughed. "Do I have to have it cut half with milk?"

Galen laughed too, remembering the indignant protests of his brother when he had been allowed coffee, but only lattes. "No, I think you can have real coffee if you want."

Galen led the way thought the shop and out to the espresso stand. "Morning, Becci," he said as she slid the window open. He heard his brother's little intake of breath.

"Good morning, Galen, your mocha's almost ready. What

does your friend want?"

Galen looked over at Rob. "Well?" When he received no answer, he gave him a discrete nudge. "Coffee?"

"What? Oh, Americano, thanks," Rob said, smiling at Becci.

"Okay." She started the coffee, then turned back looking from one to the other. "You two look alike."

"Rob's my brother," Galen said, grinning.

"You never mentioned a brother," Becci pouted, "never once."

"We haven't seen each other in awhile. Rob's been..." He stopped, unsure what to say.

"Traveling," Rob stepped in smoothly. "I was traveling a little before I finished grad school."

"Grad school? Wow, both of you? I'm impressed," Becci said, leaning out of the window to hand them their coffee, her precariously taped scarf shifting a tiny bit. "Oops." She straightened it up. "New idea, theme days. Today's scarf day, what do you think?"

"Nice," Rob breathed. Galen gave him a little kick.

"Great idea, Becci." Galen turned and walked back to the shop, stopping to turn on the open sign on the way in. Rob walked behind the counter and sank down on one of the stools. "Grad school?" Galen set his coffee down on the counter and grabbed the dust cloth.

"Yeah, finishing up my Master's, just have the thesis left."

Galen felt the slow smile spreading on his face. "Really? That's fast."

"Psychotically fast, or so I've been told." Rob grinned. "I got to college a little early, so I was ahead of the others."

"Yeah? Subject?"

"History and Lit, specializing in the sagas of Northern Europe. I thought, well..." He shrugged, a smile on his face. "It's part of the tradition, isn't it? I guess I've clung to the idea I was *Custodes Noctis* all these years. The sagas seemed a natural thing to study."

"Nice." Galen finished dusting and picked up his coffee.

"You?" Rob asked. Galen shrugged. "Before you deny something, Galen? I saw the doctorate on the wall."

"Oh, I found that in a box of cereal." Galen laughed. "I just filled in my name."

"Yeah, right. Subject?"

"History—of medicine actually, mostly Dark Ages, specializing in Western holistic traditions." Galen grinned. "I've clung to the traditions, too. It went with the Gift, and so I ran with it. I'm a Master Herbalist, too."

"Nice." Rob grinned at him. "Very nice. Can I help with something?"

"Not today, I'll put you to work soon enough, but today you are going to rest. Get it?"

"Got it."

"Good." Galen smiled and straightened the shelves, putting out the order he'd gotten the day before. He carefully set out the magical items he'd gotten, making a phone call to let a customer know one item had arrived. Rob watched him the whole time, a smile on his face, his eyes thoughtful, before getting up and wandering around the shop. Stopping before the small statue behind the counter, he looked at Galen and smiled.

"I remember this from when I was a kid," he said, running a hand over the surface.

"I moved it from the window after a break-in, but it's the same one," Galen said, fussing with the objects in the display case.

Rob watched him. "Like Dad," he said softly.

"What?" Galen straightened and looked at his brother.

"Not just herbs and vitamins and using the Gift now and then to help heal people. There's magic here, the real thing." Rob looked slowly around the room. "I can see it, you know. It has a funny shine. When I was a kid, I thought that was how all shops like this look, but they don't. Very few have real magic, that sense of actual power in them."

Galen shrugged. "Dad did most of that. Dad and Uncle Bobby. I've only added a little. I've had more time to study, since they were full Keepers and I...I..." He stopped, swallowing the pain that suddenly flared in his chest.

"Galen?" Rob came over and put a hand on his back. "What is that?"

"It's nothing," Galen started, then paused when Rob sighed. "Okay, sorry. It's an ache I get sometimes." He smiled. "All better now. And I can't take credit for the shop, it's everyone who came before, really."

"Galen..." Rob frowned. "Don't you realize you..." He shook his head. "It's nice to be back where there's magic."

Galen smiled at his brother and continued straightening things around the store. Rob wandered back and forth, running his hands over some things, picking others up to examine them closer. Finally, he settled back behind the counter and watched Galen with the thoughtful smile on his face again.

"Rob?" Galen said after a silent fifteen minutes. The silence had been comfortable, natural, like his brother had never been gone at all.

"What?"

"What are you doing up here?"

Rob chuckled. "You mean now, after all these years, knowing you and Dad and Uncle Bobby were dead?"

"Yeah."

"A friend said I needed to come here."

"Seer?" Galen raised his eyebrows.

"No, shaman actually, medicine man, Billy Hernandez. He helped me learn to control the Sight. It was out of control, my adopted family thought I was losing my mind. Of course, they thought that every since I knew Grandma had cancer, and that was when I was eight." Rob smiled. "I think they sensed something about my Gift. Galen..." Rob stopped himself for a moment, he glanced at Galen then smiled again. "No, not yet," he said softly, under his breath. Galen was sure he wasn't meant to hear.

"What?"

"Huh? Oh, nothing. Anyway, I went to a witch and she helped a little, but it was more than she could handle, you know?" Rob looked over at him, Galen nodded. "So she sent me to New Mexico and a shaman she knew there. I stayed with him for the whole summer of my junior year. He helped a lot. Then, three days ago, he called out of the blue and said I had to come here, no explanations, just I had to come." He shrugged. "So I did, I thought the least I could do was visit the cemetery and leave a stone for all of you." He smiled at Galen. "That's the tradition of the *Custodes Noctis*, isn't it? Leave a stone? I have some special ones I found in New Mexico. I guess I only need two, not three."

"Yeah," Galen said, walking back to his brother and sitting down beside him.

"Five years now, isn't it?" Rob asked. "I remember when my parents told me. I almost came up her then. I was the last of the family and I thought..." He frowned suddenly. "Who called? I remember, that same day I answered the phone once and it was just a dead line." He looked at Galen. "It was you, wasn't it?"

Galen smiled sadly, the memory of that day fresh and painful as an open wound. "Yeah, it was me."

"Galen, why didn't you...?"

"I damn near did. It was a close thing. But I was dead, remember? I thought you'd need to know, so I called expecting your mother to answer, and it was you. I knew it was you, even though your voice had changed. Shit, Rob, I... I needed you, hearing your voice...it nearly destroyed me that day, nearly took away the resolve. It was back, Dad and Uncle Bobby were gone and I was alone and I suddenly wanted the life I'd given up when I died."

"Can you tell me what happened?" Rob asked, meeting his eyes. Galen swallowed. "I'll go get us another cup of coffee, be right back." Rob stood and walked out of the shop. Galen watched as his brother spoke to Becci and turned back with two cups in his hand. Rob was smiling when he came in. "She likes you," Rob said, handing him the coffee.

"Uh..." Galen felt the blush running up his cheeks.

"She told me how you saved her friend Sandi and how you have the, I quote, 'bestest band' in the whole Northwest." Rob was smiling at him, a teasing smile. "She wanted me to know what a cool brother I had."

"I...uh..."

Rob laughed and slapped him lightly on the back. "Sorry. She does like you, though. She wouldn't take my money, so I asked her why."

"It's okay, I'll get used to it again, Brat." Galen smiled. "Thanks." He sipped the coffee for a minute. "Five years ago..."

"Yeah?"

"It was late. I'd been doing a little shopping, I wanted to send something special for your eighteenth birthday."

"You?" Rob looked at him with surprise. "You were the one who sent the gifts? I should have known."

"How? I was dead." Galen shrugged. "I'd been shopping and got home late. Dad and Uncle Bobby had already closed the shop for the day..."

PAST

FIVE YEARS BEFORE

Galen pulled his jeep in behind the building, parking next to his father's truck. The lot was quiet, the shadows deep where the glow from the streetlight brushed against neighboring buildings. Galen sat for a minute in the car, his hands still on the wheel. *Five years. He's going to be eighteen. I wonder...It's been five years, nothing has happened. I wonder... do we dare let him know?* He sighed. *Great birthday gift, huh? Little brother? You know how I've been dead?* Galen grabbed the packages off the seat and opened the door.

As he did, the old scar in his chest suddenly came to life, twisting with a new agony, breathtaking in its intensity. Galen leaned against the side of the jeep, trying to get his breath as the scar ground against his heart. "Dad?" he called weakly, knowing his father would sense the call. Unlike attacks in the past, this one slowly increased until Galen was gasping for air, trying to stay conscious long enough for his father to reach him. He thought he heard a car door slam close by, but he was completely focused on trying to stop the pain flaring in his chest.

"Take him," a voice said from in front of him. Hands grabbed him and pulled him away from the car.

"Dad! Bobby!" he yelled, knowing they would hear him.

"Good," another voice said. Galen forced his eyes open, he recognized the death scent of the thing. "Good, we have him." It was wearing the body of a woman in her late fifties, blood-red nail polish glittered on claw-like hands. She raised her hand,

and with a sick smile, placed it on his chest. Galen heard his voice scream in pain.

"Stop," Parry said from behind him.

"This one is incomplete, take those two," the woman said in the voice of the thing. Galen was dropped to the ground.

"Galen!" his father shouted.

"I'm okay," he called back, forcing himself up off the ground and staggering back to the jeep to grab a weapon. He saw the woman gesture to a group of people behind her, they moved forward as Parry and Bobby stepped between Galen and the thing. As he reached the jeep, the scar gave another twist, the pain forcing him back down. Galen braced himself against the car, waiting for the pain to pass.

"Bobby, no!" he heard his father shout as his uncle screamed. Galen forced himself up, wrenched the door of the jeep open and grabbed his sword from under the seat. Turning, he paused only long enough to take in the situation.

His uncle was lying on the ground, Parry in front of him. Bobby was bleeding, a large knife buried in his chest. Parry was trying to hold off the thing's followers. Galen shoved the emotion away, letting his training take control before he stepped forward.

The thing approached his father as Galen neared. Parry ran his sword into the thing, the blade sliding through the body with ease. It screamed as the magical blade pierced It, Its hands reaching for Parry and sinking into his chest.

"No!" Galen shoved the thing away, dropped his own sword and pulled his father's blade from Its body. The thing's followers were trying to pull the woman back into the car.

"Fools," she hissed, pulling away and stepping towards Galen again. "Take this one, we can complete it still, take this one and those two. Don't let them die on the way."

"Never," Galen said, raising his father's sword, the sword that would have been his one day. The power of the blade hummed against his hand. He swung the blade, cutting a swath across the thing's chest. It screamed, clutching at the bleeding wounds on Its body. Its followers were pulling It towards the car.

"No, no, fools, take them," It screamed in fury.

Galen could hear sirens in the distance as the thing was finally pulled into the car and, with a squeal of tires, they were gone. He dropped on his knees beside his father. Parry was cradling Bobby against him.

"Let me help, Dad," Galen said gently, reaching his hands towards his uncle. He put his hand over his father's and tried to draw the light down into his uncle's body. He focused the healing, ignoring the explosion of pain behind his eyes, ignoring the darkness tugging at the edge of his awareness. Suddenly his hands were pushed away.

"It's too late, Galen, you can't help him, you can't help..." Parry broke off, coughing, blood welling on his lips.

"Dad?" Galen put a hand on his father's arm, pain flowed up from the touch. His father was dying. "No, let me..."

"No, Galen. I can't, you know that. Not without...the bond is too strong, I don't..." His father paused. "You need to...Rob..." He moaned. Galen put his hand on his father's forehead, trying to ease the pain. "It felt something in me, you have to...Your brother...We..." Parry's head dropped down against Bobby's. "Bobby? He's dead, Galen. Bobby's gone...I..."

"Please, Dad, let me try and heal you."

"I'm dying, Galen, and even if I wasn't, you know how it works. Don't try. It would kill you...Don't deny... Galen...you have to watch out for your brother."

"Dad, what about Rob? What should I do?"

"You and your brother, Galen, you need to know...We should

have…" Each phrase was punctuated by a gasping cough. Galen shifted so he could prop his father up   and ease the gasping breaths. "Rob, you have to…" Parry cried out in pain suddenly. "Galen, please. Help, let me… I…" Tears mixed with blood on his face. "Please."

"Dad, no." Galen's eyes had filled with tears.

"Please," his father said. "I…I'm…You need to…I have served faithfully, I have walked…"

Galen put his other hand over his father's heart. "Dad…"

"Thank…Galen…" His father was gasping for air, Galen knew he was slowly drowning on his own blood.

"I'll do my best, Dad," he said quietly.

"Rob…" Parry started coughing again. "Please, Galen."

"In living we serve, in dying we serve, the line continues, we are joined with our present and our past." Galen spoke the formal words as he let the light slowly flow out of his hands, aware of the pain in his father. "You have served the world, now rest until you are called again." His father closed his eyes as Galen took the pain away, gently slowing his father's heart until it finally stopped.

* * * * *

Galen scrubbed a hand across his face, the past moving away as the room came back into focus. His brother's arm was around his shoulders, warm and comforting. "Rob, I'm sorry, they're dead because of me." Galen looked over at his brother, aware of the tears in Rob's eyes.

"No, Galen," Rob said quietly.

"I wasn't sure what to do. I called to let you know they'd died, thinking maybe you'd take that as a warning, too. I didn't know if It would come again, but I think the ritual had been broken. The first part was accomplished, I'm sure, so It could live, but what It would do with us wasn't."

Rob nodded. "I've learned a little more about what I think It is, and yes, I'm sure they went through the first part, but not the last. They need both of us."

Galen looked at his brother. "Were we right? Is it…?" He stopped, suddenly afraid of the answer.

"The Legacy, Galen?" Rob met his eyes.

"It is, isn't it?"

"I think it might be," Rob said cautiously. "We need to talk about it, Galen. What happened then, what's happening now. We have to know if this is the Legacy."

"How would we know?"

"The sagas tell us the First Emrys imprisoned an Old One in the body of a creature that walked the earth. They say that members of the line will be the fulfillment of the Legacy."

"I remember. Doesn't the world end before the line can finish it?"

"I'm not sure the world actually ends, but the Old One is released to walk on the earth again."

"Me, my fault." Galen put his head in his hands for a minute.

"I don't think it's just you, Galen, it's…" Rob started, the door banged open before he could finish.

"Galen?" Rhiannon stormed into the store. "Where the hell were you…" She stopped, looking at Rob, the color draining out of her face.

Rob stood and walked around the counter, a happy smile on his face. "Rhiannon?"

She launched herself at Rob, luckily she wasn't very big, but even with that she nearly bowled him over when she came into contact with him, her arms going around him as she pulled his head down against her shoulder. "Rob?" Rhiannon said, a smile on her face. Galen noticed something that didn't happen very often, tears were running down Rhiannon's face.

"Yeah, hi," Rob said, his voice muffled.

"Hi, yourself." Rhiannon pulled away, smiling up at Rob. "How the hell are you?"

"I'm okay. You?"

"Great, even better now." She turned to Galen. "He was the Keeper last night?"

"Yeah." Galen grinned at her. "I was a little surprised."

"Only a little?" Rhiannon laughed at him.

"Yeah, a little. What are you doing here?"

"Came to check on you, considering the day. Guess I'm not needed now." She grinned at them, then walked over to Galen and picked up the cup of coffee in front of him. She took a drink and made a face. "Mocha. You always drink mochas."

"You could try buying your own. He drinks real coffee," Galen said, pointing at Rob.

"Good boy." Rhiannon grinned at Rob, she picked up the other cup and took a drink. "Yes, much better." She hopped up on the counter and looked at Rob. "It's good to see you."

"You too." He smiled at her.

"Rhiannon?" Galen said. "Rob lost his car the other day, think you can find it?"

"Sure." She jumped down. "I'll call Greg and Caleb and we'll have it back here before tonight. What kind of car is it?"

"Jeep, like mine."

"That'll make it easy." She got a few more details and held her hand out for the keys. Rob turned them over with an odd smile on his face. She gave him another hug and headed out the door.

"It's a little like getting hit by a tornado," Galen said as Rob sat back down beside him.

"Yeah, always was. She sat with me, you know, after you..." Rob swallowed. "After you died. She held my hand, I remember. I think they'd given me something, painkillers and maybe a sedative. I was pretty hazy. Dad and Uncle Bobby took turns sitting in my room until my adopted family came for me. They must have been sitting with you, too."

"I don't remember." Galen shrugged. "It was a long time before I was aware again." Rob leaned his shoulder against him. "When I was a little better, I regretted the decision, but it was done, you know. I thought...I...We thought it was for the best. Letting you go."

"It wasn't," Rob's voice was quiet.

"No," Galen sighed. "But we thought it was. After what It did to you, to me. After what happened and what It knew, after what I heard...I thought it was best to let me die and you go. It would come for the pair of us again if we were together. And if It did, and we couldn't stop It..."

"Yeah. I know."

"Can you forgive me?" Galen's heart was pounding against his ribcage as he asked the question. Rob looked at him, meeting his eyes, with a gentle smile.

"Forgive?" Rob shook his head. "Forgive?"

"Rob?"

"Galen..." He stopped himself, still looking at Galen, then sighed. "You died because of..." Rob suddenly stood and paced away, angry. "How can you ask?"

Galen's heart sank. "Rob, I..."

The door opened, Rob glanced over as a customer walked in. He gave Galen a wild look and went in the back of the store. *He can't forgive me. I don't blame him, at this point I can't forgive myself. Ten years. But I thought it was for the best.* He forced himself up, pasted a smile on his face and walked over to his customer. Rob reappeared a few minutes later. He sat down behind the counter, composed, a smile back on his face.

They didn't have a chance to pick up the discussion again. It turned out to be a busy day. Rob fell into the routine quickly, he settled behind the cash register as if he had always been there. The stream of customers seemed to like him, too.

The day was winding to a close when Mike Silva came in. He walked over and gave Rob an intense look, took his pulse and looked in his eyes. The doctor was shaking his head and muttering under his breath when he finished.

"I hear that, you know," Galen said, carrying a jar around the counter.

"Yeah, yeah. Would you be willing to come down again?"

"What's up?"

"That girl they found...I think we're going to lose her. I thought maybe..."

"What's wrong? I thought you got to her in time?" Galen asked the doctor.

"I did, too, even with the massive blood loss, but there's something else going on, we found traces of something in her blood, and then when she does wake up, albeit briefly, she starts screaming. Being buried alive does that, I guess."

"Rob?" Galen took a step towards his brother. Rob's face had paled and he was frowning, his hands clenched. "Rob?"

His brother turned to him. "We need to go down there, Galen. We have to."

"I guess we're coming." Galen walked over and opened the door so Mike could leave, then locked up. Rob was already waiting at the back door for him when he got there. He looked sick.

"What's going on, Rob?" he asked again as they got in the car.

"We need to see her first," was all his brother said. Galen shook his head and pulled out wondering what was going on with Rob. "I was right, I knew it," Rob said under his breath. Galen glanced over at his brother, Rob was looking out the window. He turned to Galen. "I think It's here. It's coming again."

Chapter Six

Mike was waiting for them when they pulled up at valet parking. Rob had been silent during the drive down, occasionally glancing over at Galen and then back out the window. Galen was aware of each look, wondering what it meant. They followed the doctor through the hospital. The girl was in intensive care. Mike waved at the nurses and walked into the room.

Rob strode over to the bed, looking at the girl. His hands were clenched as he stood and looked at the small figure on the bed. Galen walked up beside him, aware of the emotions flowing off his brother. *And without a touch. The bond has snapped back faster than I ever thought it could. Maybe it was never broken all the way.*

The girl's eyes were open, tiny slits reflecting terror. Mike was speaking to her soothingly. Galen walked over and smiled down at her. "My name is Galen," he said, pitching his voice low, keeping it gentle. "I'm here to help a little if I can. Is that okay?" He smiled as she nodded and placed a hand on her head.

"Galen! No!" He heard Rob's shout, but it was too late. It was there, in the child, the thing that had killed his father and uncle, It was there, suddenly aware of him. The old scar twisted, pain exploded though his body as It sighed with pleasure, the cold touch of the thing pulling at him. It laughed Its sick pleasure, the sound filling his mind until he knew nothing else.

Something warm was clasped around his hand, he sensed his brother through the contact, calming the over-hard beating of his heart. *I wonder if he remembered that from training? What happened? I thought I felt It, but then what?* He was lying down, he was pretty sure of that, his head was pounding and there was an ache in his chest. Someone groaned.

"Galen?" Rob's voice was anxious, the hand on Galen's gripped a little tighter.

"Galen? Can you hear me?" Mike asked, sounding every bit as anxious as Rob.

Galen forced his eyes open. He was lying on a hospital bed, he could hear the beeping of a heart monitor. It took him a minute to realize that it was his heart that was being monitored. Rob was sitting beside the bed, his hand over Galen's. Mike was on the other side, looking down anxiously. "What happened?"

"You had a seizure," Mike said matter-of-factly, the tone in his voice anything but calm.

"My fault," Rob whispered in the same moment.

"What?" Galen asked them.

"A seizure?" Mike said again.

"My fault. I saw It, but you already had your hand down. I should have stopped you in time. I knew It was there. I'm sorry."

"What are you talking about?" Mike demanded. "He had a seizure."

"I'm so sorry, Galen. I should have stopped you. Are you okay? Did It hurt you?"

"I'm not sure." Galen paused, something was different. "Something happened. It might have just been letting me know it was there." He tried to sit up, but dropped back on the bed as the room spun.

"You aren't going anywhere for awhile." Mike put a hand on his arm.

"You suspected something, didn't you?" Galen looked at his brother.

"I had to 'see' her to know for sure."

"Hello? You two want to let me in on this? My patient had a seizure and damn near coded, you want to tell me what's going on?" Mike's tone was snarky.

Rob didn't move. "Rob? What did you need to see?"

"If she had…"

"Rob?"

Rob met his eyes. "I had to know, Galen. I had to know if this was the beginning. If she was like me."

PAST

TEN YEARS BEFORE
Day Two - Rob

It smelled wet, dank and moldy. That was the first thing that occurred to Rob. It was also very dark. *Where am I?* "Galen?" he called out, unsure. He was answered only by a far-off drip. He opened his eyes, it was very dark, a tiny sliver of light came from one side of the room. Rob sat up carefully and let his eyes adjust, breathing deeply like Galen had showed him, to help stop the fear pounding in his chest. He looked around, he was in a small room. There was a large wooden door, the light was coming under the door and through the keyhole. He was alone.

"Galen?" he called again. Nothing. He remembered the fight on the road. Galen had been hurt even before they had been stopped. He hadn't wanted to run, but Galen looked so desperate when he told him to escape. So he had run, from the fight, from his brother. *That was a big mistake. He was hurt, there was so much blood.* Rob closed his eyes for a minute, trying to get a sense of his brother through the bond they had as Keepers. He thought he felt him for a moment, just a flash, and then an odd darkness where the flash had been. *"Galen? What's going on? Are you okay? Please be okay. I'll find you, okay? You just be okay till*

86

I get there." He sighed. *Now what? What would Galen want me to do? He'd say we're Keepers—try and escape. Okay, Galen, let me see if I can.*

He walked over to look at the door. It had an old-fashioned skeleton key lock. He dug through his pockets. They'd taken his pocket-knife, but he still had some odds and ends. Rob smiled. Galen had showed him how to pick locks the summer before. It was supposedly a forbidden activity, but Galen had taken pleasure in showing him and now he was better than Galen at it. In fact, he often teased his big brother about it, telling him of his exploits with various locks. Galen would look at him with disgust, shake his head and say he regretted the day he had taught him that particular skill. Rob just laughed at him and would boast he could pick a lock. Any lock. *Okay, almost any lock, but I bet given a little time I can open any lock, anywhere, anytime.* Rob comforted himself imagining his brother's response to that statement. *"Better not, Brat,"* Galen would say and nudge him with a shoulder or lightly punch him in the arm. Comforted and feeling confident, Rob set to work, gently testing the lock. Within a couple of minutes he was rewarded by a loud click. *Ha, gotcha.* He gently pulled the door open.

There was a hallway, lit by a lone naked light bulb. Rob cautiously looked down the hall, there were stairs about forty feet from him. The room he was in was at the end of the hallway, there were three other doors along it. He slipped silently out of the room toward the stairs. As he walked down the hall, he opened the doors. *Galen might be here. I have to find him, if he's hurt he'll need my help. I can't "feel" him, though. I wonder if that means he isn't here? Or if he is unconscious.* That thought caused a ripple of panic to run up his spine. As he opened the last door he smelled something odd, a coppery smell. His brain sought to identify it, but not before he saw what was in the room. He slammed the door as the gruesome sight registered in his brain. Rob resisted the urge to run and stopped at the bottom step. There was another closed door at the top, it didn't look like it had a lock. He crept up the stairs and eased the door open. The room was empty and, across from Rob, was a door that went out of the building.

He paused, listening. He could hear someone talking, but it was muffled, coming from another room. Rob stopped for a moment, trying to hear Galen's voice, reaching out trying to sense his presence. Not hearing his brother's voice, he took a step, moving silently. *Maybe all that time Galen and I spent sneaking up on each other was a good thing.* The door was so close. He moved towards it and turned the knob. It was unlocked. He peeked out the door, making sure no one was around, slipped outside and stopped to get his bearings.

The building, it might be an old farmhouse, was bordered by forest. There was a large clearing surrounding the house that he would need to cross before he was safely in the cover of the trees. It would be a long dash. He was fairly fast these days, even though he couldn't run as fast as Galen, but his brother was tall, with legs to match. His brother assured him he'd be equally as tall, but at times like this Rob wished his growth spurt had already caught up with him. He measured the distance to the trees, wondering how fast he could cross the open space.

He paused, wondering what to do. If Galen were there, he was probably hurt, he'd need help, but Rob was pretty sure he wouldn't be enough help to rescue his brother. He thought about it for a precious minute. He wasn't sure Galen was there. And he knew what his brother would say if he didn't go. He shook his head. Galen would tell him to run, get help and come back.

Rob took a deep breath and ran for the trees. About halfway across the clearing, he heard someone shout an alarm. He thought he heard someone behind him and ran faster, it didn't work, before he got to the forest he was tackled and tackled hard. He went down, stunned.

"No you don't, kid, you're not going anywhere." A man with a thick beard pulled him to his feet. He held Rob's arm in a tight grip. Rob looked at him and what he saw caused him to panic. He struck out at the man, the way Galen had shown him, the man ducked, then yanked Rob's arm behind him, applying pressure until Rob stopped struggling. He was forced back into the house and down the stairs. The man stopped at a high shelf in the hallway and pulled down a rope. Shoving Rob back into the room he had escaped from, the man tied Rob's hands behind him and pushed him down on the floor.

"Don't worry, kid. You won't be in here all that long. The ritual will begin soon. The Other will be in here with you shortly, to spend time with you before it starts." He smiled, there was something in his smile, in his eyes, that terrified Rob.

Taking a deep breath Rob "looked" at him, using the Sight, bracing himself for what was there. The man was surrounded by a dirty black ring, tinged with the red of ancient blood. The colors, the way they looked, formed in Rob's brain not only as a visual presence, but as a smell as well. It was the smell of death. Rob recognized it, he had found a dead opossum on the road once. The man laughed at Rob's look. When he closed the door Rob heard the key turn in the lock.

Once he was alone, Rob pulled against the rope binding his hands, testing to see if he could work it loose. He struggled with it for what seemed like a long time before the hopelessness of the situation caught up with him. Determination began to give way to despair. He felt like crying. The fact that he couldn't sense his brother at all was beginning to wear on him. He'd always been aware of Galen, and this silence disturbed him enough to cause a seed of worry to start growing. Rob knew they weren't as close as their father and uncle, but still, Galen had always been there.

The key turned in the lock. A man in white pants and a bright purple shirt came in and sat down beside Rob. "I am Other."

"That's your name? What a dumb name." Rob said, trying to quell his fear. What he saw in the man caused his heart to race. He had black spots like the waitress did, but something else was there. The man had a red ring around him and a black place on his chest. Rob took another breath, calming himself, hiding what he had seen.

"I had another name, as did you Chosen."

"That's not my name. It's Rob, not chosen."

"Yes, it is now. You are Chosen and I am Other. It is the way. You will be thirteen, the Chosen age, and I will be three times thirteen, the Other age."

"What? That doesn't make sense. You know what? It's stupid."

"That is the way it is. That is how it works. I am Willing and you are Unwilling. It is the way. We get to begin with the Earth ritual in a while."

"What's that?" Rob asked, curious even though he was beginning to get freaked out.

"It will mark the Beginning. We will be bled and blessed and then we will be placed within the Earth for thirteen hours."

"What? What do you mean put in the earth?" Rob asked, terrified.

"In the ritual place and then we will be covered and will rest there for thirteen hours before the other rituals can begin."

"Do you mean we'll be buried?" He could feel his heart pounding against his ribcage. "Alive?"

"Yes, isn't it glorious?"

"Not really, no." He tried to reach out to his brother, fear making his mouth dry. Just for an instant he thought he sensed him. *"Galen, where are you? Galen? Are you alive?"* Rob reached out, trying to communicate all that to his brother. *"There is something wrong with these people. They look like death. I think they look like my death. I'm frightened. Galen?"* For just a moment he thought he heard his brother answer.

"It is a very marvelous thing to be Chosen for this ritual."

"Don't take this wrong, but I think you're nuts," Rob said, comforting himself with the image of Galen saying it.

"You will see. You will embrace it."

"My brother is coming to get me. He'll find me."

"He won't find you. Don't worry about that. I hear them. It is time." Other stood and opened the door. The man with the beard came in with a white shirt and purple pants. He dropped them on the floor and cut the rope binding Rob's hands.

"Put those on. We'll be just outside, so don't try anything funny."

"No."

"You do it or we will. You don't have any choice," the man said. The black ring around him vibrated. Rob swallowed. "Okay." He stood and picked up the clothes, waiting until they left before changing as quickly as possible. His mouth was dry, fear making his heart pound.

They came back in and placed two braziers and two golden cups on the floor. The incense smelled weird to Rob and he started feeling a little sick to his stomach. After they'd chanted something in an unfamiliar language, they stood by the brazier for a moment, wafting the smoke around themselves. The one who called himself Other picked up one of the golden cups, then held his left arm over the cup. The bearded man had a bright silver knife. He cut Other's arm and they watched as his blood flowed into the cup.

When they finished, they put that cup on the floor and picked up the second one. Before Rob could react, they had grabbed his arm and sliced deeply, holding it over the cup. He watched, fascinated, as his blood ran into the cup. *There's something strange in the incense. It's affecting my Sight. I can't see them as clearly now, I wonder what's in it. Galen will know. I'll ask him.* The thought of his brother comforted him. He was starting to get faint. They bound a purple and red cloth over the wound, picked up the cups and the braziers and led him from the room.

They took him out of the house and across the clearing. Rob noticed a small hill at the back of the house, they were leading him towards it. As they reached the bottom, they stopped and chanted, forcing Rob onto his knees for a moment before pulling him up and dragging him up the incline. Rob could see the sun setting, blood-red, over the trees. When they reached the top and Rob saw what was there, once he saw what was going to happen, he pulled violently away from them and ran. Sheer terror gave him strength to break the hold the incense had over him, his head was suddenly clear and he made a dash to escape, but was stopped before he got far. There were other people waiting along the edge of the hill, and they grabbed him and forced him back, holding him by one of two large holes dug in the ground.

"No, please, I won't try and escape again," he said desperately, tears running down his face.

He saw Other climb down into one of the holes. The bearded man put one of the braziers into it and then dragged a board over. Some of the people gathered there, all wearing red robes, began piling rocks and shoveling dirt onto the board. There was a small opening in it. Rob could see smoke curling out.

"No, please," Rob said again. "Please, don't put me down there. Please."

The bearded man pushed him down into a seated position and bound his hands behind him, carefully counting thirteen wraps before tying it off. Rob struggled against the man, against the bonds, until the man put his large hand around Rob's neck. "Hold still," he said, his voice barely more than a whisper. Rob immediately obeyed, terrified by the look in the man's eyes. *My Sight isn't right. Will it come back? If it doesn't, can I still be a Keeper?* The man did the same to Rob's legs, wrapping them from his knees to his ankles. Then he was lifted and put in the large hole. They carefully placed the brazier in with him.

"No!" he screamed. "Galen!"

"Rob!" He heard his brother's voice. It sounded in his head as clearly as if Galen had been standing next to him. *"Galen? Are you here?"* He reached out, his brother sounded so close. Knowing Galen was nearby calmed him, he stopped struggling.

They put the board over the hole, there was only a tiny slit of light filtering down. It was red like the sunset, like the blood that was soaking through the cloth on his arm. Rob heard rocks dropping on the board. The smoke from the incense filled the hole and he began to get sleepy. He was dozing, floating in a world of colors. He could smell the soil around him and the scent of the odd incense.

He must have dropped off, then come back to awareness again. He could feel fresh air winding down from the tiny hole in the board, but it was now dark outside. He thought he smelled rain. He was drifting back to sleep again when he thought he heard Galen's voice. Rob reached out for his brother, trying to sense his presence. "Galen?" he called as loud as he could. It wasn't very loud, he could barely hear it himself. He was almost all the way unconscious when he thought he heard it again.

"Rob! Answer me! Please! Rob!" Galen's voice sounded like it was coming from someplace very close.

Rob tried to call out, to answer his brother, his body refused. He tried to reach out through their bond, but he couldn't, it was almost as if it had never existed. And the darkness closed in, the colors gone, the earth silent around him. *I'm buried, like in a grave. I wonder if I'm dead?* And then there was nothing.

* * * * *

Galen was shaking. He looked at his brother, aware of the twisting of nausea in his stomach, aware of the scar alive and throbbing in his chest. *Oh gods, it is the Legacy. No.* He squeezed Rob's hand, trying to draw a little calm through the contact. Mike was staring at Rob as if he had suddenly sprouted horns. The doctor opened his mouth, closed it and looked down at Galen.

"Galen?" Rob asked quietly.

Galen looked over. "I'm okay."

"You know, I think you're lying to me," his brother said with a laugh.

"Maybe a little. Gods, Rob," Galen sighed. He scrubbed his hand across his face and looked back up. "I, Rob, is it...?" He stopped before he let the thought form again.

"What?"

"I...Rob..." Galen took a deep breath.

"Yeah?" Rob put his other hand over Galen's. "Galen?"

"I was there," Galen said quietly, ignoring the simmering fear that came every time he thought of the Legacy. "Rob, I heard you, when you screamed, right before they put you in the hole. I was out in the woods, the sound echoed weirdly, I tried to find you, oh gods, Rob, I couldn't sense you clearly enough to find you, I thought I was close, but I couldn't sense you. You disappeared. I left because I wasn't sure where you were, and I had to get a hold of Dad and Uncle Bobby..."

PAST

TEN YEARS BEFORE

Day Two - Galen

The rest stop was nearly deserted when Galen pulled in and sprinted for the phone. The need to talk with the older Keepers had become something akin to a physical pain. He was desperately worried about Rob, he thought he could sense a little of his brother through their bond, flashes of fear and pain. Galen dropped money in the phone with shaking hands, counting the rings on the other end until his father picked up the phone. "Dad..." he said softly, the worry, the fear, even a hint of his pain in his voice.

"Galen?" His father picked up on the tone immediately. "What is it?"

"Dad, it's...I...Rob." Hearing his father's voice caused what little composure he had to collapse utterly.

"Galen, what is it?" Under the slightly gruff demand, Galen could hear his father's concern.

"Rob, we stopped...Dad." He heard his voice break, grief pouring out through the words. "Dad, I lost..." He stopped himself, swallowing the lump in his throat. He took a deep breath. "We stopped for dinner last night, something weird's going on here. They ambushed us on the road and took Rob."

"What?" His father exploded, Galen knew the anger wasn't aimed at him, it was aimed at whoever had taken Rob. "Taken? How?"

"I tried to get away, we were on our way out of town and

they blocked the road. In the end, I tried to get Rob safe. It didn't work, they grabbed him. I lost him, I lost Rob." Reaching out, he tried to sense his brother, tried to send a little reassurance through the bond. For an instant he sensed Rob. "Oh, gods, Dad, they got him. I called you as soon as I could. I left you that message earlier, but I knew you wouldn't be around until about now. I started looking Dad, went out to where…I met someone she… her daughter….Once I got out of the hospital…"

"Hospital, Galen?" his father cut him off. Galen could hear the concern clearly in his father's voice. He could also hear his uncle in the background, asking what was going on.

"I wouldn't have gone at all…"

"How bad?" The concern in his father's voice boiled over into something that sounded like fear. "Galen?" He could hear a tremor in his father's voice and Bobby's anxious demands.

"Not bad." He lied, knowing his father couldn't read him over the phone, but he knew it wouldn't last long. He wanted the older Keepers to focus on Rob.

"Galen, please answer me when I ask you a question like that."

"I just blacked out at the scene, Dad, and they transported me, that's all."

"Galen, answer my question." His father's voice was suddenly completely calm. Galen could hear blind panic under the calm.

"Busted rib, face is a mess. Knife wound," he said, trying to make it sound like nothing.

"Galen?"

"I'm okay, Dad," Galen said. It sounded like his father needed reassurance. "I made contact with a woman whose daughter disappeared. I think it's connected to Rob. Dad, her daughter… Her daughter…She'd been…Dad, will that happen to Rob? Oh, gods, she'd been mutilated, she'd been…"

"What?"

"She was partially flayed," Galen said it quietly, wishing he could keep it from his father, knowing that keeping something that important from him was a huge mistake.

"Flayed? Oh, gods," Parry said softly. Galen heard his uncle repeating the word.

Galen took a deep breath, trying to calm the shaking of his hands and the sudden rush of nausea as the memory of the pictures floated before his eyes. "Whoever took her and Rob, I think...Whatever it was—it killed her. She was found in the woods, she had symbols drawn on her. They were..." He carefully described them.

"Hang on for a minute," his father said. His father was speaking with his uncle, Galen could hear his father's voice and then answers back. He couldn't quite make out the words. "Was her daughter the first, Galen?"

"No, she was the sixth."

"So Rob's the seventh?" More conversation back and forth that Galen couldn't make out. Then one thing came through the line "What? Oh my gods, no!" It was louder than the rest of the conversation. "Galen?"

"Yeah, what is it?" he said, keeping his voice calm.

"We aren't all the way sure, but we don't think it's very serious, a lesser demon called a wood hag. It can offer powers as long as you sacrifice to it. One child and one adult on the full moon."

"Dad?"

"Yes, Galen?"

"When did human sacrifice become not very serious?" Galen asked, a little exasperated. "Okay, lesser demon is maybe easy, at least for trained Keepers, but Dad, Rob hasn't really started training yet, not the more formal training. We've been working together for years, but not really training. I'm only five years into the formal training myself. I think it's serious and I suspect you're not telling me something." Galen could here it clearly in his father's voice.

"No. We're on our way, but I don't think we can be there until tomorrow."

"Dad, please answer me when I ask a question like that." He tried to keep his voice calm.

"Okay, Galen, you do need to know Rob's special, he's the seventh sacrifice."

"Can the wood hag be killed? A lesser demon shouldn't be too hard, well, as those things go."

"In a way. You have to erase the symbols. Without them it can't find the sacrifice and it'll die. You have to remove them from his skin and from around the base of the tree."

"Tree? Tree? What does a tree have to do with...And get the symbols off? Dad, her daughter, the symbols..."

"Galen, listen to me. I need you to stay calm for your brother's sake, okay?" His father said it quietly, offering comfort. "You need to get to him and get him out of there. You need to be calm. No matter what you see, no matter what he looks like."

"Dad? This really isn't helping. And think, Dad, how calm would you be if it were Uncle Bobby out there? I remember..." He stopped when he heard his father's gasp on the other end. "I'm sorry," he said, shutting off the memory of his father's desperate search for his uncle not too long before.

"They'll hang him from the tree, Galen. You need to cut him down and get those symbols off of him, understand?"

"What?" Galen hadn't actually heard anything after the word "hang".

"We'll get to you as soon as possible. I just don't think we can be there before tomorrow. The ritual—they'll be in the forest somewhere. There's a ritual tonight, too. It would be better if you found him tonight, before they start. Bobby isn't exactly sure what's going to happen. We'll try and find out more."

"Dad? What? What are they going to do tonight? Dad!"

"We don't know, Galen. If we knew we'd tell you, you know that. We're just not sure. Try and find him if you can, Galen, but be careful. And as bad as the first ritual probably is, it will get worse from tonight. We need to get on the road. Where did you call from?"

"A rest stop just outside of town. The number's…" He read the number off the phone.

"Okay, we'll call you back at this number at six in the morning." His father paused for a moment, then spoke again, his voice gentle, "we're on our way, Galen, hang on till we get there. We'll find him, we'll get Rob back, okay?" And his father broke the connection. He tried to reach out for his brother again, wanting to reassure Rob he was there, needing the contact himself. There was nothing there, just a soft velvety darkness. *"Rob?"*

He walked back to the car. "I want to head back out there, can I drop you someplace?" He looked over at Rhiannon.

"Let me come along, please. You might need help."

Galen looked at her for a long moment. Something told him taking her along was a good idea. One thing his father had drilled into his head over the years of training—Keepers trust their instincts. "Sure," he said as he got into the car.

It started raining. He drove back the way they came and took the turn onto the narrow road. About half a mile down he noticed another road turning off the right. "What's down there?"

"An abandoned farmhouse."

Galen drove by the road then stopped. He thought he sensed something, he wasn't sure what. He put the car in reverse and followed the road to the farmhouse. It was raining hard. The old building was dark, it looked deserted. Galen got out of the car and walked around the building. If anyone had been there recently, the rain had erased all evidence of their presence. He noticed a small hill behind the house. Something drew him towards the hill. He had a feeling…The top of the hill was empty. Nothing but mud and rocks and still…He thought he felt the shiver of his brother's presence.

"Rob?" he called out, his voice echoing over the forest. "Rob? Are you here?"

"Galen, what is it?" Rhiannon said, coming up beside him.

"I don't know, I just have this feeling that he's here, somewhere."

"There's nothing here."

"I can't shake the feeling, though." He sighed. "Rob?" he called again. Then, his heart started pounding. "Did you hear that? That was Rob!" He grabbed her arm.

"I didn't hear anything, I'm sorry. There's nothing here." Her eyes were compassionate, full of tears, for him, for Rob.

"No, that was him! I know it! Rob! Answer me! Please! Rob!" He listened, nothing. No one answered. Had he imagined it, that tiny sound? Taking a deep breath he tried to reach out, tried to find his brother. There was nothing except velvety darkness. Rob wasn't there. A stab of grief twisted against his heart. *Can Rob be dead?* He shoved the thought away as quickly as it formed. He'd know if his brother had died. It had to be something else. *But what?* Galen reached out to the darkness. *"Rob? I'm here, I'm looking for you, hang on."*

He turned and walked with Rhiannon down the hill and back to the car. Galen stopped beside the car, looking back across the forest. The sense of his brother was completely gone, like the dying sun. Whatever had drawn him there was gone as well. He sighed and dropped back into the car.

* * * * *

"You were there," Rob whispered, looking at Galen, a smile lighting his eyes. "You were there. It's okay, Galen, you were there." The look on his face was almost serene.

"Yeah. If Dad and Uncle Bobby had known what to expect I might have found you."

"I don't think they could have known anything at all about it, really, Galen," his brother said. "I think that group had deviated from the standard ritual, even then, even before…Like the girl tonight, the ritual has altered again, she was meant to die, her blood feeding the earth, her life giving It life to come again. I wasn't meant to die, not then, not until after…"

"My god, what happened to the two of you back then?" Mike said, aghast. Galen looked over at the doctor, he'd forgotten Mike was there.

"We had a few bad days," Rob said with a soft, sardonic laugh.

"Can I go home?" Galen asked as Mike ran his eyes over the machines beeping and whirring around him. "I'm fine, it wasn't a seizure."

"You damn near died."

"What? What? I thought you said…I'm fine now, it's not something you can treat, really, Mike."

Mike looked at him, trying to stare him down. Finally he nodded. "You can go, but I'm coming with you."

"Mike…"

"Do you want to leave, Galen?" Mike asked sternly. "Then I come with you."

"Mike…"

"Galen? Let him get you home, and once he's sure you're safe there, he can go." Rob looked at him, understanding in his

101

eyes.

"Okay." Mike unhooked the monitors and Galen pushed himself up. The room spun a little, Rob put a steadying hand under his elbow until he could stand without swaying. "Thanks. You'd better drive."

Rob helped him to the elevators. The nurse they had seen earlier that day was standing at the other end of the ward. "She's one of them," Rob said quietly.

"Yeah." Galen leaned against his brother. "We might be getting ready for a couple of bad days again."

Chapter Seven

The valet opened the door of the jeep so Galen could get in. He dropped into the passenger seat with a sigh. The old scar was twisting and throbbing in his chest. *It knows we're here, that we're together.* Rob got in the driver's side and pulled out. Galen could feel his brother's eyes on him.

"I'm okay, Rob."

"You know that I can see you're not, right?" Rob said with a shake of his head.

"Probably feel it a little, too." Galen said, looking over at him with a smile.

"Maybe a little." Rob drove silently for a several minutes. "Galen? How...?"

"How what?"

"I could always sense you, even when we were kids. Then, after you died, you were gone...How?" Rob laughed, but there was confusion and confused hurt in his voice. "Since you weren't dead?"

"I was, you know," Galen said quietly.

"I know." Rob swallowed. "I was there with you, remember?" Galen put a hand on his brother's arm, aware of the pain there.

"I remember." Galen sighed. "I do. I remember my heart stopping, I remember you holding my hand. I remember It screaming as we died, as It twisted in my chest," he sighed. "Dad did something, I think, blocked it somehow. He needed to make sure It couldn't find you. Then, when I was better, he showed me how to block it, too."

"I can sense you now."

"Yeah," Galen said, looking at him. "Something happened when I saw you, I let it go. I didn't mean to, it just shattered as I stood there, when I realized it was really you."

"It shattered? The block broke? I wonder..." Rob railed off. "I think I knew you were there. It was strange, I woke up a little at one point and I felt your hand, I thought I was dead since you were there."

"I'm sorry." Galen said again. *I wonder how many times I'll say that until he believes it?*

"Galen? You've said that twice."

"What? I'm sorry? I'll probably say it again, too," Galen said almost to himself.

"You said 'when I was better' twice. How long?" Rob's jaw was clenched as he drove, his hands tight on the wheel.

"How long?" Galen frowned.

"Galen, tell me." Rob glanced over at him. "How long until you were better? How long after..."

Galen took a deep breath. "Months." He saw Rob's shoulders sag. "I don't remember much, not at least from the beginning, after you went home. I was in the hospital there, then home I think. Dad healed me as best he could, but even with his help, it was a long time. When I was a little stronger, I could help."

"Months?" Rob sighed. "We need to talk about this." He said it so quietly Galen wasn't sure he was meant to hear it.

"Rob?" Galen was watching his brother, Rob was pale, the fading bruise on the side of his face dark against his skin. Rob shook his head. Galen sighed. "Coming back from the dead might be harder than I thought," he muttered. Rob looked over at him for a moment, then looked away with a frown.

Rob pulled the car up behind the building and walked around to help Galen out, letting him steady himself before opening the door to the apartment. Rob walked up the steps behind him, hovering a little. The scar suddenly gave a particularly violent twist. Galen stopped, he felt his brother's hand on his back, supporting him. After several deep breaths he managed to get all the way to the couch before the scar twisted again.

"What can I do?" Rob asked quietly.

"In the cupboard, there's a red bottle, can you get it?" Rob walked across the room and opened several cupboard doors before he found the right one. Rob opened the bottle and handed it to him. "Thanks," Galen said, taking a sip from the bottle. He leaned back, giving the medicine a chance to work.

"What is that?"

"Herbs and a bit of magic. It stops…"

"Stops what?" Rob looked at him, a slightly unfocused look in his eyes. "You have a spot. Where the old wound was." His hand hovered over the scar. "It's alive, moving, twisting."

"Alive?" Galen snorted. "That's exactly how I think of it. Twisting."

The downstairs door banged open, then slammed closed. Rob walked to the head of the stairs and looked down. "It's Mike." He came back over and sank down beside Galen on the couch.

Mike huffed into the apartment. "You need an elevator."

"You need to get into shape," Galen said, laughing.

Mike muttered something and walked into the kitchen, punching the button on the coffee machine before dropping into the chair across from the couch. "Don't mind me. I'm just here to make sure my patient is okay, I'll nap." He leaned back in the chair and closed his eyes. A minute later he was snoring.

"Is he really asleep?" Rob asked with a grin.

"Yes. He does that, he prides himself in being able to sleep anywhere, anytime."

"That might be a handy skill." Rob laughed. "Although I can

sleep through any philosophy seminar, anytime, anywhere."

Galen chuckled. "I think I can, too." He pushed himself off the couch, waiting as the room stopped spinning. Rob stood up beside him and followed as he walked back to the bedroom. His brother caught sight of the knife on the bed stand and walked over, picking it up carefully. Rob looked over at Galen.

"Brother to brother," he said softly, a gentle smile on his face. "You still have it."

"Of course I do. I have a box with everything you ever gave me, including the rather large collection of rocks from that trip to the ocean when you were eight." Galen opened the closet. He was aware that Rob had come to stand beside him.

"Quite a collection," Rob said with a little laugh as he looked in the closet. "A bit of everything. What's that water gun for?"

"It handy for delivering herbs and things like that."

"Looks good, too, probably scares things away without even having to shoot." Rob laughed, then looked at him. "I have a little collection myself, not much, but a few things. This is nice." He ran his hand over the falcata.

"It's my favorite, actually." Galen took a deep breath. "Rob…" His brother met his eyes and then looked at the two swords at the front of the closet.

"Are those…?" Rob asked softly.

"Yes," Galen said reverently. "The swords of the Emrys line of *Custodes Noctis*, forged thousands of years ago, passed down through the generations."

"Hand to hand," Rob whispered. He reached, unerringly, for the sword destined for him, his hand running down the scabbard, slowing as it passed over small dings and flaws in the leather. Galen rested his hand on the sword that would be his, the soft hum buzzing against his hand. He watched as Rob picked his sword up and slowly pulled the blade from the scabbard.

"It hums." Rob's voice was still a whisper. He ran a finger down the blade, passing slowly over the engraving there, Ogham, Runes, Latin, words recorded over the millennia, spells binding power to the swords, spells binding the blades to the family. Rob slid the blade back into the scabbard and set it carefully down beside the other. He looked up at Galen for a minute, a frown on his face, then looked down at the sword resting under Galen's hand. He gently moved Galen's hand aside and picked up the sword.

Galen's heart started pounding. "Rob?"

His brother smiled. "I understand, Galen. I know. I've done my homework, you know."

"Once it's done...Rob, think about this for a minute. If you do this...you've sealed your fate—our fate."

"No going back, but there never really was, Galen," he said gently.

Rob pulled the sword out of the scabbard and set the scabbard back in the closet. He let the blade rest in his palms. He met Galen's eyes and swallowed. Galen saw a flash of uncertainty for a moment. Rob took a deep breath. With another look at Galen he began the Ritual of Swords, the Latin falling easily from his tongue. He held the sword towards Galen.

Galen's hands were shaking as he reached for the other sword. He pulled it from its scabbard, letting the blade rest on his palms. He looked back up at his brother. The uncertainty was gone from Rob's eyes, replaced by a fierce determination. Galen carefully recited his part, his heart slamming against his chest as he finished and waited for Rob to complete the ritual.

"Hand to hand," Rob said, reaching out and closing his right hand over the hilt of his sword. "Brother to brother."

"Hand to hand," Galen repeated, closing his hand around the hilt of his own sword lying perfectly balanced on Rob's palm.

"Brother to brother." As the final syllable fell from his tongue, a jolt of energy, a bolt of white light, ran up the sword, up his arm and exploded in his body. The hum of the blade became a song, filling him completely, the note resonating through his body, filling him with light made music.

"You know," his brother said lazily sometime later, a slightly ironic tone in his voice.

Galen opened his eyes and rolled his head around from where he was lying to look at Rob, on the floor beside him. "What's that?"

"If they'd mentioned that particular effect, I would've made sure I was sitting down." Rob chuckled, a light, happy sound.

"Would've been nice to know," Galen answered. "We'll have to mention that to Dad and Uncle Bobby next Day of the Dead."

"We will. It's still singing."

"Mine too," Galen said, aware of the soft hum of the sword in his hand. The tone had changed. "It knows me now, not as a member of the line, but as the Keeper who wields it." The power of the blade no longer buzzed against his hand, but flowed easily into his body.

"Yeah, mine knows me, too. I never realized, Galen." He chuckled, then was quiet. They were silent for several minutes. Then Rob sighed. "Galen?"

"Yeah?"

"It's coming for us again."

"I think so."

"We need to talk about what happened."

"No," Galen said softly.

"There might be something there, something that'll help."

"Might not."

"Do you get far lying to yourself like that?" Rob's voice had laughter in it, but a serious concern underneath.

"Depends on what I'm lying about."

"Seriously, Galen, we have to talk about what happened, to you and me."

"I'm not sure that will help."

"It's the only way to know, to be sure," Rob insisted.

"Sure of what?" Galen asked, dreading his brother's answer.

"If this is the Legacy."

"It can't be."

"Do you think just by saying it isn't you can make it vanish?"

"Maybe. It's not the Legacy."

"How will we know for sure? We have to talk about this, we have to." Rob paused. "What did you say about pictures?"

"Pictures?" Galen asked looking at Rob, still trying to bring his focus back a little.

"Of Rhiannon's daughter?"

"She had pictures of the crime scene."

"So you saw the sacrifice?" Rob frowned.

"I saw the pictures of one sacrifice, yeah."

"Galen." Rob sighed.

Galen reached out and put his hand on his brother's arm. A brief flash of pain was there, the impression of old wounds, long healed scars. He let a little of the light flow down his hand. "You're right, we need to talk, Rob."

His brother patted his hand. "Thanks."

PAST

TEN YEARS BEFORE

Day Three - Rob

Rob had a headache. *I wonder if this is what a hangover feels like? If it is, I'm never ever drinking. Where am I?* Memory flooded back. The hole, the sound of the rocks dropping on the board above his head. He opened his eyes. Rob was back in the room in the farmhouse, still wearing the purple pants and white shirt. His arm hurt where they'd cut it. *There really is a cut there, I didn't dream it.* He tried to sit up and fell back down. His bones felt like jelly. He saw the brazier full of incense sitting in the corner of the room. *I wonder what's in there? Whatever it is, it's making me feel weird. It's messing up the Sight. I can't see straight, I can't sense Galen.*

He rolled over, from his back onto his side. *I thought I heard Galen. I thought he was there for a minute. It sounded so much like him. If he'd been there, I don't know, I think...Just knowing he'd been around would help. I wish he were here. If only I knew...* He started to cry. He curled up, hugging himself. *If Galen were here...* He tried to stop, but the tears kept coming. He was sleepy, the incense taking away consciousness. Rob could hear his heart beating, he listened to it, trying to calm himself the way his brother had shown him. Then, just as he was almost asleep... *"Rob? I'm here, I'm looking for you. Sleep. It'll help. I'm here, Brat. I'm coming for you."* His brother's voice played in his head, it calmed him, he let himself drift off to sleep.

The sound of the key in the lock woke him. The pretty young waitress with the black spots, Ashley, came into the room with a tray. "Time to eat, Chosen."

"That's not my name."

"It is now. You have no other name, you have no past, no future. There is only today. Today is all. Today is ritual."

"You're all weird."

"You need to eat this." She put the tray in front of Rob.

"Not hungry."

"Ah, come on sweetie. It's pretty good."

"Nope."

"Okay." She smiled, but her voice was hard. "You eat it or I force it down, how's that?"

"Yeah, sure you could."

"There's help right outside the door. Are you going to eat, or do I call them?"

"I'll eat it." He tried to sit up. He still couldn't. His hands weren't working quite right either. He tried again. It didn't work.

"Not funny. Just because you're Chosen doesn't mean you can get away with that."

"I can't, I'm trying, but I can't," he said, afraid. She had the same scary look in her eyes the bearded man had the night before.

"Fine." She raised her voice. "I need help in here." The door opened and two of the three guys Rob remembered attacking him and Galen came into the room. One of them had a large bruise on his face, and his nose was taped up.

Rob smiled. "My brother do that?" he said.

"Right before my brother knifed him," the guy said with satisfaction in his voice. "We left him on the road, he was in bad shape. Might've driven over him on the way out. Never know."

"Shut up. Galen'll be here, he'll come for me."

"Not if he's dead, kid." The big guy yanked him up and held him. The other one just lounged against the door, knowing Rob was no match for the man who held him. Ashley started spooning the food into his mouth. Rob tried to spit it out, she slapped him across the face. In the end they managed to get about half the bowl of food into him. The big guy dropped him back down on the floor.

"Don't get too comfortable, we'll be back, kid." The two men left and Ashley smiled at him, it was a terrifying smile, "Oh, yeah, we'll be back."

Rob lay on the floor. His face hurt, his arm hurt and his

stomach hurt. Whatever was in the food was not sitting well. He felt sick, he wanted to throw up. Rob wondered if he should, Galen had taught him to rid his system of poison as fast as he could, but maybe that was what they wanted him to do. He wasn't sure. Hearing his brother had calmed him, he hoped it was actually Galen, and not a trick of the incense. He was still unsure if his brother was alive. He was feeling sleepy again. *The incense, it's making me sleepy, blocking the Sight. I wonder if that's why I can't sense Galen. He'd tell me to sleep if I needed too, a Keeper has to be strong.* He drifted off.

He had no idea how long he slept. It was dark in the room except for the glow of the brazier and the light coming under the door. When he woke up, his stomach still hurt, so did his arm and his head.

"Hey," he said, hoping there was someone outside the door. "Hey, I have to go to the bathroom."

The door opened. A man came in and looked at him. "Get up if you need to go."

Rob pushed himself up. The room was spinning. He tried to stand—his legs wouldn't hold his weight. The man came over, grabbed his arm and pulled him to his feet. He manhandled Rob out of the room and into the bathroom. "Don't spend too long or try anything funny." He closed the door. Rob heard his weight settle against it. *Can't try to escape that way, I guess.*

After he'd finished, he quietly closed the toilet lid and sat down, carefully easing drawers open, hoping to find something—anything—that might be of use. Mostly there were just bits and pieces of garbage. The final drawer yielded a treasure— a large safety pin. Rob pinned it in the waistband of his pants. He didn't know what he could do with it, but he was sure Galen would want him to find something that might help in the long run. *"We're Keepers, Rob, never forget that, no matter what hap-*

pens. We're Keepers and we use what we have, anything can help."
He smiled as he remembered the oft repeated lesson. *Galen'll be happy that I remembered. That I stayed calm. He'll laugh when I tell him about it.*

He sighed and tried to stand. Since he had been away from the brazier, his legs seemed to work a little better. Rob could not only stand on his own, he could walk without the rubbery feeling in his legs. He flushed the toilet and turned on the sink before knocking on the door to be let out.

Rob was pushed back into the room, the lock clicked into place. Once back in there the incense started affecting him again. He sank down to the floor and leaned against the wall, as far as he could get from the smoking brazier. He knew he couldn't get far enough away, but he still tried. Having the pin bolstered him, he didn't know what he could use if for, but having it gave him hope.

He heard the door and looked up. Ashley came back in with the two guys from earlier in the day. She was carrying a cup. Rob looked at the two men. There was a sudden lump in his throat and he closed his eyes for a moment, relief flooding through his body. The one with the busted nose looked pretty much the same, but the other—his face was red, covered in a rash, one eye swollen completely closed.

"What're you smiling at, shithead?" he said to Rob.

"Respect the Chosen," Ashley chided.

"The little shit's smiling at me. What?"

"You don't look so good," Rob said, still smiling. "Didn't anyone ever tell you about stinging nettles?"

"What's that mean to you?"

Rob laughed. "It means a lot, more than you know," he said. He could feel tears on his cheeks. "My brother's alive." He reached out, trying to sense his brother. *"Galen? I'm here."*

The guy made to rush at Rob, but Ashley stopped him. "No, you can't. They will be here in a minute to prepare for the next ritual. Drink this." She held the cup out.

"What is it?"

"It's part of the ritual, like the food. This is the sacred drink, it has been prepared for you, it is ritual, you must consume it," she said in kind of a sing-song voice.

"Uh, let me think about that." Rob couldn't help smiling. He'd been right all along, Galen was alive. That thought gave him strength. "Nope, not thirsty."

"You do it, or we will."

"Not drinking it, sorry."

"You need to drink this," she said in the hard scary voice.

"No," Rob said, even though he knew they were going to force him to drink it. He felt braver. *"Galen? I'll be ready when you get here. We're Keepers and I'll be ready."* The guy with the broken nose came over and grabbed him, hard. He forced Rob's head back and pinched his nose, Ashley poured the contents of the cup in this mouth and they held it closed until he swallowed. The liquid was bitter and made him gag. He was nauseous again. They pushed him back down.

"They will be here in a few minutes to begin the ritual of the Sun," Ashley said to Rob as they left.

Rob lay on the floor. His arms felt bruised from where they held him. His head was starting to swim. He wondered what the next ritual was. *Sun ritual, that might not be too bad, maybe they won't bury me this time. Galen's alive.* Rob laughed to himself, thinking of the nettle rash on the one guy's face. *They underestimated us. Galen will come, he'll bring Dad and Uncle Bobby.* As reassuring as that thought was, when he heard the door he was afraid.

The bearded man and the man who'd called himself Other

came in the room. The bearded man was carrying a black tray. He put it down by the brazier, took something off the tray and tossed it into the burning embers. Other came over and sat down by Rob. His body had been wrapped in what looked like bandages. There were dark stains on the cloth.

"We will begin the next ritual. We are nearly finished. After this one, there is only the ritual of the Moon. Aren't you pleased?" Other said with a sick smile.

"I don't know." Rob could hardly focus. "Does that mean I won't have to see you anymore?"

He wasn't expecting Other to smile, it wasn't a nice smile. "That's exactly what it means. We will be taken to Her."

"Her?" Rob was slipping away from reality. He felt strange.

"The One we perform the ritual for. She will be here tonight. You will see Her."

"Lucky me." Further away.

"Enough!" the bearded man said. "We must begin." He walked towards Rob, a golden cup in his hand again. Rob knew what was coming and braced himself. They grabbed his right arm this time and cut it deeply, the blood flowing into the cup. Then they bound the arm the same way they had the night before: carefully counting the wraps and tying it in an intricate knot. They walked back over to the brazier and put the cup on the tray, chanting the strange language again.

The bearded man picked something up off the tray. Rob couldn't tell what it was. The man called out in the strange language, and the door to the room opened. The two men came in, they were dressed in red shirts. Other stood with them by the brazier. They were chanting again, waving something back and forth. Rob watched them, it felt like he was watching a movie, like he wasn't there at all. Other picked something up off the tray and they chanted again. It looked like a roll of bandages, only it was purple and red like the one on Rob's arm. *What are those for? They look like the one on my arm. Are they for me?*

The two men came over and grabbed Rob. The bearded man turned around and they began to chant again. He had something in his hand, it was glittering in the light from the brazier. The light from the embers made it look like it was covered with bright sparkles of blood. Rob could see the bearded man's eyes glittering the same way. For an instant the Sight cleared and Rob saw black spots surrounding the man. Even though he tried, Rob couldn't focus enough to see what the spots were, he couldn't tell what was happening, he couldn't tell what the glittering object was.

Rob allowed his eyes to close. *These two guys saw Galen today. Galen was with them. That makes me feel better, it makes him seem close somehow. It's almost like he's here. "Galen? Can you hear me? I'm going to black out, I think."* He tried to let his brother know what was going on. *Wait—what's that?*

Rob could hear someone screaming. The screams were terrible, terrifying—someone was in horrible pain. The anguished cry went on and on. It echoed around him, blending with the chanting, creating a single sound. It filled his senses.

Just before he lost his grip on consciousness he realized something.

That scream, it was me.

Chapter Eight

Galen was leaning with his back against the bedroom wall. Rob had moved and was sitting beside him, his shoulder resting against Galen. The sword was still singing softly in Galen's hand, the song reflecting the emotion running through him. Remembered anger and anguish caused a minor key in the sword's song.

"Rob..." he started.

"Would it help if I said I didn't remember much?" His brother's tone was teasing.

"Since I know you'd be lying, not really," Galen sighed.

"There are dark patches, you know. I don't remember portions of it." Rob looked at him, Galen saw the truth of the statement in his brother's eyes. "Part of it was that drink. I was disconnected from reality about half the time."

"Lying to me?"

"Not really. And it helped, Galen. When I thought I heard you before I went to sleep, and then seeing broken nose's friend. Nettles. Brilliant." He laughed, the note bright and happy. "I knew it was you, I knew you'd done that. It let me hang on." Rob smiled.

"I think you might have heard me, Rob, before you went to sleep."

"Galen?"

"Our connection was always stronger." Galen looked down at the sword in his hand. "I wonder how much more, now that we've done the Ritual of Swords? Now that we're the *Custodes Noctis* of the Emrys line? Dad and Uncle Bobby were closely

117

connected. I wonder what it was really like for them?" Galen glanced at his brother. "More? Less? Dad was always surprised by our connection, that I could sense you, even when we were young."

"Yeah, I know." Rob sighed, then frowned. "Hey, there were three guys, weren't there? What happened to the third, Galen?"

"He met a tiger he wasn't expecting," Galen said with a chuckle.

"Rhiannon?" Rob smiled, then frowned. "I'm sure it wasn't only a wood hag, Galen."

"You mean even before...? Yeah, I don't think so either, I sensed something in the woods and then later when I heard..."

"Heard what?"

Galen looked at his brother. "You, Rob. I heard you scream-ing."

PAST

TEN YEARS BEFORE
Night Day Two to Day Three - Galen

Galen stopped at the end of the road. The adrenaline that had been keeping him going was running out. He was tired to the point of collapse. The urge to find Rob was all that was keep-ing him on his feet.

"Galen?" Rhiannon said quietly from the passenger seat. "You need to eat and you need to rest."

"No, I have to find Rob. Dad said the ritual gets worse from tonight. I have to find him."

"If you collapse you won't do him any good. You're bleeding, you have to rest. Come back to my apartment and rest, please."

"No, you don't understand, I have to find him."

"Actually Galen, I do understand," she said softly. "I understand better than anyone, maybe. That's why I know you need to rest. You have to be ready when you find him." She laid a gentle hand on his arm. A rush of grief, of loss so great he sensed it as a physical pain, washed up from that contact. He took a deep breath, trying to ease the ache in his chest. He knew Rhiannon understood. She'd lost her daughter, not missing like Rob, but gone forever. Galen sent a tiny shaft of healing light towards her hand, she sighed and the tension in her shoulders eased a little bit.

He looked over at her and saw understanding in her eyes. "I can sleep at the rest stop, my father will call at six."

"Galen, please let me help you." She smiled her sad smile. "I need to help you, I need to…" She stopped, tears in her eyes. "I'm sorry. Sometimes I'm still a mother, you know?"

"I have to be back for my Dad's call," Galen said, looking at her. "You're right, I have to rest and maybe change the bandage. It's kind of sticky," he said, forcing a laugh, she laughed with him. "Which way?" he said, pulling out onto the road.

Her apartment was quiet, warm and smelled of flowers. When they arrived, Galen sank down onto the couch. He leaned back, trying to focus the healing on his wounds, trying to ease the pain. Rhiannon came in from the other room with a mug in her hands. She put it down beside Galen and disappeared again. He picked up the cup. Soup, homemade by the taste of it. It warmed and comforted him. She came back into the room with bandages and towels.

"I should re-bandage that for you," she said, sitting down beside him.

"I can do it," Galen said. "This is good soup, thanks."

"It was Megan's favorite." She looked away for a minute. "Let me at least look at the bandages? I am a fully qualified mom, you know." She smiled at him.

Galen looked at her. He was starting to really hurt, the healing was hard, he was distracted by the pain and it was making it difficult to focus. "Sure, thanks," he said, slipped off his jacket and pulled the mostly destroyed t-shirt off.

"What is this?" she said after she had snipped the bandage away.

"One of the guys outside the diner had a knife. And you know, now that the air's getting on it, wow, it really hurts."

"You've been walking around with this? And these bruises? Galen?"

"I think someone kicked me, I'm not really clear on that." He looked at her, she had a horrified look on her face. "It's okay, I haven't really thought about it much today." Mostly he'd been thinking about finding his brother, about the fact he couldn't sense Rob, and he always had been able to before. That fact worried him more than anything else.

"I understand," she said with the soft sorrow back in her voice. "Do you have anything to take for pain?"

"I left the hospital without the usual check-out procedures. I needed to find Rob and I didn't know who to trust, so I left." He was starting to get tired, really tired. He could barely keep his eyes open. What the injuries hadn't taken, his attempts at healing had. Exhaustion made his words sound thick.

"Well, you're in luck." She got up and came back a minute later with a glass of water. She held her hand out. "I get migraines and my doctor gives me Tylenol fours. Here, take one."

"I don't know." He needed to make sure he was up in time to get to the phone. He needed to be able to drive. *I have to be okay, I have to get to Rob. I need to ask Dad and Uncle Bobby what's going to happen, I need to know.*

"Take it. You won't be any good to anyone if you can't get up, you know?"

Galen smiled and held his hand out for the pill. "You really sound like a mom, you know that?"

"Thanks." She sat back down and cleaned gently around the stitches, then started to put fresh bandages on it. Galen had no idea what she did next. His body had finally given out and he fell asleep.

"Galen?" someone said, shaking him. "Galen?"

"Yeah?"

"You need to get up, so we can get to the phone," Rhiannon said.

"What?" He opened his eyes, he was lying on the couch. He sat up. "Is it morning already?"

"Yes, we need to get going. I have a clean shirt here for you." She handed him a t-shirt. "It's probably a little big for you, but with those bandages, it might be better."

Galen shrugged into the shirt and put his shoes on, he had no memory of taking them off. Picking up the keys, he headed to the door. Rhiannon was waiting for him. "I don't think you should go with me," Galen said.

"I have to, at least for awhile. I need to know you're okay, I need to help you find Rob. Please," she said, looking at him. Suddenly he understood. *If it was the other way around and Rob...I would need to help her.*

"Okay, but we need to get going."

He waited by the phone for nearly half an hour before it rang. "Hello?"

"Galen? Are you okay?" his father's voice was rough with emotion.

"I'm okay. Dad, I didn't find him. I thought for a moment I had, I sensed him, but then he was gone."

"Gone?"

"Yeah, there was this darkness where he'd been. I thought I

heard his voice, too, but I must have imagined it."

"I understand," his father said gently. "He might have been unconscious, Galen, or asleep. It is harder to sense someone…"

"But Dad, I always could before." He heard a frightened note in his own voice.

"Always?" His father sounded surprised. "I knew you two were different…" his father muttered, almost under his breath. "Have you found any leads?"

"There was a waitress, I think she might be involved. I'm planning to find her and her friends and ask them."

"Be careful, Galen. These're people who are serving a demon that requires human sacrifice."

"I know, Dad. I know I need to be careful, I need to find Rob."

"It's important."

"I know, Dad. It's all there is."

"Yeah," his father said softly. "I know."

"Can you tell me anything else?"

"There's a ritual today, at the thirteenth hour, try and get to him before then, Galen."

"Dad? What's going to happen?"

"Our information's sketchy, Galen. The ritual will take place outside, in the sun. It's preparatory for the final ritual this evening. That one will take place right after sunset as the moon rises. You must get to him." His father's calm voice held an undertone of steely determination.

"I will, Dad. Nothing'll stop me."

"You need to know…" His father broke off and Galen could hear another voice, Bobby, in the background. "Are you sure?" his father asked.

"Dad? What's going on?"

"Your brother might not look very good when you get to

him. But do your best to try and stay focused."

"Dad, what do you mean? How bad is not good?" Galen knew his father wouldn't have said that unless it was going to be serious.

"We really aren't sure about it, Galen. If it is a wood hag, we can take a guess. It's all assumptions at this point."

"Is there anything? Anything at all that might help?"

"If we're right, the rituals aren't pretty, Galen. They require blood sacrifice. Just try and stay focused and get him out of there. Get him down and get those symbols off of him. As long as they are there, it can still take him."

"I think the symbols were carved into her daughter, Dad."

"What?" Parry asked. Galen heard his uncle in the background. "He says he thinks they were carved into her. Are you sure, Galen?"

"I'm going on the pictures, I told you about them."

"I know. Hang on." The sound of his father's voice was suddenly muffled. All he got was the rumble of his uncle's voice and his father's replies. One word drifted through, Galen thought it was "legacy." "Get to him, get him out of there. It might be worse than we thought."

There was something in his father's voice, Galen was starting to panic. "Dad, what do you mean?"

"It's probably nothing, Galen. Bobby's, well you know how he gets," his father said gently. "Try and find him, Galen. We should be there by sunset. Where can we find you?"

"There's a rest stop just out of town. It's where I'm at now. I'll be here tonight at six. If I haven't found him, I won't wait long, Dad. I...I have to find him." He heard his voice break.

"I know, Galen. I understand," his father said softly. "When Bobby..." He stopped himself. "We'll be there as soon as we can, please be careful."

"I will, Dad. I know, I can't help Rob if I do something stupid, can I?"

"Galen?" Parry's voice demanded an answer.

"It's just, Dad, I...Sometimes..."

"Galen, you need to be careful."

"Sorry." Galen scrubbed a hand across his face. "I'll be careful, Dad. I'm getting desperate."

"I know. I do understand, Galen. I do." His father paused, Galen heard the note of desperation mirrored in Parry's voice. "Try and keep your head clear, if you can."

"I will. Hurry, Dad."

"We will." His father broke the connection.

Galen stood with his hand on the receiver for a minute, knowing his father and uncle were on the way calmed him. The bond they shared, not just as family, but as Keepers, sustained him. He walked back down and got in the car. "I need to talk to Ashley and those three guys from the other night," he said to Rhiannon.

"I know they come in about eleven every morning. You might be able to catch them then."

"That's almost five hours. Dad said the next ritual starts at the thirteenth hour. That would be one in the afternoon, I hope, if they're using a clock and not the solar cycle." Galen looked out the windshield. "What do I do? I have to find Rob. I can't just wait around. I need to do something."

"Galen?"

"Can you go back to where they found your daughter? You said her name was Megan?"

"Yes, Megan. And I can go back. I've been there so many times already. Yes, I can go," Rhiannon said quietly.

Galen sighed as he put the key in the ignition. He took a deep breath and reached out for his brother, stretching himself almost to the limit of his injured body. His heart was racing as he concentrated, he was just about to pull away, just about to let go when he thought he felt Rob. He held his breath, a sob had echoed up that contact, pain-soaked, desperate, afraid. *"Rob?"* He focused on the first healing he had been taught, reaching out to his brother, projecting every ounce of his strength into that contact. *"Rob? I'm here, I'm looking for you. Sleep. It'll help. I'm here, Brat. I'm coming for you."*

"Galen?" Rhiannon was shaking his arm.

He opened his eyes and looked over at her. "What?"

"You blacked out."

"No, no... I... uh...I was trying to sense my brother. Sorry."

"You were...?" She looked at him with disbelief.

"I, uh, Rob and I...We....I can sense him, sometimes."

"I understand." She smiled. "I do understand."

He pulled out of the rest stop and headed back down the road into the woods. It looked different in daylight, but Rhiannon showed him where to pull in. He got out of the car and walked down the path. In the morning light he could see more details. The path seemed to lead into the darkest part of the surrounding forest. It felt cold. He could feel its presence a little, the thing that had taken Megan. Galen was aware that he was walking in its footsteps, the cold like shafts of pain running up his legs. *Dad might be wrong about this. It feels, hmm, it feels old somehow. Bobby's worry might be closer to the mark. Did I really hear Dad say Legacy? There's more here than just a lesser demon.*

When he walked into the clearing where Megan had been found, he stopped, looking carefully around this time. There didn't seem to be much to see until he walked down a path that led into the forest. As he moved into the dark woods he felt something—it felt like someone breathing down his neck. Galen concentrated, reaching out, he sensed the cold touch of the thing lurking in the shadows, he thought he heard something sigh. He wondered if Rhiannon knew what had taken her daughter. *Megan* he corrected himself. Hearing her name had made it seem much more real. He walked on, winding through the dark trees. He had no idea how far he followed the path before it broke into a clearing.

The clearing was ringed by huge trees, there was a stone circle inside the trees. Thirteen stones in a ring. Two trees stood in the ring, and between them was another stone, flat like a table. *Or an altar.* There was something on it. Galen walked over. A golden cup was lying on its side in a pool of liquid. As he got closer, the flies that had settled in the liquid flew away. There was another object on the stone. A t-shirt, faded, the neck stretched. Rob's favorite. He stopped, his heart in his mouth. He knew then, without a doubt it was his brother's blood. "No!" He didn't realize he had called out until he heard his own voice echoing back.

"Galen! Galen, what is it?" Rhiannon said, running into the clearing.

He picked the object up off the altar. "My brother's shirt, the one he was wearing when he was taken." He looked up at her, his eyes filled with tears, he could feel them spilling, hot, down his cheeks. Having the shirt in his hands, seeing the cup and the liquid that had spilled from it, knowing it was Rob's blood brought it all slamming down on him. "I have to find him, I have to. Nothing matters but that." He picked up the golden cup and threw it into the forest.

"What are you doing?"

"I don't know, maybe that will help break the cycle of the ritual. Anything that might help."

"I'm so sorry, Galen," she said softly.

Galen took a deep breath. "He's not dead. There are two

more rituals, that's what Dad said. They'll need to keep him alive."

"Yes, they'll keep him alive," Rhiannon said.

"Alive, Rhiannon, but in what shape? I can't sense him, what's happening? Blood rituals mean he needs to be alive till the very end, but how bad?" Galen sighed. "I wish Dad had told me, no, if he knew for sure what was going to happen he'd tell me. He understands. If this was Bobby we were looking for…" He trailed off before he said too much, as it was Rhiannon was looking at him with an odd frown on her face. Galen calmed the panic, drawing on his training. *Rob? Can you hear me?* He reached out for his brother, there was nothing there. Silent darkness, nothing, not even a heartbeat. *Rob?*

"Galen?" Rhiannon was looking at him, tears on her face. She had her hand on his arm.

"What have they done to Rob?" For an instant it was all too much.

Rhiannon pulled him to her and put her arms around him, he leaned against her, the tears running down his face. "I don't know, Galen. The police said the worst was done to Megan the last night. That's tonight, there's still time." She sighed. Galen heard her say so softly there was almost no sound, "There has to be."

He pulled away, and looked at her with a smile. "I'm okay, Rhiannon. I'm sorry. Let's get going. We need to go talk to those friends of Ashley's."

The three men showed up at the diner at ten forty-five. Galen was waiting. He left Rhiannon sitting in the car. He watched the men park their car at the far end of the lot and head towards the diner. Galen stepped between them and their goal.

"Hiya," he said, smiling at them. "Hey, nice nose."

"Aren't you dead?" the one with the broken nose said.

"Apparently not. We need to talk," Galen said conversationally.

"Yeah, about what?" one of the other two said.

"I just want to know if you might know where my brother is?" Galen said, keeping his voice light. His hands were starting to shake as he stood before them.

"And we'll tell you why?" broken-nose guy said.

"Because I asked nicely?" Galen's heart was starting to pound.

"Yeah, right."

"Where's my brother?" *I sound so calm. I need to be careful.*

"Not here."

"Where is my brother?" *I still sound calm. I need to stay calm. I have to.*

"Yeah, not here. Bug off."

"That's not an option. I really need to know where he is."

"We're not telling you. Get lost." Broken-nose guy moved to shove Galen out of the way.

"No." Galen reached around and pulled the nine millimeter out of his waistband. "Let me rephrase the question. I would really like to know where my brother is."

"You won't find him," one of the other two said. Galen was pretty sure he was the man who'd knifed him. "He was crying last time I saw him, said you'd come. I told him you were dead."

"He knows I'm not dead," Galen said with a tight smile.

"Doesn't matter. The next ritual begins soon. They'll bleed him and cut him and then—then do you know what they do? They'll lay him out in the sun and She'll come for the first time. Just for a taste, so She'll know him tonight." And he laughed.

"Where's my brother?"

"Sorry, even if I wanted to tell you, I couldn't. She'd eat me alive." The man chuckled. "And She'd enjoy it. Not as much as She'll enjoy your brother."

Galen's hands were shaking as he struggled to stay calm. He was distracted and it cost him. Broken-nose struck out at him and caught him on the side of his head, his gun skittered across the pavement. Galen pushed himself up. *And that's it. Calm's all gone now.* Sudden rage swelled up in him, intoxicating, blocking pain, blocking everything.

Galen struck out at him, the man staggered, then one of others turned on him. Galen swung at him. He knew this was stupid, the men would be going back to wherever they were holding Rob, and Galen couldn't let his brother suffer because of him, but he wanted to let Rob know he was searching for him. Looking desperately around for his gun, he noticed the plants growing at the edge of the parking lot. When the man came for him again he tripped him, using the man's own momentum to put him face down in the patch of stinging nettles. Broken-nose swung at Galen again, connecting, Galen saw stars. He was struggling to get up when he heard a voice tight with emotion.

"Stand still or I will kill you," Rhiannon said quietly. Galen looked up, she had his gun in her hands, standing in a shooter's stance.

"You won't do anything, bitch," broken-nose's companion said and kicked Galen. As he hit the pavement, Galen heard the gun go off, the man's body dropped on him. Pain shot out from the knife wound. Galen stayed still.

"Get out of here," Rhiannon growled. "Slowly. Take him with you." The weight was shifted off his body. "Galen? Galen?"

"Here," he said, trying to sit up. Rhiannon grabbed his arm and pulled him up. "Thanks." She helped him over to the car. Once he sat down, he managed to get his eyes open. "Hey," he said. His head hurt.

"Thank god. Should I call an ambulance?" Rhiannon sounded scared.

"No, I still don't know who to trust. I'm okay."

"You don't look okay, I thought you were dead for a second."

"Um, yeah, what happened?" He was having a hard time focusing. He was nauseous. "I think I tore a few stitches, that's all."

"They left. I made them pick up their garbage before they went."

Galen remembered the gunshot. "I think you might have killed him," he said, looking at her.

"Yeah, I think I might have," she said, looking back at him. She grinned, it was a feral grin, wild and terrible. "I'm glad if I did. They're involved with the people who took Rob, who killed Megan and at least five other children."

"What time is it?"

"About 12:30," she said. "Why?"

"Dad said the next ritual took place at the thirteenth hour. We need to get back out to the forest."

"We don't know where, Galen."

"That clearing we were at…"

"That's not where they were last night. Why would they be there today?"

"I don't know. It's a start." He sat up, then dropped back as a wave a dizziness rolled over him. "Maybe you should drive."

It was almost one when she stopped the car. Galen let her help him out and they headed down the path towards the clearing where he'd found Rob's shirt. When they got there, it was empty. He stood there, desperately scanning the woods around him hoping to see something, a sign of his brother, anything.

"The guy at the diner said they would lay him out in the sun, there's no sun here. It's all shadows. There's no sun in a building, so he has to be outside, somewhere." He looked at Rhiannon, her face was bleak.

The sound started, he barely even realized it was there at first. Then it crept into awareness. Someone was screaming. It was a terrible scream, someone in pain. Someone utterly terrified. He froze, his heart pounding in his chest. The terrible scream had called his name.

The scream echoed over the forest. *That scream, that was Rob.* The realization drove Galen to his knees. The scream continued.

He took a deep breath and focused on it, focused on the pain he sensed coming from his brother in horrifying waves. Something was there with Rob, Galen thought he could smell the sweet-sick scent of death. Whatever it was recognized his brother, Galen felt that through the connection. He heard it sigh with pleasure. "I'm coming. Hang on, please hang on little brother," he said it out loud to the silent clearing. The scream stopped, suddenly cut off. But just for a second, he thought he heard his brother's voice answering him. *"Galen?"* Then silence.

Chapter Nine

They were still sitting with their backs against the wall. Galen was aware of his brother, silent, beside him. "Rob?" Galen said quietly.

"Yeah?" Rob looked over at him with questioning eyes.

"Nothing." Galen sighed. "Well, nothing, really, I just needed to hear your voice not the screams in my head."

"It's okay, I understand."

Galen shrugged. "I just…" His phone started ringing, he dug in his pocket and flipped it open. "Hey."

"Hey yourself," Rhiannon answered. "I found his car."

"Great," Galen said, smiling at Rob. "She found your car." Rob grinned back.

"Galen…" Something in Rhiannon's voice drove the smile from his face. "I…"

"What is it?"

"I found something in the car," Rhiannon said softly. "It's bad. I'll be there in about twenty minutes."

"Thanks." Galen flipped the phone closed and looked at his brother. "She found something, said it's bad, but nothing more."

"Bad? That's helpful," Rob said with a smirk.

"Yeah, it worries me a little. Rhiannon doesn't use words like bad unless it's bad. Well, worse than bad, usually apocalyptically bad."

"Even better," Rob said, then grinned. "Black Sabbath?"

"What?" Galen said, a little distracted, wondering what Rhiannon had found.

"Your ringtone?"

"Oh, right. No, it's uh, actually it's me." He laughed. "I will grant there are similarities to Black Sabbath, we cover them occasionally."

"What?"

"My band."

"Oh, right, Becci said something about the bestest band." Rob was laughing at him.

"I'm not sure about that. We do get paid. Every once in awhile, depending on where we work." Galen grinned. "As long as it's not Rat's. Of course, that's where we're playing Friday."

"What do you play?" Rob asked with a smile.

"A bit of everything. Mostly rock and metal, but a bit of everything, even a little Mariachi punk." Rob's eyebrows climbed a little with that statement. "Hey, The Urban Werewolves embrace diversity."

"The Urban Werewolves?"

"Yeah, I'll get you a t-shirt," Galen said, still smiling. "Why are we talking about this?"

"We needed a break, Galen." Rob nudged him.

"Yeah," Galen said quietly. His good humor suddenly waned, as the memories of the past, those frantic days as he struggled to find his brother rose to the forefront again. The remembered terror was beginning to take the upper hand. He knew what happened to his brother, it had haunted him for years. The fact that he hadn't been able stop it just made it so much worse. He leaned against Rob a little, sensing what was there. Rob's terror, the horror and pain at what had happened suddenly washed over Galen. He broke contact with a gasp.

"Galen?" Rob was frowning in concern.

"Sorry. Oh, gods, Rob..." Galen stopped himself. "Is there meaning here somewhere? Is there a clue, something to tell us what's happening now? Or are we just talking about the past? The old wounds? Will it help?"

"We need to talk about this."

"You sound so sure about that. Will it help?"

"It will help. We have to know what happened, to you to me, we have to face this, Galen. The answer to today is there."

"Are you sure? Or… Rob, I…" He broke off again, struggling with the sense of helplessness left over from those days.

"I heard you," Rob said suddenly.

"What?"

"I heard you, when you were in the clearing. It was…I…" Rob suddenly paled.

"Rob?"

"It was horrible, terrifying, I was trying to be brave, trying to hold on to that sense I was a Keeper, that helped too, but I heard your voice. It's what got me through, Galen. I've thought all these years I imagined it, but it was really you, wasn't it?" He smiled, before swallowing. "After that…"

"Rob?"

"I was close to giving up, Galen. I think it was during the sun ritual when things began to change. It sensed something in me…It said…They altered some of the preparations, even as they got me ready for the final ritual and that's when I almost gave up. I wasn't sure I could face it again." He swallowed, going even paler. "I knew you were looking, for me. I wanted to hold on." Guilt suddenly surged out of Rob washing over Galen.

"You were thirteen, Rob," he said gently.

"I know I was, Galen. I was a Keeper, too. Even so, I had nearly given up hope. Then I knew you were coming, I knew you were close."

"How?"

Rob looked at him. "They were scared, worried that the ritual was going to be interrupted." He put his hand on Galen's knee. "And I got your message."

"My message?" Galen said, a small smile playing on his lips.

"That you were close, that you were coming. It let me hang on, even after what had happened, even though I knew what might be coming." Rob looked at him. "It gave me so much hope, Galen. I knew if I just held on…"

PAST

TEN YEARS BEFORE
Day Three to Moonrise - Rob

There was bright light against his eyelids. Rob opened his eyes. He was lying outside. The sun was pouring down on him. *Sun feels good.* He was drowsy, he felt almost like he was floating above his body, like he could watch what was happening. *That's kind of strange. I wonder how long I get to stay outside. I hope it's a long time. I'm tired of that little room. Floating is fun. I'll have to tell Galen about it.*

Rob thought he could hear chanting—the strange language again—and he could smell the incense, but it wasn't as strong as it had been. He tried to sit up, and realized he was tied down, he couldn't move at all. He struggled against the bonds. The movement sent shafts of pain through his body, his heart was pounding as fear blended with panic.

Then…

Rob heard something moving towards him. It sounded like something dragging on the ground, moving slowly. The chanting got louder. He could hear something breathing, gasping breaths, getting closer and closer. Then he smelled death, the sick-sweet smell of a rotting animal left too long in the sun. The scent rolled over him, making him gag. Whatever was approaching smelled dead. He heard it sigh, it sounded glad. "This one is perfect," he thought he heard it say. "Wait, he's...No, it can't be!" And Rob heard something that sounded almost like a laugh. Then he could see it. He struggled trying to get away from it, completely terrified. He could feel the pain as the bonds cut into his skin as he tried to get away. It reached towards him with a clawed hand.

"No! Galen! Galen!" He heard himself screaming. "Galen!" He screamed again as the thing touched him, pain lancing through his chest from that touch. It bent towards him. "Keeper? Yes, Keeper. Oh, so long since a Keeper. Where is the other?" It sighed. He could feel its breath on him. He was slipping away, from the pain, from the fear. *"Galen, please, please, come."*

"I'm coming, Rob, hang on, please hang on." He heard his brother's voice as clearly as if Galen were standing beside him.

"Galen?" And darkness took him away from the pain and fear and his brother's voice.

The sun was gone when he woke up. He slid a hand to his face. *I can move. What happened? Where am I?* He opened his eyes. He was in the room at the farmhouse again.

He tried to roll over, he didn't have the strength. *It's my birthday. I'm thirteen. I'm supposed to start training as Custodes Noctis, a Keeper of the Night.* His hand slid to his bracelet, surprisingly it was still there, clasped around his wrist where his brother had put it. He'd asked for chocolate cake and made a point of saying he didn't need ice cream, knowing Galen always got it anyway.

"Galen?" he said aloud in the quiet room, taking comfort in the idea his brother was there to talk to. "I thought I heard you, I know you're looking for me, I know you're coming. It'd be nice if you hurried." He sighed, he wanted to talk to Galen about what had happened. The thing said "Keeper" like it knew what he was, like it knew who they were. That worried him. There was something that seemed familiar.

"Could it be in the sagas?" Rob asked his brother, wishing Galen was there to answer. "I'll start at the beginning. 'Thus it is told, in the beginning as the stones were set, as the earth turned and the leaves were touched with blood...' " He heard a sound. "Galen? They're coming back."

The door opened. He didn't hear the key turn, the door just opened. Ashley came in with the two men. She had more of the purple and red cloth in her hand, a jar and a pair of scissors. One of the men yanked Rob upright. He whimpered in pain.

"Please, let me go," he said to her, knowing she wouldn't, but hoping anyway.

"No." Her voice was cold, not human really. "The final ritual will begin soon. We have to start getting you ready. You need to be acceptable to Her."

"That thing? It's ugly and it stinks," Rob said.

She slapped him. "You can't talk that way, even if you are Chosen." She took the scissors and cut the cloth strips from his chest. After mumbling something in the strange language she opened the jar and smiled. "This might hurt a little." Her voice, like her smile, was cruel. She smeared something on him, it burned. The longer it was there, the more it hurt.

"Please, take it off, please," Rob begged, ashamed of the tone in his voice.

"Not so brave now, are you, kid?" the man holding him said. "I told your brother you were crying."

"Galen? You told him I was crying?" Rob sighed.

"Yeah, he said it figured, you were a baby." The man was laughing at him.

"Oh really? Did he say that before or after he redid your face?" Rob said. *Oh, it hurts, it hurts.* "If you think he'd say something like that, you need to get to know him better. Oh wait, maybe that's not a good idea, he might not like you much." Rob drew strength from the thought of his brother.

Ashley carefully wound the cloth around him. It bound the ointment she put on his chest tightly against his skin. It felt like fire. The man dropped him back on the floor. When Ashley turned to leave, the man kicked Rob. "That's for what your brother did. I'd do more, but She'll finish it for me," he whispered so only Rob could hear and then followed Ashley out.

He idly wondered what happened, what time it was. It felt like he'd been there for days. Finally, he drifted off to sleep. When he opened his eyes he knew that it was later in the day, even though there was no light. Something woke him, he wasn't sure what. He had the oddest sense of his brother for a moment, just a fleeting touch, and then Galen was gone.

Rob hurt. That was all he really knew. Pain was such a reality that he couldn't remember what it was like without it. It was really all there was, now. Pain and fear. He took a deep breath and stretched his senses out, looking for Galen. There was only a soft reflected silence

The door opened. The one called Other came in and sat beside him. Rob looked at him and felt himself smile. "You don't look very good."

"The final ritual approaches," Other said. Rob thought he could hear fear in the man's voice. "They will prepare us and we will be taken to Her grove," Other's voice trembled.

"You don't sound so sure, now," Rob said, glad that Other was afraid.

"It is good. It will be glorious."

"Do you believe that?" Rob asked.

"Of course."

"I don't. I think we're going to die."

Other looked at him. The look scared Rob. "Of course we are."

The bearded man came in the room. He had the brazier in his hands. *Funny, I didn't even notice it wasn't here.* He put it on the floor, he was also carrying another golden cup. He walked towards Rob. "Your brother disposed of the last cup, we need more before we can begin," he said, sounding like he was enjoying himself. Other pulled Rob's arm out and held it. The knife made another deep cut. Rob was past the point of feeling individual hurts. It was all a single ball of pain.

They wrapped his arm with the colored cloth. Rob watched, unable to really move. He watched as Other stood and went to the brazier and the two men started chanting. The bearded man had a plate or something in his hand. He put ashes from the brazier in it and then poured a little of Rob's blood from the cup into the saucer. He mixed it together with the knife, then walked over to Rob.

Other held him down while the bearded man wrote symbols on him with the knife, dipped in blood and ashes. It hurt. He knew he was crying. He could hear himself begging them to stop. They didn't. When they were done, the bearded man wrote the symbols on Other. Rob felt a little better when he heard Other scream. *I guess I'm not the only one. It hurts, please let it stop soon, please. I wonder if Galen can fix this? He helped last year when I was sick. He came all the way to California to help.*

The bearded man left Rob and Other alone in the room. Other was silent beside him. He knew the man was frightened, he could see it on his face and in the way he curled in on himself. Rob knew the final ritual was approaching, he wasn't sure if he could face the thing again, even knowing his brother was looking for him.

The door opened. The bearded man and Ashley came in,

dressed in red robes. Ashley came over to them. She had two cups, handed one to Other and he drank the contents. She held Rob up and forced him to drink what was in the second cup. He recognized the taste, it was the same stuff they'd given him before the sun ritual.

Rob realized there were other people with them. They were carrying two stretchers. They were decorated with purple and red flowers. Other stood up and laid down on one of them. They picked Rob up and dropped him on the second one. Once he was lying on it, they wrapped a rope around him, tying him to the stretcher. Then they carried him out of the farmhouse and into the woods.

Rob watched the trees go by. The sun was low in the sky. The liquid was beginning to make his head swim. *I don't think I can face that thing again, Galen. Maybe this will just let me go to sleep and I won't have to wake up again. I'm sorry. I want to be a Keeper, but I can't Galen, it was so terrible. Please come, please forgive me.* A sudden rush of guilt washed over him, he wanted to pull the words back, even though he'd only just thought them, not even said them at all. *"I'm coming, Rob, just hold on a little longer,"* Galen's voice was soft. Rob reached out to his brother. *"Galen?"*

"Sir! Sir!" Rob heard someone calling. The people carrying him stopped.

"What is it?" Rob heard the bearded man say.

"The farmhouse, it's burning."

"What!" The bearded man sounded angry. Hope started to creep into Rob's awareness.

"The place is burning. No way we can stop it."

"How?"

"It was the kid's brother. I saw that jeep he was driving parked there. He torched the place." *Galen? He knows I was there, he's coming. He's coming. It's a message. He's letting me know he's com-*

ing. He's close, he has to be. I know he'll find me, I know he will. I'll hang on, but hurry, please hurry.

"We can't let that stop the ritual. We have to go on. Find him. Stop him," the bearded man said. The stretcher started moving again. Rob let himself drift, but not too far. The knowledge that Galen was close was keeping him from completely slipping away.

They stopped again. Rob opened his eyes. The sun was starting to set, it was blood red. He was in a clearing with trees and a stone circle. There were people standing inside the stones, all wearing the red robes. Other stood up from his stretcher and walked over to a tree that was in the center of the circle. They tied his hands, threw a rope over a branch of the tree, and hauled him up until he was hanging there. Ashley was doing something at the base of the tree.

The bearded man came over and untied Rob. They pushed him off the stretcher onto the ground by another tree. They tied his hands and he felt himself pulled up into the air. He was hanging, the rope cutting into his wrists, he could feel his shoulders pulling. The bearded man drew symbols on the ground under the tree and stepped back. He shouted something in the strange language and the circle of people started chanting.

Rob heard it coming, saw it moving out of the trees, smelled the death scent of it again. It walked over towards Other. Rob could see the trail its dragging feet left in the ground. He watched as it raised its hand to Other. The man started screaming. Rob saw the thing's claws raking across Other, tearing away skin and flesh. Other was screaming, begging it to stop. Rob closed his eyes, he couldn't watch. Suddenly Other was silent. Rob knew the man was dead, he also knew the thing had turned towards him.

"No, please no," he whispered.

The chanting was getting louder. It sounded excited. He could clearly hear the bearded man's and Ashley's voices leading the others on. The thing was getting closer, he could smell it, he could hear it breathing. It sounded excited, too.

"Rob? Rob? Answer me! Rob?" Galen's shout sounded in the clearing.

Elation mingled with fear as Rob recognized his brother's voice, he took a deep breath. He knew this was going to hurt. "Galen! I'm here!" he screamed as loud as he could. He saw the thing right in front of him.

"I'm coming, Rob, hang on."

"He's here, Galen's here," Rob said to the thing. He felt the thing's hand. The pain began.

Chapter Ten

They were both silent. Galen scrubbed a hand across his face and glanced over at Rob. His brother was pale, the stark bruise standing out against his face. Galen noticed that Rob's hands were shaking.

"Rob?"

"It's okay, Galen. We need to figure out what happened, to see if it might let us know what's going to happen now." Rob looked at him. "Galen?"

Galen tried to draw a breath, the scar was suddenly awake, twisting in his chest. As it moved he thought he could sense the thing. "No, it can't be," Galen said.

Something was whispering to him in a voice he remembered, a rasping voice full of the sound of death. Memories were blending with nightmares. He closed his eyes as the assault worsened, trying to calm his breathing. The whisper was there, he could hear it, hovering just below his conscious mind. It was excited, pleased and it felt close somehow.

"Galen?" Rob's voice sounded anxious, he had his hands on Galen's shoulders, shaking him gently. "Galen?" The shaking got harder. "Galen?"

Galen forced his eyes open. "Can you get the red bottle again?" Rob was back with the bottle before Galen was really aware he'd even gone. "Thanks." He took a slightly bigger dose than usual, waiting as the spell calmed the twisting in his chest, silencing the menacing whisper. Galen looked up at his brother. "It's okay, Rob."

"How often does this happen?"

"Not often." He tried for a smile. "It's a little worse than usual."

"I can see it. Galen I thought I saw the shadow of..."

"You did?" he cut Rob off, "I thought I heard It, too."

Rob settled back beside him. "You thought you heard It?" Galen nodded. "It did recognize us, didn't It? Back then?"

"I think so. I thought I felt something that afternoon, and then later, once or twice there was this sliver of...I don't know... recognition, pleasure?"

"It knew we were Keepers, even then, even before..."

"Yeah." *I'm sorry, Rob. Saying it again.* "I think it's my fault. It sensed something in me."

"What is it?"

"I..."

"Galen? What happened to you?"

"After I heard you in the clearing, gods, Rob, I knew it was you. I sensed what was happening, I didn't want to believe it, but I knew, and I was starting to get desperate."

PAST

TEN YEARS BEFORE

Day Three Afternoon to Moonrise - Galen

The scream had stopped, although Galen could still hear the echoes of it in his head. His brother was silent, and except for that brief instant when Galen heard his name, there was only darkness. *What was that thing? It...I think it recognized something in Rob...*

"Galen!" Rhiannon was calling him from the path.

"Yeah, I'm here," He tried to stand up, his battered body was beginning to give out on him. "Rob's not here. That was him, though, I think."

"What do we do now?" she said gently, helping him to his feet.

"I don't know." Galen was beginning to fray at the edges. "I don't know. " He looked up at her, hoping she might have an answer. "What do I do?" He felt lost, desperate. *How can I ask to become a Keeper, to carry the Emrys sword when I break like this? I need Dad and Uncle Bobby.*

"We'll figure something out, I promise, Galen," she said gently. "Come on, let's go back to the car. I want to look at those stitches of yours. It looks like you're bleeding again." She put his arm over her shoulders and her arm around his waist, supporting him, carrying him. She let him lean against her. "Let's do that first. Then we'll worry what comes next. How's that?"

Galen let her help him. He drew strength from the contact. He was exhausted. Galen knew his father and uncle were on the way, he wondered how long it would take them to get there. He took a deep breath, calming himself and focusing on his training.

When they got back to the car, Rhiannon gently set Galen in the passenger seat. She knelt in front of him and eased his t-shirt up. "You're bleeding again. Do you have a first aid kit?"

"In the back," he said.

She walked around, took the keys out of the ignition opened the back and came around with the first aid kit in her hands. "This is a very complete first aid kit, Galen," she said. "Just about everything you could ever need." He could hear the question in her voice. "This looks like...hmmm..."

"Dad's a healer, he helped put that together, something for anything." He had his eyes closed and tried to focus a little of the healing into his body.

"I think 'anything' is the operative word," she said. "Galen? If I ask you something will you answer me honestly?"

"Yes."

"What did that to Megan—it wasn't human was it?"

Galen opened his eyes and looked at her. "You deserve the truth. I can never repay you for helping me, but I can give you this." He paused, searching her face. "No, it wasn't human. People helped, like with Rob. But what did it, what took Megan, it wasn't human." Rhiannon closed her eyes, Galen put his hand on her shoulder. "I'm sorry."

"It's okay, Galen. Knowing helps." She smiled the feral smile again. "Makes it easier to kill it, if it's not human."

"Humans are helping it, though," Galen said, feeling a rush of anger through his body. "Sometimes I wonder how people can serve filth like that."

"But they do," she said softly, "and they might need to die, too." She looked at Galen.

"Yeah," he said quietly. *Keepers don't kill people, or we try not to.* He leaned back again and closed his eyes.

"Galen, you need to rest."

"No, I can't."

"You have to. I understand your need to keep going, but you have to rest." She laid a hand on his cheek. He opened his eyes and looked at her. "I know, but if you don't rest now, you won't be able to help Rob. Let's at least go back to my apartment and get you another pain pill. I forgot to grab them when we left, and you don't have any in the first aid kit. You can sleep in the car, and then we'll go from there."

Galen knew she was right, his body was starting to give out. He had to rest in order to use the healing, in order to be strong enough to help his brother when he found him. If his father and uncle didn't get there in time, he'd have to heal Rob, and he was beginning to suspect that healing his brother would take all he had—and more. "You're right, let's go." He swung his legs into the car, and she carefully closed the door. He was asleep before she settled behind the wheel.

"Galen?" Rhiannon was shaking him.

"Yeah?" He opened his eyes, they were in the parking lot at her apartment building.

"Can you get out?"

"I think so, I'll try." He reached for the door. Pain lanced up his side. "The stitches tore, didn't they?"

"Yes, I did try and tape it back together. I guessed you wouldn't go to the hospital yet."

"Good guess." He smiled at her. "I think I'll just rest here. Is that okay?"

"Sure, I'll go get the pills and some water. How's that?" She got out of the car. Galen watched her walk up the stairs to her door.

He shifted in the seat, trying to get comfortable. The bandage on his side felt wet. He was still bleeding a little and his head was really starting to hurt, now that he was just sitting. The pictures of Megan were haunting him, every time he closed his eyes he saw Rob there instead of the other child. He swallowed. He focused inward, trying to direct the healing through his body, he let the warmth drift through aching muscles and open wounds as the light led him into gentle sleep.

He knew it was several hours later when he woke up. He opened his eyes. He was still in the car, Rhiannon had put a blanket over him. Galen felt a little stronger.

"Hey, how are you doing?" Rhiannon said, opening the door. She had another mug of the soup in her hands. "I have something for you to have with the pain pill, so it doesn't make you sick."

"Thanks." He took the soup and pill from her. She sat down on the edge of the seat next to him. "You shouldn't have let me sleep."

"Galen." She looked him in the eyes, so he'd know the truth of what she said. "I tried to wake you. I couldn't. I was a little scared, but you were snoring a tiny bit, so I hoped you were just asleep."

"Oh, sorry. The healing does that, sometimes," he said absently.

"Healing?" She looked at him with a frown.

"Uh..."

"It's okay, we'll worry about that later. What do we do now?"

"I was thinking, that farmhouse. I don't know, I just think...I have a feeling about it. Let's go back there and check it out." He looked out the window. "The sun's going to set soon. We need to get out there and then back to the rest stop to meet Dad and Uncle Bobby."

"The farmhouse it is," she said, getting up and walking around the car. She slid into the driver's seat. "I'll just drive till that pill starts to work. Is that okay?"

"Good plan." Galen said, leaning back and sipping the soup.

When they pulled up at the farmhouse. Galen had the feeling they were being watched. He couldn't shake it as Rhiannon helped him out of the car. He scanned the area in the front of the house but it was empty. "This is probably a waste of time, I don't know why I thought there was something here," he said as Rhiannon came up beside him.

"You thought you heard Rob when we were here last night," she said with a shrug. "This is a good place to start."

Galen smiled at her and walked to the house. He opened the door to the house and stopped. Incense, he could smell incense. Galen walked into the room just inside the door.

There was a door to the right, and an archway into the main

house to the left. He walked to the archway and stopped, turning back. The scent of the incense was stronger on the other side of the room. He walked over to the door and opened it, there was a flight of stairs. He paused, just at the edge of his awareness he thought he heard a sigh, the soft rush of air from something's lungs. The sigh carried a feeling of sick pleasure and the scent of death with it.

"Galen? There's no one around outside," Rhiannon said.

"Smell that?" He looked at her. "Someone's been here. I think they were downstairs."

Galen walked carefully down the steps. He didn't want to take the chance of a fall. At the bottom of the stairs he paused. There was a room at the end of the hallway and he knew. "Rob?" he called softly. He ran down the hall and pushed open the door.

"Oh no," he whispered. "Oh gods." The soup came up, he leaned over, the wound in his side pulling as he vomited. He felt Rhiannon's hand on his back.

When he was finished he walked into the small room. There was blood everywhere. Someone had drawn symbols, they looked like the ones from Megan's pictures, on the walls. They were drawn in blood, and Galen knew without a doubt whose blood it was.

Suddenly he was filled with rage. It was white-hot, blinding him. It cancelled out everything else. The pain of the wound in his side, the broken rib, his head, the bruises covering his body—all gone, replaced by the all-consuming, blinding rage. *No, I have to get control of myself. One of the first lessons of a Keeper, use the rage, but don't let it control you. That leads to mistakes, costly mistakes. I have to control it.* He took a deep breath and tried reaching out for his brother. "Rob?" he whispered. Nothing, just a fuzzy reflection of pain and fear. "Some of this blood's still fresh. He can't be far." Galen turned to Rhiannon. "I need to let him know I'm here."

"How?"

"Go to the car. There's a can of gas in the back. Bring it back here. We're burning this place." His voice was so soft, it surprised him.

He heard her walk back down the hallway. Galen stood in the middle of the room. *He was here. I know he was here. When? Last night? Was I this close? Oh, gods, was I this close?* He looked at the symbols on the walls. He found Rob's jeans in the corner, picked them up and held them against his chest for a moment.

"Here, Galen." Rhiannon was back with the gas can. Galen took it from her and poured it around the room. He wasn't sure if the whole house would burn, he hoped it would but he had to destroy that room. His instinct was to burn it, remove the traces of the rituals that had been performed there. It wasn't much, but it was something, and he hoped it would help slow the ritual set for that night.

"Go upstairs, I'll be right there." He took out his lighter and dropped it on the gas and ran up the stairs. He heard the fuel in the room light with a whoosh. Within minutes the whole place was ablaze. Galen reached out to his brother. *"I'm coming Rob, just hold on a little longer."*

"Galen?" He thought he heard his brother answer.

"We need to get to the rest stop to meet your father and uncle," Rhiannon said, walking up beside him where he was standing watching the house burn.

"You're right. Wait! What's that?" Galen thought he saw something. He walked to the edge of the clearing around the house. His heart started pounding. There were fresh footsteps leading down a trail into the woods. "I think they're on foot, headed back to that clearing we found earlier."

"Galen, you can't be sure."

Galen stopped by the trail and rested a hand on a tree, reaching out for his brother. "Rob, they took Rob this way. I know it. I can't explain how, but I know. I have to go. I can't leave him this time." He ran back to the car. Rhiannon had left the back open. He grabbed a shotgun and a sword, and turned to her. "Take my car. Dad will be looking for it, it was a gift. Bring him to that clearing. That's where the final ritual is. That's why they found Megan up the trail from there."

"Galen, you can't go alone."

"No, you have to go get them. I know there's something else. I have a feeling killing this thing won't be easy. I need them there, but I have to go after Rob." He was nearly crazed with the need to follow the trail into the forest. "Please. My father's name is Parry. Please."

"Okay, Galen. I'll hurry. Get to your brother. Save him." She pulled him into her arms and kissed him gently on his forehead. "Save him, Galen."

"I will." He ran down the trail into the dark woods.

The trail wound around through the old growth forest. It was dark, almost as if it were already night. Galen knew the sun was going down. He thought he must be getting close. There, he could hear chanting. Suddenly the forest was filled with terrible screams. Galen's heart was pounding. *No. That's not Rob. That's not his voice.* He ran a little further and thought he could see light through the trees.

"Rob! Rob! Answer me! Rob?" he shouted, holding his breath he waited for a response.

"Galen! I'm here!" Rob's shout answered him.

Relief washed over him. "I'm coming Rob! Hang on!" He started towards the break in the trees. Something blocked his path, racing at him. He felt the man connect with him, the fist drove into Galen's side where the knife wound was, and he dropped to his knees.

"You're going to pay for trying to stop this," the man said.

Galen looked up at him. It was one of the men from the diner parking lot. "I don't really have time for this," Galen said, trying to stand. He noticed the sword lying on the ground beside him, the shotgun was just out of his reach. He moved his hand towards the hilt of his sword.

The man walked towards him. "I'd kill you right now, but I think you should get to watch what's going to happen to that little shit first." He grabbed Galen and hauled him to his feet. Galen swung the sword, not intending to kill, the flat of the blade connected with the side of the man's head and he dropped. Galen took one last look at him before he ran in the clearing.

He reached the edge of the ring of trees. There were people standing inside the ring, the altar was covered with a purple and red cloth, two golden cups rested on the cloth. From one of the trees hung something that looked like a side of beef, Galen realized it was what was left of a human being.

From the other tree...

"Rob!" The thing was standing in front of his brother. He could smell the rotten dead scent of it. It had a hand on Rob. His brother was moaning in pain and covered in blood.

Galen raised the shotgun and fired at the thing. It pulled back from Rob towards the altar. Galen ran to the tree, madly scraping the symbols from around the base of the tree with his foot, hoping he was doing enough to destroy them. He reached up and took Rob's weight and cut the rope.

"Galen?" Rob eyes fluttered open.

"I'm here, Rob. I'm here," he said, frantically trying to get the symbols off of his brother. He could sense the thing moving behind him.

"No!" Someone grabbed him and pulled him away from Rob. It was a large bearded man. "You can't stop the ritual."

The man raised a fist and swung. It connected, and Galen saw stars. He must have fallen, the man leaned over him and wrapped his hands around Galen's throat. He couldn't breathe, and knew he didn't have long. Suddenly the pressure released. Galen took a gasping breath. The man was screaming, clawing at his own throat. A large safety pin was sticking out of the side of his neck. Rob was standing behind the man with grin on his face. "Got him," Rob said.

"Good job, Brat." Galen hit the man with the butt of the shotgun "Rob! Look out!" The thing had come back and grabbed his brother. Galen watched in horror as Rob screamed in pain and then collapsed. The thing started dragging Rob towards the woods.

"No!" Galen dove at his brother. He grabbed the thing, his hands sinking into rotting flesh. It turned on him. He fired the other barrel of the shotgun. It still had Rob in its claws. Galen grabbed his brother's arms and the thing reached a hand out towards Galen. Pain—like nothing he'd ever experienced—filled his chest. He heard himself scream, but he was still trying to pull Rob away from it.

"Keeper," it sighed, pleasure in the sigh, "the other half." Something twisted in Galen's chest, a shaft of pain stabbed into his brain. "Wait," it said. "I know this, I know you."

Out of the corner of his eye he saw the waitress, Ashley, dressed in red robes. She stood up from where the bearded man had fallen. She had a knife in her hands, walking towards where Galen was struggling with the thing.

"You don't get to stop this," she said, raising the knife to throw at him. Suddenly she was screaming. Rhiannon landed on her like a tiger, tearing the knife away. Galen saw the wild feral smile on Rhiannon's face before he looked away.

The thing was tearing at him, pulling Rob away from him. He was trying desperately to hang on through the pain and the blood that was now half-blinding him.

"Galen! Down!" his father yelled. Galen pulled Rob away from the thing, trying to get out of the line of his father's shot. Something exploded over his head. The thing turned and ran towards the forest, his father and uncle right behind it.

Seconds later a horrible scream echoed around the clearing. It was terrifying. It sounded triumphant. It wasn't human. Galen heard his father's shout. It was a wild sound. "Got the bitch!"

Galen was on his knees, holding Rob against his chest. There was no life in his brother. "Rob! No!" He tried to hold Rob's head up, Galen's hand on was resting on his cheek. "Rob? Come on." Galen focused the healing into his brother, he felt the light flowing out of him, felt it tugging at his own life. He stayed focused on Rob.

Suddenly Rob coughed and took a shuddering breath. "Galen?" Rob whispered, Galen pulled away long enough to look at his brother. Rob's eyes opened and met his, with a smile. "Galen?"

"Rob," he pulled his brother back against him.

"I knew you'd come, Galen," Rob whispered, his arms going around Galen.

"Yeah, Rob." Galen felt his body give way. The combination of the wounds, and the energy he had expended in healing Rob, had taken a toll. He fell to the side.

"Galen! Galen!" Rob said, grabbing his hand. "Hang on, I'll get Dad." Galen held on to Rob's hand. He was not about to let go. "Dad! Dad!" He heard Rob shouting. "Uncle Bobby!"

"Galen? Hang on," Rhiannon's voice came from beside him. She sounded panicked.

Someone was trying to pull Rob away. Galen held on. "No, Rob, no," his voice sounded like it was coming from a long way away.

"It's okay, Galen. It's me. I've got him, it's okay. I've got your brother," his uncle said, his voice, calm as always. "It's okay, Galen, Parry's coming."

Someone was pushing against him, against his chest. It hurt. He could hear Rob crying, his uncle comforting Rob. "Galen, Dad's coming." That was Rob's voice, he was still holding onto Galen's hand.

"Hang on, Galen," his father said.

Galen tried to struggle back to Rob. He had to know his brother was alright, he tried to reach out, but the healing left him drained. "Rob? Is he okay? Dad?" Galen asked, unable to move. His senses were beginning to dim. It was getting hard to breathe.

"Galen? Rob's okay. Bobby's got him. It's going to be fine." He felt his father's hands on his chest and head. "I've got you." Warm flowed out from the touch, lighting the dark spots of the wounds in his body, calming the pain the thing had started when it grabbed him. "Relax. Let go," his father said gently.

Galen listened, and obeyed. There was a moment more of pain and then the soft nothing of healing sleep.

Chapter Eleven

"I thought you were dead," Rob said softly.

"I thought I was, too," Galen chuckled.

"'No, Galen," Rob's voice was barely audible. "I thought you were dead. I thought you'd died there for a moment." Galen looked over at his brother. Rob was trembling, his face white as he looked down at his hands.

"Rob?" Galen curled his hand around his brother's arm, aware of the pain, the anguish those moments had caused. "I wasn't dead."

"I know, but didn't, not just then. I thought you were."

"But Dad and Uncle Bobby were there."

Rob looked at him, his eyes haunted. "When I first saw you come into the clearing during the ritual..." Rob swallowed. "And you cut me down, I...Galen..."

"Rob? What is it?"

Rob sighed. "I was so glad, but then I was scared, you looked...then I thought you died."

"Uh, Rob?"

"Yeah, Galen?"

"You aren't actually making a lot of sense, you know," Galen said.

His brother looked up at him. "You were there, that was the most important thing. That was what mattered at first. But then...But, you...Dad was...Uncle Bobby was..."

"Rob?"

"I think it was the moment when I was sure you were dead. Your hand went limp, like in the movies, you know? Uncle Bobby was scared, that calm but scared thing he did, but Galen…" Rob trailed off.

"What is it? Dad was there, you were okay. Rob what's wrong?" he said, trying to comfort his brother. "Dad was just…"

Rob looked at him, tears at the edges of his eyes, the memories reflected in haunted blue eyes. He swallowed. "Galen—Dad was crying. They both were."

"Oh, gods, Rob. All I thought was you were safe. I should have stayed with you a little longer. I tried."

"I remember…" Rob paused and looked away, across the room. "I remember I asked if you were dead. Dad looked up with a smile and said no, he'd just put you into a healing sleep so you could get all the way better. I was still frightened, I wasn't used to people telling me the truth about things like that. My adoptive parents told me my hamster had run away when it'd actually died. So I was still unsure.

"Uncle Bobby let me go, so I could get closer and see that you were okay. The affects of the incense were wearing off and I could 'see' you a little better. Dad assured me you were going to be okay, but he was still crying, so was Uncle Bobby and then I realized…"

"It was for you?" Galen said softly.

"I think so. Uncle Bobby held me and Dad put his hand on my head. It was the first time he healed me, it was always you before. It felt different, you know. I remember the pain leaving, and I tried to stay awake to make sure you were okay, but I couldn't."

"Dad was always good at that," Galen said with a smile. "He could put me out faster…He was a great healer."

"Galen," Rob said quietly, looking at him. "Even then you were…"

"What?" Galen asked, puzzled.

"You were always stronger than Dad. And your 'touch' is different somehow."

"No." Galen said softly. "Dad was..."

"Galen, don't you realize?" Rob put his hand on Galen's arm. "It's true, you...When you heal, you 'look' different, too." Galen was shaking his head, trying to deny it. "And you know Dad couldn't have..."

"No." Galen pushed himself up, trying to shove the memory away. He ran a hand across his face, and carefully put the sword on the bed. The scar picked that moment to twist, hard, Galen gasped, trying to catch his breath. The voice was back, whispering to him. He felt Rob's hand on his back, and focused on the warmth of his brother's hand, using the contact to slow the twisting of the wound. "I'm okay," he said quietly.

"Right," Rob said softly, supporting him as the pain continued. "Can I get you something? The red bottle? It's right here." Rob's hand left his back for a moment, and the bottle was pressed into his hand. Galen took a sip and waited, the pain backed off a tiny bit, the voice stilled. "Is it usually like this?" Rob asked.

Galen opened his eyes and looked at his brother. "No. Usually it just wakes up and twists."

"Wakes up?"

"It's quiet most of the year, it's only really bad around..." Galen sighed. "Sorry, nice homecoming."

"Homecoming," Rob's voice was wistful.

"Rob?" Galen winced as the scar twisted. "Let's get a cup of coffee and something to eat." He sensed they both needed a break from the past.

"Yeah." Rob turned to leave, and they both came face to face with Mike standing in the door. The doctor was pale.

"Mike?" Galen looked at his friend.

"What the hell happened to the two of you?" Mike's voice was harsh.

"How long have you been listening?" Galen asked.

"Since they started slicing on your brother. My god." Mike swallowed. "He was... You were only thirteen." Mike looked at Rob.

"Yes," Rob said softly, pushing past the doctor. Galen smiled at Mike and followed his brother into the main room of the apartment.

"But, Galen?" Mike followed them. "You were hurt, but not...Is this when?"

"When what?" Galen asked with a weary sigh. "Drop it for a minute."

Mike must have caught something in the tone of his voice, he looked at Galen for a long moment and then smiled. "I'm starving."

Galen laughed and wandered into the kitchen. He listened to the conversation Mike struck up with Rob. Mike was singing the praises of The Urban Werewolves to his brother. Galen grinned. It sounded like his friend was trying to convince Rob he should stay. Galen chuckled under his breath as he rummaged in the refrigerator for food for the three of them. "Okay, come and get it," he said a few minutes later. Rob came over and smiled, looking at the food. "Sorry, no meat," Galen said with a shrug.

"I can't stand the smell of it either," Rob smiled.

Mike looked from one to the other. "You, too? Did it happen at the same time?"

"Not during dinner, Mike," Galen said as he walked over to the table with his plate.

Rob sat across from him and looked at the doctor. "How'd you meet Galen?"

"It was about seven years ago," Galen started. "Dad and

Uncle Bobby were…" He saw Mike lean forward waiting for the explanation of how it happened. Galen had very carefully not mentioned the nature of the thing that had nearly killed his father. "Working." Mike snorted in disgust and Rob raised his eyebrows.

"Working?" his brother asked. "Something…?"

"Yeah, exactly," Galen smirked at Mike. "I was at school that day." He paused.

"They brought Parry into the ER," Mike picked up the story, noticing Galen's hesitation. "He was a mess, blood everywhere, more dead than alive. Bobby was upset. He kept trying to get to Parry, but we needed to keep him back so we could work on him."

"Bobby called, I was in class and the phone rang, the prof was pissed, but I knew he wouldn't call unless it was bad. And it was, Dad was…" Galen stopped, remembering the call. *"Parry's dying, I need you here, Galen. Now. Please. He's dying."*

"Bobby kept saying he was dying," Mike said. "He said he needed to help him. We told him Parry wasn't dying."

"He was, though, Mike, and Bobby could see it," Galen said softly. "I ran out of class and headed straight for the hospital." Galen sighed, remembering the scene that met him, Bobby frantic, his father nearly gone and the hospital staff trying to keep them away.

"When Galen got there," Mike continued, "well, it was too late, or so we told him. We were trying, but we were sure we were going to lose Parry by then. Bobby was still trying to get to him. When Galen ran in, Bobby grabbed me and hauled me away. Before security could get there, before anything could happen I saw…" He swallowed.

"You healed Dad?" Rob asked.

"Not all the way, but enough to stabilize him. Like Dad did

with us," he added with a grim smile. "Dad was there a couple of days. I stayed with him that night and the next day, helping as much as I could. Bobby wouldn't let me…"

"Let you what? Heal him all the way? Because of what you did? Galen?" Rob's voice was a little angry. "Galen?"

Galen looked at his brother, weighing what he should say. "He was worried."

"Why?" Mike asked.

Galen didn't take his eyes from his brother. "I take risks with the family I don't take with anyone else. Once I…" He swallowed, shoving it away, knowing it wouldn't stay gone. Galen knew they'd have to talk about it eventually.

"You what?" Mike said softly.

"He went too far," Rob said with no emotion in his voice. "He went too damn far trying to save someone."

"What?" Mike was incredulous. "Too far implies…"

"Yeah," Rob's voice was flat. "He…and the other…the one…"

"Rob?" Galen reached out to put his hand on Rob's arm to get a sense of what was happening, what was going through his brother's mind. Rob snatched his arm away. "Rob?"

"No." Rob pushed himself away from the table, and walked to the window looking out at the street.

Galen smiled sadly at Mike, and with a shrug, got up and gathered the dishes. He tried to ignore his brother, still standing at the window. Galen could sense the confusion and hurt radiating off of Rob. He put the dishes in the sink and grabbed a mug to get a cup of coffee. As he set the pot down, the scar woke up, twisting violently, and with it came the voice. Whispering to him. The cup slipped out of his hand. He heard it hit the floor, the sound muffled like it was coming from a long way off. Galen grabbed the counter, trying to steady himself as the old wound ground into his heart.

Keeper," the voice whispered. "Hear me?" Sick laughter filled his head. He was falling, vaguely aware hands caught him before he hit the floor. "Keeper, you let me in, you touched the girl, my child, at the hospital, and now I am here."

"Galen?" Rob's voice came from somewhere removed from him.

"Galen?" Mike sounded frantic. Galen thought he felt someone's hand on his wrist.

"You stopped me, you thought you ended it. It has just begun," the voice continued. Galen groaned a denial.

"Galen?" Rob's voice was calm, determined.

Light stabbed into his brain. Mike had lifted an eyelid. Galen groaned again.

"Not yet, they can't have you yet," the voice said. "I have something for you."

Pain drove into him, he heard his own voice cry out. His mind was pulled away from his control as It violated his awareness. He was watching, the world unfolding like a movie. *A man stood in a circle of stone. He was dressed in a tunic and hose. Galen recognized the sword of a Keeper in his hands, it sparkled in the light of a bonfire. The sword looked nearly new. Something terrifying was standing before him, laughing at him. The man was bleeding, his brother lay dead on the ground at his feet. The terrifying darkness was afraid of the man, the Keeper, afraid of what he could do. It tried to laugh, It ended in a scream.*

The vision shifted. *Rob was hanging from the tree, blood pouring from his wounds. The thing came towards Galen and touched him, the claws tracing a path through his body.* He screamed, he heard his voice, he was aware of Rob's hands holding him before he was pulled away again. *Rob was on the altar, It had Its hands on Rob. Suddenly Rob changed, no longer the thirteen-year-old, but*

*as he was now. Galen looked down at his brother's blood-stained
body. Then looked in horror at his own hands, covered in what he
knew what his brother's blood.*

"Galen!" Rob was shouting his name.

"We have to call 911," Galen heard Mike's voice filtering
down through the visions. "He's having another seizure."

"It's not a seizure," his brother snapped.

"We will kill him, you and I, we will finish it, finally, and we
will become," the voice whispered.

"Help me," Rob's voice was firm, demanding obedience.
"Hold him." Galen felt himself shifted. One of Rob's hands rested
on the back of his head, the other over his heart.

"He can't help," the laughter filled his mind, trying to pull
his sanity away, trying to take his humanity.

"I'm going to put you out," Rob's voice was urgent, "listen,
Galen, focus."

"He can't help."

Warmth flowed from his brother's hands as the sound of a
heartbeat filled his mind, shutting out the laughter, shutting out
the voice until there was nothing but the beat of the heart and
the warmth of Rob's hands and then there was nothing at all.
Galen sank gratefully into darkness.

* * * * *

"We need to get him to the hospital." Mike's voice pene-
trated the dark. "He had a seizure. We need to find out what's
happening."

"It wasn't a seizure," Rob answered.

"He had a seizure, and now he's unconscious." Mike's voice
was gruff but Galen could hear the worry under the harsh tone.

"He's unconscious because…" Rob hesitated. "I did it."

"What?" Mike said, surprised.

"It's the one healing any Keeper can do. We can help some-one sleep, away from pain, and we can help ease the end." Rob stopped. Galen felt the tiny shudder that ran through his brother's body.

"I still think…"

"It wasn't a seizure," Galen said softly. He opened his eyes, he was still propped against Rob. Mike had his wrist in a firm grip.

"Galen," Rob sighed in relief. Galen felt his brother sag.

"You remembered." Galen looked at Rob.

"Yeah…" Rob swallowed. "I haven't much since then." Galen watched as his brother struggled to get control of himself. "Yeah, I remembered."

"How long?" he said, pushing himself up and shifting so he could lean against the cupboard doors. Rob kept a hand on him, steadying him for a moment.

"Not long, a couple of minutes," Rob said, his eyes searching Galen's. "What happened? I saw…"

"What?" Galen snapped, then smiled. "Sorry. You saw It?" Rob nodded. "It said that when I touched the girl at the hospi-tal…"

"It found a way in?" Rob paled.

"It showed me…" Galen stopped, the vision of his hands covered in Rob's blood causing bile to rise in his throat. He swal-lowed, trying to keep the nausea down, it wasn't working. "It showed me…" Galen started trembling.

"Come on." Rob hauled him to his feet and pulled Galen's arm over his shoulder. He was vaguely aware when Rob pushed him through the door in the bathroom and down on the floor. Rob's hand was on his back as the reaction set in and he vom-ited. A cool cloth was pressed against his forehead. "It's okay," his brother said soothingly.

"Sorry," Galen muttered. He stayed, trembling, on hands and knees for another minute before shifting to look at Rob, crouched beside him. "Sorry," he repeated.

"Nothing to worry about." Rob grinned at him. "I lived in the dorms, so I saw it a lot in college. It was me, once or twice." He chuckled at a memory. Galen saw it flash in his brother's eyes. "Think you can get up?"

Galen nodded and Rob pulled him back on his feet, steering him carefully towards the couch. His brother helped him sit down and then hovered in front of him. "I'm okay." He smiled at Rob and then looked over at Mike. The doctor had a shocked expression on his face. "I'm okay, Mike."

"Not in any way are you okay. You had a seizure, two actually. I thought..." Mike glowered at him. "And now you're barfing your guts out? Not okay." Galen noticed his brother nodding along with the last statement.

"For the last time, it wasn't a seizure."

"Then what was it?" Mike was angry. "Galen? Well? You were seizing. Your heart stopped earlier today."

"What?" Galen looked up at the doctor. "You said..."

"I might've lied a little."

"Uh... Might want to mention that kind of thing, Mike."

"Shut up, Galen," the doctor said with a frown.

"Do you think that has something to do with...?" Rob asked.

"I don't know, Rob."

"Would you two please stop that?" Mike asked.

"What?" Rob said, looking from Galen to the doctor.

"You know. That starting to say something and then trailing off. Some of us have no damn clue what you're talking about. And some of us are your doctor and really need to know what the hell is going on." The last sentence had increased in volume so that the last word came out as a shout.

Galen grinned sheepishly at the doctor. "Sorry, Mike. We're trying to figure it out, too."

"I don't get it," the doctor said, shaking his head. He bent over Galen to look in his eyes and check his pulse.

"What?" Galen asked, looking at his friend.

"You two. Just like your damn father and uncle. Cryptic talk, nearly dead before my eyes, all those looks. You two are as bad as Parry and Bobby, maybe worse. Already," Mike grumbled.

Galen laughed softly. "Oh?"

"And I do need to know, Galen. All joking aside, something's going on." Mike met his eyes. "It has something to do with what happened ten years ago?" He paused. "And…Does it have something to do with what happened five years ago? When Parry and Bobby were killed? Galen?"

As Galen opened his mouth to reply, the downstairs door banged open. Galen froze looking at his brother.

"It's me!" Rhiannon shouted. She stormed up the stairs sounding like a charging elephant and burst into the room. Her face was red. She looked at the three of them and then walked over towards the couch. She had something in her hands. "What's going on?" she asked, frowning at Galen. "Never mind, I have a good idea." Mike sighed audibly. "What's your problem?" She turned on him and then shrugged. "Got here as soon as I could."

"Well?" Galen asked, looking at her.

"I called Greg and some others to let them know we were going to need help," she said, dropping on the couch beside Galen. She looked at him, her eyes anxious.

"What did you find?" Her gruff exterior didn't fool Galen, he saw worry and fear in her eyes. He knew something was seriously wrong without a touch.

"This was in the front seat of Rob's jeep," she said gently. She held out the object, a hospital gown. Rob grabbed it before Galen could put a hand out. "Rob? Honey?" Rhiannon's voice was soft.

Galen looked at his brother. If possible, Rob was even whiter than before. He held the gown, youth-seized and covered in the remains of dried blood. One finger was toying with a small hole in the arm of the gown. "Rob?" When his brother didn't answer Galen stood and put his hand over his brothers. "Rob?"

"It *is* back. Coming for us. We're missing something, Galen. Something that happened then," Rob whispered.

"Rob? What is it?"

"Don't you recognize it?" Rob frowned. "No, you might not. But Galen, this gown, it's mine. It's the one I had on in the hospital after the ritual in the clearing. It's the one I had on when it..."

"What?" Mike demanded. "When what?"

"When it all began again," Rob said softly.

Chapter Twelve

The room was quiet, they were all looking at Rob. "When what began again?" Mike asked.

"Rob?" Galen said softly, giving his brother a gentle shake. Rob looked up at Galen.

"I tried to tell them, but there was something wrong, I tried, Galen, I tried." Rob suddenly sounded thirteen again. "There was something wrong with Dad and Uncle Bobby."

"I know." Galen tried to gage the wave of emotion flowing from his brother, he could sense the fear, the terror the thirteen-year-old had experienced, but there was an undercurrent of something else.

"And whatever was wrong with them let it happen."

"Let what happen?" Mike demanded.

"They came for me in the hospital…"

PAST

TEN YEARS BEFORE
Day Four to Day Five - Rob

Rob was warm. There was something soft under his head. For the first time in what seemed like a lifetime he was not in pain. Something was wrapped, tight, around his chest and his arms. It smelled like a doctor's office. He heard something beside him.

"Galen?"

"Rob?" his father answered him. Rob felt a hand on his shoulder. "Rob?" Gentle warmth flowed out from the touch.

Rob opened his eyes. His father was standing beside his bed. "Dad? Where's Galen?"

"He's down the hall, in a different room. That way his snoring wouldn't keep you awake," his father said with a smile. "Bobby's with him."

"Down the hall?"

"He's just in a different room, Rob, that's all."

Rob reached out for his brother and caught the soft feeling of his sleeping brother. "He does snore pretty loud," Rob said, smiling at his father.

"Yeah," Parry smiled back. "Bobby can snore, too, so I understand. Even closed doors can't shut out the sound at times."

"I remember when we went camping last summer and I got up before Galen. I was sitting outside the tent and thought it was a bear growling," Rob chuckled, a band of pain tightened across his chest. "He's okay, though, right, Dad?"

"He'll be fine. Bobby's sitting with him so he doesn't just leap up and come racing down the hall when he wakes up."

"And he would," Rob said with a sigh. The pain was back. "Dad? Can I sleep a little longer?"

"Of course, Rob," Parry said, putting his hand on Rob's head. The warmth flowed from his father's touch, Rob felt himself starting to drift. "You need to rest. When you wake up, if your brother is up, we can all go home."

"Thanks, Dad," he said sleepily and let himself drift away.

Someone was moving quietly around in the room. "The poor dear, he went through so much," a soft voice said.

"I did hear the doctor say he would recover, though, and the scarring shouldn't be too bad," another voice answered. Rob wondered if they were talking about him.

"They said his brother saved him."

"Yes." There was something in the way the voice said that—

it worried Rob. "Yes, he did, but at what a cost. I heard that he…"

"Galen?" Rob said opening his eyes. It was hard to focus his eyes. He guessed they'd given him something for the pain, he wondered why his father had let them. *He could help at least this much.* A nurse was beside the bed, Rob looked at her. There was something not quite right in the way she looked.

She looked over at the other woman. "Get his father, please. He stepped down to talk to the doctor." She patted Rob's hand. "Your Dad will be right here, sweetheart. Just a second."

"Where's my brother? Galen?" She looked down at him. Her eyes were sad, they seemed to say sorry. "Where's Galen?" He reached out for his brother, Galen was still asleep, but there was something wrong with it, it didn't feel soft anymore, it had an odd gray tinge to it.

"Rob, lie down." His father pushed him gently back into the bed. "You have to be careful. You need to heal."

Rob looked at his father. *He doesn't sound right, he doesn't "look" right. What's wrong?* "Why won't you tell me about Galen? The nurse said…" He was fighting his father's hands.

"Rob," his father looked at him, stern, then his eyes softened. "Okay, but you have to promise you'll lie still, okay?"

Rob stopped. "Dad?" He took a deep breath. "What's wrong?"

His father kept a hand on his shoulder, there was none of the special, familiar warmth in the touch, just a hand. Rob shifted a little. It didn't feel right. "He's very sick right now."

Rob knew what that meant. It was the way adults told little kids someone was dying. "Dad?" Rob looked at his father. There were tears on Parry's face. "But, Dad, you said Galen was okay, you said we could leave when he got up." He paused, trying to stay calm. Something was very wrong with his father. "I'm thirteen now, about to start my training, you can tell me more than that."

His father sighed and smiled. "You're right, Rob." Parry sat on the bed. "Galen isn't in very good shape right now."

"I thought you said he was okay. Dad, I saw you heal him, what happened?"

"Heal?" His father looked at him with a frown on his face. "Heal? You're right. I..." Parry blinked twice and for a moment Rob thought he saw something moving in his father. "He's in ICU right now."

"Can I see him?"

"Not yet. You need to stay in bed, Rob. You were hurt pretty bad."

"I need to see Galen."

"No," his father's voice was sharp.

"Dad? How bad am I hurt? Will I be okay?"

His father sighed. "Yes, Rob, you're going to be okay. They said you'd get better, all the way better. You need some treatment, but you should be fine. You might have a few scars, but hopefully not all that many." His father looked a little sick as he tried to smile at Rob.

"Treatment? Can't you just fix it, Dad?"

"Me?" Parry blinked, confused. "No, you need something to help with the pain. The doctor said you needed treatment."

"Dad? What's wrong?" Something was definitely wrong with his father. Even though the drugs were in his system, Rob knew something was wrong. "Dad?"

"I'm sorry, I didn't even realize how bad you were until you blacked out, Rob. They had those ritual bandages on you, and the shirt. And I didn't realize how bad it really was." He broke off with what sounded like a sob. The look he gave Rob was sad. It made his father look old, defeated. His eyes were bright with tears.

"But Dad, you fixed it there, you helped me there," Rob insisted.

"What?"

"Dad?" Rob looked at his father and sighed. *I need to talk to Galen, something's wrong. First Dad says we can go home, now he says Galen is in ICU. And now he doesn't even remember healing me?*

"Now, you need to sleep. The nurse will give you something, and you need to sleep."

"Why can't you help me sleep?" Rob said a little desperately, afraid of what was happening. "Can I see Galen when I wake up?"

"No, Rob, but maybe later, tomorrow."

"Dad, I need to see him, only for a minute. At least tell me what room he's in."

"Rob," his father said quietly. The nurse came back in the room, Rob looked at her, there was something wrong with her, she had black spots around her, like Ashley the waitress. "Okay, he's in 415, just down the hall."

"Room 415?" Rob was starting to get dizzy again.

He was alone in his room when he woke up. It was quiet. He could hear a TV coming from another room, further down the corridor. The window was dark. He looked up at the ceiling. It had the kind of tiles that were full of small holes. He smiled, remembering when he'd had his tonsils out when he was seven. Galen had come to California to be with him and sat with him all day.

When the time had come for Galen to leave for the night, Rob finally admitted to his brother he was scared to be alone in the hospital. He knew his brother wanted to stay, but the rules wouldn't allow it. Galen had gently squeezed his hand and let a little healing warm Rob, then he told Rob about the holes in the ceiling. *He told me they were worm holes. He said if I was really quiet at night I might get to see the worms, they were magical and they glowed and granted wishes. I remember waiting, hoping to see them. I wasn't scared anymore.*

"Galen!" Rob said, sitting up. He was still dizzy from the drugs.

What had his father said? Galen was in room 415? Rob had to see him. He hoped his uncle was there so he could talk to him about what he "saw" in the nurse and what he sensed in his father. His uncle had the Sight and would understand. He slipped his legs over the edge of the bed and realized he was wrapped in bandages. Rob tried to stand, at first his legs felt strange at first, but after a moment he could stand. He grabbed the IV pole and used it like a cane, pushing it to the door and looking out.

The corridor was quiet. The nurses' station was to his left, there was no one sitting there. Rob breathed a sigh of relief. He looked to his right, the room numbers went up from his room. There was another set of doors with a sign "Rooms 411 to 421, ICU." Rob slipped through the doors, hoping no one would see. 411, 412, 413, 414, 415. Rob stopped outside the door. The white board on the wall said "Galen Emrys." The door was open a crack, Rob peeked in. There was only one bed in the room, so Rob thought it would be safe to go in. His brother was on the bed, eyes closed. Rob could see the gray tinge he'd sensed earlier. It surrounded Galen like an aura.

"Galen?" Rob said softly. He felt tears form in his eyes and spilling down his cheeks. He walked to the side of the bed and looked down at his brother. "Galen?" He put his hand on Galen's arm. He sensed the gentle rumble of his brother's thoughts. Rob looked around the room and out the door, he could see no sign of his uncle.

"Galen? Can you hear me? Galen?" He tightened the hand

he had on his brother's arm. "There's something wrong here, Galen. I'm frightened."

Rob tried to stop the tears, tried to focus on the training he'd had, but fear won out. He started to cry.

"Rob!" His father's voice reached him through his tears. "What are you doing?"

Rob turned, his father was standing in the door, Parry's face was red. "I had to see Galen, Dad."

"I told you he was here." His father was shouting. It was so unlike Parry that Rob felt the tears form in his eyes again.

"I had to see him Dad, I had to." Rob was crying. He realized his brother couldn't just be asleep, the shouts would have easily woken him.

A man in a uniform ran into the room. "What's going on?"

"Nothing," Parry turned on him. "My son will be going back to his room." His voice was fierce, Rob could hear it. The security guard looked at Parry and left the room.

"I'm sorry, Dad. I didn't mean to scare you. I just wanted to see Galen," Rob said quietly.

His father turned back to him. He walked over to where Rob stood beside the bed. "I'm sorry too, Rob. When you weren't in your room, I was frightened." He put his arm gently around Rob. "I should have known you'd come here as soon as you had a chance."

"I had to see him, Dad. I just wanted him to know I was here. He might be worried. You know, Uncle Bobby would worry about you."

Rob saw his father swallow and tears came to his eyes. "Yeah, but let's get you back to your room, okay, Rob? Maybe you can come back and see Galen later."

When they got back to Rob's room, he was exhausted. He was also starting to hurt again. His father helped him back into bed and turned the TV on.

"Dad? Can you help me sleep?" Rob asked, looking at his father.

"What?" his father asked confused.

"I just thought..." Rob yawned and was asleep before his father had settled into the chair by the bed.

He woke up and there was an old black and white movie playing on the TV. His father was snoring in the chair beside the bed, his body relaxed. Rob could see the dark smudges under his father's eyes, even while he slept. Rob sat up and quietly slipped his legs over the edge of the bed. He needed to see his brother, to let Galen know there was something going on. Rob was sure of that now. He pushed the IV pole quietly down the hall. No one seemed to note his passage. He went through the big double doors and back down to his brother's room. A nurse came out of the room right before he got there. Rob froze, but she didn't seem to notice him and as soon as she was gone he went into Galen's room.

His brother hadn't moved since Rob had last been in there, his uncle was sound asleep in the chair beside the bed. Rob walked over and put his hand in Galen's. "Hey, Galen. I thought I should come and visit you. I don't know if anyone told you how I am, and I thought you might be worried," he said, in case anyone was listening.

"Rob?" Just for an instant he thought he heard his brother's voice. Rob put his hand down on Galen's arm.

"Galen? Can you hear me? There's something wrong here." Bobby shifted a little in the chair. "I'm sorry I was crying last time. I was afraid, Galen." He leaned against the bed, he was tired, and the walk down the corridor had taken more out of him than he thought it would. *"Whatever is going on, Dad and Uncle Bobby are affected."*

"I just wanted to come by for a minute, Galen. I need to get back before Dad wakes up. I think he was worried last time when I wasn't there. I'm worried about you. You need to get better, Galen." And the tears started. *"I need to talk to you Galen. I need your help."* He could feel the tears running down his face. "I need to go back now, I'm a little tired, but I'll visit again as soon as I can." He squeezed his brother's hand and turned to go. His father was standing in the door. "Dad, I…" He took a step back and bumped into his uncle. Bobby jerked awake.

"Rob? What are you doing here?" Bobby squinted at him.

His uncle had the same odd gray tinge around him that his father did. "I was checking on Galen."

Parry came over and put his hand on Rob's shoulder. "It's okay, Rob. We understand, we do." His father looked at his own brother with a gentle smile. "I just wish you had let me know you were coming, that's all." He smiled at Rob. "You can't be walking around alone, what if you fell? You could hurt yourself."

"Okay, Dad," Rob said. He felt dizzy and swayed on his feet.

"Rob!" He was surprised when his father picked him up and held him against him. "Let's get you back to your room." Rob could feel his father trembling. Parry carried him all the way back to the room and placed him gently on the bed.

"Thanks, Dad," Rob said.

"You have to promise me you aren't going to try that again. I'll take you to your brother, I promise you that, Rob, but you have to promise me, too."

"Yeah, Dad, I promise." He sighed.

"Thank you, Rob," and his father sank back down in the chair by the bed. He smiled at his son. "Maybe you should see about getting a little more sleep, how's that?"

"Yeah, Dad," he said drowsily. "I think I should."

Rob closed his eyes. He was tired, but not all the way sleepy yet. He listened to his father fuss around the room, and he was pretty sure Parry very carefully pulled the blankets over him and tucked him it. Rob smiled, the gentle actions of his father finally lulling him into sleep.

Someone putting a hand on his arm woke Rob up sometime later. He sighed, thinking it was his father letting him know he was back in the room. The pressure on his arm increased. Rob tried to pull his arm away.

"You're hurting me," he said.

"That's really the point," a voice said. Rob recognized it.

He opened his eyes. The bearded man was standing beside the bed. He had a small bandage on his neck. He slapped his other hand over Rob's mouth, cutting off his shout for help. Rob could see darkness surrounding the man, black blended with the edges of his body. The pressure on Rob's arm, over the cut made by the knife, was increasing. Rob felt something tear loose in his arm. It hurt, he tried to struggle free. The bearded man held him down.

"We need to start again, I think, you and I," he said looking at Rob. There was something in his eyes. They had been frightening before, but now there was something utterly terrifying, utterly inhuman behind those eyes. Rob thought he could see the thing there. He looked again and knew it was true.

"Galen, they're here!" he called out to his brother.

Rob fought against the hand on his arm, the hand over his mouth. The bearded man shifted abruptly and took his hand from Rob's left arm and slammed it on his right. Rob felt the stitches holding that wound tear loose as well. The hand over his mouth moved up, blocking off his air. Rob started to see dark spots before his eyes.

"This is the beginning, I will be back. I need to check on your brother before I go," he said and let go of Rob. He disappeared out the door before Rob could get his wits together enough to shout for help.

Rob stood up on unsteady legs. As he moved away the IV stopped him. He tore it away from his hand. *"Galen!"* He ran down the hall towards Galen's room. When he got to the door he saw the bearded man over by his brother's bed. "No!" He shouted, hoping it was loud enough to get security.

The bearded man turned away from Galen. "This can wait." He walked towards Rob and struck out, knocking him to the floor. The impact was too much for Rob to bear. The wounds—it felt like all of them—had torn loose. He knew he was bleeding, he hurt. He heard the bearded man laugh. The laugh, the pleasure in it, sounded like the thing. The pain exploded as the bearded man placed a hand against his back. Rob moaned, before darkness claimed him he thought he heard...*No, Dad and Uncle Bobby killed it...*And he blacked out.

"How did this happen?" Rob heard his father, angry, from beside the bed. "I went down to get a cup of coffee and this happens?"

"He went down the hall again," another voice answered. "He must have tripped and fallen when he got there. The security guard found him."

"Just a fall did that to him?" His father was very angry.

"Yes, the impact from the fall tore the wounds open on his chest and back. In several places..."

"What?"

"We are worried about the damage. The doctor thinks we might need to consider something a little more drastic."

"No, not yet," Parry snapped back.

"Dad?" Rob had to force the words from him. He still couldn't open his eyes.. He tried to reach for his father's hand, he couldn't move. Something was holding him to the bed. He fought against it.

"Rob, no." His father put a hand on his shoulder. "It's okay, open your eyes and look at me."

Rob opened his eyes. His father was standing beside the bed. "Dad?" He looked at his father, "Is Galen okay?"

"What?" His father seemed surprised. "Yeah, Rob, he was okay when they found you in his room. Bobby and I had just stepped out to get coffee. Everything was okay."

"Why can't I move?" He pulled against the straps on his wrists. They hurt his wounded arms.

His father looked sick, he looked angry and—what scared Rob—he looked resigned. "They said you tore your IV out and went to Galen's room, Rob, we can't have you doing that. You hurt yourself. They had to re-stitch your arms. And those other…" His father was struggling to keep under control, Rob knew that. "You promised me, Rob. You said you'd wait till I took you to your brother."

"Dad! He was here, the bearded man—he said he was going to go to Galen. He was going to hurt Galen, I know it. I had to get there. I had to get to Galen."

"Rob, you were the only one in Galen's room. They found you on the floor. You'd fallen."

"No, Dad. Someone had to see him! He said…Dad you have to believe me." Rob was desperate, he could see disbelief in his father's eyes and the hand that still rested on Rob's arm had nothing of the "feel" of his father.

"There was no one here," the woman standing by the door said. Rob looked at her. "We've had no one on the floor for at least an hour." She turned and walked away.

"Dad," he hissed. "She's has spots."

"What?" Parry looked down at him with unfocused eyes.

"Dad! You have to believe me!"

"It was a nightmare, Rob. It must have been. After what you went through, and the drugs they are giving you..." His father looked sad.

"He said he would be back." He was struggling to sit up.

"You need to relax, or I'll have to call the nurse."

"No! No, you're right, Dad, maybe it was a nightmare," Rob said, trying to sound convincing. The last thing he wanted was to be drugged again. "Sorry, Dad."

"It's okay, Rob. I understand. Drugs can do that. Probably made you feel weird, huh?"

"Dad? I might just be starting my training, but I am a Keeper."

"What?" Parry said. Rob looked at him, the light he always saw was completely gone, replaced by the flat, sickening gray.

"I am thirteen, you know."

His father smiled. "Yeah, I know. You..." he cleared his throat. "How are you feeling?"

"Weird," he said with a little smile. "Dad? What's wrong?"

"They said...they told me..." Parry shook his head. "You can't get upset like that, Rob. I understand why you were afraid. And it's okay. After everything you went through, nightmares are reasonable, Rob. But you can't fight the restraints, you can't get upset like that. They'll sedate you again or take you away to another part of the hospital."

Rob stopped. He didn't move at all. "Take me away? No, it was just a nightmare. I'll be good. Dad? Can you help? The drugs are making me sick and I still hurt. Since Galen isn't here can you heal me a little?"

"Heal you?" His father blinked. "What are you talking about?"

"Dad?" Rob looked at him, Parry was sipping on a cup of coffee.

"Are you hungry?" his father asked.

"No, not really."

"Maybe some juice or something?"

"No Dad, I don't want anything." His father reached over and patted his hand, and it was only that, an affectionate pat, nothing more.

They had been watching the television together in silence. The station had several fairly good shows on in a row and they were quiet together. It actually felt nearly normal. Until Rob realized something was going on in the hall. He could hear people running up and down and he thought he heard an alarm or something going off. He saw his father look towards the door.

"Dad? What is it?"

"I don't know, Rob. I think I might go check it out." His father stood.

A nurse burst into the room. "We need you down the hall. Your son..." Rob could hear someone saying "call the code." The nurse pulled at his father's arm. "Please, you need to come with me, if we can't—you have to make the decision."

His father took one look at him, it was a desperate haunted look. "Rob."

"I'll be good, Dad. Help Galen." He father ran out of the room after the nurse.

Rob pulled against the restraints. He relaxed back onto the bed and looked up at the ceiling. A nurse came into the room. Rob pulled against the restraints and then looked back up at the ceiling. He lifted his head again when he heard the lock on the door click into place. Before he could react she was over at the bed and had her hand over his mouth. Rob saw movement by the door.

The bearded man was in the room with them. "Your father will be gone long enough for us to finish this first little bit. We only need a minute or two...this time." He smiled at Rob, the terrible smile, and walked to the bed. He undid the restraint on Rob's left arm and cut the bandages away with a silver knife. When he took Rob's arm in his hand the touch was painful, like the thing's claws. He said something in the strange language and then Rob saw what the nurse had in her hand. He started trembling. It was a golden cup. The bearded man raised the knife and cut deep into Rob's arm.

"We need to begin. Time is running out."

The pain radiating from the touch was excruciating. Rob could feel the blood running down his arm. He was getting light headed. The bearded man was mumbling in the language and the nurse was chanting along with him. He was beginning to panic, the memories from the farmhouse, from the rituals, were blending with the present.

He reached out for his brother and sensed him, then suddenly it felt like Galen's heart stopped. *"Galen!"* Rob felt himself sliding away.

Chapter Thirteen

The heater crackled to life, startling the four of them. Rob was sitting on the couch beside Galen, his hands were shaking, one hand still toying with the tear in the hospital gown he was holding. Rhiannon was beside him, her arm over his shoulders. Mike was sitting across from the three of them, his face white.

"Never, never in a million years did I picture this," the doctor said in a rough whisper. "What was wrong with Parry and Bobby? Usually Parry just heals people and zip, out they go. Just like you, Galen."

"There was something going on, the staff was, well…" Galen broke off. Rob looked at him. "I knew something was going on, Rob. I was trying to get to you."

"I know," Rob said with a shaky smile.

"I was too late," Galen let his head drop into his hands.

"What do you mean?" Mike asked.

"I knew something was wrong with Dad and Bobby, I could sense it the same way Rob could see it. I…I tried, but then, oh, gods, Rob, I was too late. By the time I heard you…"

Rob's smiled brightened. "You did hear me? I thought you did, I thought you answered, but I wasn't sure."

"I heard you, but it was already too late."

PAST

TEN YEARS BEFORE

Day Five to Day Six - Galen

"Galen?" his brother's voice drifted through the darkness, "Galen."

"Rob?" He thought he could hear his brother crying, and tried to answer. *"Rob?"* The darkness took him again.

"Galen? Can you hear me? There's something wrong here." Rob's voice was suddenly there again, loud, but only in his head, like the soft call in a dream. "I just wanted to come by for a minute, Galen," he heard his brother say from beside him.

"Rob? Is that you?" He tried to reach out for his brother, something was blocking him

"Whatever is going on, Dad and Uncle Bobby are affected," Rob's voice in his head said. "I'm worried about you, you need to get better Galen." He thought he heard his father's voice, there in the dark with his brother.

Galen thought he could sense someone standing by him. He could hear a rasping breath. "We're not quite finished yet," a voice said. "You and I. Not yet. You stopped the ritual and cost us—but all is not lost. No, not lost at all, Keeper." The voice laughed, the sound chilled Galen. He thought he felt a hand over his mouth, blocking his nose. He couldn't breathe. He fought against it.

"No!" Rob's voice, shrill, afraid.

"This can wait," the voice said. Galen heard his brother whimper. He tried to fight through the darkness, through the paralysis that held him wherever he was. He fought for a moment longer before he was lost again.

It was there, whatever it had been, beside him again. Galen could feel the cold coming from whatever it was. He could hear the breath rasping in and out. He smelled the death scent of rotting meat. Something touched him, a hand maybe, and pain filled him, reminding him of the touch of the thing in the clearing. He could feel it pulling his life away, feel the pain in his chest as his heart fought to keep going against the touch of the thing's hand.

"*Galen!*" A voice whispered to him in that moment, he recognized his brother.

"*Rob?*" Pain was filling him as the touch ground into his chest.

That touch won, Galen's heart stopped.

Galen took a deep breath. He was lying on a bed, he was pretty sure of that, and judging by the smell it was a hospital bed. Something was beeping with annoying consistency by his left ear. His chest hurt. Just drawing breath was agony. As he lay there memory started snaking back, curling its way through his consciousness. Rob in the car bugging him about his birthday, stopping for dinner, the fight outside the diner. Then the rest came flooding back, all at once.

"Rob!" He heard his own voice shout in the quiet room.

"Galen? Galen, thank the gods!" his uncle's voice answered him.

Galen forced his eyes open. "Uncle Bobby?"

"How are you?"

"Where's Rob?"

His uncle looked away for a split second, then back. It was enough to concern Galen. "Your brother is just down the hall."

"Is he okay?"

Again his uncle's eyes slid from him. "Yes."

"Bobby? What?"

"Your brother is okay, Galen. He's just down the hall," his uncle said, looking out the window.

"There's something wrong. I made it in time, didn't I?" He reached out for his brother and was answered by a confused jumble of pain and fear.

"He is okay," his uncle said each word carefully, but there was a deep sadness in his voice.

"Uncle Bobby? What's wrong? Didn't the healing work?"

"What?" Bobby sounded confused. Galen frowned.

"Dad's with him?" Galen asked, Bobby nodded. "When can we go?"

"We have to wait, Galen," Bobby said a little hazily. "There's something…" Bobby blinked and shook his head, his eyes coming to focus on Galen for a moment. "Galen?" And then his eyes slid away again.

Alarm bells started jangling in Galen's head. "Okay, just down the hall? What room is he in?"

"He's in room 400, Galen. You're in 415. It's just down the hall."

"If you say just down the hall again, Uncle Bobby, I swear…" Galen tried for a grin, but his uncle ignored him. "Fine, how do I look?"

"What?" Bobby looked over at him.

"How do I look, Uncle Bobby? Am I okay?"

"What do you mean?" His uncle shook his head again, like a dog listening to something in the distance.

"How am I? I can't remember much of what happened, but I know I got to Rob, I know that thing grabbed me, I healed Rob." He was starting to feel consciousness drifting away again, it was an odd feeling. "Sedated? I'm fighting sedation. Why, Bobby? Why am I drugged?"

"You'll be fine Galen. They've assured us you'll be fine." Galen closed his eyes and he thought he heard his uncle sigh, it had a catch in it. "At least you'll be fine."

What does that mean? He couldn't fight his way back far enough to actually ask the question.

The room was empty when Galen woke up. He felt heavy, the affects of the drug still in his system. He focused inwards, trying to push the drugs as far away as he could. The annoying beeping was subdued. Galen opened his eyes and looked at the ceiling. He was still drowsy and drifted along on his thoughts. His chest still hurt, although the pain had backed off a bit. He knew it wasn't gone, just removed from him a little. *I wonder where Uncle Bobby is? With Dad? Maybe he's with Rob.* His heart started beating harder as he thought of his brother. He heard the beep, beep speed up.

He tried to sit up. It wasn't very comfortable, but he managed on the second try. Galen wondered if he could get all the way to his brother's room before someone caught him, or the heart monitor betrayed him. He rolled the stop down on the IV tube and disconnected it from his hand, then turned the monitor off.

He stood up on legs that didn't work quite right and headed for the door. He looked carefully down the corridor. There was no one racing towards his room with a crash cart. He got out the door and discovered he could barely walk. Leaning on the wall, he moved slowly down the hall. He went through a set of double doors and spotted room 400. He slid along the wall and into his brother's room.

He had half expected to find his father in the room, but he wasn't. His father and uncle had probably gone for coffee. They rarely lasted more than an hour with out getting a fresh cup. He was smiling as he turned to the bed. The slight good humor didn't hold.

"Rob," he said softly. His brother was lying on the bed. A blanket was pulled over him, hiding most of his body from Galen.

Rob's face was tracked with tears. Galen pushed himself off the wall and made it to the bed. He gently brushed the tears away from Rob's cheeks. He laid his hand on his brother's forehead to get a feel for what was going on. Pain radiated up from the touch, along with the sluggish feeling of drugs. *Rob's drugged? Why hasn't Dad...?*

Galen took a deep breath and put his other hand over his brother's heart. He concentrated, working through the drugs in his own body to let the light flow, to let it seep into his brother. Galen felt the drugs shift, the sluggishness flowing into him as it left his brother's body. "Rob?" he said softly. He didn't want anyone to overhear him, and he didn't want to startle his brother. "Hey, Rob. It's me." His brother moaned a little. It was a scared, pain-filled sound. "Rob?"

"Galen?" Rob whispered.

"Hey, Rob, yeah," he said, leaning over the bed more, he could hardly hear his brother's voice.

"Galen?"

His brother was afraid, Galen could hear it in that one word, he could sense it in his hand where it rested over his brother's heart. "Yeah. I'm here. What is it?"

"Galen, they...they hurt me."

"Sometimes doctors hurt you when they're helping you."

"No. They hurt me," his brother said, his eyes hadn't opened yet. Galen focused, trying to help Rob a little more. He felt himself slipping in response.

"Rob? Tell me, who hurt you?"

"They did, a nurse and...he...hurt me...Galen...said I'm special...the know about us...I can't..." His brother relaxed suddenly.

"Rob!" Galen desperately tried to push the drugs back, away from his brother, he tried to ease Rob away from the pain. Galen focused on Rob for a minute, letting more of the healing flow into him. Rob sighed, Galen felt the pain diminish, felt more of the drugs move out. He pulled his hands away. Rob needed more, but Galen knew he had to get back to his room before someone caught him. "I'll be back, Rob," he said quietly and slipped out of the room. By the time he reached his own bed, he barely had the energy to reconnect the leads to the monitor and the IV tube. He left the drip off, not wanting any more of the drugs in his system. He let himself drift into sleep.

The annoying beeping was back. He hurt. He had the feeling some hours had passed. Galen opened his eyes. His father was sitting in the chair beside the bed. His eyes were red, like he'd been crying.

Parry seemed to sense his look. "Galen."

"Dad?"

"It's good to see you awake. You shouldn't have gone to your brother's room."

"How did you know?" Galen sighed. "I had to know, Dad. I had to see him." He looked at his father, Parry's eyes slid away.

"You should have waited, Galen. I would have taken you down there," his father said sternly. The voice sounded nothing like the man Galen knew.

"No." Galen said. The word was sharp. "I needed to see Rob. I don't feel any better after going down there. Dad?"

"What is it?"

"What's going on with Rob?"

"He's okay, Galen," his father said, looking at the heart monitor.

"Dad? Why is he sedated?"

"How do you know he's sedated?" His father turned unfocused eyes on him.

"I touched him, Dad. I tried my best to get rid of it, but I couldn't. Whatever they've given him…Hmm." Galen stopped, thinking about the "feel" of the drugs. "It feels wrong. Not just… it has something more in it than just drugs? Is that it?"

"He'll be okay," his father said, looking at his hands, acting like Galen hadn't spoken.

"Dad?"

"Galen, your brother…"

"Don't say he'll be okay. I saw him Dad, there is something wrong, what is it?"

"Galen, Rob's…" His father trailed off, and put his head in his hands. "Rob—there's something wrong, Galen." He stopped when a nurse ran into the room.

"I know, Dad, that's what I'm talking about, what's going on?" Galen demanded.

"It happened again, we need you. Now," the nurse said. Parry looked at Galen and ran out of the room.

Galen struggled up and pulled the IV out. He didn't care if the whole hospital thought he flatlined as he tugged the leads off the pads on his chest. He ran as quickly as he could to his brother's room.

His father and uncle were trying to hold Rob down. His brother was screaming, there was blood everywhere. Galen swallowed. He ran into the room and shoved his father aside.

"Rob! Rob!" He put his hands on Rob's shoulders, letting his hand curl gently around them, he focused the healing into Rob, desperately trying to reach him at the same time. *"Rob, Rob, I'm here."* He could feel people trying to pull him away. He held on. *"Rob, I'm here."* His brother stopped struggling, relaxing in his hands. "Rob," he whispered. Galen saw a nurse head towards the other side of the bed. "No! Stay back, not yet." She had a needle in her hand, he was pretty sure she planned to sedate his brother.

"Galen?" Rob whispered, terrified.

"I'm here."

"Galen, they came back," Rob said.

"Rob!" his father said, stern, frightened.

"Who did? Tell me," Galen said gently.

"They came back Galen. They hurt me again. They said 'Keeper,' they know, Galen. They know about us. It's important. They said I'm, we, you and me, spec…" He slowly relaxed in Galen's hands.

"I told you no!" He turned on the nurse who was standing by his brother. "Gods damn it. I said no!"

"Galen, calm down," his father said, putting a hand on his arm. Galen stopped dead at the touch. There was nothing there. No warmth, no light, nothing of the "hum" he associated with his father's touch. He turned shocked eyes on Parry.

"We need to let them get Rob cleaned up." His father's voice was flat, nearly without emotion. Galen glanced at his uncle, Bobby's face was gray, his eyes unfocused.

Galen looked down at Rob, there was blood covering the bandages on his arms and chest. He swayed on his feet. The dash down the hall had cost him. "I'm not leaving him, Dad."

"You need to go back to your room, Galen. I'll be there as soon as I speak with the doctor."

"No," he said. It was an act of total defiance. "I won't leave him."

"Galen," his father said. "You need to go back to your room. You shouldn't be up yet, please go back." His father sounded worried, desperate.

"Dad, I can rest here, in the chair," Galen was pleaded, begging his father to understand, hoping to break through to Parry or Bobby, hoping the tone in his voice would reach them. He couldn't risk anything more in the crowded room. He knew something was wrong, and had to stay with his brother.

His father had moved a little, leaning against the bed. "Galen, you've hurt yourself. You're bleeding, you might have torn those stitches out."

"Dad, I'm okay. Just let me stay with Rob." He was pushing away the arms that were trying to hold him.

"Galen, I'm sorry." It was his father begging him to understand, now.

"Dad, no." He looked at his father. "I need..." He saw Parry nod at someone behind him. Galen felt a sudden pinprick and the world was fading, blurring. He felt himself falling and he knew his father caught him. It felt like betrayal to Galen as he lost consciousness.

"We have discussed it. We think it would be better if he was moved..." Galen heard someone talking. It sounded like they were just outside the door.

"No, I don't want him there," his father's voice.

"Not yet," his uncle's voice added.

"We just don't think it's safe anymore."

"No." Both men spoke together.

"He's gotten the restraints off three times now. The damage is getting worse, you know that. We can't..."

"He needs to be here, we need to be close to both of them." His father sounded angry. Galen suddenly realized they were talking about Rob.

"I just don't think it's a good idea. We have him sedated, but if he gets loose again, who's to say what he might do?"

"He'll be okay." The way his father said that, Galen knew Parry didn't believe it.

"The last time, you know how many stitches it took. He's lost an enormous amount of blood. He could kill himself next time."

"I know, but we just can't let him go." The anger was gone, replaced by sadness.

"No, not yet," his uncle said again.

"If the psychotic breakdown continues you might not have any choice."

"How bad could he get?"

"This is serious...I'm sorry."

He thought he heard his father say something else, something so quiet Galen couldn't catch it.

"Dad? Bobby?" He raised his voice, hoping it would carry out the door. He looked up as they came in the room. "What's going on?"

"Nothing, Galen, it's okay." His father's eyes were red. he was making a point of not looking at Galen. Bobby glanced at him and then looked away.

"No. I need the truth. What's going on? Dad?" He looked at his father and then his uncle. Parry was looking at the end of the bed, Bobby at the heart monitor. "Look at me." And still they didn't turn to Galen.

"You're brother is very sick, Galen," his father said with a sigh.

"Very," Bobby parroted.

"Dad, I think I deserve more than that."

"The experience, Galen, it...it...it's hit Rob hard. Since yesterday, it's been getting worse. They, the doctors, are worried that he can't get away from what happened to him. He's reliving it."

"Nightmares would be reasonable after that, Dad."

"Not just nightmares," Bobby said.

"Help him," Galen said.

"We're trying," Parry said blankly.

"Dad?" Galen grabbed his father's hand, it felt cool, dead to the touch. "Why haven't you healed him?"

"What?" Parry turned unfocused eyes on Galen and then with a shrug looked away again. "He thinks the it's happening here. He's reliving what happened during the ritual. He's gotten out of the restraints."

"Restraints? What the hell is going on, Dad? How could you let them do that, he's only thirteen!"

His father looked sad, old, beaten. He was utterly defeated, and it scared Galen. "They said I didn't have any choice. They're keeping him heavily sedated, but he seems to be able to throw it off, and he's gotten out of the restraints three times now. He... he..." His father was crying. "I told them they couldn't, I wouldn't let them at first, but Galen he..."

"Dad?" Galen kept his voice calm.

"He's hurt himself."

"What do you mean? Like getting up? Or what?"

"He, they don't know how, but he—he's torn the stitches out, and he's..." His father's shoulders dropped, Bobby put an arm over the shaking shoulders. "Galen I don't, I didn't know what to do. I thought...But Galen..." His father looked at him for a moment. *He's lost. He's not there, Bobby isn't there. Something's interfering.* His father drew a breath that sounded like a sob.

"Dad? Please." Galen was trying to stay calm.

"He...He..." His father couldn't seem to finish.

"Dad?" Galen looked at his father. "Uncle Bobby?"

"He's hurt himself," his uncle said.

"What? How?" Galen snapped.

"He's gotten a scalpel somehow and..." Bobby swallowed and his eyes focused for just a moment. "I thought I saw..." And he was gone again. "He's been cutting himself, Galen."

"They want to move him to the psych ward so he can be more closely monitored," Parry said.

"No," Galen said. "No, not an option. There's nothing wrong with Rob," he said, bringing the memory of his brother in the bed, covered in blood, to mind. "He's a Keeper…"

"It might be the only way to help him, Galen."

"No. Take me down there, Dad. I need to see him."

"He's sedated, Galen, he wouldn't know you're there."

"He would know, Dad. He would, you know that." Galen tried shaking his father's arm. *He knows that. I remember when Bobby…*

"Galen, you sound like your brother. He said the same thing."

"What? Of course he did. You don't think he'd know if I was there? Was Rob here in my room, Dad? Bobby? Before I woke up?" His father and uncle actually looked at him, really looked at him, Galen saw recognition in their eyes for just a moment. "He was, wasn't he? Twice? No, three times." He paused. There was something about that third time.

"Yes he was, Galen," his father said, still focused on him. "What is it?"

"There was…" Galen looked at his father and uncle. "What was it, that third time? Someone was here. No, some*thing* was here. I don't think it was human. It felt familiar, though. The thing, that thing that took Rob, it was here at the hospital!"

"Galen?" his father said. Galen looked up, the momentary recognition was gone.

"Galen! Galen! Help!" Rob's voice slammed into his brain with physical force.

"Rob?" he said it out loud, his uncle and father looked at him as he swung his legs off the bed. They grabbed his arms, trying to restrain him as he pushed himself up. "Rob, I'm coming."

"Hurry, they're taking me. Galen, please, they're ta..kin…me… Ga…" Rob's voice faded, replaced with a cold darkness and the

edges of insane laughter.

"Dad, I need to get to Rob, now!"

"No, Galen, you need to lie back down."

Galen struggled to throw off their restraining hands. Nothing of his father and uncle were in the hands that held him.

"No, Galen," his father said.

Galen tore the leads off the heart monitor and heard it stop beeping. He pulled himself free and yanked the IV out of his hand.

"Galen, you can't." His father was desperate.

Parry stood in front of him, his uncle had placed a restraining hand on his arm again. "Dad?" he said very quietly. "Uncle Bobby?"

"Galen you can't."

"Get out of my way. Either help me or get that hand off of me." The hand dropped away. His father was staring at Galen with… "Oh, no, no, no!" Galen panicked and ran out of the room. He threw the door to Rob's room open.

Rob was gone.

"No!" he yelled. His father and uncle came up behind him. "Gods damn it, what did you do?"

"Galen…" Parry began, but it was too much, Galen struck out in his anger, in his desperation, and connected with his father. Parry rubbed the side of his face, his eyes wild. "They weren't supposed to take him yet. I was going to bring you down to see him before…But they said he…It was the only way to help him, Galen. You don't know what's been happening."

"Dad, don't you see? Bobby?" Galen felt desperate tears in his eyes. He grabbed his father and shook him, shouting, hoping his father would look at him. "You're the one who doesn't know. There's nothing wrong with him, he was telling the truth."

"No, Galen." Parry was shaking his head. Galen looked at his father, Parry looked broken.

"Dad, what's wrong with you? This is Rob we're talking about! Rob! He's *Custodes Noctis*, Dad!"

"Galen...I'm sorr..."

"No, no, Dad!" He grabbed his father's face and wrenched it around, forcing him to look at Galen. "What the hell is wrong with you?" Galen saw something in his father's eyes. "Dad?" Before he really realized what he was doing he placed a hand on his father's face, feeling what was there, trying to get a sense of it in the very few seconds he knew he had. A cold, flat dark pervaded his father. Words that didn't sound like Parry floated through his consciousness. The sense of who he was, what he was, was completely gone, like something had stripped him away and left a shell of the man behind.

Parry struggled against the touch. "No," Galen said firmly and focused everything into that touch, into his father, forcing the cold away. Bobby was tugging on him, but Galen ignored him and stayed focused on driving the darkness from his father. As the cold began to move, Galen felt the sluggishness of drugs in his father, tasted their metallic taste on his tongue. Parry was still struggling. "No, Dad," Galen said gently.

"Galen?" his father's voice was confused. Galen was starting to tremble, the healing was quickly using up his reserves of energy. Bobby was still pulling at him, his touch full of the same cold darkness that had filled Parry. It was moving, almost gone from him. "Galen?" His father put a hand over his, Galen felt warmth in the touch. "It's...I'm back." Galen let his hand drop and turned to his uncle. "No." Parry stopped him. "I've got it."

Galen collapsed on the bed as his father grabbed his uncle, placing both hands on the side of Bobby's head, he struggled against the touch for a moment before relaxing and sighing.

"Bobby?" Parry said gently.

"Present, I think," his uncle said with the half-smile that reminded Galen of Rob.

Galen groaned, his father and uncle looked at him.

"What?" Parry said, looking at Galen and the empty bed. "Galen? Where's Rob?"

"You don't remember do you? Oh, gods, Dad, Bobby..." He put his head in his hands. "That thing, it has him. It has Rob again."

Chapter Fourteen

Galen's head was in his hands, the scar was twisting happily in his chest. The closer they got to the end, the more he was aware of the movement. The pain was growing slowly, but surely, and under it all the hissing, vile whisper.

"They were drugged?" Rob asked quietly.

"Yeah," Galen said, looking at his brother.

"How did it happen, Galen?" Rhiannon asked. "I can't imagine Parry or Bobby..."

"Dad said he remembered a nurse coming in to check on Rob. She brushed past him, he said he sensed something in her, but it was too late. She must have had something in her hand. He blacked out and the next thing he really remembers was when he woke up in Rob's room."

"Nothing?" Rhiannon said.

"No, he had vague flashes, but nothing else. Same thing with Uncle Bobby."

"They knew, they had to know, that Parry and Bobby were Keepers," Rhiannon said, looking at Galen.

"Yeah, and whatever it was they were giving to Dad and Bobby, it countered their Gifts as well as removing the sense of who they were."

"But how, Galen? How would they know?" Rhiannon asked.

"They were looking for Keepers. They knew who we are, what we are. And they knew how to stop us," Rob said quietly.

"Yeah. And we knew if they had managed to get to us, we had to find Rob, save him. And fast," Galen said.

PAST

TEN YEARS BEFORE

Day Six to Day Seven - Galen

The hospital room was quiet for the space of several heartbeats. Galen's father and uncle were looking at him with shocked disbelief. Galen took a deep breath, forcing the drugs and the whispering voice out of his father had taken a grim toll on his body. "That thing, it has him. It has Rob again," he repeated, utterly defeated.

"No, Galen, that's impossible, we killed it. It's dead," Bobby said, looking from Parry to Galen. He blinked and his eyes lost focus. "No, wait…" He paused.

"What is it?" Parry said.

"I saw…I think I saw…"

"It's here, or it was, in the hospital," Galen said.

"Rob tried to tell me, I think. I couldn't…" Parry put his head in his hands. Bobby put a hand on his back. "What was wrong with us?"

"You felt cold, gray," Galen said, trying to articulate the feeling he'd gotten from both his father and his uncle. "I heard something in your head, it wasn't you. I couldn't sense you at all."

"Parry?" Bobby said gently. "We should get back to Galen's room, let them think we're playing along right now."

"You're right. We don't want to alert them quite yet," Parry said with a growl in his voice. "Not yet."

Galen pushed himself up off the bed. "Good idea." He paused as the room spun around him.

"Galen?" Bobby said. Galen glanced at his uncle, Bobby was staring at him.

"I'm okay."

"Galen, you look terrible," his father said, stepping towards him.

"It's worse than he looks," Bobby said grimly.

"Let's just get back to my room," Galen said wearily. "Can you help?" he asked his uncle, not ready for the reaction he knew he would get when his father touched him. Parry was frowning at him. Galen tried to smile.

"That bad, Galen?" Parry asked.

"Let's get to my room," he repeated, swaying on his feet. His uncle put an arm around his waist, Galen sagged against him. Bobby took his weight easily and half-carried him back to his room. The trip down the corridor passed in a blur, all he really knew was one minute he was in Rob's room and the next he was being settled gently back in his bed.

Galen's chest had started aching, and the partially closed wound in his side felt open and raw. The remnants of the drugs he had been given, as well as those he had moved from his father and brother, were pulling him down. He sighed, trying to stop the trembling in his chest. *"Rob?"* He tried reaching out to his brother, but there was only darkness where Rob's voice had been.

"Bobby?" Parry said quietly. Galen opened his eyes. His father was looking at his uncle, his hands hovering over Galen's body.

"The wound in his side isn't healing right, there's a gray film surrounding him and..." Bobby trailed off.

"Bobby?"

"There's something wrong with his heart, Parry."

"His heart?"

"The thing, it was here in my room, I remember..." Galen said looking at his father, ignoring the pain in his body. "It stopped my heart."

His father closed his eyes briefly. "I think I remember that, too."

"Be careful, Parry," Bobby said as his father dropped his hand onto Galen's chest. Galen saw a spasm of pain flash across Parry's face.

"No, Dad, you need to be able to help Rob."

"It'll take all three of us, Galen," his father said, putting a hand on his head.

"No," Galen said firmly, blocking the warmth from his father's hands. "You need to be strong to help Rob."

"Stop fighting me, Galen, let me do this," his father snapped.

"Fighting you?" Bobby's voice was full of disbelief.

"Galen, please," his father's voice was desperate. Galen still blocked the light coming from his father's hands. "Bobby?" his father said quietly. Bobby stepped to the other side of the bed and put one hand on Galen's chest and the other on the back of his head.

"No, please, you have to..." The sound of a heartbeat filled him, he started to drift. "Have to help..." He couldn't block his father any longer, he felt the warmth and the light slide into his body as he slipped away.

"He blocked you?" Bobby asked quietly from one side of the bed.

"Yeah," Parry answered softly.

"Can he do that?"

"I guess so, and he did more than that, Bobby. He brought me back even with..." Parry sighed. "He'd healed Rob a little, too. I felt the residue in his system."

"Parry, you know what this could mean."

"Yeah." Galen heard his father sigh again.

"Your sons? Our boys? Is this...?"

"I don't know. I..." The sound of the door opening stopped his father's voice.

"I'm sorry it took so long to get here," Rhiannon's voice said.

"Dad?" Galen said, opening his eyes. His father turned to him with a smile and put a hand down on his arm. Warmth flowed out from the touch.

"Hey. How do you feel?"

Galen smiled and eased himself up into a sitting position. "Better. You shouldn't have, Dad."

"I think that's my decision," Parry said, looking at him. "I'll be okay to help Rob. But we need you able to help, too."

"Want to tell me what you're talking about?" Rhiannon asked, looking from one to the other.

"Rhiannon?" Galen smiled. "What are you doing here?"

"Bobby called and asked me to come down with the pictures of Megan."

"We need to know what we're facing, Galen," his uncle said quietly as Galen swallowed back a lump in his throat. "The pictures might help." He smiled sadly.

"They might. Dad…" Galen couldn't get the words out.

"Galen? What is it." Parry asked.

"Rob's not like Megan." The lump in his throat filled with acid as he remembered the pictures. "At least not yet, oh gods, Dad." He fought back tears as they gathered in his eyes.

"Galen?" His father's eyes were concerned.

"Do you think that's next?" Galen whispered.

"What?" Parry demanded as Bobby held his hands out for the pictures. He closed his eyes. "No, you're right, not yet. Even through whatever was going on, I would have sensed that. He was hurt, but not that." He looked across Galen to his brother. "Bobby?"

Galen glanced at his uncle. Bobby face was paper-white as he flipped through the pictures. Galen saw a tear work itself lose and trickle down his cheek. "Gods, Parry." Bobby swallowed. "I'm so sorry, Rhiannon."

"The time for sorry is past, now's the time to kill," Rhiannon said, her voice fierce.

"How do we find him again?" Parry asked the room at large.

"They took him for a reason. I think the ritual's changed. They're seeking to complete something else. Oh no, oh gods, no." What little color was left in Bobby's face had drained away.

"What?" Parry and Galen asked together.

"Parry, it might... Oh gods, it might be the first step. Not just a sacrifice now, but the ritual to let it walk the earth in human form. They need Rob for that and they need..." He stopped himself and looked at Parry.

Galen looked from his uncle to his father. Parry was shaking his head. "They need me, don't they?" Galen said quietly. "It's why I was sedated, why it came in my room. It was testing—tasting—me wasn't it?"

"No," Parry whispered a soft denial. "No."

"That's it, isn't it, Bobby?" Galen looked at his uncle. "They need...oh, gods." His mind was replying the scene in the clearing and the moments in Rob's room. He realized all three of the others were staring at him, waiting for him to finish. He met his father's eyes. "It knows."

"Knows?" Parry and Bobby said together.

"About us, about me and Rob. It knows what, who, we are. It's how they knew to drug you. It recognized me, and Rob said it knew we were Keepers."

"Keepers?" Rhiannon asked.

"What?" Parry asked, ignoring Rhiannon. "It knew...? Bobby?"

"Yeah, it's worse than we thought."

"What the hell are Keepers?" Rhiannon said indignantly.

"It said 'the other half' when it touched me during the ritual. It knew. And now they need me to complete the ritual."

"Galen..."

"Keepers? Hello? Want to answer me?"

"It's the perfect way to find Rob..." Galen said urgently.

"What the hell are you talking about?" Rhiannon grabbed Parry's arm and shook it. Galen watched his father's face change as Rhiannon's rage and grief touched him.

Parry was completely focused on Galen "Out of the question. No, absolutely not, no." His father was shaking his head slowly.

"Dad, Bobby, it's the only way." He glanced over at his uncle. "Tell me what I need to do."

"No, Galen," his father whispered.

"I need to know what's going on," Rhiannon said angrily.

"Will they come for me?" Galen asked his uncle.

"Yes. Part of it has already been accomplished. The sacrifices before this, what they did to Rob here..." His uncle looked at him with bleak eyes. "How can we ever ask his forgiveness for letting that happen, Parry?" He cleared his throat. "If they can get you...They probably already have that arranged."

"Okay, so what's the plan?"

"No, Galen. No."

"Please? Please tell me what you're taking about. I have a right to know," Rhiannon begged.

Galen ignored her and focused on his father. "Dad..."

"No, Galen." His father looked at him. "I can't let you."

"Dad..."

"No."

"Uncle Bobby..."

"No," his uncle said.

"I can't, Galen. I can't." Parry drew a breath. "I let Rob...I can't lose you."

"We can handle this Galen. Let us," Bobby pleaded.

"Dad, Uncle Bobby, I have to, I don't have a choice."

"No. No! Of course you have a choice. Galen, Bobby and I can handle it." His father looked away. "You died yesterday, Galen. When I was healing you I felt that. It damaged your heart somehow and you died. I can't, Galen, I..."

"Dad, I understand."

"No," Parry said softly. Galen wasn't sure if he was disagreeing with his statement or denying the whole situation.

"Yes, I do, I understand. And I'm sorry, I really am. But you know as well as I do, we have no choice. We have to get to Rob before it's too late. What if Rob dies? And Dad, this thing, if it's—we can't let it lose on the world. We have to stop it. It's..."

"No, Galen."

"Dad..." Galen looked at his father, saw his determination to get to Rob, his determination to keep Galen out of it. Galen put his hand on his father's leg, opening himself completely to Parry. Galen waited until his father's eyes met his. "Dad, I have to do this, I have to."

"No, Galen." Parry was still shaking his head.

"If something happens to Rob, something that I might have been able to prevent..."

"Galen, they'll kill you."

"You two, you have to know, you have to understand. If Rob dies, it doesn't matter if they kill me."

"Galen, you don't mean that."

"If they kill Rob...It doesn't matter. You know how I feel. You have to know."

"Galen...no." His father was trying to deny it. Galen glanced at his uncle. Bobby was shaking his head in unison with Parry.

"You know it's the truth. What if it was one of you?" Galen felt tears in his eyes.

"You and Rob…" Parry began.

"You aren't…" Bobby continued. Rhiannon opened her mouth to say something and snapped it shut.

"But we are," Galen said. "We are."

"You can't be."

"We always have been. I heard him. Not a feeling, but words. More than once. That's how I knew he'd been taken. He called out to me."

"Galen…" His father was shaking his head.

"Dad, you know it's true. And if it were Bobby, what would happen?" He looked at his father. "If Bobby died? You would hunt it down, hunt the people serving it down and then, when it was over…"

"If I lived that long?" Parry dropped his head, his eyes bright with unshed tears. "When it was over I would hand you my sword and I'd join Bobby."

"Yes," Galen said softly. "How can you think it would be different for me? You trained me, trained Rob a little already. We're Keepers, Dad. It's who we are, what we are and our brothers are part of that. I couldn't go on without him." Parry looked up at Bobby, their eyes meeting for a long moment, then Parry sighed and nodded.

"I…" Galen sighed. "What's the plan?" he said gently.

"I still don't think this is a good idea."

"Are you just saying that because you think you should?" Galen said, smiling at his father.

Parry laughed. "Yeah, I guess so. They'll come here for you. I don't know where they'll take you. I don't know where they had Rob."

"An abandoned farmhouse, Rhiannon showed me," Galen said, smiling at Rhiannon

"They'll take him there, then," Parry said.

"They can't." Galen grinned.

"Why?" Bobby asked.

"I kind of torched the place."

"You kind of..." His father smiled back at him, and looked up at Bobby.

"Good job," his uncle said.

"Yes, very good. One less place for later," Parry said.

"Excuse me?" Rhiannon piped up. They turned to look at her. "I hate to interrupt the back slapping, but can you please tell me what's going on?" She glared at them. "Pretend I have no clue what the hell you're talking about. Start from there. What are Keepers? What is that thing that killed my Megan?"

"We're not sure what it is anymore, Rhiannon," Bobby began. "It was a lesser demon called a wood hag, but something's changing."

"It's not human?"

"No, but the host will be." Parry's voice was sad.

"I know, Dad, but this human is serving that filth. Allowing..."

"Keepers don't kill humans, Galen," Bobby added.

"We do, sometimes, you know that." Galen looked at them. "Sometimes we have to."

"Back to the question—what are Keepers?" Rhiannon asked. "Do you hunt things like the demon?"

"Not usually," Parry said. "We usually hunt bigger things. *Custodes Noctis* hunt the things that the dark creatures fear."

"Of course," Rhiannon said looking at Parry for a minute, then she turned to Galen. "What?"

"Think of it this way. There are demons like the one that took Megan and there are people who hunt those things. Then there are *Custodes Noctis*, the Keepers of the Night. We hunt the things the demons fear, the things the demons serve. The dark that the night fears."

"Ah, I think I understand. Some people hunt little things like house cats and you hunt things like tigers."

"Yeah, I guess." Galen smiled at her.

"And if you don't want to kill the humans," Rhiannon paused. "I will. You just get the boys safe," she said, looking from Parry to Bobby.

"Thank you," Parry said quietly, acknowledging the gift she offered. "We can do it. If we can even find him, we still don't know where they have him now."

"Follow them. Wait till they take me and follow them. Simple."

"I don't like it," his father said, then held up a hand to stop Galen's protests. "But it's all we've got."

"It'll be okay," Galen said. "Do you think they'll go back to the clearing where they held the first ritual?"

"It's as good a guess as any," Bobby sighed. "We can try and follow them, but if something happens we'll head for the clearing."

"So we have a plan." Galen smiled, trying to still the pounding in his heart. He was afraid—for Rob, for his father and uncle, for himself.

"Galen?" Bobby said softly.

"I'm okay, sorry." His father put a gentle hand on his chest, calming the slamming of his heart. "I'll be...What do you think they'll do?" He had to ask, he didn't want the answer, but he had to ask. "Will I be like Megan?"

"Oh, gods, Galen..." Bobby grabbed his arm. "I...I don't know."

"Promise me something, please, Dad," Galen said, looking at his father. "Promise me you'll help Rob first, no matter what happens to me, you'll help Rob first."

"Galen…"

"Please, Dad. I can focus the healing enough to keep myself stable while you heal Rob. Please, promise me."

Parry put his head in his hands for a minute. "Okay."

"Thank you." He knew what he'd asked of his father, what it had cost Parry to agree. "You three should go get a cup of coffee or something. They might be waiting for you to leave. And I need to get this over with. I need to get to Rob and I don't want you hurt if they come now. You need to be able to follow them."

"Good idea," Rhiannon said walking to the door.

"Galen…" His uncle pulled him into a tight hug. "We'll be there, you won't be alone."

"I know." He returned the embrace and then turned to his father. Parry pulled him tight against him and Galen felt the healing light warming him as his father held him. "It'll be okay, Dad," he whispered. "Just don't make us wait too long."

His father pulled away. "Right. We'll see you soon." He and Bobby turned and walked out of the room without a backwards glance. Rhiannon shrugged and followed them.

Galen stretched out on the bed, wondering if he'd see them again. He reconnected the IV to his hand without turning the drip back on. *Rob? We have a plan, we're coming.* He reached out, trying to sense his brother. Silent dark was all that was there. No warmth, nothing of his brother at all. Galen sighed and let his eyes close. He'd been listening to a radio playing from somewhere down the corridor when a man with a beard came into the room. He had a doctor and the nurse Galen remembered from his brother's room with him.

"Good," the man said. "We can begin soon."

Galen sat up. The doctor moved quickly across the room and grabbed him, forcing him back down onto the bed. Galen struggled against the hands, trying to make it as believable as possible. The nurse grabbed his arm, Galen felt a cold touch in the woman's hand, he felt the sting of a push against the port in his hand. And that was all.

He could smell damp burned wood, the scent twisted through returning consciousness. There was also the scent of gasoline. *Maybe I'm in a garage?* Galen opened his eyes. He was in a small room. There was light coming under the door, but no windows, nothing to let him know what time of day it was. Galen pushed himself up. He was still dizzy from whatever they'd given him. He thought he could smell the incense he remembered from the farmhouse coming under the door. Galen wondered how long he'd been out as he slid over to the wall and levered himself up. He was leaning against the wall, waiting for his head to stop spinning, when he heard the latch on the door turn.

He launched himself at the door, knocking down the man who was on the other side. Galen looked around. It might have been a garage or a converted stable. He guessed he was back at the farmhouse—or at least where the farmhouse had been. Galen remembered there were several outbuildings, and hoped Rhiannon would do the same.

There were two doors to his left and three to his right. He turned right and started opening them, looking in, not finding what he was looking for. He headed back the way he'd come, realizing too late the man he had knocked down was up again. He sprang at Galen.

Galen took a swing, knowing it was futile, and braced himself for the hit he knew was coming. It caught him in the stomach, he felt the nearly healed wound in his side pull and his legs went out from under him. He felt himself lifted and dragged back across the floor. "Rob! Rob!" he shouted, hoping his brother would hear, and would know Galen was there, too.

He was tossed back into the room. He hit the floor hard and

just stayed still. As he lay there, he tried to reach out for his brother again and just at the edge of his awareness caught a tiny hint of Rob. Pain, fear, despair. *"Rob? I'm here. You're not alone."* That was what came through strongest from his brother, the fear he was alone.

The door opened, Galen looked up as the bearded man came into the room. He had a brazier in his hands, it was smoking and Galen knew it was the incense he had smelled at the farmhouse. The man put the brazier down and set a golden cup beside it. The incense drifted around the room, Galen blinked as his mind tried to identify what was in it. *Frankincense, myrrh, pine? Maybe pine, that might be hellebore...*

Another man came into the room, carrying a tray. Galen couldn't see what was on the tray. There was a third man, Galen recognized him.

"Nice nose," he said with a smirk. The man kicked him. "Where're the other two? They both dead?" He was kicked again.

"Stop!" the bearded man said. "We must begin."

The two men wrenched Galen up off the floor. He tried to get a sense of them through the touch, but he could barely "feel" anything. *The incense, there's something in it, it's stopping the Gift.* The man with the broken nose pulled the hospital shirt off of Galen. They pulled his left arm out. The bearded man started chanting.

He watched as the bearded man picked up the cup. Galen looked in it and felt relief wash over him when he realized it was empty. The chanting continued. The bearded man approached him. He had a silver knife in his hand, held the cup under Galen's arm and sliced deeply into his forearm. Blood ran into the cup. Galen heard himself swearing at them. He felt a little disconnected. *Hellebore and, hmm, what else is in that incense. It's affecting me pretty fast.* When they were satisfied that they had enough blood, they put the cup back by the brazier. *I wonder how they decide that? Is there a line in there, "fill to here with blood"?*

The chanting increased in volume. The men holding him tightened their grip on his arms and pulled them away from his body. The bearded man had the knife in his hand again. He took a golden saucer from the tray and put ashes from the brazier in it, then poured a little blood from the cup. He dipped the knife in the mixture and turned to Galen with the saucer in his hands.

Galen closed his eyes, waiting for what would come. He jumped when he felt something run down his chest. The chanting got louder. Another trickle of the liquid down his chest, another and another. The bearded man put his hand over Galen's heart. He felt the cold of the thing, then the hand was pulled away. The chanting went on. *I think they're carving symbols into me like Rob.* Galen sagged. *Well, that wasn't too bad.*

Then he felt the touch of the knife again.

It slid slowly along the path of the liquid, drawing a line. The knife stopped its downward path, then...*Oh gods no.* It slid under his skin and started back up. The knife paused, twisted and began to move again. He heard himself screaming, unable to stop the sound.

He didn't know how long it went on. He was still conscious, but only just, when they stopped. They wrapped him up in something, then lifted him onto his feet and dragged him out. He was dropped into another room, unable to move. Galen thought he heard something, he listened, someone else was in the room with him.

"It was my birthday," a voice whispered, sounding like it was talking to itself. "I wish Galen were here. I wonder what they'll do to me? That scream a little while ago, it sounded like Galen. I

213

wish he were here, I don't want to die alone." The voice paused for a minute, Galen heard a sob. "Dying alone will be hard."

Not believing his ears, Galen pushed himself up onto his right arm. He looked over… "Rob!" He crawled to his brother and gently turned him over. "Rob?" He was limp in his arms. "No. Come on Rob." Galen lifted a shaking hand to Rob trying to get a sense of how badly his brother was injured. He found a pulse, faint, but there, and nothing else. He pulled his brother against him and put his back against the wall so he could support Rob's weight. Galen tried to focus the healing into his brother, but he couldn't bring the light to his hands. The incense had blocked the Gift. "Rob?" he said gently.

"Galen?" Disoriented, confused, still limp, nearly lifeless in his arms.

"Rob, I'm here, it's okay. Can you hear me? I'm here. It's okay."

Rob whimpered. "Galen?"

"I'm here."

"Can you help me a little? It hurts."

"I know. I'm sorry, Rob…I…"

"The incense? It affects you too, you can't heal me, just like I can't see."

"I'm so sorry, Brat." He gently pulled Rob up and put his brother's head against his shoulder. Galen put his cheek on the top of Rob's head. "Dad and Uncle Bobby'll be here soon. I'm sorry," he said again.

"It's okay, Galen. We're together."

"No matter what, we're together." He let his head rest against Rob's. "I'm sorry Rob, this didn't go quite as planned, but at least I'm here with you, at least we're together." And he let his eyes close.

Chapter Fifteen

"My god," Mike whispered, the words coming out in a sigh of horror. Galen blinked, he'd forgotten the doctor was even there, forgotten he'd been speaking, the past had suddenly been so close. The old scar was twisting, the pain shooting out from the wound almost in anticipation of what it knew was coming. Mike gave him a wild look and walked over towards him, tugging at his shirt. He pulled it up and ran his hand along the old scars on Galen's chest. "You were...they..." Mike swallowed, looking sick. "I always wondered, you know, but I never really believed. My god, Galen, they flayed you."

"Only a little." Galen tried for a laugh, it came out strangled, his heart had started pounding suddenly. He took a deep breath trying to steady himself.

"Galen?" Rob said softly from beside him. Galen looked over, his brother was frowning, his eyes unfocused. Galen knew Rob was "looking" at him. His brother put a hand on his shoulder.

"I'm okay, Rob."

"No, you're not," Rob said, squinting. "Something..." The wound suddenly twisted, deep, driving pain into Galen's chest. He thought he might have cried out. "Galen?" Rob said anxiously.

The voice was back, whispering to him, trying to force his mind away from his control. "Time, nearly time, I have waited long years for this, Keeper. Our time has come," It said. Galen was gasping for air, he could hear Mike shouting, he felt Rhiannon's hand on his. "Very soon we can finish what you began. Very soon I will have my time, you will give me the gift and we will walk together you and I, you will know me."

"No," Galen heard his voice. Rob's hand left his shoulder and the warm presence of his brother was suddenly gone. He felt himself shifted. Someone was holding onto his wrist. Mike's voice was anxious, talking to Rhiannon, she was answering, but the words had ceased to make sense.

"They trapped me, held me, but now...now our time is near. We were so close once and you took that away. Not this time. Soon, soon Keeper you will be mine," It continued.

"No." His own voice again, harsh and grating against his ears.

"Yes, yes, soon. So much to answer for, a long line of pain from you and yours, but you will give me the gift. You denied me once, but you cannot stop it. They made the mistake of keeping you alive and now you are mine...finally mine..." The voice sighed, a sick pleasure in the sound as pain stabbed into Galen, like the blade from so long ago. "Remember this? Yes, you thought you ended it, but..." Laughter filled his mind.

"Drink," Rob's voice overrode the laughter. Galen felt something pressed against his lips. "It's the red bottle." His brother's voice was coming from far away.

"Very far away, you are nearly mine now, that will not save you. Nothing can now. Too late, he is mine, you are mine, and soon I will be back to walk and rule as I once did. We have a small task for tonight, Keeper. Something I need to know."

"No," Galen's heard his voice, it had a finality to it. He tried to steady himself, tried to focus and despite everything, he felt his heart slow a beat.

"Galen? What's going on?" he heard Rob's voice, anxious, demanding an answer.

"Yes, yes, my Keeper," the voice shrieked in his head. Galen remembered the sound.

"No." Galen wasn't sure he had spoken aloud. "Rob," he said to his brother, again unsure. His heart slowed. "Rob, something...." The voice was screaming.

"Not yet. This doesn't happen now." Rob's voice had an edge of steel to it.

"Rob... It wants something," Galen whispered, wondering if anyone heard him. Another beat slower, he could feel the world slipping away, it felt familiar.

"Yes, perfect, my Keeper." The voice had the edge of laughter in it.

"How if I'm dead?" Galen asked the voice.

"Your death is later, my Keeper, this is a test," the voice said.

"What's happening?" Mike was shouting.

"He's dying," Rob snapped. "No, Galen, I won't let you."

"Dying? How?"

"I don't know. Galen are you doing this?"

"Doing what?" Mike shouted.

"Galen, no, please no, honey." That was Rhiannon.

"Rob," the word sighed out of him as the world began to fade. "Don't..." The laughter began to increase in volume. Another beat slower. Mike and Rhiannon's voices faded to murmurs.

"No, Galen." Oddly, Rob's voice seemed clearer. There was warmth on the old wound, flowing out, pushing the pain away. The voice was suddenly confused, the laughter fading to a hush. Part of the pain flowed away, outwards. "Galen?" Rob's voice overrode the pain, the laughter, the angry screams of the voice. There was a pleased, almost triumphant, undercurrent in the voice, but It was angry that it was being slowly silenced. Galen tried to focus.

"No, Galen, not now, not this time," Rob's voice played in his

head. *"I won't let it happen."*

"It wants this, Rob."

"It doesn't get your death. Not tonight, Galen," Rob's voice was hard, determined.

Galen felt the thing's hissing voice pulled away from him. *"No, Rob, what are you doing?"* Galen's heart wouldn't slow and further, something was gently blocking it, holding him there. *"Rob, Dad and Bobby made a mistake…"*

"Yes, they did," his brother answered, the words loud in his mind. *"But it's not the mistake you think."*

"It wants this, whatever you're doing. Stop, please, Rob."

"Trust me." The warmth flowed beyond the old wound, numbing it. Galen recognized the affects of his spell, but something else was working on it as well. The voice had been pulled away, like a splinter pulled from a wound. He could still sense the edge of it somewhere, but it was away from him. *"Trust me."* Galen took a deep breath. He struggled against the warmth, against the light, trying to block it like he had his father. *"Please, Galen, trust me."*

Galen let go, stopped trying to fight it and let the warmth fill him. The world slowly came back, he was aware of the couch under him. The room was warm, the fan must have come on, there was a soft breeze against his face. He could feel Rob's hand where it rested over the old wound. Warmth was still flowing from that touch, the darkness and cold had seeped into his brother a little. "Rob?"

"It's okay, Galen." His brother's voice was soft. "Are you back?"

Galen opened his eyes and met Rob's slate-blue ones. "How?" He tried to sit up, Rob held him down with gentle hands. "How?"

"How what?" Mike said, his voice snappish. Galen heard

profound relief under his friend's sharp tone.

"How did you...?"

"You showed me." Rob's voice was quiet.

"I...?" Galen sighed. "It wanted that, Rob. It was testing you."

"I know."

"You know?" Galen raised his eyebrows. "What?"

"Galen, it's part of it, part of..."

"No." He shook his head.

"You want to tell me what just happened? Maybe let me in on what the hell's going on?" Mike's voice was climbing in volume. "Maybe mention that whole dying thing to me?"

"No," Galen said.

"Yes," his brother said at the same time. "They're there."

"What?" Rhiannon asked, laying a hand on Galen.

"The answers we were looking for, they're here, in what happened at the end. Galen, you need to tell me."

"Rob..."

"Then I'll tell you."

PAST

TEN YEAR BEFORE

Day Seven - Galen

Galen was leaning against the wall in the small room. Smoke from the brazier had filled the room, making it hazy, making him hazy. "I wonder what, exactly, is in there? Something's blocking our Gift. Was it designed with Keepers in mind? And if it was, what does that mean?" Galen said quietly, more to himself than his brother. Rob shifted slightly in his arms, moaning. "It's okay Rob. I'm here."

"I know," Rob answered him. "Sorry."

"Sorry? Why?"

"That you have to be here because of me."

"Nothing to be sorry for, Rob." Galen sighed. "Dad and Uncle Bobby'll be here soon."

"Think they'll make it in time?" Rob's voice seemed older somehow, accepting of what was happening.

"Yeah." Galen shifted. He tried to focus a little of the healing into Rob, into himself, but the Gift was completely gone. The grayness he had sensed in his father and uncle was there where the light had been.

"We won't get a chance to be Keepers together will we?"

"We will, Rob," Galen said.

"I have a funny feeling we won't, Galen." His brother sighed, a sad sound. "I need to tell you something Galen, something about…"

Before his brother could finish, the door opened. Two men came in, pulled Rob out of his arms and dragged Galen out of the room, out of the building. There was an open space, it looked like it had once been a garden. They pushed him up onto a flat stone.

They pulled his hands down, he felt something wrapped around his wrists, then he was tied down, essentially immobile. There was pain, brief, intense, sharp, then something warm flowed across his chest, down onto the flat stone.

The chanting was getting louder. Galen heard someone approaching him. A cold draft blew over him. He recognized the smell of the thing. The bearded man stood over him and smiled. "Let us get to know your heart, She and I, so we can prepare for the last." He said something in a language Galen didn't recognize. Galen could see the thing's eyes behind the man's.

The man lifted a hand, the chanting got even louder. Galen could feel the cold of the thing. The man put his hand against Galen's chest, Galen ground his teeth together against the wave of pain. It felt like the hand was going into his chest, through flesh and bone. "Keeper," the man whispered. "Yes, Keeper," his voice was filled with pleasure. Galen desperately tried to still the scream rising in his chest. He didn't want to give them the satisfaction. The hand closed. It turned in his chest. And he heard himself. The scream was torn from his throat, involuntary, necessary. The hand withdrew.

Galen felt his body sag in relief. He was untied and half carried-half dragged back to the room where his brother was. They closed the door as they left, he heard a lock turn.

He was close enough to where his brother lay to touch him. He put his hand on Rob's shoulder. "I need to rest, just for a minute, Rob. Then I'll figure out how to get us out of here," he said, his voice was rough, his throat hurt. "Just give me a minute."

"Galen?" Rob shifted until he was resting against Galen, their shoulders touching. "You're bleeding."

"Just a little, not much," he said gently. "I think it's near the finish, Rob, we have to get out." He closed his eyes and let the incense fill him for a minute. He knew it would help take the pain away. He let himself drift a tiny bit. "I just need to rest long enough to get something back," Galen said.

"I wish I could heal you, Galen," Rob said quietly. "I want to talk about that."

"About what, Brat?" Galen was not quite aware, drifting on the cloud of incense.

"Our Gifts."

"What about them?"

"I... The incense is making me sleepy."

"Me, too, Rob. Rest, we'll need everything we have in a little while."

"Okay." Rob reached over and put his hand on Galen's arm.

They came back sooner than Galen had expected, it felt like

mere minutes. He raised his head and tried push himself upright. It didn't work. He watched as they picked his brother up and took him out of the room.

"No," Galen said as they closed the door. He tried harder, he'd made it clear to his elbows when they came back in. They grabbed him and dragged him out of the room. He was carried out into the open space again.

Rob was already there, he'd been placed on a flat stone, Galen assumed it was the same one he'd been on before. He could see the stain of his own blood on the stone. He realized there were other people in the garden, too. Galen knew this was it, the final ritual, he hoped the elder Keepers were close. The bearded man approached Rob. Galen could hear his brother whimper, reacting to the thing. The man was saying something in the strange language, the others around the garden were chanting.

"Rob! Hang on!" he called out, hoping to break the ritual. One of the men hit him in the side. He tried to stay lax in their grip, hoping they'd let their guard down for a minute.

The bearded man stood over Rob. He held his hands out and then placed them on his brother. Rob reacted to the touch, he was straining against the bonds that held him as his body instinctively pulled from the pain. Then he screamed. There was blood where the man's hands touched Rob's chest, Galen could see the bright stain growing on his brother's shirt.

"Wait," the man said, the thing's voice loud in the startled cry. The bearded man turned from Rob and walked to Galen. The man stopped in front of him and the thing's eyes searched Galen's.

"I'm going to kill you. It'll probably be the last thing I do," Galen said softly, sure of that now, knowing what it meant. "But I am going to kill you."

The man—the thing—laughed. "I doubt that. Nothing can

kill me soon, if what I felt was correct."

He reached out and touched Galen, a hand on his head, a hand on his chest over his heart. The thing was laughing now, Its pleasure apparent in the laugh. Galen fought the touch, fought to stay conscious. He could feel the hand in his chest, he could feel blood from the touch, it felt like his life was flowing away. Galen was open, vulnerable for an instant and the thing violated his mind. He screamed at the intrusion. The thing thrust into his consciousness and then It stopped. Galen heard the man sigh, ecstatic.

"Emrys," the man said. "I was right, what I felt in the boy. You are Emrys." The thing turned away, back towards Rob. The pain retreated a little. The man had Its hands on his brother again.

Rob reacted to that touch, Galen acted in that moment.

He pulled away from the men holding him and dove towards the stone where Rob was lying. Galen pushed the thing's hands away. He could sense movement behind him, but he didn't care. He was focused on his brother. Galen tore at the bonds, got one, then the other loose. The thing's hands were on Galen's back, reaching in. Galen heard himself screaming. He pulled on his brother and managed to roll him off the stone.

The man—the thing—shrieked "No!" in Its voice, in the man's voice.

Galen stood over Rob, blocking the thing, the others who were there, from his brother. The bearded man was angry, the thing inside the man was furious, Galen could see that in the thing's eyes looking at him from the man's face.

"Not this time, Emrys," the thing said, hatred in Its voice. It was reaching for him. It was there now, the thing, more and more in the man. Galen could smell It, feel the cold reaching out to him. He could see It in the eyes and hear It in the voice. The man was disappearing into the thing.

It reached out and touched his face, Galen clenched his teeth, still trying to block It from his brother. The other people in the clearing were standing back, afraid of the thing that stood in their midst. It slid Its hand down to his throat. He heard Rob whimper.

"I'm going to kill you," Galen whispered to the thing.

"You're already dead," It said.

"Then there's nothing to lose."

The thing tightened Its grip, slowly, almost gently, searing through skin. Galen took a deep breath.

"Galen!" His father's voice carried into the garden.

"Here!" From the way his father's voice echoed, Galen knew they were still a ways off.

"We're coming!"

The thing pulled Its hand away. "No, they won't stop the ritual."

"Just did," Galen said, trying to keep the dark edges away, the darkness reaching for him.

"No! There are other ways, Emrys, Keeper. I won't lose, not this time." It turned from him and ran into the building. Galen followed. He could hear Its breathing as he moved down the hallway. It was in the room where he and Rob had been held. He hesitated for half a second, wondering what it wanted in that room. Galen spotted an old farm tool on the wall. He grabbed it. When he entered the room, the thing stood and came at him. Galen felt something push against him, pressure in his chest. "I don't have time for that right now," he said. It was bad, he knew it was bad.

The thing was shrieking at him, the man's voice blending with the thing's. It reached out and twisted whatever was there in Galen's chest, smiling as he did it.

Galen took a deep breath and raised the scythe. He struck out, using the weight of the tool to help his swing. The thing, the man, collapsed screaming, clutching what was left of a leg. Galen struck again. It screamed at him, wordlessly. Then, "This is not over," It said quietly, trying to rise, falling back and reaching for him again. It touched his ankle, Galen dropped to his knees and struggled back up. "This is not over."

Galen used the scythe to shove some oily rags over to the thing, where It was writhing on the floor. "Yeah?" He tipped the brazier over, the rags caught. The thing screamed. "How about if you burn? Is it over then?" He watched the flickering flames for a minute, until the thing—the man—was dead, and the room was filled with the stench of burning flesh.

Galen could feel the blade in his chest, becoming more aware of it as he staggered down the hallway, out of the burning building. The others in the garden were standing by Rob. "Get away from him!" Galen lurched towards them "Get away." He made it to Rob. They stood back unsure of him.

Broken-nose guy started coming towards him. "You stopped it, I can't let you..." The man stopped suddenly, a look of surprise on his face, then he fell forward, sliding off Bobby's sword.

Galen was falling, finally.

His father caught him. "Galen?"

"Took you long enough, Dad," he said, feeling his father's arms around him, holding him. "Rob?"

"He's here," Bobby's voice answered. "Oh gods."

"What?" his father said.

"I...my gods," Bobby said again. "Parry..." Bobby's voice was anguished.

"Is Rob okay?" Galen asked, relaxing. His head dropped against his father's chest. He could hear Parry's heartbeat, he tried to focus on it, tried to draw a little of the healing from his father. "Dad?"

"Bobby?" His father shifted, Galen cried out in pain. "Can you move him?"

"Yeah, Parry, sure." Galen could hear Bobby moving, he heard Rob whimper.

"Don't hurt him," Galen said, it was getting hard to speak. "Is he okay?" Galen was aware of his brother the instant they laid Rob beside him. He reached a hand out, and put it on his brother's chest. Felt the heartbeat, felt the chest rise with a breath. "He's alive," he whispered, then he felt something that terrified him. "No, Rob. Heal him, Dad," Galen said desperately, afraid of what he had felt in his brother.

"Galen, hang on." A hand brushed whatever was in his chest. "We have to pull it out. Galen? You still there?" his father asked.

"Yeah, Dad, sorry though, not much longer I think." He let the darkness in a little.

"Go ahead, Bobby," Parry said. There was a tug against his chest and then the blade was torn from him, the passage pulling at him like the thing's claws digging through his chest. "Dad, no, you promised," Galen said as he felt the warmth from his father's hands beginning to heal the wounds on his body.

"Rob is…" There were tears in Parry's voice. "You did good, Galen."

"Thanks, Dad." The darkness crept in further. He was trying to hang on. His hand was lying on his brother, he tried to let the light flow into Rob.

"No, Galen!" His father's voice was desperate.

"Dad? What's wrong?" Galen struggled against the healing, trying to block his father.

"Not this time, Galen," his father said sternly. "Not now." And suddenly, like a light being turned off, the world was gone.

Chapter Sixteen

"He'd never done that before. I didn't know he could," Galen said, looking at Rob.

"Dad didn't want you to try and heal me, Galen. He knew."

"Knew? Rob?" He tried to sit up again, Rob's hand held him in place. "I'm okay," he grumbled.

"Are we going to cover the 'you know I can tell you're not' thing again?" Rob said with an sardonic smile.

"Of course he's not," Mike growled. While Galen had been speaking the doctor had produced a stethoscope and was pressing it on Galen's chest. Galen tried to bat it away. "Stop that," Mike said, smacking his hand.

"Rob?" Galen asked.

"You know what I see."

"What?" Mike snapped.

"Rob's like Bobby, Mike," Galen said patiently, watching his brother.

Mike peered over at Rob. "Like Bobby?" He smiled suddenly. "Tell me then."

Rob swallowed and looked at Galen, asking permission. "Maybe it will get him off our back," Galen said, frowning at Mike.

"I'm your doctor."

"Fine. Go ahead, Rob."

"He has a spot," Rob said.

"A spot?" Mike asked, peering at Galen.

"Where the blade went in and where…It's the old wound," Rob continued. Mike tugged at Galen's shirt again, pulling it up to reveal the old scar. Galen was watching their faces, they both turned paper-white at the same time. "My gods, Galen," Rob breathed. Mike opened his mouth and closed it again, swallowing convulsively.

"Rob?"

"It's...I..."

"What the hell is that?" Mike said, looking from Galen to Rob.

Galen could feel something wet on his chest, the air from the fan had cooled it enough for him to notice. "Am I bleeding?" he asked curiously. Mike swallowed again and then bolted for the bathroom. "Something I said?" Galen asked with a smile, trying to ease the lines of worry on his brother's face, trying to stop the near panic he could sense flowing off of Rob in huge waves. Rhiannon got up and walked to the hall closet, coming back with a towel. She carefully folded it and laid it on Galen's chest. "I am bleeding?" Galen met Rob's eyes.

"Black blood," Mike said, coming out of the bathroom. "You're bleeding black blood and..." He stopped himself as he pulled a cup from the cabinet.

"They can see me now, where I rest near your heart. Thanks to what your brother did, they can see me a little now," the voice was back, whispering to him again.

"What Rob did?" Galen addressed the voice aloud, Rob looked at him.

"What?" Mike said, coming back to look at Galen again.

"Galen?" Rob put his hand on top the towel. Warmth flowed out from the touch, silencing the voice. "Is it talking to you?"

"It was," Galen said. "How?"

"How what?" Mike was annoyed.

"He...it's like the healing, feels a little different, but he shouldn't be able to do that at all," Galen said, looking from the doctor to his brother.

"He put you out earlier," Mike said.

"Yeah, all Keepers can do that, like we can all..." Galen stopped himself as he saw a spasm of pain cross his brother's face. "But this is different. Rob?"

"I...uh..." Rob smiled sadly. "It happened then, I think. Something snapped in me during the ritual. Then later at the hospital, before..." He paused. "I heard Dad and Bobby talking, about the Legacy and about us. And I heard..."

"What?" Galen said gently.

"It was in me, then. That's why Dad wouldn't let you heal me, that's why he couldn't heal me."

"Parry could heal anybody," Mike said defensively. "You're both here, he must have healed you."

"No. Dad healed Galen, there was no hope for me. It had..."

"What?" Mike said.

"It had invaded me during the ritual. It was in me, I had a wound a lot like the one Galen has now, only the thing had done it with its hands. It wouldn't let Dad heal me. It wanted me to die..."

PAST

TEN YEARS BEFORE

Day Nine - Rob

The antiseptic smell of a hospital or doctor's office crept into his awareness. There was a soft hissing sound that seemed to be connected to the gentle breeze against his nostrils. Something was beeping, an irregular beat. Sometimes when the beep paused too long, Rob would feel a spasm of pain and something that sounded like a pleased sigh in his head.

"I can't heal him, Bobby," his father's voice drifted over to him.

"Can't?"

"There's something blocking me. When I put my hands down, it pushes me away."

"It's what I saw? After the ritual?"

"I think so, I...gods, Bobby, what do we do?"

"Nothing, they can do nothing," a voice suddenly hissed in Rob's head. He recognized it—the thing from the clearing, from the ritual in the garden, was speaking to him. "You are mine now, and soon, soon, we will finish what was once begun, child, Emrys. They did well to choose you, though they didn't know, couldn't begin to understand what this means to me," the voice said.

"I don't know, Parry. Do you think...? What we suspected? Is it...our boys? Your sons?"

"The Legacy?" his father whispered.

"Could it be? After so long?" the thing's voice purred.

"Dad?" Rob said, the word came out as a small whimper. "Dad?" he tried again.

"Here," his father said gently. Rob felt his father's hand on his forehead. "Can you open your eyes?"

Rob fought the glue that was holding his eyelids closed. He managed to get them open, the light was blindingly bright, he closed them again, aware of tears trickling down his cheeks. Taking a deep breath, he tried again, blinking away the involuntary tears. "Where's Galen?"

"Yes, where is the other?" the thing said.

"He's asleep right now, Rob."

"Dad?" Rob felt panic twist in his chest, the thing laughed at him, Its voice hissing against his heart.

"He's here, look." Parry shifted so Rob could see the other

bed in the room. His brother was curled on his side, facing Rob, his eyes closed, his face peaceful. Rob could see stripes where flesh and skin had been removed, and the remains of a hole in his chest where a blade had been. The ghost hilt of the blade was still in his brother's chest. He could also see the shining marks where the wounds had been carefully healed.

"He's okay?" Rob asked, knowing the answer, but wanting to hear it anyway.

"Not for long," the voice hissed.

"Your brother'll be fine, Rob. He should be awake soon." Parry smiled at him. "If you can sleep a little more, maybe he'll be awake next time you are."

"Okay, Dad," Rob said. His uncle came up on the other side of the bed. "Hi, Uncle Bobby."

"Hi yourself," his uncle said gently. Rob smiled.

"Just relax, Rob," his father said. Parry put his hand back on Rob's forehead and put his other down on his chest. Rob saw the light flowing to his father's hands. He also saw it stop before it could enter his body.

"No, he doesn't get to heal you. No, my Emrys child, you are mine," the voice laughed.

Rob saw his uncle move a little and he heard something beside him beep. Warmth flowed into him, not from his father's hands, but up his arm. *Drugs, they gave me something to let me sleep. Dad wants me to think it's him so I won't be frightened.* He started to reach out for his brother, but a pleased sigh from the thing inside him stopped him. "No, you don't get Galen. No," he told the thing in his head.

"Not yet, but soon," it hissed at him.

"Never." Rob drifted into sleep.

A warm hand was resting on his the next time he drifted to the surface. He'd been having nightmares, he'd known he cried out, and he was sure he heard his brother answer. Rob opened his eyes and looked over. Galen was sitting in the chair beside the bed. "Galen?"

His brother turned from watching the hall. There was a frown on his face, but it smoothed into a smile. "Rob. How do you feel?"

"Tell him, tell him how you feel. Tell him about me, tell him about this," the voice laughed. Pain suddenly ground into his chest. Someone screamed.

"Rob, it's okay." He felt his brother's other hand on his chest. Warmth flowed up against his head and his body. "No," Galen said. There was something that felt like a push, almost like Galen had shoved him, then warmth flowed into him.

"Galen?" He wasn't sure if he said it out loud or not.

"It's okay," his brother answered, Galen's voice clear in his mind.

"You can't heal him," the thing hissed. "The child is mine, Emrys."

"No," Galen said firmly.

"Wait, wait…" the thing was pleased. "It can't be. Not just Emrys, but…"

Rob felt a shift in himself, pain was flowing out of him, he somehow knew it was flowing into his brother. "No, Galen."

"Let me, Rob, please."

"Galen!" Rob heard his father shout, his brother was wrenched away from him. Rob opened his eyes. Galen was struggling against Parry, trying to get back to Rob. "Galen, no."

"Let me go, Dad," Galen's voice was hard, sharp as a blade. Rob saw a flash, it looked almost like the healing light from his brother and then his father staggered a little.

"Galen?" Parry's voice was shocked.

"Parry?" Bobby almost shouted.

232

"Stop him, don't let him..." Another flash of light and Parry dropped to the floor. Before Galen could get back to Rob, Bobby blocked him.

"Sorry, no, Galen, you can't." Before Galen could react Bobby struck out, the punch sending Galen down.

* * * * *

"They stopped me, I'm sorry, Rob," Galen said, looking at his brother. He could see Mike out of the corner of his eye. The doctor was shaking his head, a stunned expression on his face.

"They were right, Galen," Rob said.

"Rob?"

"They were right. They should have put you in restraints and sedated you until I was dead." Rob stood and strode across the room. He stayed with his back to Galen, facing the wall.

"Rob?" Galen repeated. He pushed himself up into a sitting position. The room spun for a minute. Rhiannon put a steadying hand on his elbow. With a deep breath Galen managed to get onto his feet. Black spots danced before his eyes as the maniacal laughter of It increased in volume.

"What's going on?" Mike said, putting a hand on Galen's chest. "You shouldn't be up."

"It's okay, Mike."

"No. Nope. No way," the doctor said, trying to push Galen back on the couch.

"I had to, Rob..." Galen looked at his brother. Rob still refused to turn around.

"Had to?" Mike demanded. "Had to what?"

"This has something to do with what's going on now, doesn't it?" Rhiannon asked.

"Rob." Galen was still focused on his brother.

"You should have let me die," Rob grated out.

"I heard Dad and Uncle Bobby…"

"I did too." Rob turned back to him. "I did too, Galen. They thought…I think they suspected…If they'd let me die…"

"They…We…Oh, gods…" Galen took a deep breath as the scar twisted. He could feel the cold black liquid oozing slowly down his chest. "If I hadn't…We both would…"

"You don't know that, Galen." Rob's voice was harsh.

"I do, Rob."

"Dad and Uncle Bobby…"

"It wasn't in them, Rob, you know the truth, you have to," Galen was pleading, begging his brother to forgive him.

"Galen?" Rob said with a frown on his face. He was moving towards Galen when the room suddenly twisted around Galen, wrenching him sideways and down. Rob caught him and eased him onto the couch.

"It told me, Rob."

"Galen…"

"When I…It told me, it's why…" Galen said.

"Why what?" Mike's shout caused them both to turn towards the doctor.

"I had to, Rob. Please…It told me, and once I knew, I had to…"

"Galen, I'm going to kill you in a minute," Mike growled.

"That's what we're talking about, Mike," Rob said, his voice grim.

"What?" Mike was surprised.

"It killed him," Rob said, meeting Galen's eyes.

"No, Rob, it didn't kill me. I had to kill it."

PAST

TEN YEARS BEFORE

Day Nine - Galen

"What happened?" Bobby's voice drifted into Galen's awareness.

"I'm not sure, Bobby, I think he somehow used the healing," Parry's voice was shaky.

"Is it true, then?" Bobby said, awe and fear in his voice. "Our boys. Parry…"

"I know. How do we tell Galen?"

"Parry," Bobby paused.

"What is it?" When Bobby didn't answer, Galen heard his father's voice take on a desperate note. "What?"

"When Rob dies, Parry, we're going to lose Galen."

"What? No, they haven't gone through the Ritual of Swords, they've hardly trained together, they aren't bonded yet."

"No they're not…but these boys…I don't think it matters." Bobby paused. "And the healer…Galen…You know."

"Yes." His father's voice was strained.

"The thing…if it's what…if this is the Legacy, Parry, Galen will die."

"Both of them? No, Bobby, no."

"It needs the healer, too. If it were the other way around we might be able to protect Rob, but…Galen's tied to him too closely already, and it would come close for Rob. I…Gods, Parry." Bobby's voice cracked. "If you could heal Rob…"

"I can't, Bobby."

"I know, it almost killed you."

"I have no idea how Galen managed even what he did." Parry sighed. "How do we kill it?"

"The vessel has to die, but if this is the Legacy, when Rob

dies and Galen…It Becomes."

"There's nothing we can do?" Parry said, anguished.

"No, it's in both of them, Parry. That blade—it left a trace in Galen, and as long as it's in both of them, there's nothing we can do. Rob dies, Galen dies."

Galen opened his eyes. His father and uncle were standing by Rob's bed. Bobby had his arm around Parry's shoulders. "Dad?"

They turned to face him, Parry brushing tears off his face. "Galen."

"How's Rob?" Galen sat up. "Did I help?"

Parry nodded. "He's sleeping, Galen. You did help."

"Thank the gods," Galen closed his eyes for a minute. "I'll do a little more…"

"No, absolutely not," Bobby said.

"Or you'll hit me again? Nice left, by the way," Galen said, looking at his uncle.

"Sorry about that." Bobby smiled sheepishly. "I wasn't sure grabbing you was a good idea."

"Probably not," Galen said, smiling back. "Sorry, Dad. I'm not sure what happened, I just needed to get to Rob."

"I know." Parry laid his hand on Galen's arm.

"I'm okay, Dad, except for the black eye."

"I just wanted to be sure, you know that," his father said, patting his arm.

"I know, Dad." Galen took a deep breath and looked at them. "Rob's dying."

"No." They both shook their heads.

"I felt it. I can feel it. His heart, it's not working right. I felt drugs, too, not your healing."

"I can't, Galen."

"What?"

"The thing won't let me, it blocks me."

"I..." Galen stopped. "It tried to stop me, but I pushed through it, why couldn't you do that?" Galen looked at his father, Parry was frowning at him.

"It hurt Parry," Bobby said. "When he tried to force it. I thought..." Bobby swallowed. "He's telling the truth."

"Dad?"

"It's true, Galen. I'm sorry. I...You have to..." Parry broke off. "Galen..."

"Parry?"

"I..." Parry turned and strode out of the room.

"Galen?" Bobby looked at him.

"We'll be okay," Galen said gently. Bobby squeezed his arm and followed Parry out of the room. Galen waited for a count of ten before slipping out of bed. He walked over to Rob's bed and laid his hand on his brother's head. Pain, the sluggish metallic feeling of drugs and a deep darkness flowed up the touch.

Galen rubbed his hands together, focusing the light, breathing deeply. He put his hands back on his brother and pulled the light into his hands. He met the hard wall of darkness.

"No, no healing, nothing. No, not this time, Emrys. He dies, then soon you will both be mine," a voice hissed at him.

"No," Galen said. He forced the light against the wall, pushing, he felt the darkness push back. Taking a deep breath, he stabbed through the wall. The healing flowed from his hands, running into his brother's body. Rob moaned. "It's okay, Rob, it's me," Galen said softly. He guided the light, letting the healing fill his brother until he came to the ruin of Rob's heart.

"You can't heal this, Emrys Keeper. He's still mine. When he dies, when you die, I can walk again," the voice said.

"I can and I will," Galen said, focusing on Rob's heart. Pain lashed up the contact, slamming into his body, making the scar on his chest where the thing had stabbed him twist. It recognized Itself there and laughed, the sound filling Galen's head.

"Yes, yes, soon. I am with you, with him. Soon," It hissed. Galen ground his teeth together and tried to force his way past the black spot. "No!" It said. The healing suddenly stopped, a black spot in Rob's heart pushing the light away. Galen tried to start the light again, aware of blood dripping from his nose.

"You can't stop me," he told the hissing voice.

"Galen!" his father's shout surprised him. Parry grabbed him an instant later.

"No, Dad," he wasn't sure if he said or thought it.

"Galen, no."

"Yes," Galen said firmly. With a deep breath, he used the contact with his father to pull the healing light from Parry. He heard his father's gasp, felt the convulsive grasp on his arm. Somehow he knew his father couldn't pull away.

Galen forced himself back to Rob's heart, back to the black spot hissing in his brother's chest. Galen saw It, twisting and turning in Rob's heart, waiting like a serpent to strike with the last of Its poison. He grabbed It, the thing struggled with him as he tore It out of Rob's heart, pulled It up, out of his brother and into his own body. It was screaming as It flowed into him, running up his arms, Galen forced It into the scar Its knife had left. He held It there as he guided the last of the healing through Rob.

"Break the contact, break it," Parry said desperately.

"Parry?"

"Do it now, Bobby."

"No!" Galen shouted as Bobby pulled him away from Rob.

"Let go, Galen, let go. I can help your brother now, let go." Galen could feel his father's arms around him as he was guided back to bed. "Why?" Parry said sadly.

"Had to, Dad," Galen said opening his eyes. The world was washed in red. *Blood vessels broke maybe?*

"Galen..."

"I heard you, this is the only way. I die, It dies, Rob—you can help Rob. He'll make it."

"Galen, let me heal you," Parry said, rubbing his hands together.

"No, Dad, It has to die before It can walk. Before It can finish the sacrifice. This is the only way."

"Die, Galen, but let me...You just have to die for a moment..." Parry said eagerly.

"Yes, yes, good plan," It whispered. "Die, sacrifice yourself and then come back. Perfect. Let that happen." It was laughing with joy.

"No, that won't work, trust me. It won't work. You have to keep Rob alive. If he dies..."

"If he dies what you did means nothing. No, it means you helped me, made it easier." Laughter filled his head.

"It's not in Rob anymore, is it, Bobby?"

"No, Galen," his uncle said sadly. "It's not there at all, there's just a little scar left."

"Good," Galen sighed.

"It's in you, Galen," Bobby said. "Parry..."

"I know, I was there." Parry shook his head.

"Promise me, Dad. Promise you'll do..."

Parry laid a gentle hand on Galen's head. "Of course, you don't have to ask. We'll do everything we can, we'll send him back to his family. He'll be safe there. We can keep an eye on him, but stay away, that way if it's still out there...He'll be safe."

"Thank you, Dad, sorry." Pain ground into the scar. "Can you...? If I help?"

"Sleep?" Parry put his hand on Galen's chest. He saw the

spasm of pain cross his father's face as his hand brushed the scar. The sound of a heartbeat filled Galen. He knew it wasn't his. As he'd healed Rob, his heart had absorbed the damage. Sleep claimed him.

The soft sound of someone crying woke Galen. "Rob?" he said. That's what he thought he'd said, all he heard was a groan that sounded like an "r". *That won't work.* "Rob?" he tried again.

"Galen?" Rob said with a sniff. "Galen?"

"Are you okay?"

"Galen?"

"Are you okay, Rob?"

"He won't be, soon, soon, soon," the voice whispered to him. Pain ground into his chest, twisting the scar, making his heart beat frantically. He heard the change in the heart monitor.

"No," Galen told the voice. "Rob?"

Galen heard the springs on the other bed squeak, a moment later Rob's hand settled on his arm. "Galen? Did you say something?"

"He will be mine again, you are mine. We will walk together you and I," the voice said.

"No," Galen said again.

"No? You didn't say anything?"

Galen opened his eyes, blinking against the brightness of the light. Rob was standing beside the bed, tear streaks on his face. "Rob? Are you okay?"

"Galen," Rob squeezed his hand.

"Are you okay?" Galen asked, desperation in his voice.

"I guess," Rob scrubbed tears off his face. "I feel better. But Galen…"

"What is it?"

"You're dying."

"Rob," Galen began.

Rob sat on the edge of the bed. "Don't lie to me, Galen. I can see it. I know what happened. I can see your heart, I can see the handle of the blade, it's still in you and now that thing—It was in me—It's in you now." He looked at Galen, his eyes mature in his still youthful face. "I told you we'd never be Keepers together."

"I'm sorry."

"I knew, Galen, I just never thought...I thought it would be me." The maturity was still there, but tears began streaming down his face. "Galen..."

"Come here, Brat," he said gently, holding his arm out to his brother. Rob leaned forward, into the embrace, then collapsed against him, sobbing. The thing in his chest purred with pleasure and tried to push beyond where Galen was holding It. He kept It there, knowing that his time was fast running out. "You can't have Rob," he told It silently.

"No!" It screamed back. "No, not when I am so close."

"Yes," Galen told It. He held Rob gently as his brother sobbed against him. Tears had worked free from Galen's eyes and were running down his cheeks. A gentle pressure on his hand, where it rested on Rob's back, marked the return of his father and uncle. The four of them were silent except for the sound of Rob's sobs. "We're going to die soon," Galen told it.

"No!" It lashed out at Galen, pain exploded through his body. He cried out, fighting the thing as It tried to escape the prison in Galen's chest. The pain was reaching the unbearable point when it diminished a bit, just enough for Galen to open his eyes and focus on his family.

"I need to go," he said to Rob. His brother's hand was resting on his chest.

"I know," Rob said, tears running down his cheeks.

"Dad? Uncle Bobby?" Galen looked at them. They walked

to the other side of the bed. Parry put his hand on Galen's head, Bobby's hand rested on his shoulder. "I...." He stopped for a minute, then started again, falling back on the formal ritual. "I have served faithfully, I have walked the path chosen for me, I ask for release, for rest, until I can serve again."

Parry shifted his hand to Galen's chest. "I don't know..."

"I'll help," Galen said, forcing the words out as the thing writhed and screamed in his chest.

"In living we serve..." his father began.

"No," Rob said suddenly.

"What?" Bobby said.

"It's my right, as his brother, as the Keeper that served with him."

"Rob, no," Parry said gently.

Galen met his brother's eyes and saw a wisdom beyond his age. Rob looked back, defiant, pleading. "Rob?"

"We didn't live long together as Keepers, Galen..."

"No, Rob," Bobby said quietly.

"Yes," Galen said, looking at his father and uncle. "It's his right, his place, Dad. He..." Galen couldn't go on, the thing was screaming, pushing against the bonds he was holding it in. "Please." His father nodded and moved his hand away.

"In living we serve, in dying we serve, the line continues, we are joined with our present and our past." Rob spoke the formal words, Galen felt his brother's gentle touch against his heart, slowing it. Rob grabbed his hand and held it tightly, to the point of pain, as Galen focused and helped his brother stop his heart. He could hear his father and uncle reciting the formal words as the world began to slide away. "You have served the world, now rest until you are called again."

"No, no, no," the thing was screaming, fighting him.

"Yes," he told It. "Yes. We die now."

He could feel himself dying, he could feel It dying with him. Galen's felt his heart stop. He was aware for another moment, aware of his brother's hand on his, aware of his father and uncle, then he let himself go—dropping gently down into a glimmering black pool surrounded by white light and a soft song.

* * * * *

He could still hear the song playing softly in his ears as he focused on the present again. Mike's face was white, Rhiannon was crying softly, Rob was sitting beside him, his hand resting on Galen's arm.

"You died?" Mike said.

"Yeah," Galen said softly.

"You think that's the kind of thing your doctor should know?"

"Dad healed me," Galen said, hearing the bitterness in his voice. "He wasn't supposed to, if he'd left me dead, Rob would be safe. The *world* would be safe and he and Bobby would still be alive." Galen sighed.

"Too bad," It whispered against his heart. "Too bad he didn't leave you dead, my Emrys Keeper."

"It's talking to you," Rob said quietly.

"Yeah."

"What?" Rhiannon asked. "What do you mean?"

"It infected him again," Rob said, looking at her. "While we were at the hospital."

"Infected?" It was offended. "No, no, returned to my rightful place. We will be great, you and I, when we Become, when we walk this world together."

"No." Galen focused inward, trying to stop the pain, trying to still the voice.

243

"Drink, Galen."

Galen felt the bottle pressed against his lips, he sipped blindly, wondering when he closed his eyes. The thing was fighting against his spell, but he knew It was losing the battle, It was screaming defiance, but the voice was getting quieter. "Rob?"

"Sleep, Galen, let your spell work, I'll entertain our guests," Rob's voice was gently ironic.

"Thank you." He opened his eyes and smiled at Rhiannon and Mike. "Sorry, long day."

"He's right, Galen, you need to sleep. You were up a lot of last night," Mike said.

"And the night before that, too," Rhiannon added. "You can't run on no sleep, no matter what you think and no matter how many coffees you get from Becci."

"I don't know if it's the coffee or Becci that perks him up," Rob said with a chuckle.

Galen sighed and closed his eyes, listening to the conversation flow around him as exhaustion, pain and the spell combined and pulled him away to the first dreamless sleep he had known in ten years.

Chapter Seventeen

Sunlight filtering through the curtains woke Galen. He stayed unmoving, enjoying the few moments before he was fully awake, those moments when the bed was perfectly comfortable, exactly the right temperature, the pillow perfectly soft. He also let the dream he'd been having wash over him again—Rob home, and all that went with it. *Odd I had that dream, it felt... maybe because it's my birthday? I miss him more at birthdays.* He shoved the thought away as he stretched a little. The clink of dishes pulled him fully awake.

"Rhiannon?" he said, opening his eyes. He was lying on the couch, the quilt pulled over him.

"I sent her home. She wanted to stay, and really? Getting rid of her can be quite a trick," a soft, sardonic baritone answered him.

Galen sat up and looked into the kitchen, blinking away the tears that were suddenly in his eyes. "Rob?"

"Are you okay?" his brother asked, frowning in concern.

"I...uh..."

"Galen? What's wrong?" Rob looked at him, his eyes unfocused.

"I... Sorry." He pushed himself up, swaying. "I need to take a shower before we open the shop," he said quickly, trying to hide the sudden emotion.

"What?" his brother said. "Galen? Lying doesn't work."

"It's stupid," he said, turning towards his room.

"Galen?" The soft question wouldn't let him walk away.

"It's stupid, Rob." He cleared his throat as his voice hung up on the name. "I thought it was a dream."

"A dream?" Rob frowned, then his face smoothed out as comprehension lit his eyes. "Nope, not getting rid of me that easy," he said with a grin. "I don't think you should work today."

"I have to open up."

"You can barely stand."

"People expect the store open."

"And I doubt you could heal anyone today," Rob continued, undaunted.

"The shop needs to be open, Rob," he said, grabbing the wall as the room flipped over.

Rob looked at him for a long moment. "Fine, I'll do the heavy lifting and the running. You just tell me what to say. About time I started learning anyway," he said easily. "Go take your shower."

Galen grabbed some clean clothes and headed into the bathroom, turning the shower on and letting the steam heat the small room. Stepping into the shower, he let the warm water run over his shoulders, easing the knot of tension tied at the base of his neck. He glanced down at this chest, the scar had altered. It was black and pulsing, like something breathing or the beat of a heart in the center of the scar. It ached, right at the edge of a throbbing pain, but it had diminished from the night before. The voice was quiet, even the soft whisper gone for the moment.

"Hey, you drown?" Rob banged on the door.

"I'm okay, Rob, just getting out, sorry." He quickly toweled off, and before pulling his shirt on, he taped a gauze pad over the black wound in his chest. He'd grabbed a dark t-shirt, just in case the wound started seeping the black fluid again.

Rob was waiting in the living room when he got out. His brother glanced at him, his eyes unfocused. Galen smiled, knowing there was no way to hide the black wound from Rob's Sight. "I need coffee," Galen said, hoping to distract Rob. He headed down the stairs and into the shop.

"I can go get it, Galen, you should…"

"Don't, Rob, I'm okay." Galen frowned at his brother as they walked through the store and over to the coffee shop, daring him to say something.

"Yeah, you're okay. Just great."

"Morning, Galen, Rob," Becci said, leaning out the window.

"Holy shit," Rob said under his breath.

"What's the theme today, Becci?" Galen asked. She was wearing black hotpants, fishnet stockings and two small skull stickers—just enough to cover her nipples—and nothing else.

"Oh, it's Goth fantasy." She smiled at him as she started his coffee. "Americano for Rob, right?" Rob nodded. Galen shoved an elbow in his brother's ribs.

"Breathe," Galen said under his breath. "You're turning red."

"Thanks," Rob said, his breath coming out in a long sigh. "Nice outfit."

"Oh, do you like it? It shows off my tattoos." She turned so they could see the patterns decorating her back.

"Nice," Rob said, smiling.

Becci smiled and put Galen's coffee on the ledge. She set a cupcake beside it. "Happy birthday, Galen," she said, shyly.

"Thank you, Becci. It's Rob's birthday, too."

"Is it? But you're not twins? Weird." She put Rob's coffee down beside Galen's. "I didn't know. Can I give you a flavor? Whipped cream? A muffin?"

"Galen can share." Rob smiled. "He always takes the bigger piece though, even when I asked nicely," Rob continued. Galen stared at him—he sounded like he was six.

A chocolate muffin appeared beside the cupcake. "I didn't make this, but they're pretty good."

"I was kidding."

"It's your birthday, you need something. And calories don't count on the big day." She winked. "Come back for seconds later."

"Thanks, Becci," Galen said, picking up the cupcake and his coffee. The world spun, he took a deep breath and walked carefully back towards the shop, aware of Rob hovering behind him. "I won't fall down in the middle of the street."

"You never know." His brother opened the shop door and held it as Galen walked in. "Sit down," Rob said. "I'll open up. I remember how from before." He smiled as he set his coffee and muffin on the counter, then opened the curtains and turned on the sign. He walked back over to Galen and leaned against the counter. "Happy birthday."

"Happy birthday, Brat. I don't have anything for you, yet. I was planning on shopping yesterday."

"Galen," Rob swallowed. "I…" He cleared his throat. "I have my brother back, I don't need anything else. I don't have anything for you, either."

"Will you—can you forgive me?"

"Forgive you?" Rob asked, his eyes clouding. "Galen…"

"I'm sorry, Rob, I shouldn't ask."

"Shut up," Rob snapped. Galen blinked in surprise at his brother's harsh tone. "You've asked me that before, and Galen…"

"Rob…"

"What part of shut up do you not get?" Rob said, his eyes flashing. "You don't need to ask, you have…I can't…I thought… It's me…"

"You aren't making much sense, Rob."

Rob took a deep breath. "You died for me, Galen. How can you think…?" Rob shook his head. "I didn't know, Galen, I didn't hear that."

"What?"

"That it was in both of us, that it needed both of us. That you'd die, too. I've thought that if I'd just died then, you wouldn't have."

Galen shook his head. "I'm sorry. There wasn't time to tell you. And Rob, I would've died, had it been in me or not."

"You don't know that, Galen. Your Gift might have..." Rob trailed off.

"It's our way, isn't it? *Custodes Noctis?*" Galen sighed. "I don't think the Gift would have helped."

"Galen..." His brother took a deep breath.

"Hey, what kind of coffee you want this morning?" The shop door banged open and Flash came in. He stopped, looking from Galen to Rob and back again. "Oh my god."

"Flash, this isn't the best..."

"Oh my god, the brother." He took three large steps over to Rob and pulled him into a quick embrace. Galen had to chuckle at the look on his brother's face. "Good to see you, kid," Flash said, letting go and slapping Rob on the back. "How'd it happen, Galen?"

Galen smiled. "He was in the hospital, Mike called."

"You and hospitals, kid. How I saw you last time." Flash smiled at Rob.

"What?" Rob looked at Galen. "Galen?"

"This is Flash. He plays bass in The Urban Werewolves."

"Hi," Rob said.

"Hi, he says. Damn, Galen." He looked at Galen. "Just damn."

"Yeah." Galen smiled at his friend.

"You were responsible for one of the biggest scares I've ever had, kid," Flash said to Rob.

"Flash, shut up," Galen said.

"What do you mean?" Rob asked.

"Shut up, please, shut up."

"We were playing a big party," Flash said, ignoring Galen. "We were taking a break, kicking back, having a drink, you know. Chatting. There was this girl...Never mind. Galen and I were talking and all of a sudden..."

"Shut up!" Galen practically shouted.

"He just drops. Eyes roll up in his head and he was down. It took a second for it to register, you know. Then I checked him, I think one of the girls was screaming. Galen wasn't breathing and I couldn't find a pulse, but I'm not very good at that. I was getting ready to start CPR and he takes a big breath. A few seconds later he was awake, but disoriented and muttering about 'got to get to Rob.' I had no idea what he was talking about."

"Galen?" Rob turned to him.

"The car wreck, three years ago. I'm not sure where you were when it happened, but I can tell you the moment your heart stopped for a few seconds." Galen tried smiling. "Flash insisted on coming with me."

"Yeah, like you could've driven yourself anywhere at that point," Flash snorted.

"Coming with you?" Rob said softly. "You were there. I thought...You were there. It wasn't a miracle recovery, it was you."

"Yeah, I...I should have stayed, but..."

"You were worried. You needed to stay away. You needed to stay dead. That won't work anymore." Rob frowned. "You told me, when you saw me the other day the block shattered, why not then?"

"I'm not sure."

"I might know," Rob said with a smile.

"Coffee?" Flash said. "No? Sarah's coming on, I'll be back."

"That's a strategic retreat if I ever saw one." Rob glanced at Galen.

"Probably, but he does have the hots for Sarah. She comes on about now, and she and Becci work together for awhile." Galen looked away. "You have to go, Rob."

"What?"

"You have to go, It's coming for us again. For me. You have to go. If this is the Legacy…"

"It is, Galen, I'm sure of that."

"Then you have to go, Rob, you have to. We can't be the two that bring that thing back, let It walk again."

"We already are."

"No, no, you have to go."

"You know I can't, Galen. I appreciate the offer, but you know I can't." Rob smiled. "I did suspect you'd try and send me away, once I knew you were alive."

"Gods, Rob." Galen sighed, suddenly understanding. "You… the Ritual of Swords. You forced it. You knew."

Rob shrugged. "I thought you might try and send me away, once the euphoria passed. I have no intention of going, Galen, sorry. We needed to perform the ritual anyway. It was time." He laughed. "Actually, well past time."

"We can break the ritual."

"Do you think you can…? Galen…" Rob looked at him. "It's too late, anyway."

"No, you can go." Galen grabbed Rob's arm, his brother tried to pull away, but it was too late for that, too. He stopped and looked at Rob in horror. "What did you do?"

"It has to be in both of us, Galen."

"No, Rob, no. If this is the Legacy…"

"It is, that's what I'm telling you, this is the Legacy. I thought it was, I've thought that for years. What I remembered, what happened, what…" He sighed.

"But it can't be us, we can't be the ones that free that thing…"

"It was mistranslated, somewhere along the line the saga became corrupted."

"Someone's corrupt?" Flash said, coming back in. "Sweet. I love corruption." He put three coffees down on the counter. "You both look like you need more. I had Sarah make them with an extra shot in each."

"Is that my usual with an extra shot or your usual with an extra shot?" Galen asked.

"What?" Rob said, sniffing the coffee.

"I like my coffee a little stronger than Galen," Flash said, slapping Galen on the back. Galen stumbled. Flash and Rob grabbed his arms and led him to the stool. "What's going on?" Flash asked, frowning with concern.

"I'm okay," Galen grumbled.

"Right, okay, uh huh." Flash picked up his coffee. "You believe he's okay?"

"No, not at all," Rob said. He handed Galen a coffee and looked at him.

"Rob," Galen sighed, and took a sip of his coffee. "How many shots are in here, Flash?"

"Oh, I don't know, eight or nine probably." He shrugged. "It's good for you. It'll put hair on your chest."

"It'll put hair on my tongue."

"That too." Flash grinned. He looked from one to the other. "I'm glad you're here, kid."

"Why?" Rob asked, sipping his coffee and making a face. "Yikes."

"I've been worried," Flash said, dragging a stool out of the back and sitting down.

"Worried?" Galen looked at Flash. "About what?"

Flash frowned. "Well..."

"This isn't one of your 'I'm worried about you because you aren't partying' things, is it, Flash?"

"Let him talk, Galen," Rob said quietly. Galen glanced at his brother. Rob was watching Flash's face with the unfocused look that meant he was using the Sight.

"I've had this funny feeling lately, and this guy was hanging around your shop—once in the morning and once at night. Then that thing with your chest the other day. I know it gets bad around this time of year, but you've never been so bad I had to fetch the meds for you." He paused. "And I, uh..."

"Are you blushing?" Galen chuckled.

"Probably. I had a friend do a reading, you know."

"Tarot?" Rob asked.

Flash shook his head. "No, she uses Runes. It was a little vague."

"Runes usually are."

"But it was something along the lines of death and destruction and end of the world stuff."

"I told you that strip club would be the end of you." Galen tried laughing. His brother and his friend frowned at him.

"The reading was for Galen, wasn't it, Flash?" Rob said, looking at Flash.

"Yeah, I've been trying to think of a way to bring it up, without sounding crazier than usual."

"Flash?" Galen asked, looking at his friend with surprise.

"Sorry, man, I..." Flash shrugged. "Then the brother is here? I'm worried. I talked to Mike and Rhiannon, too."

"You've all been keeping an eye on me. Damn." Galen stood, steadied himself on the shelf for a minute and paced away. He sighed, it was hard to make a dramatic exit when you had to wait for the world to stop spinning. He walked behind the curtains at the back of the shop and sat down at the table. Galen could hear Rob and Flash talking, their voices low, intense. A minute later Rob came back.

"Flash is going to keep an eye on the shop so we can talk."

"Rob, I don't want to talk. We've talked enough. I..." Galen put his head in his hand. "Coming back from the dead was a mistake. I should have healed you and left like before."

"You said the block shattered before you healed me."

"It did. I couldn't stop it. I'm not sure why."

"I might know why."

"You said that before, Rob. What? And why, damn it, Rob, why?"

"Why did I say it?" Rob looked at him.

"No, why did you...how did you?"

"Oh." Rob looked away, staring out the window on the door. "It has to be in both of us, Galen. You said that. I didn't know, not until now. I knew you wouldn't..."

"Let you take part of that thing into yourself? You're right." Galen could feel anger simmering, threatening to boil over. "You act like you had this all planned out, but until I touched the girl, It wasn't in me, not like now. It's been a little worse since Dad and Bobby died, when It came for me that time."

"Galen," Rob took a deep breath. "I don't think It came for you, not that night. I'm pretty sure it thought you were dead until that moment."

"What?" Galen asked, aghast, five years of guilt pressing against his heart.

"It wanted Keepers of the Emrys line, Galen. As far as It knew there were only two left."

"Dad and Bobby," Galen whispered. "It came for them."

"I think so. It fits with what I've uncovered." Rob looked at him. "After hearing what happened to you ten years ago, knowing what happened to me. Yes, Galen. It came for them, not you."

"I thought...It was our birthday..."

"It was their birthday, too," Rob said gently. "It wasn't expecting to find you, It wanted them, hoping they might be enough to let It walk."

"You say that like you don't think it would've worked."

"I don't think it would, it's what I was telling you, about the Legacy."

"We can't be that pair of Keepers, Rob, we can't. It can't be us that frees that thing..."

"From the prison the first Keeper, the first Emrys, trapped It in?" Rob shook his head. "I've wondered how Dad and Bobby missed that. The sagas say It was imprisoned in a lesser demon, possibly a wood hag. Until last night I thought they hadn't known, but they did, they suspected even before the second ritual, when you blocked Dad's healing."

"Suspected?"

"That it would be you and I..."

"No, Rob." Galen was shaking his head, trying to deny it, terrified his brother was right.

"They were right, but Galen, they were wrong, too," Rob said, meeting his eyes.

"They shouldn't have brought me back, they should have left me dead."

"That's not it. They should have let it happen, let the Legacy begin."

"We can't be the two that release that thing, Rob," Galen insisted.

"That's what I've been trying to tell you, we already are."

"What do you mean?"

"It was set into motion then, Galen, ten years ago. We have

to finish it, the Legacy." Rob sighed. "We, you and I, have to finish it."

"Rob?" Galen asked, letting his hand rest on his brother's arm so he would know the truth.

"Galen?"

"Is that why you're here? Now?"

"Yes," Rob said quietly.

"You said you were here because of a call from a friend."

Rob shrugged. "He did call."

"You said he told you to come."

Another shrug and a wry smile. "I lied."

Silence stretched between them for a long moment. Galen looked at Rob, fighting a growing wave of panic. He could sense his brother's calm certainty, his determination. Galen pushed himself up from the table and walked to look out the back window.

"Galen?" Rob asked.

"Rob," Galen began. He sighed, shaking his head. Something dark flitted at the edge of his vision. He turned his head to look, but nothing was in the parking lot but their two jeeps. "Why are you here?"

"Galen…"

"Why?" he asked again, aware of the first hint of simmering anger bubbling in his chest.

"The Legacy," Rob said quietly.

"What?"

"I'm here to fulfill the Legacy, Galen. It's why I…"

"What?" Galen whispered, the anger boiling over. He turned to face his brother. "You're here to do what?"

"Galen…"

"I died to stop that. You know I hated Dad at first for saving me? I was so terrified that I was the one who'd let that thing loose on the world again. I tried to die again, but Dad blocked that too, like he blocked our bond. I couldn't...I tried...I didn't want to become..." Galen stopped, the anger pressing against his chest. "Dreading what would happen, and then losing Dad and Uncle Bobby. To stop the Legacy from happening. Denying what I was, who I was supposed to be. Ten years, Rob, ten. With that ache of the broken bond throbbing in my chest every damn day. And now you're back and you want to let that all happen? Make everything I did..." He picked up a jar from the shelf and threw it against the wall, watching as it shattered.

The scar was suddenly awake, twisting in his chest, the thing resting near his heart purring with joy as his rage reached It. Galen closed his eyes and pressed his hand to his chest.

"Soon, soon, my Emrys Keeper. Soon we will walk together," the voice whispered. "We will Become. See, see who we are." The vision unraveled, pictures playing in his mind like a slowly unfolding horror film. *Rob lashed to a stone altar, covered in blood, something dark hovering over his body. Galen saw that it was himself there with blood on his hands. The vision shifted, something ripped through Galen's chest, out of his body, exploding into the night, a shadow rising above them both, roaring jubilant defiance.* "No," he groaned. "Never." *Black fire was consuming him, burning him away.*

"Galen," a soft voice said, breaking through the vision. Something that felt like the gentle drops of a spring rain washed over him, slowly dousing the fire. "Galen?" The soft voice silenced the other that was screaming with glee, driving the vision forward. "Trust me." The vision was pulled away. "Galen?"

"Oh, gods," Galen groaned. Awareness was replacing the black-tinged vision, the horror slowly retreating. A warm hand was resting against his forehead, another on his back. He leaned into the support. "We can't stop it, can we?"

"We don't want to," Rob said gently. Galen opened his eyes. He was crouched on the floor, Rob kneeling beside him. Rob eased Galen into a sitting position, guiding him back to rest against the wall. Galen watched as his brother got a bottle of water out of the small fridge, then sat down beside him. "You always drank sparkling water," Rob said with a smile as he opened the bottle, waiting as the bubbles settled before handing it to Galen.

"Thanks. What happened?"

"When you lost your temper, It found an opening, I knew it was only a matter of time, I was hoping what I did would last a little longer," Rob said with a grimace. "Sorry."

"What you did?" Galen looked at his brother. "When you took part of It into yourself?"

"Yes." Rob met his eyes. "Galen, we have to talk."

Galen shook his head. "Why, Rob?"

"We have to," his brother said simply.

"What? No, it can't be us, we can't be the two…"

"We always have been, Galen. I think Uncle Bobby was beginning to figure that out."

"He was always obsessed with the Legacy. I remember grandfather getting into an argument with Bobby when I was nine. Bobby insisted he'd see the Legacy come to fruition in his lifetime."

"He knew, I think, when you blocked Dad's healing. You shouldn't have been able to do that." Rob nudged Galen with his shoulder. "The problem was the saga, the translation was corrupted."

"No." Galen shook his head. "What do you mean? About the saga?"

"Finally heard that?" Rob chuckled.

"What?"

"I said it twice." Rob smiled at him.

"But what do you mean? I thought it was pretty clear. 'The Saga of Emrys', it tells of the birth of the Keepers, then the Legacy, how the first of the Emrys line imprisoned the thing and how a pair of future Keepers will let It free and It will walk to rule again. After a time of darkness another pair will banish It forever."

"Right. Only the translation's wrong," Rob said, excitement sparkling in his eyes and flowing off of him in waves.

"How can it be wrong?" Galen shook his head. "You'd think if it was wrong, someone would've noticed."

"You'd think so, wouldn't you? But I think it was so accepted as truth, no one wanted to question it."

"But you did?" Galen asked skeptically.

"I told you about my studies, the sagas of Northern Europe? I'm writing my thesis on the Emrys Saga, so I've been following it through the source material, all the way back to the first time it was written down."

"And?" Galen couldn't help smiling at Rob's enthusiasm.

"I found an error, in the text about the future Keepers who release the thing and then the pair that banish It. It's always been assumed that it was two different sets of Keepers, the word used in the original saga is related to a variant of an older tongue that..." Rob trailed off with a sheepish grin. "You probably don't need to know all that. What I'm trying to say is the word in its original form didn't mean two different sets of Keepers, it meant the same two at different times."

"No, Rob, no. It clearly states that after the first pair dies, the other arise to banish It." Galen saw his brother open his mouth to reply, but plowed on. "And the second pair, Rob, they're different. They have..."

"Powers not seen since the first Keepers? Not used in millennia. Yeah, I know. I think Uncle Bobby was…"

"No, it clearly states…"

"That the first pair dies?" Rob was grinning at him. "I know that."

"Then how?"

"We both have, Galen. Well, it's on a technicality, but we both have."

"I don't think the accident and your heart stopping for thirty-nine seconds really counts as dying, Rob."

"That's not what I'm talking about," Rob said, the smile gone from his face.

"Rob? I'd have known."

"No, you wouldn't, Galen." Rob laid a hand on Galen's arm. "You were wrong, you know," he said gently.

Galen's heart was pounding. "How?"

"The bond was too strong."

"Rob?" Tears were suddenly pooling in his eyes as his heart labored against a tight band of pain.

"It's how it's always been, Galen, for *Custodes Noctis*, from the first Emrys to all the other families, until today."

Galen was shaking his head, trying to swallow around the lump in his throat. "Rob?" he repeated.

"I always knew it would happen. I'd seen it when I was about six. It why I knew we'd never be Keepers together. I was ready, that's why…" Rob paused. "I managed to hold on long enough to help you. I had a hold of your hand so tight it hurt. Then there was this flash of pain and nothing but this shimmering black lake and a song. I remember being sad when I left the lake, when Dad brought me back. There was this emptiness, this silence, where you'd been before, so I knew you were dead." He smiled. "I'm glad I was wrong."

"But if you knew I was dead, Rob, why are you here? How

could we have been the pair? How could we...?"

"I summoned you," Rob said with a shrug.

"What?"

"The early Keepers, according to the sagas, could raise an army of former Keepers of their line. I found a text that had the spell. That's why the block shattered when you saw me. I'd summoned you, and you couldn't block me anymore."

"What? What kind of magic were you playing with, Rob?"

"I summoned you. I don't have quite the power to..." He stopped and looked at Galen. "The spell calls the Keeper back. The line from the formal farewell? 'Until you are called to serve again'? They meant that literally. So I called you back. Once the spell was finished—well, I was sure I'd done it wrong. You hadn't appeared. That's when my friend called and said I needed to come here. He knew about the spell, he helped, but I'm sure the summoning broke the block, you had to be 'visible' to me."

"He helped? What?"

"I had the text of the spell, but that was all. It was missing some of the information I needed to complete the spell. So I called him. He helped me control the Sight, remember? And he knows about the vision. He thought we could find the answer in the past. All we had to do was access it. So, he guided me."

"Guided you? How?" Galen frowned.

"The way shamans always do, a combination of things." Rob stopped for a minute.

"Do you have any idea how dangerous...?"

Rob shrugged. "Had to be done."

"Rob, people go insane...the drugs..."

"It's over, Galen, scolding me about it now won't stop me." He laughed softly, then sobered. "But we found the answer there, in the past. He'd written it down, but I didn't need that. It was part of me. So, I went home and waited for the right time. And

I summoned you."

Galen sighed and looked at his brother. "No, Rob, it can't be us. The Keepers who banish It, they're different."

"And you think we aren't? That's what Bobby realized, Galen."

"What?"

"My Sight is different than other Keepers. I talked to Uncle Bobby about it, and I talked to another Keeper. That's why I went to the witch and shaman. I can 'see' like other Keepers with the Gift, but I can also 'see' other things, including visions of the future and the past." Rob paused. "In the past, so the sagas say, both brothers could heal. The elder had the Gift to use on everyone, the younger had a lesser Gift, mostly designed for his brother, but it does work on other people, although only for little things. And as you know, I can heal a little."

"So, you're special, Rob."

"Galen," his brother sighed with exasperation. "I have been trying to tell you…"

"No."

"You have power, Galen, real power. Not like anyone else I've ever seen. Not Dad, not other Keepers. You used the healing as a weapon. That was once part of the Gift, but deemed too dangerous and so it was suppressed. You have visions, you can 'see' a little, even though you deny it. I told you, this shop has the funny shine of real magic, Galen. You. Not Dad, not grandfather, you."

Rob shook him. "Do you think just anyone could make a spell to control that thing? Do you honestly think just anyone can block an experienced healer? And do you think Dad was the one who blocked our bond? He couldn't Galen, it was you. All along, it was you." Rob looked at him, meeting his eyes. "And think about it, we performed the Ritual of Swords."

"Yeah?" Galen looked at Rob, trying to absorb what this

brother was saying.

"Without the Elder Keepers, Galen."

"Yeah?" Galen said again. "We did, oh gods, I hadn't…"

"Do you know the last time that happened? That a pair of Keepers performed the Ritual without the others there to guide the release? To help channel the power?"

"Rob, it can't be…"

"The First Emrys, Galen. That was the last time."

"No."

"Do you think by saying that you can change all this, Galen? I told you, we already are the Keepers of the Legacy. This is all part of the Legacy. It began ten years ago, it ends now."

"Rob…" Galen stopped. "No, it can't be, I've spent how long denying it?"

"It's true,' Rob smiled. "Bobby knew, I think."

"Dad did, too," Galen said with sudden certainty. "He tried to tell me the night he died."

"It wasn't time yet."

"It is now?"

"Yes."

"We can't let It become, Rob."

"We have to, it's the only way to banish It."

"But Rob, I saw…" Galen tried to convince his brother.

"I know, I've seen it too. It has to happen so we can banish it."

"So what do we do?"

Rob smiled. "I was thinking we could start by raising an army."

Chapter Eighteen

The bell in the shop rang as someone came in, Galen heard Flash's deep voice answering questions. He leaned against the wall, looking at Rob in disbelief. "You're going to raise an army?"

"No," Rob answered.

"But you just said…"

"You're going to raise the army, Galen. I can help, but you're the one who has to do it."

"No." Galen shook his head.

Rob put his hand on Galen's shoulder and gave him a little shake. "Yes, Galen, you are."

"Rob, I can't."

"You can, do we have to start this conversation again?" Rob smiled.

Galen smiled at his brother. "What?" he asked as Flash stuck his head through the doorway.

"Do you have monk's hood?"

"Yeah, it's behind the counter, labeled Wolf's Bane, *Aconitum Napellus*." Galen started to push himself up. "Maybe I should help."

"Maybe you should sit your ass back down," Flash said with a frown. "I can help. And I know all the ones with the skull and crossbones are poison." He disappeared back into the shop.

"He likes playing in the shop." Galen grinned at Rob.

"He was enthusiastic when I asked if he'd watch it while we talked. Galen, we need to be ready. This is happening tonight."

"Give me a minute, Rob. I've spent the last ten years trying to avoid the Legacy."

"I know." Rob stood and offered Galen his hand. Galen let Rob haul him to his feet, then followed him out into the shop. "We need a few things for the ritual." Rob wandered behind the counter and started collecting things. Flash finished ringing up the customer, escorted her to the door and came back to stand beside Galen as he watched Rob.

"What's he doing?" Flash asked.

"Apparently he's planning on starting an apocalypse," Galen said with an uncertain chuckle.

"What?" Flash gasped. "Galen, can I talk to you?" He tugged on Galen's arm.

Rob turned and smiled. "Why don't you get some coffee? I'll watch the shop till you get back."

Flash nearly ran towards the door, and, after a quick smile at Rob, Galen followed. Flash yanked the door open and pulled Galen outside. "He's doing what?"

"I was a little glib, Flash."

"I told you about the reading, Galen. End of the world stuff, and you were right in the middle of it." Flash looked back at the shop. Rob was standing behind the counter watching them. "Is he okay? I mean, he's your brother and all, but Galen is he okay?"

"I thought... He's okay, Flash."

"How can you be sure?"

Galen smiled. "How the hell do you think?"

"Because he's your brother? Not good enough." Flash looked at him. "Galen, you haven't seem him for how long? And he shows up on the anniversary of your Dad's death? How can you trust him?"

"I can, and not just because he's my brother, it goes with the Gift." Galen paused for a minute, a sliver of doubt creeping into his brain. *What if I'm wrong? What if It's doing something to Rob and I can't...*

"What?"

"What what?"

"You were thinking about something, Galen. I saw it." Flash shook his arm. "What's going on?"

"I wish I could explain, Flash. It would take too long. Later, okay? Rob and I need to perform a ritual..."

"Magic? In the shape you're in? Galen..." Flash frowned. "I remember..."

"It won't be like that, Rob's here to back me up," Galen said softly, the incident Flash mentioned suddenly playing in his head. "Rob's here. It won't be like that." He wondered if he was trying to convince his friend or himself.

"Shit, it nearly killed you."

"I know. It won't be like that." Galen sighed. "There was something wrong with that spell, Flash. It was like it was broken, not working right and it exploded.

"So it's not a spell like that one?"

"No." *Not at all, it's much bigger and, oh, hasn't been done in probably a thousand years.*

"That bad?" Flash put his hand on Galen's shoulder. "Galen..." Flash said softly. Galen could sense his friend's concern flowing out from the hand resting on his shoulder. "Tell me."

"I can't tell you everything, not right now." Galen paused as Flash sighed. "There really isn't time. But it has to do with why Dad's dead. Why I told you I had to stay dead to Rob all those years ago."

"Why you have a big wet spot on your chest?" Flash touched the spot, his fingers came away covered in blood and black ooze. He looked at his hand in horror. "What the fuck? Are you going to die? Galen?" He shook his head. "I'm not leaving. Not while you do the ritual, not for awhile. Get used to it. Until I'm sure that you're okay, that the brother's not wrong."

"Rob's not wrong," Galen snapped.

"How can you be sure?"

"Because I am. Gods damn it, Flash." Galen grabbed his friend's arm and pulled him back towards the shop. He slammed the door open. Rob looked at him with surprise.

"Galen?" Rob asked, walking around the counter.

"Come here," Galen snapped.

"Galen?"

Rob walked over, a frown on his face. "What is it?"

"Flash is worried," Galen said angrily, looking at Rob. He could feel concern and confusion radiating from his brother.

"Galen..." Flash said.

"Shut up." Galen took a deep breath and laid his hand against his brother's chest, over his heart. Galen reached out, let the light flow. Rob looked at him for a minute then closed his eyes. Galen let his eyes close as well. He could feel the thing where it rested in Rob's heart, pulsing as the connection grew. The voice was whispering to him, Galen ignored it. He could feel his brother's sense of purpose, of certainty that what they were doing, what was happening, was right. *"I'm sorry, Rob,"* he said silently through the connection.

"It's okay, Galen. I understand. I wondered how long you'd wait. You always were a little suspicious."

"I don't doubt you, Rob."

"You need to know what It's done to me. You need to know if I am influenced by It. I took It into me after the Ritual of Swords. You have to know. I understand," Rob said gently. Galen sighed. He felt the answering sigh echo in his brother.

"My Emrys Keepers!" the thing suddenly shouted. Agony twisted in Galen's chest. He heard Rob moan. "Yes, yes, yes. This is better than I hoped, better than I could wish for. Power!" It shrieked. The vision started.

"No," Galen said audibly, his voice sounded odd.

Rob was tied to the stone altar, a crowd had gathered, frenzied chanting rang through the air, ecstatic, nearly orgasmic in tone. Galen stood beside the altar, blood covering his hand. Blood was flowing over his brother's body as the darkness rose above them. A sound, like the flapping of giant leathery wings filled the air. The crowd's chanting increased a pitch. Galen raised bloody hands and plunged them down... "No," he heard his voice again. *Rob looked at him, a gentle, sardonic smile on his face.*

"*It's okay, Galen,*" his brother's voice echoed in his head. "*Let me...*"

The vision abruptly changed. The darkness was screaming in fear, the sound of Its wings beating frantically in the air. There was a shout, a challenge to battle, Galen recognized his voice as having given the shout. He raised his sword, the army behind him charged. The darkness, the beings suddenly gathered around It, shouting a challenge in reply.

"We'll defeat it," Rob said softly. "We'll defeat all of them."

Galen had heard the words, not in his head, but audibly. He opened his eyes. "Rob? Are you okay?" Galen could feel the pain as the thing twisted in his brother's chest, mimicking the twisting agony in his own. They were on the floor, Galen's knees ached from where he had collapsed on them.

"What the fuck was that?" Flash demanded from beside him. Galen looked at his friend. Flash had his hand on Galen's back, a terrified expression on his face. "What did I just see?"

"What?"

"I think he got dragged in when he touched you, when we fell." Rob patted Galen's hand where it rested on his chest.

"Galen?" Flash whispered. "What the hell's happening?

What was that thing?" Flash blinked.

"It's an Old One," Rob offered.

"What?" Galen and Flash spoke together, Galen whispering a denial, Flash chuckling a little.

"An Old One. A dark force, like a demigod. It ruled on earth, wreaked havoc, created chaos, fed on humanity…"

"So it's bad?" Flash said, looking at Rob.

"Worse than bad, Flash." Galen looked at his friend. "It's the end of the world stuff the reading was about."

"When I said end of the world, or when she did, I guess I thought…uh…I don't know, it was metaphorical or something. I didn't think it meant the actual end of the world!"

Galen chuckled at Flash's offended tone. "It's the actual end of the world." He frowned at Rob. "Did you guide that vision?"

"Yeah," Rob smiled. "I told you that I lived and worked with a shaman. Guiding visions is one of the things they do best. He taught me…I can also…"

"What?" Flash said, his eyes narrowing suspiciously. "Can you influence people?"

Galen took a deep breath, Rob stopped him with a look. "Yes," Rob answered quietly. "I can guide visions, dreamwalk."

"Dreamwalking is dangerous, Rob," Galen snapped.

"We're missing the point here. He can influence people, Galen. He could be influencing you." Flash was glaring at Rob.

"He's not."

"How can you be sure?"

"Because I can be," Galen growled. "He can't alter…"

"How do you know?"

"Flash…"

"Galen!" Rob stood and dashed out of the room.

Flash looked at Galen. "What was that about?"

"I don't know." The thing was suddenly alive, twisting in his chest, agony grinding against his heart. Galen gasped, trying to stop the movement. The dark center of the thing was sending tendrils out, a spider's web slowly filling his chest. "Don't touch me Flash," he managed to get out, fearing the contact would allow It access to his friend.

"Here, Galen." A bottle was pressed against his lips. He drank, feeling the spell slowly work through his body, the tendrils stopped their seeking movement, though they didn't retract. Galen took a deep breath. The voice was whispering happily, anticipation growing in Its laughter.

"Galen?" Rob asked softly. "Are you there?" He put his hand on Galen's back. Warmth flowed into Galen.

The voice sighed. "Power, power, power. Yes. Better than I hoped. Much better. Better even than the first."

The warmth changed, pulsing with white light, silencing the voice. *"Not yet,"* Rob's voice was loud in Galen's mind. *"Not yet."*

"I'm okay," Galen said, opening his eyes and looking at Rob. "Thanks." Flash looked from Galen to Rob. "I'm okay, Flash."

"Uh huh. Galen…"

"Don't start again, Flash. Rob can't alter…"

"What?"

"It's hard to explain. It goes with the zapping I do, he can't change how I perceive him through that, and there's more, Flash. You didn't know Dad and Uncle Bobby, but, we…" Galen broke off, wondering how to explain who they were to his friend. Flash was shaking his head.

"I'm on Galen's side," Rob said, looking at Flash. "Believe what you want. Galen? We need to perform the ritual before it's too late."

"Galen, no. You can't. Even if you trust him. You can't. Last time…Shit." Flash was frowning with concern.

"Last time?" his brother asked as Galen pushed himself up, Rob put a hand under his elbow to steady him.

Galen shrugged. "It was a little rough, Rob, but I figured it out. The spell was wrong, I didn't find out until too late."

"How bad was it?"

"Bad," Flash answered for Galen.

"This is different, I told you. Rob's here." Galen smiled at his brother. "I have a small garden in back, will that do? I assume we need to be in contact with the earth?"

"Galen…" Flash put a hand on his arm to stop him.

"Watch the shop, okay?" Galen smiled. "I'll explain everything later." Galen turned and walked slowly out of the shop. He could hear Flash's deep voice and Rob's baritone answers. His brother's voice sounded angry. Galen shrugged and wandered across the parking lot to his garden.

He sank down on the bench and looked around. The garden was full of plants. The cold weather had done some damage, but the mints were still growing. The valerian and pleurisy root towered over the soft gray-green alecost and dark green wood betony. The aconite and mandrake were drooping from the cool wet weather. He smiled and took a deep breath, the scent of wet leaves and decaying berries drifted on the air, touched with a slight scent of mint, hyssop and lavender. A sense of peace flowed over Galen as he sat there. The twisting agony in his chest and the voice that accompanied it were suddenly quiet. He sighed and closed his eyes.

"Galen?" Rob asked softy. Galen opened his eyes, his brother was standing at the edge of the garden. "Everything okay?"

"Yeah." He stood and stretched. "This part of the garden is bolted."

"Bolted?" Rob walked into the garden, stopping beside Galen. He looked around and sighed.

"Magical plants to protect the garden."

"I can see that," Rob said with a smile. "I can feel it too. It's not just the plants, you know."

"Bringing that up, again?" Galen smiled at his brother. "We'll see."

"I do see." Rob walked out of the circle of plants Galen had been sitting in, to the other side of the garden. "I can see this, too."

"What?"

"You've channeled a lot into here. It's concentrated magic. It will focus whatever ritual or spell you perform here. It looks almost like a vortex."

Galen laughed softly. "I'm glad, most of the time, that I don't see the world the way you do. I think I'd be nauseated a lot of the time."

Rob chuckled. "Yeah. That's one of the reasons I went to Billy. I've learned to turn it off and on now, like Uncle Bobby did. I'm always aware of auras around things, but I can turn most of it off. I can shut down visions too, if I need to. There for awhile…" Rob trailed off and Galen had a brief impression of flashing colors, shouting voices and blood. "I was losing my mind, Galen," he said softly. "I didn't understand what I was seeing. Uncle Bobby couldn't help. I called more than once, you know."

Galen walked through the garden to his brother. "What?"

"I think he thought it was because the bond was broken, because of what had happened. I was trapped somehow." Rob shook his head.

"I'm sorry." *How many sorrys is that now?* Galen stopped himself.

"It wasn't your fault. We need to start." Rob carefully laid the things he gathered in the shop down on the ground. "I grabbed the—our—swords. We need them for this."

"Rob? If we need them? You used this spell to summon me how?"

"It wasn't nearly as big, you know, and I used my knife and bracelet." Rob pulled the small knife from his pocket. "You gave them to me, the traditional gift. They didn't have as much magic, but there was enough."

"There was only a little protective spell, Rob."

Rob snorted. "Galen..." He walked over and laid his hand on Galen's arm. "Look at it." Galen felt an odd jolt, the connection between them altered a little. Suddenly the world looked different. The knife in Rob's hand was gleaming with a bright silver light, fluid, like mercury flowing around the small object. Galen blinked. Rob's bracelet had a similar shine. The garden, near the bench, had a soft curtain shimmering around it, the place where he stood was a swirling mass of colors. Galen swayed, dizzy, as the thing in his chest purred with pleasure.

"Rob?"

"I wish I could show you yourself, Galen. I'm not sure how I'd manage that." Rob smiled, letting his hand drop away.

"I..." Galen swallowed.

"Yes, yes, power, true power. Unlike any Keeper I've had. I've waited for you my Emrys," It whispered against his heart.

Galen grabbed his brother's arm and pulled him towards the bench, towards the part of the garden he'd bolted against evil. As they stepped through the ring of plants the voice fell silent.

"If you think that is just the plants, Galen, you're crazy." Rob stopped and rubbed his chest. "Nice to have It quiet."

"How bad is it?"

"Nothing like what you experience. It hurts, but..." Rob met his eyes. "I'm sorry."

"Why are you apologizing?" Galen punched him lightly on

the arm. "It can't hear us here. What do we need to do?"

"The spell is mostly in Latin," Rob began and carefully outlined what they needed to do. When he was finished he looked at Galen. "Ready?"

"No."

"Once It becomes Galen, once It returns to Its form as an Old One, Its servants will appear. The ones who served It in the past. Conjured by Its return. We'll need an army to defeat them."

"Still not ready, but we don't have much choice. Okay." Galen took a deep breath and walked to the part of the garden that he'd seen swirling with power. He picked up the herbs and items Rob had gathered in the shop and placed them carefully on the ground. "Rob?"

"I'm here, Galen, I'll help as much as I can. I don't have the power for this."

"I don't either," Galen said softly. Rob sighed, but didn't say anything. Galen lit the candles, softly reciting the first part of the spell Rob had given him. His voice took on the sing-song he always used when casting, the words slowly forming into a song as he spoke. His voice grew stronger as the song, as the spell, flowed through him. Power pulsed around him, touching him with hot sparks of energy.

"Rob?" he called softly. His brother stood beside Galen and handed him his sword. Galen took it, feeling the power run through his hand. He continued the spell, no longer needing the written words Rob had given him. He instinctively knew what was needed, and the words flowed out of him in a song. He let it fill him, the light flowed around him, pulling him with it. His hands moved of their own accord. He was aware of his brother standing beside him, Rob had his own sword in his hand. The power in that blade resonated through Galen's, resonated through Galen. Pain from somewhere burned white-hot against his arm, the light coalesced around him, the song grew, voices joined his and then the spell exploded outwards in a flash of light so bright it seared his skin and blinded him.

"I'm sorry," his brother said softly. The ground was hard under Galen's back, someone was winding something around his arm. "Galen?"

"Did it work?" Galen opened his eyes. Rob was bending over him, his face paper-white, wrapping his arm in a piece of cloth. "What happened?"

"Galen..." Rob gave him a wild look.

"Did it work?" He looked around, half expecting to see a crowd around him. "I thought I heard voices. Are they here?"

"I don't know," Rob said quietly. "Galen, are you okay?"

"I'm not sure. What's wrong with my arm?"

"You cut it."

"I did? Huh." Galen looked down at the bandage. "I don't remember that from the spell you gave me."

"It wasn't there." Rob flashed him a panicked look. "Galen..."

"What?" Galen pushed himself into a sitting position, his brother put a shaking hand behind his back.

"That spell..."

"What? It was the one you gave me."

Rob was shaking his head. "No. It started out that way. The same one I used when I summoned you."

"But? Help me up."

Rob stood and pulled him to his feet. "But...You started singing."

"I always do when I cast."

"It wasn't Latin, Galen. I think I recognized part of the language, it's an old European tongue. But that wasn't in the spell I gave you. I tried to stop it, but you held me back."

"I don't remember you grabbing me."

"I didn't, Galen, I couldn't get close enough. You held me back. Then you cut your arm with the sword. I caught the word for 'rise' and 'blood' but it went so fast." Rob bent to retrieve their swords. "I…"

"What?"

"I…" Rob looked at him. "Galen…"

"Can we try a whole sentence? I have a headache." Galen tried to focus the healing inward. The light failed to appear.

"Galen?" Rob walked to him and put his hand on Galen's head, Galen could feel his brother's hand trembling where it rested against his forehead. Gentle warmth flowed into him, and stopped the throbbing behind his eyes. "What's wrong? You look funny," Rob said, looking at him.

"It's the spell. It drained me. It'll take awhile to recover."

"I'm sorry."

"Why are you apologizing?"

"I had no idea, Galen." They walked together towards the shop. "I had no idea you…" Rob shook his head.

"What?" Galen put a hand on his brother's arm to stop him, "Galen…I…you…"

"Rob? What?" Galen looked at his brother, tried to get a sense of him through the contact. The Gift was still silent, just a soft hum. He caught the very edges of disbelief from Rob.

"I knew, but I never suspected…My gods, Galen, do you realize…?"

"Are you okay?" Flash pounced on them. They walked into the back of the shop with him.

"I'm fine, just a headache." Galen stopped by the fridge and grabbed a bottle of water.

"What happened to your arm?"

"The spell required blood," Galen replied easily, knowing it was true. The memory of the pulsing power tingled through his hands.

Flash grabbed his arm and pulled him into the shop and shoved him down on a stool. "Galen?" He turned to Rob. "Is he okay?"

"I'm not sure," Rob answered. His face still was still white, his hands shaking. He looked at Flash. "I'm sorry."

"Would you stop saying that?" Galen snapped, then smiled as a customer came into the shop. "Why don't the two of you go get coffee and something for us to eat?" Galen handed his brother a twenty dollar bill, hoping the walk would help remove the shocked expression from Rob's face. "There's a sandwich shop down the block. Tell them it's for me, they'll know what to make."

"Veggies with cheese," Flash muttered and shook his head in disgust. "Don't know how you survive on that shit. Yech."

"I survive on it too," Rob said. He smiled at Galen. "We'll be right back."

Galen watched them go, then walked over to the young woman who had come in the shop. He helped her find the herbs she was looking for, and recommended a protective amulet. Rob and Flash were back as he was finishing up the sale. Rob looked at him with the unfocused look and shook his head. He handed Galen a cup of coffee and pulled a stool up to the counter. Flash settled beside Rob on the other stool. They exchanged a look and then turned to Galen.

"What?" he asked, looking at them. "Rob? Flash?"

"We've been talking," Flash started.

"Save me," Galen said, taking a bite of the sandwich.

"Well, we have," Rob chimed in.

"And?"

Rob shrugged and looked at Flash. "We think it's best..."

"We? I thought you didn't trust him only five seconds ago, Flash," Galen frowned at his friend.

"Yeah, well, I changed my mind. So there." And Flash stuck out his tongue.

"Nice," Galen snapped, then sighed. "Whatever you two have decided, just let me eat in peace, okay? Before you pack me upstairs and lock me in my room or...or whatever..."

"We just thought it would be a good idea to call Rhiannon and let her know what's happening, maybe Mike too," Rob said.

Galen looked at his brother, Rob met his eyes. Galen saw the resolve he'd seen earlier, but there was something else, an undercurrent of fear. *It's getting close. As sure as he is, there's no way this will be easy on either of us. As sure as his is, there's no way to know if we survive. We will need help. The summoning didn't work.* A soft voice from somewhere whispered to him. Galen turned his head. "What?"

"Call Rhiannon?" Flash said.

"No, what did you say?" He looked at Rob, the voice had sounded like his brother.

Rob shook his head. "Galen?"

The voice whispered to him again, the words flowed over him, too soft to become intelligible. Galen glanced around the shop. "Galen," the gentle voice whispered.

"What?" he asked again.

"Galen?" Rob frowned at him with concern.

Galen looked at Rob, then smiled. "Rhiannon, not a bad idea. She'd kill us if she missed this party." Galen pulled out his phone and called Rhiannon.

"Happy Birthday, honey," she said when she answered.

"Thanks. It's tonight."

"We'll be at the shop in twenty minutes. I'll call Mike, always good to have a doctor along."

"Rhiannon? What's with you and Mike?"

"Nothing, Galen, nothing at all," she said. Galen could hear a smirk in her voice. "We'll be there soon, don't leave till we're there."

"Right." He flipped the phone closed and looked at Rob. "She's on her way."

"Good," Flash said.

Galen smiled at him and turned back to his sandwich. Rob watched him. "I'm okay, let's eat. We might not have another chance." Galen could hear the thing chuckling happily against his heart. He could hear the soft, gentle whispers from somewhere else.

"Galen?" Rob was looking at him, he frowned then glanced around the shop, following Galen's look. "What?"

"I'm not sure." Galen shrugged. "Let's eat. You used to be all about the food, Brat," he said, a teasing note in his voice.

"Yeah, I did." Rob smiled, still watching him. He seemed to sense Galen's need to change the subject, and turned to Flash. "Becci told me you two have the bestest band in the whole Northwest."

Flash grinned. "Now if Sarah would only think that," he said with a sigh and launched into an enthusiastic appraisal of the group. Rob snuck smile at Galen as Flash talked. Galen let the talk flow around him as he focused inwards, trying to sense the Gift. It was still dark, inactive. There was a small hum, but nothing else. Galen wondered what the spell had actually done. He sighed. The soft whispers were still just out of hearing, although he heard one call his name again. He finished the food and sipped his coffee, idly watching two men and a woman walk down the street outside the shop. They turned and came across the street.

"Time, my Emrys Keeper. Time," the thing sighed with pleasure.

Galen stood, Rob turned to look out the store window.

"Galen," he said softly. "They're coming."

"A little sooner than we planned, Rob," Galen said. He looked at Flash. "Go, get out."

Flash looked at him. "What?"

"Get out now!" Galen shouted at his friend.

It was too late. The door slammed open, the three came into the room. One of the men held a gun in his hand. He fired at Rob, Galen heard the *phftt* of a dart. The gun was turned on him, the dart hit him, dragging him down into the dark before he could react.

Chapter Nineteen

The sound of water dripping beat its way into his brain, each drop impacting with a near physical violence. There was an acrid stench in the air, nearly covering a damp, moldy smell that seemed to seep up from the floor Galen was lying on. He groaned.

"Don't move." Rob pushed him flat on the floor. "Let the drug wear off a little more. Trust me."

Galen opened his eyes to complete darkness. Panic flared. "Rob?" He reached out for his brother, his hand came into contact with Rob's chest. "I can't see." He heard panic in his voice.

Rob grabbed his hand. "It's okay. We're in a cellar. There's no light."

"Good." Galen shifted, nausea washed over him in a huge wave.

"Trust me, you want to hold still," Flash grumbled from beside him.

"Flash tossed his cookies before I could stop him, or help him," Rob said, putting his hand on Galen's head. The nausea backed off.

"Thanks. Good job, Flash."

"I'm a barfer, you know that," Flash said.

"All too well." Galen sat up. "You say we're in a cellar?"

"Or something like that. I'm sure we're underground. The wall on the far side of the room is dirt," Rob answered.

"Part of the ritual?" Galen asked.

"Yeah, they need to bury us."

"What about bleeding us?" Galen reached out behind him,

his hand came into contact with a wall. He moved so he could lean against it. The thing in his chest was grinding against his heart in joyful anticipation.

"You have been bled my Emrys for this. Not for everything. Now we wait. Only a little more time and we walk," It said with a deep pleasure.

"Galen?" Rob asked quietly.

"Did It talk to you, too?"

"Yeah, It said only a little more time and you will see what I can become, what my Emrys will give me." Rob paused. Galen sensed his brother's hesitation. "What did It say to you?"

"It said only a little more time and we walk. Rob…"

"It's okay, Galen, it's supposed to happen."

"Would you like to tell me what's going on?" Flash snapped. "I think we have time."

"Flash, I'm sorry," Galen began.

"Yeah. Okay, you know I had a date with Sarah for tonight, right? If this ruins my chances with her, I'll kill you."

"Thanks. It's hard to explain Flash, it has to do with…" Galen stopped. The thing in his chest gave an excited twist. He took a deep breath. Rob put a hand on his shoulder.

"With…?" Flash asked.

"Hang on," Galen said, straining to hear anything beyond their breathing and the drip of water. Without thinking, he reached out with the Gift, he could sense someone approaching. "Company."

A door opened and light flooded into the room. Galen blinked, letting his eyes adjust to the sudden light. He looked around, it was a small room, one wall was, as Rob had discovered, dirt. A large stone rested against the exposed wall. The room was empty except for the three of them and the stone. A ladder led up five steps to the door. "Back away from the steps," a woman's voice drifted down to them. Rob moved so his back was resting against the wall next to Galen.

The woman came down the ladder, she had a gun in her hands. Galen recognized her, she was the nurse he and Rob had seen as they left the hospital. "Stay there. Okay, bring it down." A small man came down the ladder, carefully carrying a tray. He put the tray down and then reached up for something else. As soon as the brazier was handed to the man, Galen recognized the scent of the incense.

"I bet that's my frankincense. Bastards," Galen said under his breath. Rob chuckled.

The woman walked over towards them and gestured with the gun. "Stand up." They stood. She walked towards them, stopping in front of Flash. "This one is useless."

"Gee, thanks," Flash muttered. She struck him, Flash made a move to grab her and the gun was shoved in his face. "Okay." He put his hands in the air. "I get it."

She walked to Rob and smiled at him. "I remember you. Your friend killed my sister." She laid a hand on Rob's chest. Galen looked over as Rob's eyes rolled up. His brother moaned. "Yes, good." She pulled her hand away and turned to Galen with a cruel smile.

Galen could sense a tiny sliver of It, in her. "Your sister was Ashley?"

"Yes." She stood in front of him, her eyes searching his. "We've been waiting for you. Bring the tray." The small man slithered forward. He held the tray up for the woman on it were two silver cups and two bowls of grain. She picked up the bowls and handed them to Galen and Rob. "Eat." They scooped some of the grain out and ate some. It had a bitter undertone that Galen tried to decipher. He knew he recognized it, he just couldn't place it. When the bowls were empty, she handed them the cups.

Galen turned to Rob. "Cheers, Brat."

Rob raised his glass with a smile. "Cheers."

"This isn't a joke," the woman hissed. "Drink."

Galen clinked his cup against Rob's and drank. He handed the glass back to her. The spell the cup contained was already working on him. He could feel the first tingle of it running down his arms. *Not just herbs then. And like the incense designed to alter the Gift.*

"Put these on." She handed a red robe to Rob and a black one to Galen. "We'll be back." She turned and left, the small man scuttling behind her. Galen glanced down at his robe, black shot with dark red threads, the fabric shimmering like blackened blood.

"Nice," Rob said, pulling his shirt off and shrugging into the robe.

"Are you nuts? What are you doing?" Flash demanded.

"We have to go through with the ritual," Rob explained as the cellar door slammed closed plunging them back into the dark, lit only by the eerie glow from the brazier.

"Why?"

"Hard to explain, Flash. I will later, promise." Galen pulled on the robe, the smooth fabric sliding over his skin. The spell tingled along his legs.

"You'll explain later? Yeah, you already said that."

"Flash…" Rob said. "It's a little complicated."

"I'm listening…"

"Galen?" the soft, gentle whisper asked.

"What?" Galen said.

"Galen?" Rob put his hand on Galen's shoulder.

"Did you say something?" he asked his brother. The voice sounded like Rob.

"Galen?" the whisper came again.

"Or think it?" Galen said.

"No, could it be the thing?"

Galen shook his head. "Sounds completely different, the thing hisses."

"Yeah, it does." Rob rubbed his chest. "It's quiet right now."

"I know, like It's waiting for something. Are you okay?" Galen asked, trying to get a sense of his brother. The incense and the drink were affecting him.

"So far, a little tingly. You?"

"Same. Rob..." He sighed. "Can you smell that?"

"What?"

"I think this is going to be bad. Whatever's coming, they don't want us to go into shock," Galen said, looking at his brother.

"What do you mean? Smell what?"

"It's in the incense. Opium. It's not what's blocking the Gift, but I think it is helping the thing get better access to us."

"It's quiet for some reason." Rob absently rubbed his chest.

"Yeah, something big is going to happen, It's waiting, building Its strength for whatever's coming."

"What's coming?" Flash asked in a deceptively quiet voice.

Galen looked at his friend. "I'm not sure. Rob might have a better idea."

"Is it like what I saw in that vision?" Flash looked at Rob.

"Probably something like that. It was once like a god, It ruled on earth, and an ancestor of ours banished it to a lesser form."

"And if all that made sense to me, I'd ask what are you two doing?" Flash said, looking from one to the other.

"We're going to let It become what It once was so we can kill It," Rob said softly.

"Why didn't your ancestor kill it? When he had the chance?" Flash seemed dubious.

"Rob? You know the sagas better than I do," Galen said.

"He couldn't. According to the saga he tried, but he didn't have the power to actually kill It, all he could do was force It into the wood hag."

"Why couldn't he kill It?" Flash asked.

"I…" Rob began. "The sagas are unclear."

"His brother was dead," Galen said, remembering the vision the thing had shown him.

"That's not in the sagas, Galen."

"No, but that's what happened. His brother was dead, he was dying, he couldn't kill It, so he left It to us. The Legacy was clear, there has to be two Keepers to face It." Galen looked at Rob. "Two of us, Rob."

"Yeah. Galen…"

The door slammed opened again, light flooded down on them. The woman and small man came down the ladder, followed by ten other people. They filed into the room, standing by the large stone. The woman and small man stepped over to Galen and Rob. She laid her hand on Rob's chest.

"Rob!" Galen moved towards his brother when Rob moaned and dropped to his knees.

"Stay back," she hissed in a voice that sounded like the thing. She drew a silver knife and slashed Rob's arm. The small man scuttled forwards and held a golden cup underneath, letting the blood flow into the cup.

"I'm okay, Galen," Rob said through clenched teeth.

"Silence!" she demanded. She looked in the cup and nodded to the man. He handed it to her, then bound Rob's arm in black and red fabric. She walked to the large stone and began chanting, pouring the blood onto the stone and the ground around it. The others began chanting with her. Galen remembered the sound of the language from ten years before.

"It's talking," Rob whispered. Galen looked down at his

brother, Rob's eyes were closed and he was holding the arm they'd cut. "Galen, I'm sorry..." Before Rob could finish, two men came down the steps, grabbed Galen and pulled him over to the stone. Galen heard Flash's protest and Rob's anxious voice trying to calm Flash down.

They pushed Galen down onto the stone. One of the men held him down while the other bound one arm to an iron ring on the stone and the other to similar ring in the dirt wall. They wrapped a black and red cord around his legs, holding him immobile against the cold, flat stone. Galen looked across the small room and met his brother's eyes. Rob gave him a small smile. Galen's heart was pounding against his chest, the thing was beginning to hiss, a rhythmic hiss, like the chanting of the people in the room. The woman approached, she smiled at Galen and held the small knife over his chest.

"We begin what was begun, we undo what was done, we give of ourselves to achieve what will come," she said, plunging the knife down into the scar where the thing was hissing and writhing in anticipation.

"Yes, yes, my Emrys, it is time. It is time. Soon, very soon we walk, very soon we become." It was nearly singing.

The woman turned to the others in the room. "The vessel has already given what was needed. She made the perfect sacrifice, her gift was not wasted. He is here. Let it begin."

"Yes, yes, my vessel she that held me cradled in her heart," the thing hissed. "See what she gave." *The vision unfolded, a woman in her late fifties standing beside an altar, the child Galen had touched in the hospital was tied to it. The woman was whispering to the child, telling her of the things she had done, of what she was giving. She laid her hands on the child and the girl started screaming. The woman sank to her knees, her life flowing away. Her voice joined the screams of the child as darkness ran over her*

*body and into the child. The woman sighed and fell to the ground.
The child was lifted away from the altar.*

Galen blinked as the vision ended. He looked around the
room, sensing the others that had been there as the thing had
lodged in the child, waiting for him to come to heal her, waiting
for him to touch her so It could invade. The chanting increased
in volume, some of the people were swaying as they chanted.
Rob was still on his knees, his head cradled in his hands. *"Rob?"*
Galen reached out for his brother, the incense was blocking the
Gift. *"Rob?"* he tried again. His brother lifted his head. *"I'm here,
Galen."*

"The moment of our joining has begun," the thing hissed
happily.

The woman with the knife called out, cut her hand and held
it down on the bloody wound in Galen's chest. He felt the small
sliver of It in her slither down her arm and into his chest. Pain
ran out from the point of contact, shivering along his body. She
lifted her hand and staggered to lean against the wall, a smile on
her face. The small man approached, cut his hand and laid it on
Galen, more of the thing was transferred. Each of the remaining
ten did the same thing, each walking away obviously drained, all
with a smile of joy lighting their face.

It was hissing now, Its voice full of the same joy reflected
on the humans' face. It twisted with delight, sending shafts of
pain, of hot agony, lancing through Galen's body. "Yes, yes, your
family took my life. You will pay before we become, my Emrys,
before the final Joining. Yes, yes."

"We will wait until the appointed hour, and then at last He
will be free," the woman said, walking towards the ladder. The
others turned and followed her. The door closed, leaving them
in the dark again.

"The dark will remain, my Emrys. Once I become, we will

rule a world filled with dark. The Old Ones will walk again," It hissed against his heart, sending a grinding agony through his bones. Galen groaned as the visions began, he tried to stop them, but they welled up. *The Old One was there, standing in the circle of stones, the Keeper before It. The Old One was afraid, the Keeper was chanting a soft spell. It roared defiance, reaching out with a huge clawed hand it ripped at the Keeper.* Pain shot through Galen's body, he struggled against the bonds holding him, fought the voice as It hissed in his chest. He was losing himself to It, he could feel pieces slipping away into the abyss of darkness.

"Galen," the soft, gentle voice whispered. "Galen, fight it."

"Galen?" Rob's voice asked. Galen opened his eyes, he could just make out his brother in the dim light from the brazier. "Fight it." Rob untied the ropes holding Galen and pulled him up and away from the altar. He guided Galen to the far corner, away from the brazier, away from the stone. "Galen?" Rob asked again, his voice desperate.

Galen fought his way past the vision, focusing on the sound of his brother's voice, focusing on the warmth of Rob's hand resting on his back. "I'm here," he said, his voice rough. "My throat hurts."

"Probably because you were screaming," Flash said.

"Screaming?" Galen looked from Flash to Rob.

"Yeah," Rob said softly. "Galen…"

"It's all in me, except for the last in you, Rob," he said to his brother.

"I know."

"Did you know?" Galen demanded, trying to ignore the thing as It sang in his chest, dancing happily as It pulled Galen away bit by bit. "What are you doing?" he asked as Flash pulled off his t-shirt and Rob began tearing it into strips.

"Trying to…" Flash looked away, swallowing convulsively.

Galen looked down at his arms, the symbols carved on his body ten years before were bleeding again, the slashes on his arms open and dripping blood.

"Did you know?" he repeated, grabbing Rob's arm.

"Know what?" Flash asked.

"About the final part of the ritual. The part in Rob has to be in me to finish this. Rob…"

"I know, Galen." Rob looked at him with an sardonic smile. "But we'll stop it before anything bad happens."

"Before anything…" Flash sputtered. "Hello? In a cellar? Galen's bleeding? You're bleeding? Crazy people with knives? And there's more? Are you two nuts?"

"Yeah," Rob sighed.

"Galen?" the soft gentle voice whispered. "Galen?"

"What?" He looked at Rob. "What?"

"Galen? What is it?"

"You don't hear that?" Galen demanded.

"The thing? Yeah, I hear It. It's happy," Rob said, looking at him with concern.

"No, no—the other voice. It sounds like you a little."

"I don't hear anything." Rob looked around. "The Sight isn't working right. The drink and the incense…"

"Yeah. Rob, how can you fight if I succumb? Will that kill you?"

"I don't know, Galen. We just won't let that happen. If you're right, we both have to be there to kill It."

"Rob…" Galen paused. "It'll be like the visions, won't it?"

"I think so. You have to go through with it, no matter what."

"I know, we have to stop this before…All of It is in me, except that last part, if we die will it stop?" Galen asked on sudden inspiration.

"I'm not..."

"Try and die, my Emrys, this time it won't work. It's come too far for a simple death to stop me. Die and I become, live until I become. Either way, it will happen," the thing said.

"I guess that answers that," Rob said.

"Yeah."

"Galen?" the gentle voice whispered again.

"What?" he snapped. Rob frowned at him.

"Galen, Rob's right. It has to become so you can defeat it," the soft voice whispered.

"I'm going insane," Galen muttered.

"Galen?" Rob finished winding Flash's shirt around the slashes in Galen's arms.

"Galen?" the soft voice said.

"What?" Galen shouted.

"Galen, we're here. We'll help, trust Rob. Trust us," the soft voice continued.

Galen blinked, the voice was suddenly more than familiar. He finally recognized the soft tone, the gentle call. He looked wildly around the dark room, hoping to see the owner of the voice. Tears sprang into Galen's eyes, he looked at his brother. "Dad?" he whispered.

"What? Galen? What is it?" Rob gave him a shocked look.

"Dad?" he whispered again.

"Yes, we're here. You called. We're here, Galen. All of us," his father answered him.

Chapter Twenty

Galen shifted so he was leaning against the wall. Rob had torn another piece of the t-shirt off and was pressing it into the bloody wound in Galen's chest. The thing was hissing, twisting in ecstatic joy against his heart. Galen was drowning in Its voice as It sang, pulling the dark into Itself, pulling it into Galen. He closed his eyes, trying to listen to the other voices—his brother, his father—that the thing was trying to silence.

"Dad?" he asked. "You're here?"

"Yes, I am. Bobby, others. You called," Parry said.

"Galen?" Rob asked, looking at him.

"I...I'm hearing voices, Rob. It sounds like Dad."

"It is me, Galen," his father's voice had the hint of laughter in it Galen remembered.

"He says he is Dad. You don't hear him?" Galen asked. Rob shook his head. "How do I know, Rob?"

"You performed the Ritual of Calling, Galen. It must have worked."

"No." Galen was shaking his head, hoping to hear the gentle voice again, trying to focus on his brother's voice.

"Soon, soon it won't matter, none of their voices will matter, it will be only you and I," It hissed joyfully.

Galen heard Rob gasp. "Rob?" He opened his eyes and looked at this brother. Rob had his eyes closed, his face reflecting horror and agony. His eyes were moving rapidly behind his lids. "Rob?" Galen grabbed his brother's arm in a tight grip. "Rob!"

His brother drew a ragged breath, he opened his eyes. "Sorry," Rob said softly, rubbing his chest. "It's talking to me again."

"It was a vision," Galen said with certainty.

"Yes." He met Galen's eyes, his face bleak. "I…I'm sorry, Galen."

"Sorry?" Flash snapped. "Sorry about what?"

"It showed me…" Rob looked away. "Galen…"

Galen smiled. "Yeah, I know. I think I've known for awhile."

"I thought it would work, I thought we were the ones…" Rob said, a note of apology in his voice.

"We are, the ones who start it."

"Galen…"

"Hello?" Flash grabbed Galen's arm. "What the hell are you two talking about?"

"It's going to…" Rob swallowed, his eyes filled with tears. "It's going to…"

"It needs both of us, Flash, but once the part of It in Rob is transferred, It doesn't need my body anymore."

"What the fuck does that mean?" Flash growled.

"Galen…" Rob said quietly.

"I'm losing myself already, Rob. It's taking everything." Galen felt It twist, the pain shooting through his body. "It wants to…"

"Galen," his father whispered. "You have to hold on, you have to fight it."

"How? How can I fight It?" Galen asked desperately. Rob looked at him with a frown.

"You can, we're here, let us help," his father said.

"How can you help?' Galen asked.

"Galen?" Rob put his hand on Galen's arm. "What's going on?"

"Dad's talking to me."

"Your dead father? He's talking to you?" Flash asked. "Okay, I give up, this is now officially fucking insane."

"Like it wasn't before?" Rob's voice was sardonic.

"No. Not like this. Galen zapping people is one thing, the occasional spell, mostly small—only that one big one, some odd people frequenting the shop, the herbs and whatever he does after dark with all those weapons. That's one thing. Or several. But talking to dead people?"

"I've talked to the dead before, Flash," Rob said. "They can be pretty helpful sometimes." He chuckled. "Once I remember…"

"You talk to the dead? This just keeps getting better."

"They can be helpful," Rob said defensively.

Galen heard Flash respond, but the words flowed around him. He closed his eyes. It was talking, singing, shouting in joy as It pulled more and more of him into Itself. The combination of incense, the ritual food and whatever had been in the cup was beginning to affect him. It sensed that and began talking, visions swam through his mind, horror upon horror filling his body with agonizing pain, filling his mind with a growing pleasure.

It was slowly Becoming. Galen could feel It breathing in the wound, twisting as It waited to work Itself free and walk on the earth once more. His brother's voice had faded into a low rumble, the thing singing in his chest now had the upper hand. He struggled against It. Pain shot out from the wound, running though his body like a river in flood. "Enjoying this?" It said, Its voice slowly gaining power. "Yes, power. Your power, My Emrys."

A rough hand slapped his face, the stinging blow a mere pinprick in the writhing mass of pain filling his body as It twisted, growing slowly, filling him with more and more of Its darkness, the black tendrils were creeping slowly towards his brain. Another slap. "Galen!" Hands grabbed his shoulders. "Galen!" Rob was shaking him, Galen opened his eyes, the room was brighter, light streaming down from the open door. "They're coming. Galen, can you hear me?"

"Rob?" he asked, the name was nearly meaningless.

"They're coming. The final ritual. Just hold on, okay?" Rob squeezed his shoulders.

"Nearly gone."

"No, Galen. You're not." Rob gave him a gentle shake. "No." Tears were running down Rob's face. "I'm sorry I got you into this. I thought it would be easier, when I summoned you…"

"Because I was dead," Galen said, knowing the truth of it.

"If you were dead, it would be hard to…"

"Die? Yeah, that's what It plans. Can you help me up? I'd like to face this on my feet." Rob nodded and pulled him onto his feet. Flash put a steadying hand behind his back. "Rob?"

His brother smiled. "We got to be Keepers together, after all," Rob said, his voice soft, somehow sounding like his thirteen-year-old self.

"Yeah, Brat." Galen pulled his brother against him in a brief, tight hug. He gave Rob a gentle slap on the back and turned to Flash. "Told you—you should've run."

Flash smiled. "Nah. They would have run me down any-way."

"If you get a chance, go, okay? Don't look back, just go," Galen said urgently.

"Too late for him, My Emrys Keeper. Far, far too late." Its voice was strong, nearly a shout.

"Here they come," Rob whispered from beside him.

"We're waiting, Galen. We're here," his father whispered. Galen felt a feather-light touch brush his shoulder.

"Take him," the woman said, pointing at Rob.

"I'll go," Rob said, pulling away from the men who'd grabbed his arms. "Galen?"

"Time!" It screamed. Galen walked blindly towards the

stairs, past the woman and up the ladder. He heard Flash protesting behind him, heard Rob's urgent voice talking to Flash, calling Galen's name. They meant nothing. The time had come. The Becoming had begun.

Galen walked out of the small structure into a glade of giant trees, their huge trunks dwarfing the people gathered beneath them. Torches lit the scene, casting strange shadows through the clearing. The wind was whispering through the trees, a soft voice singing ancient praises of the dark, of the Old One. Night had fallen, a few stars glittered in the sky and the moon hung, blood-red, over the clearing where the people had gathered. Galen moved forward. A circle of stones was placed around the clearing, he could hear the power humming through the menhirs. A flat stone stood in the center of the circle, a large upright towered over the stone. Two huge braziers stood at each end of it, wafting the incense over the entire clearing. Galen walked towards the stone.

"My altar," It said, Galen heard his voice say the words.

He ran a hand over the smooth black stone. "Yes," he said to the night. "Perfect." The woman stepped beside him and handed him a cup, gold and copper glittered in the light of the torches. He took the cup. *Rob's blood.* How he knew, he wasn't sure. Pain shot through him with the thought. "No, the time has come, we begin," he said, Its voice ripping at his vocal chords.

He raised the cup over his head, tipping it and letting the blood flow out in a thin stream. The people around him began chanting he could hear their voices raised in the old song of praise, the words altered from those that called the wood hag, but still it was the same language, unchanged for five millennia. Galen walked around the stone as the chant washed over him, the darkness rising above him, moving with him.

He could sense other creatures lurking just out of sight.

"They wait for me, My Emrys," he said. His voice joined the others as he sang the prayer of the final joining. The incense wafting from the huge braziers skewed reality even further. A small part of him identified the smells, chided him to move away from it. He took a deep breath, the heady scent filling him with pain, with pleasure, as It danced on his heart.

Galen held out his hand, his sword was placed on his palm, the power of the blade ran through his body, brushing the thing as It leapt and danced in his chest. He held the sword aloft. "Bring the other," Its voice tore out of his throat. He tasted the coppery taste of blood as the words flowed out of him. He heard someone shouting behind him, he recognized Flash's voice. The shout turned to screams. Galen wanted to turn, to see what had happened, but It refused to let his body move.

Rob was beside him. "Hold on, Galen," he said quietly. With a defiant look at the men standing on either side of him, he reached over and took his sword from the woman, then lay down on the stone and placed his sword on his chest. "The sword is still singing," he whispered. The men came forwards and bound Rob to the altar, wrapping his body in the black and red cord.

"Now, now we will be Joined. We are become, we will be free," Galen said. Rob looked at him, a frown on his face.

Galen stepped forward, the thing moving his body towards the stone. He laid his sword on the stone, on Rob's left. He lifted the sword from his brother's chest and laid it on Rob's right. The dark was hovering over him, swirling around him, the chanting was reaching a fevered pitch.

Galen raised his hands, the chanting increased, the woman beside him nearly shrieking in joy. The wind suddenly changed, whipping the smoke away from Galen. He blinked. "Too late, we are Become," the thing said in his voice. He looked down at Rob, his brother met his eyes with a gentle smile. As far gone as he was, Galen could see the pain on his brother's face. "I'll try to heal you," Galen whispered to him.

Rob shook his head. "Let the ritual play out."

"What was taken is now returned, what was broken is now joined," he chanted, the thing's voice tearing at his throat. "I'm sorry," Galen whispered. "Now!" the thing shouted. Galen raised his hands.

And plunged them into Rob's chest.

Rob screamed, Galen felt the blood flowing hot over his hands, felt the movement of his hands as they passed through Rob's flesh until they came to rest deep in his chest. He could feel Rob's heart beating frantically against his hand. Rob was screaming in pain. The thing began to climb out of Rob, up Galen's arms. It was pulling parts of Rob with It, his Sight, his healing, his power.

His life.

"No," Galen said and tried to focus the light into his brother. The dark was filling him like a black cloud obscuring the sun. He took a deep breath and forced the light down one hand and into Rob. The thing was filling Galen, the black tendrils had reached his brain and were forcing their way into his consciousness. Galen focused every bit of healing left to him down his arms and into his brother. He slowly withdrew his hands, Rob's heart was barely beating, his brother had stopped breathing. "No," he said. Rob was nearly gone.

"Let me help," his father said softly. A warm hand was suddenly on his back. Galen knew it was Parry.

Galen pulled the light out of his father, as he had ten years before, he could see the light in his hands as it flowed into Rob. It was like he was watching through two sets of eyes, his own and the thing's, and each got something different out of the sight before them. Rob was dying. One part of him was filled with joy with that knowledge, the other with an almost paralyzing grief. "Rob?" Another hand touched him and he reached out and drew the light out from that touch as well. Power rippled through him, brushing him like the wind on a lake. The thing recognized the touch and tried to pull Galen's hands from Rob. In a last desperate moment, Galen focused part of himself through the light, hoping against hope that this plan would work.

The thing tore his hands away from Rob. "We are Become!" Galen screamed, blood running from his mouth from torn vocal chords. The chanting reached an orgasmic level as the thing twisted Itself through the last bit of Galen. He screamed, his voice blended with the thing's as a black cloud gathered over his head. He was chanting, the power he'd pulled from his brother, his own power, blending together to wrap around him. The power whipped around him, buffeting him with its fury. The swirling power focused to a single shaft and impaled him, running through his body in a huge surge.

Its moment had come. It ripped out of Galen, exploded out of his chest and into the air above him, Its huge form hovering over the clearing, Its breath stirring the trees, Its great wings beating with the sound of a thousand drums. "Finish it!" It screamed.

Galen forced himself up onto his feet and reached for his sword.

"Finish it! my Emrys, you are ended, end the other and we are Become!"

Galen lifted his sword and turned to the altar. Rob was covered in blood. Galen looked down at his hands, they were dripping his brother's blood, splashing drops on the altar as the thing screamed to finish it. The sword glittered in the light, the hilt was cool against his skin. He raised it, and looked at the thing perched on the huge stone at the end of the altar. "Finish and it is done. Finish, my Emrys." Galen swung the sword towards his brother. Rob's eyes were open, he smiled at Galen as the sword sliced down.

"Yes!" It screamed, then roared in fury as Galen slid the sword through the bonds holding his brother to the stone. He grabbed Rob's sword and pushed it into his brother's hands as the thing reached down and grabbed Galen in a huge clawed hand. It lifted him and slammed him into the ground.

"Galen!" Rob shouted. Galen looked towards his brother, Rob had rolled off the stone and was pushing himself up. A scream pulled Galen's attention from his brother, he twisted and saw something dark tearing at Flash.

"Help Flash," Galen called.

"Galen…"

"Flash, Rob!" Galen got a hand under his body and started to push himself up, his arm gave way and he collapsed back onto the ground. The thing laughed, the sound rattling the stones around the clearing. The power humming through the circle resonated through his body.

"My children are here," the thing said. Galen looked around, small spots of flickering darkness were popping into the clearing, tattered black rags fluttering in the breeze. Another one of the creatures dropped towards where Flash lay on the ground. Rob ducked as it swooped on him, striking out with his sword. Galen watched as his brother impaled the creature tearing at Flash, its dying shriek was answered by the other creatures filling the air, the clearing reverberating with their keening voices.

Galen tried to get up again, his arm wouldn't bear his weight. He glanced down at himself, the robe was torn, a giant slash ran down the length of his chest. Taking a deep breath, he managed to push himself onto all fours and crawled towards his sword. He could see it, a few feet away, where he'd dropped it. The metal was gleaming softly in the light of the torches, the smoke from the incense drifting down like fog, partially obscuring his vision. As he crawled towards the sword, he muttered an old spell he'd picked up from a passing Rom witch. A small breeze puffed against him and blew the incense away. He reached for the sword, his hand only inches from the hilt.

His hand was stopped. Four of the creatures landed on him, slamming him to the ground. Claws dug into his arms, he was pulled up and into the air. They carried him back to the altar, dropped him onto the stone and then settled on him, pinning him to the black surface. Another landed on his body, running a sharp talon along the wound in his chest. It chattered something to the Old One perched on the huge stone at the end of the altar, It laughed, gesturing for the creatures to continue.

The creature sitting on his chest put a hand against Galen's face. He felt it seeking, digging through his brain, looking for something. It chattered happily, having found what it was looking for. It turned to the Old One and said something, waving a bloody claw. The thing waved a huge hand and the small piece of darkness perched on Galen's chest flitted away, the creatures holding him down began humming, their voice blending with the chant still ringing through the clearing.

The Old One drifted down from Its perch and walked on huge taloned feet towards Galen, the impact of each step sending jarring pain through his body. It stopped beside the altar and turned towards the people gathered at the edges of the clearing. "The time has come, my people, I walk. With this last moment I am free, with this last moment I am Become, I am yours again and you are mine!" The chant rose, becoming a scream of delight that bounced around the clearing. Galen thought he saw movement to his left, but he couldn't be sure.

The thing turned back to him. It looked down at him with eyes shifting like smoke. Red to black and back again, like molten rock bubbling under blackened lava. "My Emrys," It whispered to him, Its voice grating like gravel dragged across a rock. It ran a gentle, almost loving hand down his face, gently cupping his chin before resting Its hand on wound It made when it tore Itself free. "Power, my Emrys, so much, more than any before, and I have had Keepers, my people have fed me Keepers over the years, but never the right ones, never my Emrys," It sighed, a blast of fetid breath washing over Galen, making him gag. "*My* Emrys." It laid a hand on his head and a hand on his chest imitating the stance used by *Custodes Noctis* healers.

In a ghastly mockery of the healing, darkness, rather than light, began flowing down from the touch of the thing. Oily black light slid through Galen's body, cold, filling him with darkness, pulling the last bit of Galen Emrys away, into Itself. Moments later, It pulled Its hands away. "It is accomplished!" he heard It shout. Screams of joy filled the clearing as the thing raised Its huge wings and pushed Itself into the sky. The creatures pinning him to the stone rose aloft with It, dancing in the air in a flitting ballet.

"Galen!" A trembling hand was laid on his arm. "Galen?" He turned nearly unseeing eyes towards the owner of the voice. He knew he should recognize him, but the face, the voice, were meaningless. "Can you hear me?" Even though he heard the words, he shook his head, somehow knowing the man would understand. He heard him, but the words made very little sense.

"Gods," the man said, looking down at the ruin of his chest. "Galen..." The man closed his eyes. "I understand why now. I hope what you left with me was enough to bring you back." A warm hand came to rest on his forehead, the man still had his eyes closed, his lips were moving in a soundless whisper. Warmth flowed out of his hands. Slowly, bright white light began to fill him, pushing the dark cold away. A spark of something slid into him, running through his body with an electrical shock.

He could feel the trembling hands on his head and chest, he opened his eyes and looked at his brother. "Rob," Galen said softly, laying a hand over his brother's.

"Galen?" Rob opened his eyes.

"It worked," Galen said, smiling.

"Good." Rob scrubbed a shaking hand across his face. "Good."

"Can you get my sword? Before It realizes what's happened?"

"Yeah," Rob said, bending to pick the sword up from where Galen had dropped it. He handed Galen the sword. "Galen, your chest…"

"Let's finish this first, Rob. Help me up." Rob slid a hand behind his back and help him sit up. Galen took a deep breath, trying to focus healing into himself. The pain backed off a tiny bit. He swung his legs off the altar.

Movement caught his eye again. He glanced towards the forest beyond the small building and saw a flash of light in the dark. Galen nudged Rob, his brother looked over as well. The flash again, this time Galen realized what it was. "Rhiannon. She's waiting for a signal." Rob nodded.

"We're waiting too, Galen," his father said. Galen saw a shimmer of silver light beside him.

"Rob and I have to kill the Old One, the others will have to take care of everything else," Galen said.

"We understand," his father said.

Galen looked at Rob. "Ready?" His brother nodded. Galen raised his sword. The Old One caught the movement and turned in the sky, diving down towards them, the dark creatures flowing down behind It chattering and shrieking as they descended. The thing slammed into the ground with enough force to topple some of the stones lining the clearing, the creatures dropped down beside It. Galen took a deep breath, "Now!" he shouted.

The clearing suddenly shimmered, silver light began pouring into the dark circle of stones. The people surrounding them stopped chanting. One of them screamed as Rhiannon burst from behind a tree, sword in hand. The woman who had led the ritual turned towards her. She dove towards Rhiannon, pulling a knife from her belt as she ran. Rhiannon stopped, looked at the woman, held her sword in front of her and waited. Galen could hear her counting as the woman plunged towards her. Rhiannon looked over at him with a grin, pulled out a gun and calmly shot the woman.

The Old One screamed with rage. The dark creatures were fighting for their lives as the shimmering figures moved between them. Galen recognized his father and uncle, and the man from his vision, the first Emrys. Dark and light swirled around him, the sounds of screams, of shrieks, of death flowed over him.

His entire focus was taken up by the thing as It approached them.

Rob put his hand on Galen's arm. *"I'll move to the rear,"* Rob's voice played in his head.

"Okay, be careful," he thought back. Rob nodded and slipped to the side. One of the silver figures moved in front of Rob, blocking his brother from view. The thing struck out at the shimmering form. Galen heard a scream of pain and the light was abruptly gone.

"Yes, My Emrys, yes, I can kill them, my children can kill them," It said, dark laughter bubbling out of It.

Galen looked around, the battle was raging, bright light blending with darkness, disappearing as one or the other was killed. The air was full of human screams, defiant battle cries and the shrieking of the dark creatures as they died. Galen's focus wavered for an instant when he realized a figure curled on its side was Flash.

The thing acted in that moment, swiping at him with a huge hand, claws like steel catching him and lifting him away. He felt himself move through the air and then slam down against a stone. A silver figure bent to help him up, the hands holding him were no more than a whisper of warm air. He met the sparkling emerald eyes and smiled his thanks. A gentle breeze wrapped around him, he felt a tiny shiver of energy radiate out from the touch. "Thank you," he said, the figure dipped his head in acknowledgement and turned to slice through one of the dark creatures in an easy swing.

Galen forced himself back towards the Old One. It was waiting by the altar, watching the battle around it, occasionally reaching out to cut through a fleeing human. "Fools, abandon me now and die," It roared.

Rob had edged around behind It. He looked over and caught Galen's eye. *"Wait for me, Rob,"* he thought, hoping it would reach his brother. Rob smiled and nodded.

"Right, you wait for me, too," Rob answered.

"Yeah, we need to kill it together. Our swords have to pierce It at the same time."

"That's not in the sagas."

"Yeah, well, fuck the sagas." Galen saw his brother blink at the unaccustomed profanity. Galen grinned, then grimaced as his legs dropped out from under him. He tried to force himself up, knowing he was very nearly at the end of his ability to keep going. One of the dark creatures landed on him, tearing at him. "Galen!" his father shouted, he realized he heard the shout audibly. Galen felt flesh tear before the creature was cut in two. Hands pulled him upright. "Galen, can you go on?" Parry asked.

"Yeah, can you and Bobby try and keep them off Rob and me while we finish this?" The shimmering form of his father nodded.

Galen walked slowly back towards the altar. The thing watched his halting progress, he felt Its amusement ripple through him, the black tendrils were pushing at him again. *When Rob brought me back, there must have been some of that thing left in me.* Galen took a deep breath.

"What do you mean? Some of It is still in you?" Rob demanded, his voice a shout in Galen's head.

"I can feel It, still in me. I might not have as much time as I hoped."

"We will finish this, Galen," his brother said firmly. Galen caught the edges of his brother's fear, pain and determination to go on. Galen nodded.

As Galen approached, the thing reached out again, tearing at him with Its claws. Galen fell to his knees, but forced himself up again. He saw the shine of Rob's blade on the other side of the Old One. Rob was moving slowly towards It. His progress was stopped when one of the dark creatures drove him to the ground. Galen started to move towards his brother when Bobby descended on the creature. Rob stood. *"I'm okay, Galen, just a scratch."*

Galen was aware of his father sliding along behind him. He drew strength from the fact his family was together. The thing saw Parry as well. Galen felt anger swell through him as the Old One recognized his father. Galen fought the connection with the thing, fought the urge to draw his father closer to the thing so It could kill Parry.

"You can't kill me, my Emrys."

"I can." Galen said, stopping before It. *"Get ready, Rob."* It thrust Its hand towards him and grabbed him in Its claws. The sharp points drove into Galen's body like blades of dry-ice, so cold they burned as they punctured his body. He heard his voice scream in pain, but stayed focused on It, hearing Its laughter in his head. Silver shimmered beside the altar, many feet below where the thing held Galen. His father and uncle were protecting Rob.

"I have your power, I own your life," It said, pulling him closer. The black light was flowing into him again, ripping away pieces of himself. He swallowed, trying to focus.

"No," he said quietly. "This ends now."

"Yes, yes it does, my Emrys," It threw Its head back and laughed.

"Now!" Galen shouted. He thrust forward with his sword, driving it into the Old One's chest, impaling Its heart. Darkness flowed up the sword, burning him, the thing was screaming. Galen felt Rob's sword impact the thing, felt the blade slide through his body. It shrieked a horrifying sound. Clawing at the sword in Its chest, It looked at Galen, anger seething in Its eyes. Galen twisted the sword, driving the blade into Its body with the same motion that It had ground against his heart.

He was falling.

The thing dropped him as It fell, toppling down, black blood pouring from the sword wounds. Galen saw his brother perched on Its back, his hand still on the hilt of his sword. The thing screamed and reached for Galen, tearing flesh away from his throat.

The dark creatures suddenly stopped, their shrieks growing in intensity as they flitted towards the fallen Old One. They landed on Its body, hundreds upon hundreds of them, landing like a swarm of beetles, their wings rustling as they perched on Its body. They patted It with clawed hands, a keening shriek rising through the clearing.

With a final scream, still defiant, It died. The dark creatures rose as one, tearing pieces of the thing's body with them. As they popped out of existence, Galen realized they had dismembered the Old One. All that was left was a pool of black liquid, slowly congealing on the ground.

"Flash!" Galen forced himself onto all fours and crawled towards Flash. He turned his friend over, the creatures had done a lot of damage before Rob had driven them away.

"Hurts, Galen," Flash whimpered.

"I bet," Galen said softly. "I'm sorry." He laid his hands on Flash, letting the light flow. Flash sighed and closed his eyes, Galen tried to stay focused on the healing, consciousness was rapidly fading, flowing away from him like the blood dripping on the ground in front of him. The last of the light slid out of him. Flash's wounds were already healing, the pain gone from his friend's body.

"Galen! What the hell are you doing?" Rob pulled him away from Flash. "Gods, Galen."

"Too late for me, Rob," he whispered, "had to save Flash."

"Galen!" Mike's voice was rough with emotion. Galen felt a hand pressed against the wound in his chest. He cried out in pain.

"No, no, that won't help," Rob snapped.

"He's bleeding out, Rob. I have no idea how he lasted this long!" Mike was shouting.

"Honey, honey, hang on," Rhiannon said quietly. Galen felt her take his hand in hers.

He was gently lifted, propped against his brother, a warm hand was placed on his head. Rob was focusing the healing into him, he could feel Rob's lungs taking some of the effort of breathing from his own. Rob put a hand on his chest. He felt the light begin to flow out of his brother. The darkness left in Galen by the thing blocked the light. "Can you help me?" Rob asked, tears in his voice.

Galen opened his eyes. "No, sorry. Rob..."

"No, Galen, no. Not again. Not this time." Rob looked around the clearing. "Dad!"

Parry appeared beside them. "Galen, no."

"Heal him, Dad."

"I can't, Rob. I can help, like I did during the ritual, but I can't heal by myself." Parry's shimmering form glittered with tears. "Can you help, Galen?"

"Nothing left, Dad." Galen drew a shallow breath, the healing that had been blocking his body from pain, from keeping him from going into shock, from bleeding to death, was gone. "Sorry," he said again. *How many times is that?* "Rob..."

"Help me," Rob said, his voice harsh.

"We need a healer, Rob," Parry said as two more shimmering figured knelt beside Galen. One was his uncle, the other was the man from his vision, the first Emrys. Galen nodded to the man.

"I can heal. Help me, Dad," Rob said. Parry put shimmering hand over Rob's, Galen closed his eyes as he felt the light flow into him, warming him. The dark still blocked the healing. He knew that he only had moments left, he tried to fight back towards his family. "Rob, I'm sorry. I..."

"Shut up, Galen," his brother growled.

The healing suddenly changed, strengthened. Power slid into his body, driving the dark away, shutting it off in a small place. The world was fading, drifting away on the bright light, sparkling like a thousand twinkling stars against the dark night. *"It can't be completely removed. I'm sorry,"* a deep voice whispered. *"I never learned how. My brother—it took him completely before I could stop it. I never thought to pull part of him into myself as you did during the ritual. It saved you, that spark you left with your brother. Rest, Galen Emrys. Rest."*

"Galen?" Rob said desperately.

"Galen?" his father's anxious voice joined his brother's.

"Rest, Galen. Rest until you are needed," the deep voice whispered. *"Rest."*

"Galen?" A drop of water fell on Galen's face.

"Rob," he said to his brother. "We got to serve as Keepers. We finally got to serve together as Keepers."

The light flowed into him and he finally let it carry him away.

Chapter Twenty-One

A nightmare pursued him through the velvety darkness. Claws glittering with blood pulled at him, pain shot through his body with each assault. Galen cried out, his voice muffled. Warmth and healing light would drift through him after he called, a gentle voice spoke soothingly to him. *Rob.* Once the light left him, the nightmare would begin again, over and over. The dark creatures perched on his chest, holding him immobile as the thing slowly took away everything he was, pain pushed him closer to the light, to sounds—but he couldn't breech the darkness.

"He needs to be in the hospital," Mike's voice drifted down through the dark.

"Why?" Rob's voice was harsh, exhausted.

"Why? Oh, I don't know. Those wounds? Coma? None of that seems like a reason to get medical care?"

"He's getting medical care, you're here."

"He needs…"

"What? What does he need, Mike?" Rob shouted. Galen could hear desperation in his brother's voice.

"A vent would help…Take some of the stress off his body, the lungs…"

"Mike?" Rob's voice was suddenly quiet. Mike kept talking. "Mike?" The doctor kept talking. "Mike!"

"What?"

"He doesn't need a vent."

"It would help him heal…He needs…"

"I've been breathing for him since the ritual," Rob said softly.

Galen let himself drift through the dark sea. He could feel the air moving in and out of his body, and knew what Rob said was true. *He's assisting my heart, too.* The dark was tugging at him again, the nightmare images washing through him, threatening to push him into the abyss.

"You're what?" The shock in Mike's voice caused a ripple of amusement through the dark waters holding Galen captive.

"Breathing for him. The hospital can't help this, Mike," Rob said gently. "His wounds are healing, you know that. It's what happened during the ritual." Rob sighed. "I can help heal the physical damage, and some of the psychic injury, but even with Dad's help it's not enough. We need Galen." *Dad? He's still here?*

"Rob…"

"Don't start, Mike," Rob snapped. "Sorry."

"It's okay, but Rob, Galen is…"

"We just need to bring him back far enough to help us. If he'd just come back a little further, he could put himself in a healer's trance."

"Can't you do that?"

"No, I can heal a little, with Dad's help a little more, but neither of us has the power Galen does. We need his help." Galen heard a moan, it took a moment for it to register that it was his own voice. "Galen? Hang on." A warm hand was placed on Galen's forehead, light and warmth flowed out, the dark was pushed away.

The nightmare began again. The Old One was talking, pulling Galen with It as It moved across the earth, leaving pieces of Galen behind as It moved, filling him with Itself. Slivers of memory moved through him, his own blending with remnants of the thing. He tried to focus, tried to move through the dark sea. Rob's words flitted across his mind. The weariness in the tone caused concern to bubble through the inky night. Galen fought his way free. Light touched his eyelids. Pain flowed through him, part nightmare, part real. Something warm was resting on his arm. "Rob?" No answer. Galen tried to draw a breath. "Rob?" he heard his voice that time, a dry rasp in the quiet room.

The warmth tightened on his arm. "Galen?"

"Yeah."

"Galen?"

"Yeah," he repeated. He tried to open his eyes, they felt glued closed.

"Hey." Rob's voice was soft.

"You okay?"

"Yeah," Rob said. "I'm okay, you're not."

"I know."

"Can you..." Rob stopped. Galen heard his brother clear his throat. "Can you heal?"

"I..."

"The healer's trance? The sagas say..."

"I've never used it before, Rob. No one has used the healer's trance in centuries. I'm not even sure I know how to..."

"Try," Rob whispered. "You have to at least try."

Galen tried to focus the light, tried to pull it into himself, it hovered just out of his reach. "Can you help?" he asked quietly.

"As much as I can."

"Thanks," Galen said. Rob laid his hands on Galen's forehead and chest. Before Galen focused the light, he reached out, trying to get a sense of his brother. Exhaustion washed up through the contact, Rob was very near the end of his endurance.

"I'm okay, Galen, take what you need," Rob said. "Please."

"Rob..."

"You're dying, Galen. If you can't heal, I'm gone anyway." Rob paused. "Please," he said simply. "I'll be okay." Galen still hesitated. Rob sensed the hesitation and white light suddenly flooded Galen's body. "Use it," Rob's voice was harsh.

Galen waited for the space of three heartbeats, the light flowed through him, he caught it and focused it, sending shafts through his body. Consciousness began to waver, to shift, he was floating on the light, warmth filling his body. A soft song began, it sounded like the song of his sword. He drank in the healing like a man lost in the desert finding water. It filled him, altered him. Right before it pulled him away, he focused a tiny bit of it back into his brother. He heard Rob's soft sigh as he drifted away, carried on the song and the light.

Consciousness began filtering back. Galen was aware of an ache in his chest and neck, the fact he was breathing for himself, the bed under him and a warm hand resting on his. "Rob?"

"Galen?" Flash answered. "That you, man?"

Galen forced his eyes open. "Flash?"

"Welcome back, shit, man, you had me worried." Flash grinned.

"Rob?" Galen coughed, his throat was unbelievably dry. Flash grabbed a bottle of water off the bedside stand, slipped a hand behind Galen's head and held the bottle so he could take a sip. "Thanks. Rob?"

"Sleeping." Flash sat back in the chair beside the bed. Galen glanced around. He was in his own room. "He was about at the end. He wouldn't leave." Flash chuckled.

"What?"

"The kid wouldn't go, even though he was pretty sure you were going to be okay. I tried, Rhiannon tried…Mike finally managed it." Flash laughed again.

"Drugged him?" Galen felt an answering smile on his face.

"Oh yeah. Out like a light." Flash glanced at the clock. "About fifteen hours now."

"Good, don't let him get up too soon, okay?" Galen looked at his friend. "Flash…"

"We'll talk about all this shit later, Galen. And don't do something like apologize. You saved my life. I know it, even if you deny it. So shut up and rest. I'll keep an eye on the brother and the shop. Rhiannon's down there now. Oh, your Mrs. Barkley came by looking for you. I told her you were sick. She bought some ginger and catnip and said she'd be back."

"She needs her arthritis treatment. I zap her," Galen said. "Flash?"

"Yeah?"

"Could you give me a hand to the…"

"Sure." Flash pulled him to his feet and helped him to the bathroom. By the time Galen was back in his room he was exhausted. "You need more rest," Flash said softly.

"Yeah," Galen said, letting his eyes close. He called up the healing and felt it respond immediately. The light flowed through him as he dropped off to sleep.

It was raining.

Galen could hear the water falling on the metal balcony outside his window. He sighed, listening to the musical sounds of the drops, enjoying the quiet, the soft feeling of the bed. There was a lingering ache in his chest. He ran a hand over it, feeling the rough texture of scar tissue. With another sigh he opened his eyes. He was alone in his room, he glanced at the clock. *Ten thirty? I hope someone's in the shop.* Galen took a deep breath and pushed himself up, waiting for a moment, then he put his feet on the floor and carefully stood.

He walked through the quiet apartment. The scent of coffee and toasted bread hung in the air. Galen paused by the door to Rob's room, the bed was made with military precision. Galen smiled, remembering the mess that his brother left when he was younger. He grabbed a couple of towels out of the linen closet and walked into the bathroom, turning on the shower and letting the steam heat the room before stepping under the hot water. The water helped relax the tight muscles along the edge of the scar tissue.

When the shower cooled he stepped out. Wiping the steam from the mirror he looked at the damage on his chest and neck. He ran a finger along the slash on his throat, turning his head to get a better look at the deep purple scar. Something shimmered at the edge of his vision.

"It was a fatal wound," his father said quietly.

"I know," Galen said. "So was the one on my chest."

"Yes."

"You and Rob saved me. Thank you."

"I only helped. Emrys helped, too. Galen…"

"Yeah," Galen said, knowing what his father meant. "Me and Rob, you and Bobby suspected all those years ago. You should have popped in to tell me."

"Suspected is different than knowing, and I couldn't come until I was called."

"Are you planning on hanging around?" Galen asked with a smile.

"We've been talking about it, and we think we might." Parry's form shimmered with gentle humor. "If you don't mind."

"I've been hoping you'd haunt the place for years."

"Good." A soft touched brushed Galen's shoulder. "You need to eat."

"If you're going to start bossing me around, Dad, maybe…" Galen laughed, his father's form shimmered with laughter and slowly dissolved. "I'm glad you're back."

Galen padded back to his bedroom, carefully stretching before he got dressed. The scar across his chest pulled his shoulder.

He rotated the arm, trying to loosen the tightness. The room spun around him, he put a hand on the wall waiting for the dizziness to pass. His father was right, he did need to eat. He got dressed, walked through the apartment and down the stairs to the shop, automatically glancing out the back window as he passed the door.

Galen could hear voices, his brother, Flash and a woman, talking in the shop. He paused by the curtains that screened the back from the shop and waited, pulling the fabric aside to look in. Rob was moving a little slow. Flash seemed his usual self, but Galen could sense an edge of weariness in his brother. The bell on the door tinkled as Flash escorted the woman out. Galen pushed aside the curtain and stepped into the shop as his brother turned back towards the counter.

"Galen!" Rob smiled and walked quickly towards him, pulling Galen against him in a tight hug. "Hey."

"Hey, Brat," Galen said, leaning against his brother for a moment.

Rob stepped back, tears sparkling in his eyes. He left his hands on Galen's shoulders, searching his face. "Should you be up?"

"I think so, about time, don't you think?" Galen laid his hand on his brother's and let a little healing light flow through the contact. Rob closed his eyes briefly. Galen felt the exhaustion still weighing Rob down shift.

"Thanks, but that's enough for right now," Rob said, giving his shoulders a squeeze and letting his hands drop.

"Hey, man." Flash came over and slapped him gently on the back. "I'll get some coffee." Flash smiled and headed out the door.

"Sarah working?" Galen asked with a laugh as Rob led him to the stool behind the counter. "I'm okay, Rob," he said gently. Rob leaned against the counter, Galen ran his eyes over his brother. He could see a scar at the edge of Rob's collar. Galen pulled the t-shirt down a little. "I do that?"

"The thing did it, Galen. Not you."

"I know, Rob, it's just…" Galen sighed, the memory of his hands sinking into Rob's chest suddenly fresh.

"Your hands, I know."

"You know?"

"Yeah, Galen, but you healed me, too. I never thought…" He stopped as Flash came back into the store, carrying three cups. Rob frowned. "I'm not sure coffee should be the first thing…"

Galen reached for the cup Flash held out. "First Dad, now you." He grinned. "I should be okay, unless this one of Flash's…"

"No, it's one of your wimp specials. I even had whipped cream put on it." Flash shuddered. "Whipped cream."

"Thanks," Galen said with a smile. He sipped his coffee and looked around the shop, enjoying the quiet comfort of the store. A thought wound its way into his brain. "How long?"

"A week tomorrow," Rob said softly.

"Yeah," Flash echoed.

"I'm glad you're up today, though. I wanted to make sure you were up and around before…"

"Before what?" Flash growled.

"You weren't planning anything stupid were you?" Galen asked, looking at his brother.

"What?" Rob and Flash said in unison, Rob's voice innocent, Flash's demanding.

"You weren't planning on going and cleansing the circle where the ritual took place without me, were you?" Galen met his brother's eyes, knowing that was exactly what Rob had planned.

"Uh…"

"No, Rob. I won't let you." Galen frowned.

"It has to be done," Rob said, frowning back. "You know that."

"It does. But not alone. Gods, Rob, you know better than that."

"What the hell are you talking about?" Flash asked, looking from one to the other.

"The place where the ritual took place needs to be 'cleansed.' That kind of thing leaves a huge scar on the earth, and it has to be removed or dark forces can use it as a gathering point. It also removes the possibility of the Old One's minions returning to that spot," Rob explained.

"Okay, sounds like a good idea." Flash paused. "I bet it's not easy."

"No, and that's why he doesn't go alone," Galen said.

"No, Galen. No," Rob growled.

"Rob…" Galen began.

"You can't, Galen. It's too big a risk."

"You'll need my help, Rob. You can't muster the power by yourself to cleanse that circle without help. Dad and Bobby won't be enough."

"Even with Emrys' help…" The fight left Rob, Galen watched his brother's shoulders slump.

"It has to be me," Galen said softly. "Keepers work together, I have to be there."

"Galen, I…" Rob swallowed looking away.

"I know, Rob. I understand. You're worried what being back there will do. If the darkness that's left will affect me." Galen laid his hand on his brother's arm. "You'll be there to stop that, if it's needed."

"No!" Rob shook his head, pulling away. "I won't, Galen. No.

I'm going alone."

"You're going alone over my dead body." Galen pushed himself off the stool and stood in front of his brother. The world suddenly revolved around him, he swayed. Rob caught him under the elbows and guided him back to the stool. Galen put his head in his hands, waiting for the dizziness to pass. "I might need to eat something," he mumbled through his hands.

"Yeah," Flash piped up. "Soup. You need soup. I'll be back."

"Are you fighting with me just for the hell of it?" Galen asked, looking up at Rob. His brother was frowning with concern. Galen watched the emotions playing on Rob's face, ending with a half-hearted smile.

"Probably. I know we have to go together. It's how we work, but…" Rob looked away.

"What?"

"I just found you again, Galen. Then, after the ritual, I was sure…" Rob swallowed, then looked at Galen, bright tears sparkling in his eyes. "I was sure I'd lost you again."

"I'm not lost."

"I know, I'm just worried about what'll happen if you go back."

"I won't hurt you again, Rob, I won't let that happen."

"You didn't do it, the thing did it," Rob said very slowly, very patiently like he was explaining something to a child.

"Rob…"

"We're done talking about that, okay?"

"Rob, I…"

"I said we're done." Rob stuck his fingers in his ears and started humming. Galen chuckled, then laughed, lightly smacking his brother on the chest. "Well, that's settled," Rob said, letting his hands drop, grinning at Galen.

"The other's settled, too. I'm coming with you."

"Yeah." Rob smiled. "I actually had no idea how I would manage it. You're the only one with enough power to cleanse the place."

"You aren't going to start that again, are you?" Galen sighed.

"Galen," Rob said, shaking his head. "After everything, you still doubt that you're..." He trailed off with a shrug. "I won't convince you of it, will I?"

"There's nothing to convince me of, Rob."

"The Legacy? Defeating the Old One? Coming back from the dead? Any of that ring a bell?"

"I know, but...Okay, fine, I might need more convincing," Galen laughed. The door to the shop slammed open, Galen got up, knowing who to expect. Rhiannon walked quickly across the store and pulled him into her arms. He held her for a moment, when he pulled away there were tears on her cheeks.

"Good to see you up, honey," she said gently.

"Good to see you, too. Are you okay?"

"Me? I'm indestructible, you know that." Rhiannon hopped onto the counter. "Flash has soup. He was right behind me."

"I was, until you ran," Flash grumbled from the door. "Thanks for the help." Flash walked over to the counter and put two large bags down. "I got some kind of potato soup thing for you." Flash dug a Styrofoam cup out of a bag and handed it to Galen. "Veggie sandwich for Rob and real food for me and Rhiannon."

"Thanks," Galen said, settling down on the stool.

"So what's the game plan?" Rhiannon asked around a mouthful of sandwich. "Rob and I need to go cleanse the circle."

"No," Flash jumped in. "You and I and Rob need to go cleanse the circle."

Galen snuck a glance at his brother, Rob quirked his eyebrow at him. "No, Rhiannon, we need to do this, you and Flash can come with us to cleanse the circle," Galen said, emphasizing the "us."

"You just got out of bed," Rhiannon said with a frown.

"And I'm coming with you."

"Rob?" Flash said.

"He's coming." Rob shrugged.

"We settled it a minute ago," Galen said with a smile. "When's moonrise?"

"Just before midnight," Rob said. "You can finish your soup, take a nap and I'll wake you when it's time to go."

"Rob? You weren't planning on not waking me were you? Maybe trying it for yourself after all?"

"It's tempting, but no. You need to be there." Rob laid his hand on Galen's shoulder, meeting his eyes. Galen felt the truth of his brother's statement, as well as an undercurrent of fear.

Galen felt an answering shiver of fear in his heart.

With a deep breath, he smiled at Rob and opened his soup, content to listen to the others talk before heading up the stairs and back to bed, wondering what the night would bring.

Chapter Twenty-Two

The rain had stopped by the time they reached the site of the ritual. The all-pervading damp was still there, sending a soft ache into the scar tissue on Galen's chest. He rolled his shoulders and looked out the window at the dark place. He could just make out the ring of stones in the glow cast by the headlights. Something that felt like an inaudible rumble flowed through him, the remnants of the ritual, of the Old One, still moving through the place. Galen could sense the emotion from Rob. His brother was worried. "I'm okay, Rob," he said quietly.

"Yeah." Rob looked over at him, then laid his hand on Galen's arm. "You're lying."

"Not too much," Galen said, smiling. "It has to be done."

"I still wish you'd let me do it," Rob muttered. Galen looked at his brother as another set of headlights swept over the place. He raised his eyebrows and met Rob's eyes. "Okay, fine." Rob grinned. "Rhiannon, Flash and Mike are here."

"We don't really need babysitters." Galen got out of the jeep and walked around to the back, waiting for Rob to open it.

"They seem to think we do," Rob said, laughing. His mood was catching and Galen felt an answering chuckle in his chest. "I guess I could've messed with Rhiannon's car, but then I would have had to sabotage Mike's and Flash's."

"And take their credit cards so they couldn't rent one," Galen added.

"So, letting them come along seemed like a better idea." Rob opened the back. "I got everything I think we need."

"I'll say," Galen said, looking into the jeep. Rob had their

323

swords, several additional blades, a large box full of herbs and charms and some smaller items scattered in the back. Galen reached in and grabbed his sword, pausing as the song flowed up his arm and behind his eyes. He leaned against the car for a moment as the dizziness passed. "I wonder how long that goes on?"

"I don't know." Rob picked his sword up and closed his eyes. "It could be inconvenient."

"I didn't notice it during the ritual," Galen said as they walked towards Rhiannon's car.

"We might have been a little distracted at that point."

"Maybe." Galen laughed softly. "I'm not sure what's going to happen, maybe you three should stay back here," he said as they approached their friends.

"Yeah, sure. Of course we will." Flash looked at him. "Not."

"He said it." Rhiannon smiled.

"I agree," Mike chimed in.

"Fine," Galen said, smiling. "Just be careful, and if something looks like it's going sour, for gods' sake, run. Promise that."

"We'll run. Right guys?" Flash said, looking from Rhiannon to Mike and back again.

"Flash..." Galen growled.

"Oh, no. Fuck no, not leaving you, Galen. Just get over it. Okay? You and Rob are the pros, we get that, but we're here to back you up, and back-up doesn't run."

"Especially the doctor," Mike said.

"Right," Rhiannon agreed.

"Okay," Rob said, "but be careful." He turned to Galen. "Are you ready? The moon's starting to rise." When Galen hesitated, Rob put a hand on his back. "Galen?"

"I'm ready." He looked at Rob, trying to ignore the growing tingle of darkness simmering beneath his feet.

"What?" Rob asked.

"Nothing." Galen walked towards the circle, memories of the ritual playing in front of his eyes. He stopped at the mark the Old One made when it fell. Darkness flowed out of the ground, running up his legs, exploding in his chest. He felt the impact with the ground as his knees slammed into the earth.

"Galen!" Rob's hand was on his arm, supporting him.

"It's okay."

"No, no, it's not. This was a mistake. Rhiannon!"

"No, Rob. Help me up. We have to cleanse this place. If we don't…" Galen broke off, wondering if he should tell his brother what was left lurking under the blackened soil. "Help me up." Rob pulled him to his feet and left a steadying hand under his elbow. "I need the herbs." Galen held out his hand before his brother could object.

"Okay." Rob acquiesced too easily. Galen looked at his brother for a long moment. "I heard you, Galen. About what's left," Rob said softly. "I'm not sure you can keep stuff like that from me."

"That might be a pain in the ass," Galen grumbled. He took the black velvet bag of herbs from Rob. Galen carefully sprinkled the area where the Old One had died, then walked to the altar. The vision of his hands sinking into Rob's chest was suddenly before his eyes. His hands started shaking as a sense memory—warm liquid, the resistance of Rob's ribs—crept into his awareness. He took a deep breath and covered the altar with herbs.

"I have the candles. I already lit them at the place where It died." Rob carefully put the candles onto the altar. He lit them and turned to Galen. "Are you sure?" He smiled. "Of course you are. I'm ready."

Galen placed his hands on his sword, right hand on the hilt, left holding the blade. He stopped. "I've never done this before,

Rob," he admitted.

"Have you ever raised an army of the dead before?" Rob clapped him on the back. "Just start. I'm sure it'll be like the other."

"How will you know…"

"What to do?" Rob finished for him. "I've read the ritual. Remember I planned to do this by myself. I'll follow your lead, Galen."

"As will we," Parry's form shimmered into existence beside them, joined an instant later by Bobby and a third man. Galen recognized him—the First Emrys.

"Thank you," Galen said. He took a deep breath and tightened his hand on the hilt of the sword. He let his eyes close, aware of the pulsing of dark evil under his feet, slowly filling the circle again. With another breath he began to sing, the song flowing out of him as if it were part of him. Reality wavered, the song grew in intensity.

He felt Rob's hand on his shoulder, heard his brother's voice join his. Power surged through him, light began to pool at his feet, he heard other voices, a counterpoint to the song he and Rob were singing. The power began to build, the light slowly engulfing him. The darkness was pushing in on him trying to reach him through the light. A single cold claw of the dark touched him, he thought he felt himself fall, but he wasn't aware of his body. The song filled him completely, surrounded him.

Galen continued, waiting for the moment, and it was suddenly there. He let the song change, and the power that had been gathering exploded outwards, washing the circle in a huge wave of light, chasing the darkness away, from the shadows of the stones, from the dark place where the Old One had died. Galen felt a shriek echo out of the earth, a final strand of something lashed out, wrapping him briefly in the dark, then disappeared into the night.

"What are you doing? Check on Galen first," Rob's voice was harsh. "Help me up."

"He's alive, Rob," Mike answered. "Galen?"

"I know he's alive," Rob snapped. "Galen?" he said gently. Galen felt his brother drop down beside him, then Rob's hand on his head and chest a moment later. White light flowed out, touching the spots of darkness lingering in his body. The light increased. "Thanks for the help, Dad, Emrys," Rob said. Galen let the healing flow through him, floating a little as it took away the ache in his head and chest. "Galen?"

"Here," Galen said, opening his eyes. "You have blood on your face."

"I got hit by a piece of the altar," Rob said with a grin.

"What?" Galen held out his hand, Rob helped him sit up. He looked around. "What happened?" Galen asked, looking over at Flash. His friend was sitting on the ground, shaking his head.

"You... You just... I mean, I knew... I saw during the other ritual... But I never thought..." Flash stopped every few words, Galen wondered if his friend thought he was finishing the sentences.

"Flash?"

"Holy living fuck, Galen," Flash said, focusing on him.

"I'd like to agree with that," Rhiannon said, crouching down beside Galen.

"What?" Galen looked at his brother, Rob quirked an eyebrow at him. "Well, Brat? What?"

"Galen, I never... And I was..." Flash continued.

"Did he get hit on the head?" Galen asked the group at large.

"We all did," Mike said. Galen noticed cuts on the doctor's forearm.

"I just don't... I mean... It fucking exploded." Flash was shaking his head again.

"What exploded?" Galen said quietly, suppressing the urge to shout at them. "Rob?" His brother pulled him to his feet.

"The altar and the stones, Galen."

"They what?" Galen looked over where the altar had been, nothing was left but an indentation in the ground. The circle of stones was gone, the clearing scattered with bits of broken rock.

"Exploded," Rob said.

"Exploded?" Galen walked to the indentation, the echoes of darkness were gone from the place. He felt a tiny whisper of something, then it was gone, slipping through the night.

"Exploded. Blasted apart like you'd filled them with dynamite," Rhiannon said, walking up. "You did it."

"No, Rob, Dad, Bobby and Emrys did it." Galen put his arm around her and gave her shoulders a squeeze.

"No, Galen Emrys. You did this. You did what I couldn't, what none of us could." The First Emrys was there in front of him. "We helped, but you did this. You and your brother." He reached out and laid a shimmering hand on Galen's shoulder. "We will wait until you call us to serve again." He slowly disappeared, his form blending with cloud-muted stars.

"He's right, Galen," Rob said quietly.

"He is indeed. We'll see you at home," Bobby said, Parry nodded.

The whisper touched him again. Galen closed his eyes and focused on it. It was connected to the place, somehow, but the echo was faint. He concentrated, reaching out along the line of the connection, feeling his way.

"The first clearing," Rob suddenly said.

"What?" Galen opened his eyes and glanced at his brother.

"The first ritual, the very first, Galen. There's something still there."

"Dad and Bobby cleansed the place," Galen said, shaking his head. "And you'd think if there was anything left, it would be at the farmhouse, at the place of the second ritual."

"We need to go back," Rob said quietly. "If we go now, we can be there by tomorrow moonrise. Maybe a little sooner, depending on speed limits." He grinned at Galen. "You can sleep in the car."

"I don't need to sleep, Rob. I'm fine."

"Well, I'm not," Flash said from behind them. "You don't think you two are going anywhere without us, do you?"

"We can handle this," Rob said.

"I'm sure you can, doesn't mean we aren't going," Rhiannon said, frowning at them.

"Thank you," Galen said quietly, looking at their friends, a rush a of gratitude warming him. "We need to do this alone."

"Galen…" Flash met his eyes for a long moment. "Okay, Rhiannon can drop me off and I'm going to go get drunk. Really, really stinking drunk. I'll see you in a couple of days, assuming I'm not in an alcohol-induced coma."

"Flash?" Galen looked at his friend.

"It's okay. I'll be fine by the third shot." He walked over and gave Galen a brief hug. "I'll make sure the shop's open at ten tomorrow morning."

"Thanks." Galen watched Flash walk towards Rhiannon's car. "I'm okay," he said to Mike as the doctor pulled a stethoscope out of his pocket. "Go with Flash."

"Galen? Are you sure?" Mike was peering at him.

"Yeah, I'm sure." He smiled and waited as the doctor followed Flash.

"I'll see you later, honey," Rhiannon said. She pulled out her keys and walked away.

"Do you think they're heading home?" Rob asked.

"I think they're going to wait about half an hour and follow us, actually. Rhiannon knows where it is." The whisper was back, pulling at him. "We need to go, you're right," he said to Rob. His brother nodded. Galen picked up his sword, looking at the blood on the blade. "Where did that come from?"

Rob shook his head, laughing. "Your hand, genius." Galen looked down in surprise at the slice in his hand. The wound was already healing.

"You're getting good at fixing things like that," Galen said as they walked to the car. He put his sword in the back and dropped into the passenger seat with a sigh. "Do you want me to drive?"

"I'm fine, you get some sleep."

"I don't need to sleep," Galen grumbled, the words were hardly out of his mouth before he heard a soft snore. *Was that me?*

Sunlight on his face woke him. Galen looked out the window, forest was slipping by, broken occasionally by a single house or pasture. "Hey," he said quietly.

"Welcome back." Rob looked over with a grin. "There's coffee in the thermos."

"Thanks." Galen poured himself a cup. "When did we get coffee? And a thermos?"

"I always have a thermos. I stopped for coffee about an hour ago. I figured you'd have to get up soon."

"What time is it?"

"Just after noon. We can stop and eat if you want."

"Let me have some coffee first," Galen said, sipping the hot liquid. "Not bad."

"Truck stop coffee's always good. How do you feel?"

"Good. A little headache, but that's all." He smiled at his brother. "How are you?"

"Hungry." Rob grinned. "But other than that, good. So, are we asking as a matter of form?"

"What?" Galen grinned back, knowing what his brother meant. He could feel the connection with Rob, stronger than it had been in the past, stronger than it had been even the day before. They were quiet for a long time. "Rob?"

"Yeah?"

"Why did you think it had to be at the first clearing? Not where the second ritual was? Dad and Bobby cleansed both places."

"I know." Rob glanced over at him. "The second place…" He trailed off, his face sad.

"Rob? What?"

"I…" His brother reached over and laid his hand on Galen's arm. He felt the connection alter like it had in his garden, the world shifted and he knew he was seeing through Rob's eyes. A memory unfolded. *It was dark when he arrived, the place still had the stink of the fire there, the one Galen had lit, the one the bearded man had died in. The remembered stench of burning flesh filling his lungs as he walked towards the altar place. Rob paused, looking around, it hadn't changed much in ten years, really. The last vague echo of the darkness that had touched the place was still there. Tears filled his eyes, his chest was aching. It had taken his brother, Galen had died in his stead. Rob began chanting, the darkness shifted beneath him. It moved away from the place, moved to where It, the thing that had killed Galen, now resided. It was time for it to end. Rob was weeping as he destroyed the last physical evidence of the ritual, of the place where so much had ended.*

"Gods, Rob," Galen said, coming back to himself, tears on his face. He looked over at his brother. "You destroyed it, but not the first clearing?"

"I couldn't, once I was there. I just couldn't bring myself to walk down the path, knowing it was the place where it all began, where my life ended, really."

"Rob," Galen began, but didn't know what to say. The grief from the vision was still there, pressing against his heart. He laid his hand over Rob's and let the healing light flow into his brother.

"Thank you," Rob said quietly. "I didn't know how to tell you."

"There's less of a chance for misunderstanding when you do it that way. That's a trick you'll have to show me."

"I will, and you'll have to show me how to make stones explode." Rob laughed, the bright carefree laugh Galen remembered from when they were young. "That bitch! I thought I lost her."

"What?" Galen turned around, Rhiannon's car was behind them.

"You were right, they followed us, but I thought I ditched them."

"You didn't really think we'd lose her for long, did you?"

"I tried," Rob sighed. "She seems to be part bloodhound though, or something." He looked at Galen. "Should we just invite them to eat with us?"

"It would save them hiding behind menus."

"Sounds like a plan." Rob turned on the blinker to let Rhiannon know they were exiting. She followed them to the restaurant parking lot, and their friends met them at the door.

"You weren't planning on sabotaging my car while we ate?" she asked, grinning at Rob.

"No. I already tried that."

"You what?" Galen asked his brother.

"He took a couple of sparkplug wires while I was in the bathroom." She scowled at Rob. "Flash and Mike were asleep at their posts or something. I come out, no wires and these two sipping coffee."

"Luckily, she had an extra set," Flash said with a grin.

"I'm beginning to think you have a whole engine in your trunk." Rob held the door.

"Yeah," Rhiannon said distractedly.

"Rhiannon?" Galen put his hand on her shoulder, bracing himself against the wave a grief. "What is it?"

"Megan…" She trailed off and cleared her throat. When she looked up at Galen her eyes were bright. "We stopped here, ten years ago, the day before she was taken." Mike put an arm over her shoulders.

"We can go someplace else," Rob said, turning back towards the door.

"No, it's okay." Rhiannon shook herself. "I'm okay, let's eat." They followed the hostess to a booth. Galen trailed behind, aware of a sudden tension in his brother. Rob was all smiles, teasing both Galen and Rhiannon as they ate and joining in with Flash and Mike on an assessment of the women in the diner. Galen watched his brother, for all the joking the other emotion was there the whole time.

"Rob?" Galen said after the meal, when they were alone in the jeep.

"Yeah?"

"What is it?" He looked over at his brother, there was a tightness around Rob's mouth.

"Going back. I never realized it would be…"

"This hard?" Galen finished for him. Rob looked over with a frown. "I know."

"It all ended there, Galen. If that hadn't happened, if I hadn't let myself get taken, we could have been serving all these years.

We could have been together." A tear found its way down Rob's cheek.

"I'm sorry," Galen said softly. *And that makes a thousand, I think.* Seeing his brother so broken, still aching from the wounds of the past, tore at Galen. "I thought…"

"You thought you were doing what was best, I know that, Galen. I don't blame you." Rob looked out the windshield, frowning.

Galen reached across the car and put his hand on Rob's arm, letting his brother's emotion flow through the contact. Something was there, something that had been there all along. Under the grief, under everything was guilt, soul-killing in its intensity. "No!" Galen said. "Rob, no!"

"You keep saying you're sorry, asking me to forgive you, but it's me, Galen."

"No!"

"How can you ever forgive me?"

"There's nothing to forgive, Rob."

"I let myself get taken."

"I failed you that night. They took you, I should have stopped them," Galen said quickly. He knew his brother didn't hear his words.

"And then you died for me. For me, Galen. I know you were trying to stop the Legacy, but Galen…" Another tear wound its way down Rob's cheek.

"Rob…" Galen was at a loss for words. He looked over at his brother, Rob was focused away from him. Galen was silent.

They arrived at their destination four hours later. Rob had been silent, lost somewhere Galen couldn't go. He'd tried to reach his brother every way he could think of, even turning the radio to an all easy-listening station. Nothing would shake Rob out of the mood that had descended on him. His brother parked the jeep and opened his door without saying anything to Galen. He walked to the back and pulled out their swords.

Galen sighed and got out of the car. The forest was quiet. It smelled warm, living. He took a deep breath and walked to where his brother was standing, staring at the forest with unseeing eyes. "You sure you want to come, Rob?"

Rob was silent for so long, Galen wasn't sure he was going to answer. Then Rob looked over at him, meeting his eyes. "Yeah, Galen. I need to," he said. "I'm sorry. Shutting you out wasn't helping." Rob's eyes looked old. *This experience, no matter what's happened now, what we've done, it's taken something from him.* Rob smiled at him. "You need help and I need to help."

"Now what?" Flash said, getting out of Rhiannon's car. She'd parked beside the jeep and the three of them got out and walked over to Galen and Rob.

"This way." Rhiannon turned onto the path that led to the clearing. She led the way as the trail wound around through the trees. They stopped at the first clearing, where Megan had been found all those years before.

"I never thought I could let her go, never thought I could get beyond this place," she said softly. She looked at Galen. "I think I finally can, because of the two of you." She stood on her tip toes and kissed each of them lightly on the lips, then turned away. She put a small offering—flowers, a small plush kitten—down on a flat stone.

"I can finally walk away from here, Megan is at peace. I can be too." Rhiannon was silent for several minutes. They stood with her, Flash put an arm over her shoulders. She smiled at Galen, tears running down her cheeks.

Galen noticed when his brother moved closer and leaned against him. He glanced at Rob, his brother's face was tight with grief. Galen gently nudged Rob with his shoulder. "We need to go," he said softly.

"We'll wait here," Rhiannon said, looking at them then frowning at Mike and Flash daring them to defy her.

"Fine, we'll wait here, but if we hear anything that sounds bad, we'll come running," Mike said.

"One peep and we come running," Flash confirmed. "Got it?"

"Got it." Galen looked at them. "Thank you, having you here—it means a lot."

"Yeah, it does," Rob said quietly. "Let's go."

Galen took the lead, following the path as it brought them to the clearing where the ritual had taken place. As they got closer, Galen could sense the tension in his brother. They walked out into the ritual clearing. Rob stopped, looking around, swallowing.

"Rob?" Galen said softly.

"I...it'll be okay, Galen." He walked over and put his hand on the tree that Galen had found him hanging from. Rob looked up at the branch, part of the rope still dangled there, frayed broken and weather-worn, but still there. He looked over. "Galen?"

"We're here together, Rob," Galen said softly, hoping to reassure his brother. It was as if the thirteen-year-old was standing there, too. The pain in his brother was almost too much to bear.

"I..." Rob looked away. "It's still there," he said, walking towards the stone altar that stood in the center of the clearing. Galen felt the whisper of darkness again. It was trapped there, in that clearing, in the stones and earth. The thing that had taken Rob, the wood hag, part of it still echoed there. Rob stopped before the altar then pushed at it, harder, and harder, a desperate, frantic motion. Galen started moving towards his brother as the depth of Rob's emotion hit him. He got to the altar faster than he thought he could. Rob was crying, shoving at it. He looked up at Galen. "I can't move it. I have to destroy it!" Rob's voice was determined, but under that Galen could hear the younger Rob, frightened, full of panic. "Can you help me?"

"Of course." Galen put his weight against the stones. They didn't move for a moment, then slowly, slowly began to shift. The stones fell, breaking apart with a sharp sound that echoed over the forest.

Galen listened to the echo, remembering—he looked around the clearing, seeing it not as it was at that instant, but the place as it had been. Empty, with Rob's shirt and blood on the now destroyed altar. Empty except for the sound of his brother's scream. Empty except for the vision of his brother hanging from the tree.

"Galen?" Rob said from beside him. "I'm sorry."

"No sorry needed," he said quietly, feeling the truth of that settle in his own heart. "No blame, no apologies. It had to happen the way it did."

Rob looked at him for a long moment. Galen felt the steady hum of their connection, Rob nodded. "You're right. It had to happen so we could stand here, so we could serve together as who we were meant to be," Rob said quietly.

"It did."

"Do you want to start?" Rob asked, handing Galen his sword.

"Together this time, I think, Rob."

"Are you sure?" Rob looked at him.

"Very sure." Galen took a deep breath and let the song rise in him. The clearing was filled with the sound of their voices, with the hum of the swords and the light, twisting around them, touching the forest. There was no explosion this time, just the light touching the edges of the dead trees ringing the circle. A small fire began. Galen knew that it would only burn those parts of the circle touched by darkness.

The song wound to its end. Rob looked over and smiled. "Can you get that down?" He pointed up at the rope.

"I think you can reach it," Galen said softly.

"I know I can, but I think you need to," Rob said, his voice sure, the hint of sadness, of grief and guilt that had been there gone.

"You're right." Galen pulled on the rope and broke the end of the branch off with it. He reached in his pocket and handed Rob his lighter. "You burn it."

"Thanks, Galen." Rob lit the end of the rope, watching it burn. Then, turning to Galen, he smiled. "This is the last of it. It's finished."

Somehow Galen wasn't sure this would finish it, the small whisper of darkness was still there, nearly gone, just a tiny echo in the sounds of the earth. He wondered if it was always there, that whisper, that voice of the things the night feared. That sound of the things he lived to stop. For the moment he let it pass, instead drinking in the healing that was needed for his brother. For himself.

"It all ended here," Rob said softly, looking at him, his eyes bright in the flames as the clearing burned around them.

"It all begins here, too," Galen said.

"*Custodes Noctis.*" Rob was smiling at him, an open candid smile.

"Yeah, Keepers, together."

"About damn time." Rob slapped him on the back. "Is it nice to be alive?"

"Yeah, I'm glad my death's over, Rob. Thanks. It's nice to be back and be what I, we, are supposed to be."

"Yeah, and let me repeat. About damn time." Rob chuckled, the soft sound became a laugh. Galen joined him.

As one they turned to leave. When they reached the last turn in the path, Rob glanced back at the clearing, the smoke rising gently above the trees. The forest felt warmer, smelled cleaner. Rob stopped, and stood looking back down the path, back towards the clearing. Galen walked back and stood beside him. His brother leaned against him. They stood together, watching the fire that was still burning, then turned and walked down the path to where their friends were waiting, out of the dark forest towards home.

Acknowledgements

I would like to thank everyone who has read this in its many stages. Your encouragement kept me writing.

Special thanks to Matt Youngmark for amazing design work. Dennis and Sammy for editing and helping me find the right words when I needed them. Sheila for finding the right wording when I needed it. Jane for amazing enthusiasm and plans. Phoebe for blurb extraordinaire. Also huge thank you to those that have supported me through all of this: Pooh, Sheila, Carol, Phoebe, Bev, Jane, Sifi, and my family and friends. A special acknowledgement to JA and JP who have no idea they are here, but without whom I might never have taken the first steps that led to this book.

Dedicated to Dennis for unflagging love, support, humor when I needed it and very generous patience. Sammy for love, support and sisterhood.